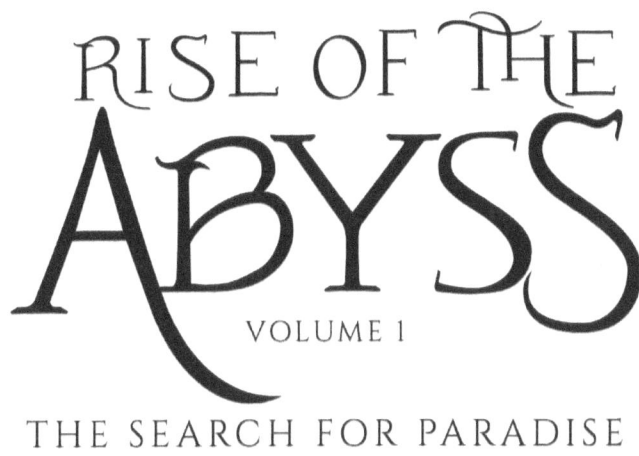

RISE OF THE ABYSS

VOLUME I

THE SEARCH FOR PARADISE

NEGUS LAMONT

Print ISBN: 9780920583029
ISBN: 978-0-920583-02-9 (print)
ISBN: 978-0-920583-04-3 (Amazon)
ISBN: 978-0-920583-06-7 (Kobo)
ISBN: 978-0-920583-08-1 (Apple)
Masani Press
Toronto, Ontario

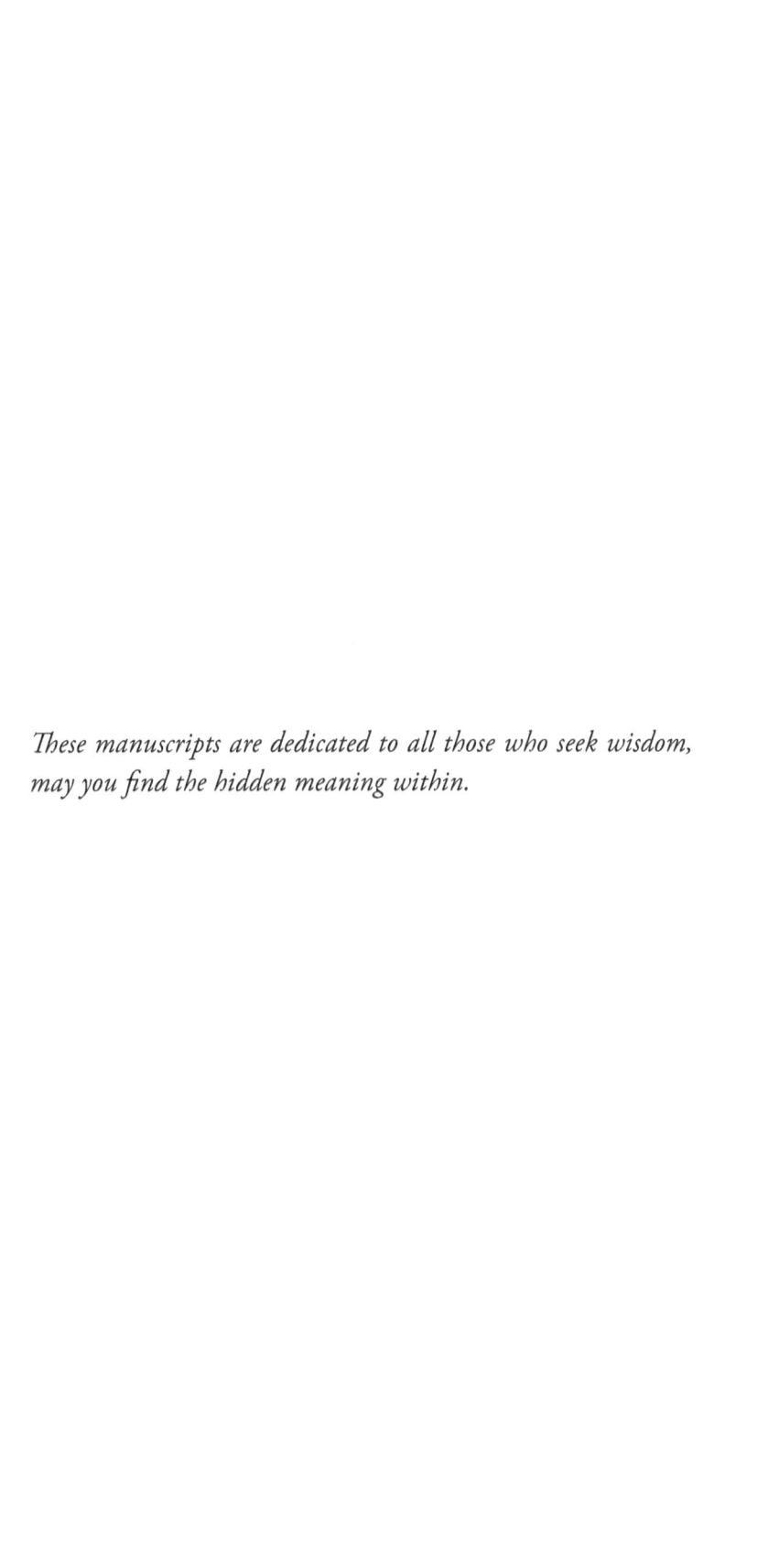

These manuscripts are dedicated to all those who seek wisdom, may you find the hidden meaning within.

PROLOGUE

THE FIRST GREAT world turn occurred when Lelanos was divided into four major guilds; the Lion in the north, the Fox in the east, the Elephant in the south, and the Crocodile in the west. Each guild had twenty five percent of the world's territory under its command. The Lion Guild was known for their courage, leadership, and ferocity. Thus, they were the most respected. The Fox Guild was known for their cunning tactics, adaptability, and ability to win under the direst of situations. Thus, they were the most feared. The Crocodile guild was known for their ancient magic, efficiency in battle, and stern training. As a result, they garnered the most malice out of the four guilds. Finally, the Elephant Guild was renowned for their patience, business acumen, and stability. Thus, they were viewed as the most trustworthy of all the guilds. For eight world turns this stalemate continued as each guild was too afraid to launch an attack on an opponent. One day the stalemate ended due to a shift in power.

Donta Ivory furrowed his brows, "What do you mean…every single member of the Fox Guild is dead?" The messenger bowed with fervor, "Our spies in the Lion Guild have confirmed it. Jarvan Hartengale VI found their last sanctuary and eliminated every single one of them." Donta slammed his claymore into the ground causing the earth to shake, "Including their mysterious guild leader?" The messenger lowered further. "Yes, even their guild leader, the one who is said to be so fast and deadly that none has ever laid eyes upon him and lived to tell the tale. It was said to have been a battle to rival the gods. Jarvan VI was severely injured in the process but he emerged victorious."

Donta sneered and asked, "How can the tale have been told if none has ever lived after seeing him?" Beads of sweat dripped down the messenger's forehead. He stammered, "I don't...know..." Standing up Donta paced the floor. "Of course, you wouldn't know. What can you tell me of that senile brother of his? The one I fought in Hell's Arena!" The messenger dropped to his knees. "My apologies master. He is reported to have died as well, once again at the hands of Jarvan VI".

Donta continued to pace the floor back and forth as he dragged his massive claymore. "This is unacceptable. When an honorable opponent surrenders they are not to be eliminated like vermin. The women and children are not to be stepped upon like something one finds at the bottom of their boots. There is no justice in this war." A single tear streamed down his face. He clenched his jaw as he lifted his claymore above his head, slamming it on the floor. The claymore shattered into two pieces. He handed both chunks to the messenger. "Deliver the hilt to the Lion Guild's Jarvan Hartengale V and deliver the blade piece to the Crocodile Guild's Dominus Bourbon. Let both know that the Elephant Guild no longer has any interest in world domination and will withdraw our claim to supremacy. The messenger's eyes widened as he gripped the two pieces of the once destructive weapon. From that day forward Donta became known as 'The Elephant's Sorrow.' The Lion Guild declared war on the Crocodile Guild following the withdrawal of the Elephant Guild. These two powerhouses have been engaged in a bloody and heated war ever since.

CHAPTER 1

JAMES

JAMES IVORY SAT atop the wooden bench with his back straight, arms crossed, a slight frown, and his lips pursed. His grey robe was modest yet elegant at the same time, an attribute the elephant guild had perfected. The hut was expertly crafted with ivory walls and oak wood seats lining the outer layer. The rare red soil caressed the bare feet of all who entered and threatened to sing one to sleep. The accused knelt before the bench with his elbows turned in and hands extended. Judgment can't be escaped where the Elephant Guild is concerned. To break one of the five sacred tenets of the guild is to evoke the wrath of the guild, this often comes in the form of James Ivory. "It seems I need to reiterate the five sacred tenets for everyone to hear. This is the third time a tenet has been broken in the last world turn. 1. A member from our family will not directly interfere with the actions of another guild, the punishment is death. 2. A member from our family will not indirectly interfere with the actions of another guild, punishment is expulsion. 3. A member from our family will not have sexual relations with a member of another guild unless they are married, punishment is castration/mastectomy. 4. Failing to report a guild member who has violated any of the tenets, thirteen days of starvation. 5. Compromising the integrity of the guild, punishment is the Tribune."

The crowd simultaneously yelled, "Strong, self-evident, and resolute. We are united and pursue a single purpose!" James stood up, his massive body towering over the defendant. He addressed him, "You have failed to report a member who broke tenet number three. Do you accept your punishment?" Several members of the crowd opened their mouths wide and raised their eyebrows. A few raised their fists and clenched their jaws at the disgusting news that had befallen their ears. Screams of boos echoed throughout the courtroom. "Quiet!" James' thundering voice boomed throughout the room essentially silencing it, the whimpering of the lone tenet breaker was all that remained. "What do you have to say for yourself?" James asked.

"I am ashamed for I have brought dishonor to our guild. I have failed to uphold our values and have broken one of the five sacred tenets. I realize that starvation is but a small price to pay for failure to conduct myself in a manner deemed worthy of this crest. I humbly accept my punishment and vow to regain the respect of my peers," said the humble guild member. Everyone in the court room stood up in angst, the moment they had all been waiting for.

"Deep in my heart love is felt alive. From the depths of my soul I know we will thrive. Though the world may shake due to their greed and their pride, we will survive elephantidae proboscidea!" James exclaimed slamming his gavel against the desk. The ground beneath the court room shook and a small apple tree sprouted from the ground in front of the defendant. The cheers of the crowd were interrupted by a Raven which flew directly to James. After finishing the letter, he tore up the parchment stood up and left without a word.

James had not been in the capital city of the world since he was a child. He had told his father that one day he wanted to move to Larimar for it was the greatest city he had ever seen. His father scolded him heavily but said something that he never forgot. *When one goes to such great lengths to display beauty there is often the most putrid of inner turmoil's underneath.* Larimar was known for its extravagant tournaments, magnificent architecture, and diverse population. The tiles were made of marble, the light blue hue created a calming affect that had a way of sweeping through anyone fortunate to step foot into the city. The buildings were made of onyx and quartz stone, with a unique gem stone in the center for identification.

Ravens spiraled back and forth between houses carrying messages from lovers and friends to the ancient secrets of a guild. What James loved most about the magnificent city was the food. The bazaar was filled with the rarest of delicacies, from fish caught at the outskirts of Crocodile territory, to mushrooms picked from 'Death Ravine.' The city wasn't nicknamed, 'The Breath of a Goddess' for nothing. *What a wondrous place...I wonder if I will have time to explore this city in all its splendor.*

While walking through the bazaar he gazed upon the sea of different guild crests, most of which he could not identify. *It seems the Elephant Archives need to be updated, from what I know there are supposed to be ten unique guilds housed in this city, but these crests say otherwise. How can so many guilds coexist with their own values and customs? Father said such a thing would be an elephant's brew for disaster.*

"Who sent me the urgent raven!" James demanded, his thundering voice traveled throughout the fortress. "It was I, your honorable Judge James," squeaked a tiny shrew of a man. Pursing his lips James continued his inquiry. "What has transpired that required my immediate attention? I have journeyed for five days straight from Grande to deal with this matter, it best not be trivial," said the gigantic figure. "Please sir, do not be vexed for I would not have requested your assistance if it was. You are the most reputable judge in the entire guild and the only one capable of dealing with this issue. I would have written to your father had you not arrived in such a timely manner. This matter is worthy of attention from only the guild master or his son." The member stood there with his hands on his head, blinking repeatedly.

James took a deep breath unfurled his brow and placed a hand on the old man's head tilting it gently, in a low and even tone he asked, "What matter has troubled you so?" The man paused for a few moments and then he replied, "I can't speak the words for they are too great a task for a man as lowly as myself. Please follow me so that I can show you what has happened." James nodded his head and followed the old man through the fortress.

The fortress in Larimar was not a traditional Elephant Guild structure. It was a massive building with large twists and turns. The design was in the shape of an Elephant's head. "It seems you have done well with the fortifications of the walls," said James. "Yes, sir. It is exactly as your father had instructed. The walls are built to withstand a massive siege and hold a tactical advantage in the city. There are several large mountains behind it to prevent any attacks from the rear. Praise be to your father who always has the survival of the guild at the forefront of his mind." James nodded and replied, "I notice the barracks are heavily stocked with weapons and armor."

Beaming proudly the member tilted his head back and gloated, "The Larimar division of our guild holds about fifteen percent of our members but has the ability to house and supply fifty percent. In addition to this we keep a large surplus of food and water in case of an emergency. A man such as myself has no idea as to what kind of emergency could befall our guild." James smirked, "It seems the possibility of an emergency is foreign to anyone in the guild, save for my father. As far as I know, the Elephant Guild has only lost a member due to expulsion or death from old age. Praise the Elephant Deity that we enjoy stability, reliability, power, dignity, and honor. Our vow of neutrality is a great service to the world for we do not abuse our spirit power." The member nodded in agreement and replied, "We have arrived." The light was dim, and the smell was horrendous but as far as James could tell he was standing in front of a jail cell. The man in the cell was all skin and bones, it was obvious that he had been starved for longer than any man should have been. He reeked of rotten flesh, as if he had been cursed with decay magic.

James clenched his fist and the earth beneath them began to shake. "Why has a family member been kept under such horrible conditions?" A tall slender figure emerged from the darkness, accompanied by a group of young members. The tall man placed his hands on his hips and answered promptly. "It was my doing, he has committed the most egregious of sins. He violated sacred tenet #1; directly interfering with the actions of another guild. The members under my supervision wanted to execute him on the spot, however, I deemed it necessary to bring in a judge to make the final decision. The only way for me to calm their anger was to lock him in this cell. I had no other choice, punish me if you will but please help us. This bastard shows no sign of remorse!" All the members got on their knees and bowed before James.

Turning away abruptly, face burning, yet hands still clenched James said, "I…don't…no need to bow, please stand up." One by one the members stood up each one more sluggish than the last. James approached the cell and motioned for them to release the prisoner. Upon further inspection, the prisoner was worse off than he initially thought. His eyes were drooping, the beard unkempt, and he had large red spots covering his skin. Curling his upper lip and shaking his head to the side he asked the man, "What is your name?" The man's head and body stood erect with hands curled into a fist. "Surely you jest, to ask the name of a dead man is to give hope to the hopeless. I will not tell you my name. I accept my fate, get it over with now," said the man. The other members looked at James awaiting his decision.

"Do you know who I am?" asked James. The man responded, "I know who you are. They call you the honorable James Ivory and you are expected to be the successor of the forever neutral Elephant Guild. Why do you continue to question this condemned man?" The man bowed his head. James took out his flask and handed it to the accused. "I wish to understand what you did and why you did it, a man should be understood before he meets his end." Taking the flask, he gulped the contents without hesitation. "Please tell me your story and I will listen with open ears."

The man softened his posture. "Ok…I guess. Myself and two other members were walking through the Kintip district when we came to an alley way. We were blocked by the scene of a young girl being molested by a member of some guild. She was screaming for help, but people just kept passing by. I couldn't recognize his clothing, nor could I see his guild crest. However, I am sure the young girl was guildless because she was wearing the mandatory orange gown. No one cares about guildless people in this city; they are treated worse than animals. The other two members with me were about to leave when…I don't know…something came over me. I rushed in and began beating the man, I punched and kicked him until all I saw was blood. The other two members grabbed me and pulled me away before anyone could see us. She doesn't know it was an Elephant Guild member, at least I don't think she had time to see. I don't know…

what came over me, but I am not sorry…I did what I did, and I stand by it. So…there you have it…I guess," he sighed heavily and shrugged his shoulder.

James' palms began to sweat as he bit his lips. Slowly he reached for his large war hammer. He clasped the ivory handle and then stopped. Sweat gushed onto the handle as his other hand began to shake. "What are you waiting for? He is to be executed on the spot," said the supervisor.

James shot him an errant glance, but he knew the man was right. He took a deep breath and withdrew his weapon from its straps. With one swift motion, he slammed his war hammer against the ground. The earth beneath the culprit engulfed him. He stood there as the man with no name drew his last breath.

CHAPTER 2
JARVAN VII

THE MORNING LIGHT beamed down into the bed chambers of the prince where he rested. After a night of drinking and fraternizing with two female companions from the Deer Guild he could still taste the bitterness of the ale and feel the chalk-like texture of the meat between his teeth. Slowly Jarvan VII sat up and rubbed his head, his temples pulsated at an alarming rate.

He took note of three empty bottles on the floor, a platter of the city's finest cheese on the marble nightstand, and the naked bodies of two servants. He nudged the one he had dubbed green eyes and prodded her awake. "It's time for you to go, make sure to clean up before you leave." The green-eyed servant smiled and nodded before gathering her clothes. He gazed at her medium sized breasts, slim waist, and toned thighs. Above all, he liked the way her round eyes matched the innocent features of her face, a true doe if he had ever seen one.

The second one began to stir beside him under the covers. She was a bit thicker with large breasts, a medium sized waist, and a voluptuous ass that had threatened to tear through her servant's robe. Jarvan was quite amused with this one as she was shy at first. He liked the shy ones, for they always resist his initial advance thinking he has approached them under jest. The large breasted one woke up and smiled, eyes beaming with delight at the monumental night that she had experienced. Jarvan responded with the kindest words he could muster. "I no longer require your presence, time to leave." The large breasted one nodded and began to gather her things. By the time the second one had finished putting herself together the room was spotless.

The two servants bowed and left, loud giggles could be heard down the hall. Jarvan walked towards his bathroom, his bare feet caressed the black and yellow marble tiles. He passed by the life size crystal lion named 'Akili.' Dragging his hands over the refined sculpture that represented his guild he smiled proudly. The hot water caressed his skin, as each drop of water splashed against his muscular body he began to hum to himself. *What shall I do today?* He thought to himself.

This was a common question that came with a common answer. He stood in front of his mirror and looked at his reflection with deep satisfaction. "Mirror, mirror on the wall, what should the crowned prince do before he falls?" Jarvan's question was met with silence. "Should I go to the tavern where the common guilds drink in my name? Or perhaps I should head to the brothel where the women swoon at the slightest gaze? Maybe today is the day I finally defeat that intrepid father of mine in that game he is always playing?" His questions were met with more silence. "Woe is me, for I live in a world where mirrors can't speak, tis a sad day when my reflection is the only thing that can please me." He stared at his reflection some more. "Does not the Sparrow desire to fly across the forest? Does not the Squirrel desire to climb trees, and frolic in the grass? Should not the Lion desire to hunt the Crocodile to taste the succulent meat upon his tongue?" He slammed his hands against the sink, causing two chunks to break off.

Jarvan heard soft knocking at the door. Putting on his black robe with a lion crest on the back he walked towards the entrance of his bed chambers. Looking down he saw a pitiful young servant boy with a sullen look on his face. "You're late yellow hat, my breakfast ought to be cold by now." The boy mumbled to himself, thick beads of sweat formed across his forehead. Growing impatient with this farce Jarvan placed a hand on the boy and told him he will not be punished, but he is to slow down and repeat himself. "Mmm…mm…milord, I was on my way with your meal when I saw a handful of soldiers returning from the campaign on the Crocodile Guilds final stronghold. None of the soldiers who returned were the famed Golden Triad generals that left, to make matters more perplexing they were carrying three bloody boxes. I was shocked that such a small company of men would return with news of a victory, but for the Triad generals to fail would be unheard of!"

Jarvan's left eye twitched as his grip on the young Deer servant tightened. "Milord, you're hurting me…," the boy whimpered. Realizing his folly, he released the boy and told him to take the food and share it with his guild members in the kitchen. "Make sure you tell no one of what you saw." The boy nodded with glee and took the cart of food away. Jarvan stood there in a daze with his hands at his side. "Three bloody boxes? Could it be the Triad Generals have failed?" He ran his hand through his long golden hair. "We have lost many men to this Gatticus, but for all three generals to perish at his hand…" He shook his head in dismay. "I refuse…the mighty Lion is not so weak that we could lose the remaining of our famed generals to this heathen."

Jarvan Hartengale VII entered the throne room clad in his magnificent gold heavy armor with white trimmings. The ground beneath his feet illuminated with every step. A magical halo of swords hovered above his head indicating a secret power that he kept under tight guard. His white cape shimmered elegantly while magically fading into flakes of light.

The entire throne room stared in awe as it was rare for Jarvan to wear his armor away from battle. He sat down at his usual spot just below his father Jarvan Hartengale V and Queen Aeterna. The spokesman for the soldiers stopped talking when he realized Jarvan had entered the room in his armor. Jarvan motioned his hands to indicate the soldier should continue, while his father merely observed. His piercing gaze often stopped men dead in their tracks.

The spokesman continued with his fatal tale. "We were ordered to stay back so that we could bring swift news of our victory. We waited for ten days and still no army had returned. On the eleventh day, a behemoth of a man carrying an axe in the shape of an anchor came before us. It was him and four other members of the Crocodile Guild. We immediately recognized him as the legendary General Gatticus. When he approached us he said, if that is the best you can do in the sea soon we will reclaim our cities on the land. Afterwards his soldiers handed us these three boxes and said to deliver them to our emperor before they rot." The hair on Jarvan's neck began to rise, his eyes became bloodshot, and the light below his feet flickered. Hesitantly, he said, "Open the boxes."

The three soldiers holding the boxes complied and slowly opened them, one by one each box revealed the head of a Triad General. Those that had vision of the contents covered their mouths, word travelled throughout the room that the Golden Triad had been eliminated. The emperor's piercing eyes scanned the room, causing the murmurs to subside. Jarvan's armor became unusually warm, he didn't have to look back to know what had happened.

"So...you mean to tell me that when faced with the man responsible for the defeat of our guildmates you turned tail and ran?" Jarvan glared at the soldiers. One of the soldiers asked, "Milord...what...do...?" The prince interrupted him. "Not to say that you would attempt to at least take the life of the general who has caused us so much grief. Countless of our men have died to this man, including my uncle the late Jarvan Hartengale VI or perhaps you have forgotten all about him?" The soldier bit his lip. "I could never forget the guild's pride and joy, for he was our greatest warrior...it's just..." Jarvan stepped forward. "Oh, how amazing it must be to lack the pride, honor, and dignity of the Lion yet be privileged enough to wear the guild crest." Jarvan turned to his father. "I suggest we expel them from the guild for their inability to uphold the guild's values." His father's face remained stoic. "They are to be executed publicly for lack of discipline, you should have trained them better." Without a moment's notice, the soldiers were carried away by the royal guards. The prince motioned for the court to clear out.

"Father, I believe it is time for me to lead a campaign against the Crocodile Guild. All the other generals have failed and brought disgrace to our sacred crest. There is much glory to be had and all hail to the Lion Spirit, it is up to me to take it." Jarvan kneeled before his father, his hands tightened into a fist. His father shook his head. "Again, I must deny your request to head a campaign. I can't risk you traveling such a great distance as this will invite ill thoughts at the sight of us using our trump card. When the time is ripe you will set foot on the island of Tem." Jarvan raised his head slowly and stared at his father in disbelief. "I can't accept this decision. What possible risk could there be? The time is ripe now!" The emperor placed a hand on his shoulder. "You see, a large portion of power comes from the belief that one does not need to use all of it to accomplish an objective. When the lead Lion needs to go out for a hunt the vultures descend from their trees. It is best to let the ones at the lower pack bring our prey to our doorstep."

Jarvan stood erect with his chest puffed out, "You speak in riddles when the time for decisive action has come to pass! Do you not wish to see me have my glory on the battlefield? Perhaps you feel that this General Gatticus who continues to be a thorn will cut me down as he did your brother?" The emperor furrowed his brows and replied, "I have already sent word for the Wasp Guild to send a general and a massive force for a joint campaign. They will assist a military force led by Captain Warda. There is nothing left to be said on this matter." Jarvan kissed his teeth before mustering the only words that his father would hear. "I understand."

The emperor stood up, walking stick in hand. Slowly he made his way to the Volute table, where he motioned for the queen to join him. Upon reaching the exit, Jarvan was blocked by his older brother Octavius Hartengale. "Hello brother!" he gloated with a large smile across his face. "I suppose father denied you again? Hmm, it's such a shame that you must stay in the capital with us normal folk. Heu heu heu." Jarvan winced and shouted, "Begone with you foul vermin! I am not in the mood for your riddles or games." Octavius leaned in closer and taunted, "No games, just an acute observation. Father doesn't want to send you to your death, I mean everyone knows it. You aren't good enough to eliminate the Crocodile General. In fact...I'd rather put my coins on the ambitious Captain Warda." His bony index finger crept towards Jarvan's face. "Remove your finger from my face at once!" Jarvan exclaimed. Octavius snickered, ignoring his younger brother. With lightning speed Jarvan grabbed his older brother's finger and twisted it. His brother screamed out in pain.

"No matter where I am, you will always be the forgotten son. No matter how hard you try to be relevant you will always amount to nothing. You'd be smart to remember that the next time you point at me, Octavius the first and only of his name!" As Jarvan walked away he could hear his brother's whimpering at the loss of movement in his finger.

In his room Jarvan paced back and forth. *I am more than good enough, I just have to convince father. I can't leave the fate of our guild to some Wasp general or an overly ambitious captain. What could father be thinking?* As far as Jarvan knew his father had only one weakness and that was the problem that he had always faced. The only way he knew to defeat his father was head on with sword and shield in hand, but he would never dream of such a thing. When it comes to wits his father was unmatched. *There has to be someone who can talk some sense into him, there just has to be.* Jarvan kept replaying the events in the throne room and came up with nothing. He removed his armor and laid on his bed, the smell of lavender crept into his nostrils seemingly to calm his frustration. It reminded him of the night before with the two women from the Deer Guild.

It is typically frowned upon to fraternize with the servant class, but those green eyes were calling him. Besides he was the great Jarvan Hartengale VII who would dare to draw his ire? "Pragma Aeterna!" he exclaimed aloud. *There is only one reason why he would invite her to face him in volute. The weakness of many men is a woman for only they can calm the heart and ease the storm that is a man's troubles.* As he contemplated on these words an eerie sensation filled his essence. He sat down with his head in his hands. *What if she won't help me? I know that we are from separate guilds. I from the mighty Lion Guild and she from the elegant Swan but I see her as a mother. I know not how she views me.* He let out a loud sigh as he laid on the bed. *But what choice do I have? I have to go to the only person that will listen to my plight.*

∽

The next day Jarvan waited outside the entrance of the courtyard. The queen approached him wearing an elegant pink dress adorned with gold stars. "Queen Aeterna, I wish to speak with you on a matter that has troubled me for quite some time," Jarvan beckoned for his step-mother to sit beside him on the wooden bench "I hope one day you will desire to call me mother. I love you as if you were my own and I am here to listen," she said taking a seat beside her step-son. Jarvan smiled warmly and replied, "It means a lot to me to hear you say that, you and I have not had a chance to speak as often as I would like. I have something I wish to discuss with you and it is difficult for me to do so." Pragma smiled, "You can tell me anything."

Jarvan nodded and continued, "The weight of this loss has taken its toll on my heart, to hear that thousands of my guildmates have perished at the hands of these heathens. To find out that the training of my soldiers has not come to bear fruit, redemption should be mine!" He gripped the edge of the bench firmly, light emitting from his hands. "I agree, but I don't think I can be of much help. I don't usually meddle into the affairs of your guild. The same way your father rarely interferes with the affairs of my own," she said as she placed a hand on Jarvan's shoulder.

Jarvan lowered his head and sighed, "I would give up all of my possessions for a chance to walk upon the island of Tem with sword in hand. I would even forgo the crown that is promised to me." The halo above his head started to rotate. "Oh my, I certainly hope that wouldn't be necessary. I can see just how much you are hurting, I will do what I can." Jarvan leaned in to give his step-mother a hug. "Thank you, mother," he whispered. As he embraced his step-mother the same eerie sensation returned, only heightened. Ignoring the feeling he embraced her with all his might.

The royal family gathered in the throne room to greet the Wasp Guild forces. The emperor played a game of Volute by himself. Jarvan VII was sparring with four members of the royal guard. Octavius was hunched in the corner by himself with a book in hand, while Lamia Hartengale and Pragma Aeterna gazed out the window. "They are here!" Lamia said jumping up and down. The rhythmic chanting of the Wasp Guild could be heard long before they could be seen. Octavius perked up slightly. "It says here that the Wasp Guild is known for their numerous and complicated formations. They wear black and yellow light armor with Wasp wings at the back. These enchanted wings allow the wearer to hover momentarily, the Wasp members often use this feature to reposition during an attack.

This is rather fascinating." While deflecting a blow with his shield, Jarvan scoffed. "Enchanted wings that allow the user to fly? I'll believe such a thing when I lay eyes upon it."

Lamia giggled, "I suppose we will find out soon enough, here they come!" Octavius continued with his reading. "It says here that each Wasp member carries a weapon unique to their guild known as the 'Nest of Wasps,' a mid-ranged weapon that shoots out small explosive balls of Kazrite Ore." Jarvan raised an eyebrow. "Not possible, Kazrite Ore is used to strengthen weaponry, armor, and light candles. How can they turn it into a weapon? Free me from your tales of fantasy." Soft knocking could be heard at the door. "Enter Azreal Glycerine from the Wasp capital of Sentia!" the court announcers loud voice boomed throughout the hall. It was a well-known fact that the Wasp members were typically shorter than the average citizen in Larimar, but they made up for the lack in size with strict discipline, poise, and exceptional health. Expectations were high to see who the Wasp Guild would send for the first inter-guild military campaign.

"Greetings all....my name is Azreal Glycerine...umm...so...I'm here for the war." The emperor, the queen, Lamia, and Octavius erupted into a fit of laughter. Azreal had spiky black hair with yellow streaks at the side, his armor was mildly impressive although not very sturdy, and he was shorter than anticipated. Additionally, one of the wings on his 'armor' was clearly damaged. The squadron that accompanied him bit their tongues while covering their mouths. The emperor stood up and pointed at the young Wasp 'general' and said, "You will be following the orders of my son for this campaign." Picking up his board game he exited the room. The rest of the royal family followed suit, leaving Jarvan VII alone with Azreal and his squadron.

Azreal walked closer to Jarvan. Upon closer inspection, his armor was merely cloth with mismatched patches sewed in. Jarvan squinted, the veins in his temples began to show. "Why does your cloak look like something you found in the trash?" Azreal dusted himself off and stammered, "W...well...this is my grandfather's cloak. Truth be told I am the general of the Kazrite Mining Operations. I was recently transferred to military general for this campaign." Jarvan sat back down, stomping his feet in the process, his hands rose simultaneously. "I'm almost afraid to ask but why were you transferred?" Azreal's heart began to race, his breathing quickened, and his pupils began to dilate. "I created a new weapon that makes better use of Kazrite Ore, care to see a demonstration?" he said, beaming a massive smile. Jarvan rolled his eyes while waving his hand.

Assembling the new weapon he had on his back, Azreal explained, "Currently the Nest of Wasps is used as a propulsion mechanism to launch several different aura imbued bolts in a direction, however, this mid-range weapon isn't very accurate and thus hits the intended target sixty-five percent of the time. The large area of effect offsets the accuracy. I thought to myself what if I create a mechanism that shoots one large Kazrite Ore over a long distance and have it explode upon impact. This would give a hundred percent accuracy as well as large destructive power. The way it..." Jarvan cut him off. "I don't care, just finish the demonstration. I will stand over here and you aim it at me. Don't miss!" he added. "Yes...m...milord." Azreal's muscles tightened, his eyes blinked rapidly and his mouth tensed. The wasp general aimed for Jarvan's hand and fired. The ore went far left destroying one of the queen's favorite sculptures. "S...sorry milord," Azreal mumbled.

CHAPTER 3

ORIANNA

IN THE FAR west lies the great city of Passerine. Once belonging to the Crocodile Guild, it was rebuilt to better suit the needs of the Raven Guild. The city is located on the coastal line where large cliffs peer down into the ocean. The walls of the city were made up of pure white limestone with gold intertwined between the seams. Passerine served as the hub for all communication between the prominent guilds.

Located in the middle of the city was a massive Sequoia tree which they called the Great Hub. The tree was so massive that depending on the time of day it could block out the sun. The only ones who could set foot in this tree are the Raven Guild high council members. These members were identified by their white robes and blue chains. Eventually out of respect the raven members started calling them the White Ravens and it became the most sought-after position in the city.

Malikai's eyes became the size of saucers as his eyebrows raised. With a dry expression he commented, "You seem to be pleased with yourself brother...I take it you didn't fail miserably." Tamriel furled his eyebrows and spat on the floor and cackled, "Well Malikai, the fact that I am here in the hub means I have passed the exam. In fact, my score was twice as high as the other nine applicants. The new spell that I created is one that rivals mother's. Though how the likes of you managed to get in here five years before me is beyond preposterous."

Malikai's arms tensed up, his face turning red. "I don't know what pre…preparestous means….but I can show you the new meaning of a blade to your face. That would do well to fix your crooked nose." Tamriel placed a finger on his crooked nose and questioned, "The likes of you show me something new? Now let me recall, when was the last time you did anything of note…now I remember. Mother used her connection with our clumsy sister to get you into the exam. Although I admit, combining wind magic with dual wielding was rather unique. It pales in comparison to what I have done on this monumental day." Tamriel placed his hands on his tome and asked, "I suppose you want to know what I did? I'll tell you. I created the very first curse spell with healing magic, quite the feat. It makes your pathetic dual wielding look like mere child's play."

Malikai withdrew his weapons and exclaimed, "I'll show you child's play!" "Brothers no! Please don't fight!" Orianna attempted to rush in between the two but tripped on her gown. Malikai enchanted his dual short swords with wind magic. Laughing, Tamriel took out his book of incantations and chanted the destructive words that neither Malikai nor Orianna knew the gravity of. Orianna was paralyzed, her lips trembled, heart beat increased, and tears poured down her chin. "Please stop…fighting is bad!" she whimpered. Seemingly as if the Spirit Deities had answered her call a large wind barrier came between the two brothers forcing them to stop.

"What is the meaning of this?" A tiny wrinkled figure carrying a large winged staff emerged from the darkness. Her question was met with silence. "I asked you fools a question. Oh…I see, Tamriel you are too high on success to smell your own farts and Malikai you are too drunk on ale to speak without a slur. Then there is you….all mighty oracle. Clumsy little girl get off the floor and fix yourself up! How you became the oracle is both a blessing and a curse. Such a foolish little girl you are." Looking up to the ceiling she clasped her hands together. "Why have you forsaken me all mighty Raven Deity. To have children who are magically inclined but stuck in the brains of toddlers." Her eyes shifting from Tamriel to Malikai to Orianna. Her wrinkles disappeared, the lines on her face subdued to show a young woman in her thirties. The bags underneath her eyes became light blue eye shadow. "Come you pathetic children of mine, we have a prophecy to hear."

The Clairvoyance Room was a medium sized room located in the middle of the Great Hub. It was a room that was constantly lit using eternal spirit fire. It is rumored that should the fire ever go out it would signify the end of the Raven Guild. The spirit fire is one of the few forms of fire magic the Raven guild possessed. Four times a year the high council members would leave their separate quarters and convene in this dimly lit room. Excluding the oracle all members must drink an elixir used to raise their spirit level. Immediately after drinking the Elixir of the Spirit the members must surround the oracle and wait until midnight for the transformation.

This day was a special day for it was the beginning of a new world turn and thus time for the first prophecy of the year. The group gathered around Orianna while they waited for midnight. She sniffled and placed her hands against her thick thighs. "Is…is it close to midnight?" she whispered to Tamriel. Tamriel responded with silence. She looked at her feet and counted to one thousand. Her veil hid the tears streaming down her face. "One…two…three…four…five…" The bones in her neck fused together. Every time she transformed it was a different set of bones that fused first. She clasped her gown tightly. "Six…seven…eight…" This time it was her spine being rearranged. "990…991…992…" She let out a loud scream as the wings sprung from her back. Two streams of blood covered her face as the transformation was nearly complete. Her eyes rolled to the back of her head and her third eye opened. The aura from the deity filled the room with blue light. The light from the spirit fire burned out momentarily. The deity floated above the ground as the wings flapped. A furious wind blew throughout the room.

"Bow before the Raven Deity!" Commanded the deity. The group laid their heads down on the floor and closed their eyes, waiting to receive the blessing. "*Iktar rak more star nam ro mien nos.*" As the words entered the members' ears the divine light filled their bodies. Blood spilled from Tamriel's ears, nose, and mouth but he remained still for to defy the command of a Spirit Deity was to invoke its wrath. The Spirit Deity flew to the ceiling and unleashed a strong blast of wind pushing back all ten members of the high council except Corvus Jackdaw, Tamriel Duskbringer, Solaire Duskbringer, and Malikai Duskbringer. It continued to speak in the divine tongue, "*Kim rok tor nor more nal viema alagora notta nief nefsto. Tel gall na me illvune, jinseal illianosk amarak. Geburn duva emrit akal pour tasno jinseal…"*

The deity disappeared in a flash of blue light and Orianna's body dropped towards the floor. Malikai dived forth catching his sister in the process. Her gown was bloody and her face was pale. "What happened, why did it stop mid-sentence?" Tamriel asked. Solaire charged towards her daughter and grabbed a lock of hair and answered in a dark tone. "You pathetic girl, the god took mercy on your weak body." She flicked her daughter's nose.

Orianna woke up as the blood on her face cleared away. "You know, you are too hard on your children," said Corvus. Solaire contorted her face and screeched, "They need to learn eloquence and endurance, when I need advice from a frail brown old man like yourself I'll ask." Corvus rebuked, "Umm….perhaps we should get on with the interpretation then graceful old hag." Solaire glared at him but opened her book of translations and compared it with her notes. Her hands tensed up. "This…cannot be!" she exclaimed. She paused a moment and began to start over. Her hands shook violently. "It says here…that…for the guild to survive we must kill the emperor. Then it goes on to say something about Elephants rampaging at night." She slammed the book on the ground.

"What does that Elephant part mean?" asked Corvus. "I don't know, but what does it matter? The emperor must die so that we can survive. Nothing else matters." The other members regaining consciousness agreed. The wrinkles on his forehead became more prominent. "I understand all of that about the emperor but are we so despicable that we would betray our benefactor after all these years?" the old man asked as he stroked his beard. Orianna raised an eyebrow and questioned, "Mother, what does he mean by benefactor? I thought we're simply allies." Solaire's right eye twitched and a snarl appeared across her face. "Keep your mouth shut girl, you forget your place!" said the old cleric. Corvus stroked his beard at a rapid pace. He commented, "I think we should wait until the second prophecy before we make any moves to betray him." The other members spoke amongst themselves. For the first time in history the Raven Guild was divided on what to do after a reading.

CHAPTER 4

LORD VEGA

THE FIVE CLANS of Pacifia have traditions and customs that transcend time and thus do not gauge it the same way humans do. This world made primarily of water is one filled with treacherous creatures. Lord Vega was a riddle even to his own clan. He often sat in his underwater cavern staring at the darkness. His large wings caressed the back of the cave while his trusty companion laid beside him. His weapon was never far from his side. He enjoyed practicing the language of man in solitude. He stood up and waved his claws about. "Ma nom ez Lord Vega Z." His fascination with the human language was unusual to the other clans, but he had ordered all the leaders to learn the language. The human language was thought to be primitive and their obsession with the things they called 'music, dance, and acting' were thought to be foolish. His teacher Odessa of the Undines had taught him the best she could but being a Krynn there are certain human sounds that he could not make. Although the five clans were divided into separate sanctums the elite members often gathered for feasts.

Additionally, they gather whenever a clan wishes to challenge another to a gauntlet. This is an event that happens very often as to rise in status is the goal of every clan. It brings great fortune to the entire race and overall much more safety. The lowest clan is required to live in the outskirts of the sanctuary and thus is vulnerable to the Elite Beasts. These Elite

Beasts are enormous monstrous creatures that can't be controlled by the Undines. He picked up his spear and waved it with slight force. A large whirlpool sprang forth. "Surrender or perish!" he yelled.

Sitting back down he looked at the picture book Odessa had made for him. The contents displayed pictures of the exploits of man. He looked as the one called Jarvan VI journeyed deep into a cavern like his own. In this cavern, he met an old scraggly human with a bunch of fur coming out of his face. The man held no weapon but his aura glowed bright pink and a smaller creature covered in fur appeared before him. Lord Vega's eyes clicked twice as he peered at the scribbles. "Fuh-ox," he pronounced as he turned the page. The page depicted a fierce battle between this scraggly man and Jarvan VI. Jarvan VI took his massive 'Spi-Ear' and fought off the beast while the one they called Deathbringer countered with an onslaught of punches and kicks, however, the furry man was eventually defeated. The final page showed the furry man smiling as he drew his last breath.

The tentacles on Lord Vega's head rotated wildly as he tried to figure out why a furry who has just suffered defeat would smile. Odessa had taught him that humans smile when they are pleased. This smiling concept was something that has spread throughout Pacifia and the clans would do something which resembled a smile. He picked up the newest 'buh-ok' that Odessa has created for him and studied it. This one had a picture of a giant island with a Crocodile on the cover. The title said Tem. The island of Tem had pictures of vicious storms, large 'm-ound-tins', and his favorite sea beast Charbydis. Lord Vega's tentacles pointed straight up and his main orifice transformed into something resembling a smile. Charbydis was a ravenous sea beast that the Undines had given to the humans of the Crocodile Guild.

Lord Vega stood and walked towards the entrance of his cavern. He closed the book and placed it on a rock. "Who dares to disturb me?" his hands gripped his spear. Upon seeing him clasp his spear Odessa bowed to the floor. "Lord Vega I have come to inform you that I have returned from the land of the humans with news." Lord Vega motioned for her to continue talking. Odessa took a few steps back and to the side keeping an eye on his spear. "The Crocodile guild has started the Nidas. Soon their young children will be trained in the arts of scholastics, warfare, stealth, hunting, and athletics. The ones who fail will be discarded." Lord Vega's tentacles rotated. "That is not enough death, their ocean must run red if we are to wage war upon land." Odessa nodded. "Yes, Lord Vega. I will devise a plan immediately. There is something else…" Vega's eyes changed color. He thundered, "Speak!"

Odessa continued, "My scout has heard rumblings…" Lord Vega pointed his spear at Odessa's throat and bellowed, "Swiftly!" Odessa bowed once again. "There are a few members of the Cretin clan who believe that your inability to wage war against the humans after fifty of their world turns is due to your cowardice. Some have even begun to say that your fortitude has…weakened." She took a few more steps backwards. The tentacles on Lord Vega's head rotated furiously. "They think me weak?" he questioned. Odessa nodded her head and prepared for the immense power to follow. Lord Vega put down his spear and turned around, he picked up his favorite book and began to analyze it. Odessa turned to leave when Vega started to speak. "None would dare challenge me. They all cower in fear, as they should. Make haste and tell the humans of this Raven Guild that I wish them to kill the man on the cover." Odessa inched closer to inspect the book cover. "That's….the emperor, their greatest ally."

He looked up at her, the temperature of the water decreased rapidly. "And?" he queried, as his eyes turned dark red. Her hands quivered as she removed her human clothing, praying that her legs would fuse quickly. "They will certainly refuse to betray their closest ally and benefactor after such a long period of time." Her legs finally fused together and a large blue and gold scaled fin appeared. She swam a little further away from the great Krynn lord. He grabbed his spear and slammed the base against the ocean floor. Ten whirlpools erupted outside the large cavern. "If they fail to kill the cunning Jarvan Hartengale V they will inhale the mutilated corpses of their offspring as the Goba peel the flesh from their brittle bones!"

CHAPTER 5

JARVAN

JARVAN SAT IN his seat leaning on his hand while caressing his chin. His armor gleamed under his own light as his sword and shield laid next to his chair. He let out a low hum while his other hand tapped against the arm of the chair. "Again!" he yelled. Azreal raised his weapon and aimed it at the young man Jarvan identified as yellow hat. Yellow Hat stood in front of a giant marble block with an apple on his head. The servant shook uncontrollably as Azreal took aim. Beads of sweat streamed down his forehead while he made every effort to balance the apple on his head. Azreal's hand trembled slightly but his eyes were focused and his breath steady. He held his position waiting for Jarvan to issue the command. Jarvan raised his hand. Azreal slid his finger onto the trigger. Yellow Hat steadied himself. Jarvan lowered his hand. "Free!" Azreal pulled the trigger. The projectile flew true as the air surrounding him became warm, it spiraled and exploded against the marble wall slightly to the left of the Deer member. A gust of debris blew the apple off his head, but he caught it before Jarvan could take notice.

Jarvan stood up and stormed over towards Azreal grabbing him by his collar. His face became red while the light beneath his feet flickered in a frenzy. "Mistakes like that can get everyone killed. To fire prematurely is to waste the ammunition of not only you but your entire brigade. Following the wrong command on the battlefield is one of the worst things you can do."

Azreal tensed up and tried to explain himself. Jarvan released him and stormed back to his chair. "Do it again and this time aim true and listen with intent!" Jarvan turned to Yellow Hat and pointed to him. "If that apple falls off your head again you will get well acquainted with the Brown Hats in the stables!" Azreal took another Kazrite ball from the large pile and loaded his weapon. He wiped the sweat off his brow and shook his shoulders. He steadied his shoulders took aim and this time held his breath. Jarvan raised his hand for the hundredth time. "Fire!" The projectile spiraled accompanied by a large stream of orange aura, it whizzed and knocked the apple from the Deer member's head. The Kazrite ball exploded dead in the middle of the target painted on the wall. Azreal ran over to Yellow Hat and the two started to jump up and down. "I did it, and you're alive!" Azreal exclaimed.

A scowl crept across Jarvan's face. He stood up and walked over towards the two buffoons. "You still have about two hundred kazrite balls over there. You must repeat that two hundred times in a row without fail, otherwise we are starting from scratch. A great army can carry a poor general, but a poor general can't lead said great army. Do you want to be a great general or a poor one?" Azreal stopped celebrating and stood erect. His brow lowered, and his face creased. Jarvan had never seen Azreal look this serious before. "I will be the greatest general the Wasp Guild has ever seen!" Azreal declared.

The moonlight streamed into the throne room, it reeked of sweat, meat, and Kazrite dust. Jarvan and Azreal sat around a large golden table with a map laid out on top. Tiny little ships were placed in different formations. Jarvan had large bags underneath his eyes while his hair was unkempt. The puffiness of his face was clearly visible to Azreal but he made no mention of it. Azreal's stench was mouth gagging, his cloak laid on the floor while he wore a Deer Guild robe to keep warm. Yellow Hat walked into the room holding his breath. He pushed in a cart of assorted cheese and refined deer meat. Jarvan grabbed a handful of cheese, stuffed them in his mouth, and murmured an issue of gratitude. Yellow Hat bowed and ran out of the room. Azreal grabbed for the cheese but Jarvan slapped his hand away. He mumbled, "Not for you." He then pointed towards the meat. Finishing the food in his mouth he stared at the board again.

The green ships were labeled Crocodile Guild and were laid out in a defensive formation. The large ships were bunched together in the middle of the circle, while the smaller ships were laid out evenly in a large radius. "Why are they laid out in such an odd formation?" asked Azreal. Still chewing Jarvan replied, "This formation has been consistent from the first naval battle and has been undefeated thus far. General Gatticus is a well-known land general however his area of expertise is naval warfare. This has been the crux of our problems. We do not own any ships of our own and our members have little to no experience with naval warfare." Azreal wiped the sweat off his brow. "So that is why the Lion Guild spends countless resources on purchasing ships from your coastal allies the Raven Guild." Jarvan winced. "Yes, I suppose that is common knowledge. In addition to our inexperience in the water the ships that the Raven Guild provides are not built for battle. Because of this we are essentially sitting ducks against the massive battleships of the Crocodile Guild." Azreal placed a finger to his lips and commented, "Their ships are rather odd looking."

Jarvan nodded in agreement. "The Crocodile guild uses large ships that are reinforced with Corundum. This mineral is the hardest mineral in the world and can only be found on the island of Tem. Because of this reinforcement the Crocodile Guild has a defensive formation that is near impenetrable. Whenever a ship gets within range they are bombarded with a sea of arrows." Azreal scratched his head and asked, "Ok, can we go over this one more time? With the addition of my army we won't be sitting ducks. The problem is that our rams will be completely useless once they get in range. The strength of your guild is your prowess on land. Did I get all of that?"

Jarvan looked up at Azreal as both his eyes began to twitch, yellow light formed. With a lack of impatience, he replied, "Yes, for the fiftieth time. Yes, that is correct!" Azreal backed up a bit while he covered his mouth. "Well….this is just a side scratching moment, if only you guys could just pounce on them." Jarvan steadied himself before looking to the ceiling and scratching his head. Azreal looked around wildly at the ceiling. "Are…" Jarvan raised his hand, interrupting Azreal. "Shh, I got it." Azreal closed his eyes before reaching for another piece of meat. "If we forgo the addition of the rams we will save rooms for boarding planks. These planks will be reinforced, and we could use them to board the crocodile ships from a long distance, because of their massive size and weight, they won't be able to turn in time. We issue out a barrage formation." Azreal rubbed his forehead and asked, "A what?" As he was about to take the last piece of meat Jarvan snatched it up. Azreal looked at Jarvan with dismay.

Ignoring Azreal's annoyance, Jarvan continued. "We will set our formation in a triangular formation and make a rush straight to their flag ship. Instead of having our larger ships in the back we will put them in the front. That way we will be able to withstand the onslaught of arrows. You go and calculate how many large ships we will need and how many small ones. The ships are to be divided equally between the Lion Guild members and the Wasp Guild members. Both guilds will share equally in the risk. Put the best soldiers in the vanguard. Make sure the flag ship is the biggest and most reinforced, you and I are going to be at the head of the fleet."

Azreal shook, his tongue became dry, and a single drop of sweat inched slowly down to his nose. Feeling flustered, he asked, "O...ok... may I ask why are we in the vanguard?" Jarvan inched closer to the man who smelled of mold and replied, "A great leader will always lead by example." Azreal wiped his forehead nervously. Sensing Azreal's discomfort, Jarvan asked, "What's wrong with you?" Azreal readjusted his collar, looked to the floor, and bit his lip. Slumping down in his chair Azreal sighed, "Well...it's just...if I'm going to be in such mortal danger, I would have liked to have felt the pleasures of a woman at least once." From the depths of his heart Jarvan laughed and said, "Oh...my waspy friend, that is something we will have to rectify."

CHAPTER 6
JAMES

JAMES HAD BECOME somewhat of an expert on the layout of Larimar. As he walked throughout the city he noticed several things he had not taken note of when he had just arrived. Members of the guildless class roamed the streets of Larimar in their orange gowns. The misery of poverty apparent on their faces. *I will have to update the records. It seems one became guildless when they had the inability to manipulate aura and thus could not be accepted into a guild.* James ran his hands through his ivory colored hair. *It's unfortunate that aura manipulation is a talent that is often passed down through the bloodline. If only more people were able to learn this skill...* He stared up at the sky. A deep raspy voice whispered in his ear. *Darkness.* James looked around wildly. Scratching his head, he shrugged. "That was odd..." he whispered aloud.

James realized how fortunate he was to not only be born to a family who had a strong history of aura manipulation but to also be born in one of the most influential guilds in the world. He always thought his life was a difficult one for he had the burden of thousands of people relying on his guidance and judgment, but this was something that paled in comparison to the trials and tribulations of those who were guildless.

What can I do? My guild is not open to outsiders. If only I could help these people. His feet ached and his tongue desired reprieve, but he kept walking. The massive war hammer that had always seemed light to him felt like a burden upon his mind. James' cowl covered his insignia as he didn't want anyone to know he was in the city. His father would reprimand him for coming to Larimar without his squadron. Once again, another aspect of the world James did not understand. As far as he knew the Elephant Guild and Lion Guild had always been allies so why would he need a squadron for official guild business? He stomped the ground as he looked around to find something to occupy his mind. He walked over to a carnival game.

The high striker operator looked at him with wide eyes and cackled, "You're quite the big boy, aren't you! Dehehehehe." James smirked and handed him three lion dollars. The golden coins flashed with the lion insignia. One was flipped onto its tails and contained a swan insignia. This was another thing he had not noticed previously, not that it mattered. The game was simple, it required the contestant to pick up a wooden hammer and hit it against a gong. The little swan would fire across the pond to the other side depending on how hard the gong was hit. The further it goes the better prize that was won. Before James could take his turn a large behemoth of a man pushed him out of the way and exclaimed, "I go first little man!" The man's gold armor reflected the light right into James' eyes, the giant's gold Lion insignia was clearly visible. The operator grabbed his knickers and said, "Captain...W...W...Warda no problem." Scrutinizing the hammer Warda chuckled, "Hahaha tiny little hammer, like this tiny little man's hammer. Ho Ho Ho." He clasped both his hands and slammed the hammer against the gong creating a loud echo that carried throughout the bazaar. The swan shot across the pond and nearly made it to the end but fell short.

The operator handed Warda a large crystal swan. Warda dropped the hammer to the floor with a grotesque smile. James took the large hammer with one hand and stretched his wrist. With one hand, he slammed the hammer against the gong. The hammer instantly broke and the swan shot straight to the end breaking against the edge of the pond. The operator and Warda gasped in astonishment as James waited for his prize. The operator handed him a gorgeous crystal necklace. It was wrapped with white gold and had a swan design on the pendant. Warda lowered his brow and balled his fist. He pushed his crystal swan toward James and bellowed, "Trade, now!" James looked at him and scowled. "I think not Mr. Warda. I won this fair ivory and I would be doing myself a disservice if I gave it to you."

Warda grabbed the necklace out of James' hands and walked away with both the crystal swan and the necklace. James' eyes turned white while green vines wrapped around his arms. He removed his cloak and the ground beneath Warda shook. He reached for his ivory war hammer and withdrew it from its strap. Four giant pillars sprung up in front of Warda blocking his path. Warda turned around in time to see a massive hand made of clay spring up from the ground, grabbing his wrists. James walked over slowly and took the crystal swan out of Warda's left hand. He placed it on the ground in front of him. Afterwards he took the necklace and placed it in his pocket. James turned around and walked a few paces. A massive tree sprung forth from underneath the swan suspending the swan twenty feet in the air. He turned around and looked at Warda and smiled. "I hope you know how to climb as well as you know how to run!"

James returned to the fortress in a much better mood than when he left. His shoulder became loose as a surge of energy rushed through his shoulders. He walked in to see three members excitedly grabbing their weapons. James looked around the room and looked at the supervisor and asked, "Did something happen?" The supervisor raised his eyebrow and answered, "Uhh...no...we're going to the Pilgrim's Inn to celebrate the justice you carried out when you first arrived." James' heart sank as he stared at the men in disbelief. "You guys are celebrating by going to the brothel?" Regaining his composure, he realized this was a common thing in Larimar. He had always heard of the 'Fly Girls' in the Butterfly Guild and of the Elephant members who loved to visit the brothel. Naturally they were restricted from sexual intercourse with these women, but they could enjoy the entertainment. What made matters worse was that up until two weeks ago this was on his death list.

He stood there conflicted at the dilemma that he was now in. The hypocrisy of the whole thing now became evident. The deep raspy voice returned. *How is it pious to watch women of another guild dance and grind on you but it be wrong to have sexual intercourse with them? How can it be justice to kill a member for preventing a woman from being raped?* James shook his head as if to shake the raspy voice away. The supervisor leaned in closer and whispered, "Certainly, the all great judge James will join us, it would be an honor to have you accompany us on this outing." James looked at the man and nodded slowly. He kept replaying what had happened the night he killed his family member. The look of defiance was something he had never seen before. No family member had ever failed to accept their punishment without remorse. He couldn't have fathomed such a thing, but it happened. It happened to him and that was all he could think of. "We stay static but at what cost?" The supervisor turned to him and asked, "What did you say all honorable one?" Realizing he spoke aloud James regained his composure and replied, "Nothing, I was just saying this city is beautiful." A second member laughed hysterically and exclaimed, "Wait until you see the Fly Girls!"

The Pilgrim's Inn is the most popular brothel in the entire world. It is believed that the Butterfly Guild practices a rare form of magic that allows them to stay young forever, because of their everlasting beauty the members often have an excess of suitors. The most desirable out of all members are the ones who manage the operation. The guild is run by the Mora family, a family of women who all play different roles in its day to day operations. James went to the brothel even though he knew his father would not approve. Although it is not technically against the rules it would be unethical for the lead judge of the guild to be caught in a place like this. James shook his head and waved off thoughts of his father. He was determined to see what was so special about these famed Mora sisters.

Stepping into the brothel was like stepping into a portal to another world. The scent of lavender and lily filled the nose while the eyes were met with the most beautiful view imaginable. The brothel was filled with beautiful flowers and its guests were all laid about on large purple sofas. Several women stood on stage dancing to some odd music that James could not identify. He immediately became enamored with the beauty of the women. The other guild members rushed over to the stage excitedly and ordered a table. James slowly walked over to the bar and ordered a shot of tequila. *It is frowned upon for Elephant members to drink outside of the guild halls. To be seen intoxicated in public is in poor taste.* This time his father's voice echoed. He clenched his teeth. "Better make it two shots instead….in fact…just leave the whole bottle," he said to the bartender. James downed a shot. It had been over five years since he drank. *A sober mind is a sober body, and a sober body is a healthy one.* He downed two more shots. *The Elephant Guild is the best guild in the world; it doesn't matter if no one else knows that, we know it.* He downed three more shots. *One day you will understand what I go through when you have kids of your own.*

James placed both his hands on his head. A young lady with a slim waist, large breasts, and large buttocks approached him at the bar. She sat down and placed a hand on his thigh. "You seem like you could use some assistance, care to pour me a drink?" His hands shook as he licked his lips. His heart began to beat faster, and he swallowed deeply. He stammered, "N…no…thank you." He had not had sex in over six years. *Celibacy is the true mark of a man. A ten-year vow of celibacy before you choose a good strong Elephant woman is the true test of a man.* His father often preached these words. The young lady while still smiling did a bow and left. He downed five more shots, before he knew it, the bottle was finished.

He placed a few more Lion dollars on the bistro table. The bartender slid the bottle over and shook her head. This time another woman walked over wearing black latex. The latex collar gripped her neck tightly and the straps held up her bra. Her figure blossomed through the rubber as her thighs gleamed under the pink lighting. She wore black gloves that went up all the way to her armpits. His jaw dropped as he took one more shot and watched as she poured herself a drink. She smiled and caressed the rim of the glass, "My name is Eros…what's yours, big poppa?" Regaining his senses, he shook his head. "Please… leave me alone." As he reached to pour himself another shot she grabbed his hand lightly. "You seem to be down on something, why don't you tell me what's on your mind?"

James stared at her for a moment, his eyes darted back and forth as he scanned the room. "Well … the thing is…I heard…about a young girl who was guildless and being taken advantage of. This happened right in the middle of a busy alley way." Eros covered her mouth and let out a loud gasp. She finished her drink and reached for another. "That's horrible, it's so sad the way guildless are treated in this city. They are treated worse than the rats found in stables. Though I admit…I'm not surprised. I mean there are some things that go on in here that I'm not proud of either." James sat up straight and looked this woman in her eyes. "What do you mean?" She looked around and placed a hand on his. "I can't tell you right now. Come tomorrow morning when it isn't as busy."

CHAPTER 7

ORIANNA

ORIANNA'S ROOM WAS not the room of an adult. She had stuffed purple dragons scattered around her room, a giant sculpture of Jarvan VI whom she absolutely adored, and her clothes were scattered across the room in various piles while food laid about in a corner. The room smelled of fermented herring, something she had gotten used to. It was a large room that granted her much space to lay about her waste. Orianna removed her veil and stood in front of her mirror. Her mouth was firmly closed, brow lowered, with a slight frown. "I am NOT worthless! I am NOT worthless! I am NOT worthless!" she exclaimed as she walked back and forth, her boots clopped loudly against the stone. She sat down on her bed and placed her head on her hands. "I am completely worthless...I...should....I should just die." Tamriel whom was creeping outside her doorway entered and retorted, "Ya...you're right, you should just kill yourself." Orianna opened her mouth as her eyes widened. "Are you...s... serious?" she stammered.

Tamriel crept closer and sat beside her on the bed. He placed a hand on her shoulder and whispered in her ear. "It's simple really, if you die the Raven Spirit will choose someone else to be the oracle and we won't have to deal with your nonsense. If you kill yourself, you will be doing a great thing for the guild." He stood up and handed her a dagger with a Raven design on it. "Think about it, I'm sure mother would be quite proud of your sacrifice. After what you did I can only imagine what other failures we should expect from you. At least you would be saving the family from more embarrassment and discord. That must count for something. I mean do you enjoy being a failure in her eyes?"

He slinked off into the distance before turning around one last time. "At least clean up this filthy room before you do it, I'd hate to be the one chosen to discard of your wretched body." He cackled as he walked away. Tears streamed down her face as she sat on the bed with the dagger in her hand. She stared at the engraved markings of a Raven and pondered what it meant to be the Raven Guild oracle. She thought about all the pain she had endured for the sake of her prophecies. But above all she thought about the gift she had been given.

I was given the gift of prophecy for a reason. I may not know what that reason is, but I know I am destined for something greater than what I have achieved. If I were to end my life now, things will never get better. I struggle with this depression but I will not let it get the better of me. No, I am not worthless…at least…I don't think I am. Orianna placed the dagger on the floor and laid on her bed. *I will give it back to my scum of a brother in the morning. I will prove to him and the rest of the guild that I am the best Oracle the guild has ever had, above all I will prove it to myself.*

Each guild has a Spirit Deity that acts as a patron for its members. This patron provides access to enhanced magic using one's aura. When a guild member manipulates their spirit levels to harness the power of a deity they can perform various forms of magic. As their spirit depletes they become more fatigued to the point of passing out. It is believed that angering the patron deity of your guild is the worst offense a member of a guild can do.

To risk the ire of this ether world being is to put your very existence at risk. One's existence could be divided into three parts. These three parts are the consciousness, body, and the spirit. When someone uses their aura for magic they intertwine their spirit and body with the deity. However, in Orianna's case she lends her consciousness, body, and spirit to the deity which often has a catastrophic effect on her health. Each time she allows the deity to merge with her being she shortens her lifespan significantly.

"CRZZZZKKKKK!" Orianna jolted upright, her eyes rolled to the back of her head. She turned swiftly to the edge of the bed and stood up. Her feet moving on their own paced towards the mirror where her eyes rolled forward. She attempted to look around but was stuck, she tried to let out a loud scream, but nothing came out. Her eyes were glued to the mirror and her mouth sewed shut. The mirror flickered, as blue waves shimmered across the refined glass.

An entity with the head of a white raven appeared. It titled its head and began to speak, *"Ak nok don nick flak she."* The deity stopped and stared at the expressionless face of the oracle and then it spoke, *"Find the twins before the Elephant clips the Lion's tail."* Orianna screwed up her face and opened her mouth in dismay. Her possessions in the room floated one by one. First her clothes on the floor, then the pile of food in the corner, then the bed in the back, until all her items in the room were levitating except her desk and the mirror. Blood trickled down her nose and her head throbbed. Her ears rang while her feet felt as if they were on fire. The Raven Deity bellowed, *"FIND THE TWINS BEFORE THE ELEPHANT CLIPS THE LION'S TAIL."*

Tears streamed down her eyes as she nodded her head absentmindedly. She yelled, "Yes...ok...ok...please...stop!" The Raven disappeared, and all her items came crashing down. Her bed smashed to pieces upon impact. Orianna collapsed to the floor. Malikai rushed into the room with both of his swords drawn and asked, "Is everything ok?" He looked around to see her room in complete disarray. Orianna used the desk as leverage while she stood up "N...no...she...came back," she stammered. Malikai sheathed his weapons and walked into the room. "Who came back?" She grabbed him by the shoulders and shook him. "Th...the... Raven Spirit! She came back...and said we have to find the twins before the Elephant clips the Lion's tail." Malikai covered her mouth and whispered, "Shh! Don't ever mention that word around mother. She will kill you if she hears anymore talk about Elephants." Orianna pushed her brother off while standing straight, looked him in his eyes and furled her brows. "It is my duty as the oracle to pass on the message to the guild speaker!" Malikai looked at her as his heart dropped. He walked past her and started to clean up.

৵

Orianna walked into the dining hall where the high council was enjoying a meal. Malikai looked at her and shook his head. She ignored him and continued to walk towards their mother. Before Orianna could say a word, a Raven flew through the window and landed on the table in front of Solaire. She removed the parchment from its legs and read it aloud. "The high council's presence is requested at the western gate by the coastline. There is an urgent matter that requires your attention." The high council including Orianna left the dining hall to head to the coastline. Malikai approached Orianna and grabbed her arm. "I'm telling you, do not tell her about the vision of an Elephant. It won't bode well for you. Please just keep your mouth shut." Orianna brushed him off and quickened her pace. She approached her mother once more. This time Tamriel interrupted her. "Hello Orianna, what a surprise to see you here in such amazing splendor. I would have thought you'd be bedridden by now. I suppose it's a blessing. All praise the great Raven Spirit!" In the clear tone of sarcasm. He turned to their mother and engaged her in conversation. By the time they had arrived to the coastline Orianna was exhausted, the Raven Spirit took a larger toll than she could have imagined.

Her natural ability to heal herself was mediocre at best and thus she was starting to feel an after effect. The group was greeted by a large crowd staring off into the distance. A large grotesque figure approached. It was a giant monster shaped like a whale with beady eyes and an enormous mouth. Its mouth was lined with a plethora of jagged teeth. Inside of the mouth was only darkness. On top of the hideous beast was a woman but her entire body was blue with shiny gold scales. The creature barged into the coast line while simultaneously destroying the western wall, by this time the entire crowd had scattered and only the high council stood by.

Solaire had created a large barrier which protected them from the impact of the creature's arrival. The woman on the creature looked at the crowd that had fled and shook her head. "Greetings Raven Guild my name is Odessa, my last name is not one you would be able to pronounce so I will forgo that. I have come here to pass on a message from the lord of the five clans of Pacifia. Where is your guild speaker?" Solaire stepped forward, while Malikai and Tamriel stood beside her albeit slightly behind. "I am as you see me, speak quickly so you can take your leave." Odessa tilted her head and smiled the most innocent of smiles. She raised her hand and the sea monster tilted upwards. It shot a large stream of water from its mouth into the air. For several moments, nothing happened. Tamriel took another step forward. He pulled out his spell book and smirked. Before he could find the right page a massive stream of water slammed into the closest building to them and flooded the city.

Tamriel put his book away and took a few steps back to join the rest of the high council. Odessa once again turned her attention to Solaire and started to speak again, this time in the language of the deities. "*Ak nok ro jist navo soma ilget ravune jistfu.*" She then jumped down from the monster and tapped the barrier. The barrier disbursed into a shower of light. She walked up to Solaire and grabbed her by the collar. Malikai went to draw his swords but water shot out from his throat. He made gargling sounds as he struggled to breathe. Odessa turned to the entire high council. "My lord's message is very simple…. you are now under his dominion and you must prove your worth. Kill the emperor or suffer pain a thousand times worse than death." Odessa released Solaire and granted Malikai the oxygen he so desperately craved. She took her leave.

While walking back to the Great Hub, Orianna approached her mother once again. She stuttered, "M…m…mother I…know this is a bad time…but…I had another prophecy." Solaire stopped and turned to her with staff in hand. Orianna continued, "Th…the Raven Deity said that we have to find the twins before the Elephant clips the lion's tail…I don't know wh…" Solaire raised her staff high above her head and swung. The staff came crashing down against Orianna's head knocking her unconscious.

Orianna awoke with a sharp pain in her head, indicating that she had been healed but not by her mother. She squinted as she tried to make out whose room she was in. It was remarkably clean and smelled of the ocean breeze. She stood up only to sit back down again. Her head started to spin as she struggled to keep down her lunch. Corvus Jackdaw entered the room with a cup of steaming tea and crackers. He leaned closer to inspect his work.

"It seems I am a bit out of touch. I admit healing is not my forte. Dehehehe." His mouth revealed he was missing more than a few teeth. Orianna clasped the tea and sipped it. She whispered her gratitude. "Do you remember what you said to your mother to make her so angry? She hit you over the head and then stormed off." Orianna nodded. Corvus' face became sullen as he continued to inspect her wound which had not fully healed. "I'm so sorry to pressure you, but would you be remiss if you told me?" Orianna nodded and said, "The Raven Deity came to me in my bed chambers and spoke the rest of the prophe...." Corvus' eyes widened as he took a seat beside her.

"Please go on, I won't get angry." Orianna continued, "He said that we have to find the twins before the Elephant clips the Lion's tail. Why does my mother hate the Elephant Guild so much?" Corvus' face dropped and he rushed to his closet where he began to rummage through his things. He pulled out a book and flipped the pages. He popped open the book and placed it on the floor. He then drew a circle around it with three more circles. A few moments later the image of a Fox appeared. "This is a depiction of the Fox Deity. The Raven Guild used to be under the Fox Guild's patronage. For many world turns we had sought our independence. Donta Ivory found this out and offered to support the Raven Guild in our endeavors, in return we would hand them several magical tomes that contained secret enchanting techniques. The Raven Guild did as we had agreed but he backed out of the deal at the final moments. After reading the tomes he said that the curse magic the Fox Guild used was despicable and not something he could condone. Somehow the Fox Guild learned of our betrayal which forced us to flee into the gaping mouths of the Lion Guild. Many of our members died during our escape, including your father. Your mother places the blame on Donta for these death's but above all she blames him for the situation we are in now."

Orianna widened her eyes in disbelief and asked, "What do you mean? I thought we were in a wonderous situation." Corvus shook his head. "In your world that is correct. However, the elders do not agree with such a perspective. We want nothing more than to be free of servitude. To be called upon like servants when we're needed for healing is not something any of us enjoys. We wish to heal on our own accord. This is something that we will never accomplish. Perhaps your generation will find a way." Orianna grasped the sheets tightly and murmured, "That doesn't give her any right to be so cruel to me and my siblings. What of this prophecy?"

Corvus shook his head once again. "If the Raven Deity says it is your duty to search for the twins then that is what you should do, I just don't know what role the Elephant or Lion Guild will play in your search. We will be heading out today. The emperor has ordered the elite from all the reputable guilds to attend Lamia's birthday, so you are expected to come. I don't know if we will find the twins there, but that is the best place to start."

CHAPTER 8
LORD VEGA

LORD VEGA SAT in the corner reading the latest tale from Lelanos. This one detailed the exploits of General Gatticus and how he defeated the Triad Generals. He laughed as he reached the part where Gatticus cut off the head of the first general. Lord Vega's arms tensed up as he placed the book down and grabbed his spear. "Odessa is that you?" Odessa emerged from the darkness and bowed. Lord Vega had been waiting impatiently for the news of the Raven Guilds compliance. He walked closer as his massive armored body towered over her. His large claw grazed her shoulder while he tilted his head downwards. "Rise and speak freely."

Odessa did as her lord commanded and stood up. The scales on her skin turned purple as she smiled. "It is my pleasure to inform you that those humans have witnessed the power of the five clans, they will comply." Lord Vega nodded but remained tense. He motioned for her to enter his cavern. From the outside it looked small, however upon closer inspection it was a vast cavern with ample room. Inside laid numerous books that Odessa had created for him. In addition to his spear there was a jewel encrusted trident. This trident was known as the trident of the divine and was Lord Vega's most prized possession. He had only used the trident once in battle, however it caused catastrophic damage.

Lord Vega and his trident annihilated the sixth clan which chose to wage war on the Krynn when he became their leader. The only taboo topic in Pacifia is to speak of this forgotten clan for it would enrage any Krynn within earshot. To do such a thing would be to invite death to their doorway. The trident rested against the wall and gleamed in a multitude of colors. Her jaw dropped as her pupil dilated and a sparkle appeared out of the corner of her eyes. Odessa licked her lips as she inched closer to the Trident.

Lord Vega turned to her and waved her over to sit on the bed. Odessa nervously sat down and asked, "Is…is…there something I can assist you with my lord?" she stood erect and bit her tongue. Lord Vega attempted to smile and sat on the floor of the cavern with his legs crossed. "I want you tell me every single detail. How did they react? what happened? Who was there? What did the high council do?" The massive figure crossed his hands against his chest and his eyes switched over to something Odessa had never seen before. The pupils of his eyes turned light green as he sat there in bliss.

Odessa looked down and cleared her throat. She stammered, "O… okay…well when I arrived the Raven members dressed in black…." A large Cretin member swam into the cavern and threw a scroll on the floor in front of Lord Vega. The tentacles on his head twirled furiously. He looked at Odessa who immediately picked up the scroll and read it. Odessa's scales turned dark red as she read the scroll. "It…it…umm…" She started to bite her lips as the scroll dropped out of her hands. She looked at Lord Vega then looked at the Cretin messenger and questioned, "Are… you…guys…sure?" The Cretin messenger looked at Lord Vega and took another step inside of the cavern. He smashed his claw against the wall causing several books to fall out of place.

"The Cretin clan challenges the Krynn to the gauntlet for supremacy over the five great clans of Pacifia!" the Cretin messenger declared. He clapped both of his claws together and began to walk side to side while clicking his claws. The tentacles on Lord Vega's head turned dark blue. Odessa repositioned herself into a far corner of the cave. Lord Vega stood up and grabbed the Cretin messenger with his right claw. The moisture from the Cretin's body left him as a mixture of aura and water entered Lord Vega's claw.

The dry limp carcass of the Cretin messenger sank to the floor. He stepped on the body and a loud crunch echoed throughout the cavern. His eyes now dark blue he turned to Odessa and pointed to the exit. "Leave!" With her whole body covered in red scales she immediately swam out towards the exit. Upon leaving she realized she witnessed something that she never thought possible. Someone dared to challenge the Krynn to the Gauntlet. This was the moment she had been waiting for. She has made each Gauntlet more difficult than the last to gauge the strength of the five clans. However, Odessa had always wanted to see how her beasts would stack up against the lord.

Lord Vega's claw turned dark blue as he walked towards his Trident of the Divine. The tentacles on his head still twirling wildly he caressed the handle and stared at the jewels on the trident. His hand gripped the trident turning the entire handle dark blue. He twirled it around causing rifts in the water. He slammed his trident against the cavern floor and a massive whirlpool emerged outside the cavern. He walked towards the exit and bellowed, "They…think…me…weak!"

The four leaders from the five clans sat in a circle surrounding the sacred crystal. Several stone tables laid side by side while the leader of the Undines, Odessa Skaomin sat with her fin to the side waiting patiently for Lord Vega to arrive. Her elegant gold scales shimmered under the beam. She had a pet beast by her side. Her second in command stood behind her with a large tome in hand ready to complete her task.

The Undines pride themselves on their magical acumen and spend much of their time training their beasts and pitting them in competitions. The very best of these beasts are chosen by Odessa for the Gauntlet. The leader of the Goba Sdogr Karshin could be viewed sharpening his four knives as he dived into the massive feast in front of him. He grumbled, "Nom nom nom! I'd wait for Vega…but he takes too long." Odessa tilted her head and remarked, "You mean Lord Vega…I'm sure it was a slip of the gill." His arms flailed back and forth as he grabbed meat after meat barely giving himself time to breathe. "Yes…Lord Vega." Sdogr was a gruesome creature who was constantly eating a variety of meats from the most dangerous beasts he could find. He often got injured in the process of hunting elite beasts but would gladly give his life up for a taste of their precious meat. He was formidable with his four blades.

The Goba are comfortable with their current position in the five clans, because of this they spend a majority of their time practicing the art of witticism and enjoy their days lounging about. The master of the Mari whispered to his clanmates. Melas' tentacles caressed the ground while his massive claws made hand signals to his clan members. The Mari was the only clan to have a separate language from the other five clans.

The Cretin leader Ayrsh Degusol argued with several Krynn members while the remaining Cretin elite did their celebratory claw dance. Their claws clapped as they moved side to side and they turned their heads 360 degrees. The Cretin were the most power hungry out of all the clans and were constantly in a chaotic state due to their inability to agree on a long-term leader. Ayrsh clicked both his claws together and declared, "When I am lord of the five clans I will allow all who wish to travel to the human world free passage. It won't just be the Krynn and the Undine elite. The Goba will be allowed to hunt above sea level while the other clans can fish to their hearts content. The reign of the mighty Cretin will be long and prosperous!" Members of each clan whispered amongst themselves.

Lord Vega entered the marked area trident in claw and looked at the facade they called a united dinner. His mouth curled as he rolled his claws into a massive fist. He looked at the Cretin leader yelling at his Krynn members while the intrepids danced side to side. Dancing was something that he knew humans did but it looked disgusting to see the Cretins do it. His eyes turned black. He grasped his trident firmly and swam upwards. He tilted his trident downward and took aim. With enormous force Lord Vega aimed his trident towards his target. In a flash of red light, the weapon spiraled through the water, a large popping sound could be heard in the distance as it streamed towards Ayrsh.

Ayrsh looked up just in time to see the trident spiraling towards him but he only had enough time to open his large crusty mouth. The trident smashed into the edge of the table in front of Ayrsh causing a massive rift that cut down the middle of the table. Lord Vega swam towards the group and yelled, "Insolent!" His tentacles appeared in a jagged formation while blue aura leaked from his right claw. The entire area became silent while Odessa's pet beast ran off into the distance. He raised his right claw slowly and turned his claw towards Odessa. "Begin!" Odessa stood up and grabbed the tome from her second in command. Her pupils dilated as a smirk appeared across her face. She turned to Ayrsh and eyed him from top to bottom. "Is it true that the Cretin wish to challenge the Krynn for supremacy over the five clans?" Ayrsh looked towards Melas and then looked towards his clan mates who stood quietly. "Yes. That is correct, for we are the mighty Cretin!" The group behind him began to do their celebratory dance once again.

Odessa turned to Lord Vega to see him standing upright while the rest of his clan sat behind him silently. "Lord Vega will represent the Krynn for the Gauntlet," said a Krynn member. The Goba whispered amongst themselves. Sdogr shouted, "Beg Lord Vega to go back to sleep should the Cretin!" The Goba laughed amongst themselves. Lord Vega shot them an errant look immediately silencing the group. Odessa read from the tome. "This Gauntlet will consist of three challenges where the winner is expected to win 2/3 of them. The first challenge is a race which will be through Volcanic Grove. The two entrants will ride a Rift Clamor that they choose out of the thirteen ones available. The second challenge will be treasure retrieval where the two entrants must enter into the territory of…an Elite Beast." Whispering could be heard once again. Odessa continued, "The Elite Beast for this trial is Hydrosta. The contestants must enter her territory and steal one of her fresh eggs. The eggs can be identified by their crystalline structure with a green streak across them." Ayrsh sat down with his claws resting on the table.

"As you know Hydrosta is one of the most dangerous Elite beasts within our grounds. The winner of that trial will be doing a great service," Odessa continued with her explanation. "The final trial for this Gauntlet is a duel until submission, but if the member with the most points dies during the final challenge they fail the Gauntlet and the survivor will be the victor." Odessa turned to Lord Vega who nodded his approval. She then turned to Ayrsh who glanced at Melas one more time both eyes flickering madly. Melas stood in the distance with what resembled a smile. A Cretin member nudged Ayrsh who eventually nodded in agreement. Odessa turned towards Lord Vega and the Krynn once again and declared, "The Gauntlet will commence when the first Hydrosta egg hatches, this should happen very soon." The two leaders nodded in agreement.

CHAPTER 9

JARVAN

AS JARVAN ENTERED The Pilgrim's Inn a bar maiden dropped her tray to the floor breaking several glasses. Staring at Jarvan's halo her face turned red. A woman dressed in a pink and white top walked over with a broad smile on her face. The top squeezed her breasts together while her leather pants accentuated her thick thighs. The smell of lilac filled the lungs of the young men. Azreal's pants became a bit snugger. "Welcome once again Monsieur Hartengale, may I direct you to your usual area?" Jarvan nodded. "I do apologize, she is new and as such is not used to seeing a man of your stature." Jarvan shook his head and commented, "Good help is ever so difficult to find." The woman led the two of them to a large pink sofa surrounded by flowers and several bottles of the world's finest wine. She adjusted her skirt and turned to Azreal, whose eyes were fixated on her large breasts. She walked closer to him and caressed his thigh. Jarvan grabbed her hand and quipped, "He's off limits to you and your ways Madam Ludus." Covering her mouth with her hands and leaning away Madam Ludus asked coyly, "Who me? I'm quite the innocent little butterfly," she said winking at Azreal. His face turned bright red as he bit his lips and moved his hands to cover his pelvis.

Jarvan looked at her and cleared his throat. "Sure, whatever aids you in your sleep during these cold nights." He waved his hands slowly and continued, "I'll have you send for my dear Philautia and surprise me with two others, and for my friend here he will have the Gemini Twins." Azreal's muscles tightened as his mouth became tense. His sweaty palms touched Jarvan on his shoulder and he stammered, "T...t...two? But... it's...my...first...time." Madam Ludus' face perked up as she cooed, "Oh sweetie the Gemini Twins will take real good care of you." She let out the most devious of laughs. Jarvan pushed Azreal's sweaty palms off his glorious armor, wrapped his arm around his neck, pulled him closer and whispered, "You'll be fine, trust me!"

Jarvan walked towards the sofa where Azreal sat with his legs crossed, dawning a massive smile. The Gemini twins surrounded him on both sides. Two empty bottles of Domaine Elegance laid across the table while a third was being opened. Jarvan motioned for the women to leave. The twins did as he commanded. Azreal's face beamed brighter than Jarvan's halo while his eyes glistened under the candlelight. He exclaimed, "I think I'm in love!" Jarvan placed a hand on Azreal's head and smirked, "Well you certainly look like a new man, though I must warn you, women like that require more than the average woman you're used to seeing walk around the street. They require someone who knows how to handle their every want and desires while being a rock during the difficult times."

Azreal tilted his head upwards to meet Jarvan's straight face and asked, "How do I become such a man?" Jarvan took a deep breath before sipping his glass of wine. "I suppose it is up to me, the great Jarvan Hartengale VII to show you. We will have plenty of time on our way to crush the pathetic Crocodile Guild!" Azreal nodded his head with fervor.

CHAPTER 10

JAMES

AS JAMES ENTERED the brothel he noticed Azreal Glycerine from the Wasp Guild sitting with two women drinking a bottle of wine. James has had several dealings with the Wasp Guild since he became an Elephant Guild judge. *I really hope he didn't see me. I have no interest in hearing complaints on this eve.* The members of his guild often got into disputes with Wasp members over territory. Although the Wasp Guild was under Lion Guild land many of their mining operations threatened the borders of the Elephant Guild. These land disputes often manifested in the form of unsanctioned duels. Often James would have to pardon his members for they were defending the honor of their guild. Unfortunately, the emperor does not do much in restraining the Wasp Guild and this is currently one of the more pressing issues that strain the two guilds relationships. According to James' father the Emperor and his guild are a vessel which contains all that is wrong with the land. James could only imagine what the emperor says about his father.

James walked over to the back where Eros was waving him in. He removed his large brown cloak to reveal his under armor. He decided to leave his armor and war hammer at the fortress for fear that it would draw too much attention. He stood at the doorway and peered inside the room. It was dimly lit with scented candles and a large black lamp. Eros smiled,

"Welcome to my sex dungeon," she said as she grabbed him by his massive hand and pulled him inside.

She caressed his shoulder with her hand and walked James around the room. "This is where I spend quality time with my special clients." The room was filled with chains, whips, ropes, and a large black chained leather swing in the middle. His heart raced, breath quickened as his pupils dilated. He stared at the leather swing and grabbed it by the chain. James tugged on the chain testing the strength of the suspended swing and commented, "It...doesn't...umm...seem that sturdy." Eros smirked and asked, "Would you like to try it?" The voice of his father crept into his mind. *An elephant judge must uphold their integrity under the most tempting of situations.*

His muscles tightened while sweat poured out of his palms. Feeling flustered, he muttered, "I think I'm fine." Eros raised her eyebrow and stepped in close to the honorable judge James Ivory, her breasts pushed up against his stomach. She went upon her toes and leaned in to whisper in his ear. "You know, it isn't against the guild rules to receive the punishment of my whip. I've had several unnamed Elephant members come to me for penance. I mean, the faith in your code of ethics is so strong that even members who have gotten away with crimes still seek punishment." Her breath smelled of mint.

James took a step back as blood rushed towards his genitals. He stammered, "S...s...sure. I mean...just for a bit." Once again, his father's voice came raging in his head like a rogue Elephant. *A man must stand his ground under pressure for pressure is a man's burden to hold in the direst of situations.* He walked over to the front of the swing and removed his shirt. Before he could position himself, Eros motioned for him to remove his wool pants as well. She strapped him in one limb at a time, first his left leg, then his right leg, then both his arms. The swing had him suspended forward with his rock-hard buttocks exposed. The chains clasped tightly against his bare skin chafing his wrists. She walked around him, caressing every single inch of his muscular body. She looked at James in the eyes and brought her lips within inches of his own, she whispered, "You're a strong man, you don't need a safe word." She picked up a piece of elderwood from her desk and placed it inside of his mouth. "There's a good boy, let Madam Eros take real good care of you." She winked and licked her lips.

Eros picked up a leather flail from her desk of punishment and rubbed it against his pelvis. The bulge in his pants throbbed rapidly. Eros licked her lips again. "Oh my I guess your muscles aren't the only thing that is Elephantine!" James squirmed in the chains as his cheeks turned bright red. She brought the flail to his back and rubbed it against the back of his neck, goosebumps emerged all over his skin. She raised the flail backwards and struck, a loud smack traversed the room. James could only muster a small moan through the elderwood. Eros shook her head and threw the leather flail to the floor. "Tsk...tsk...tsk...not good enough. Not good enough at all." She turned around and rummaged through a large chest marked dangerous. He struggled to turn his neck but could not get vision of what was going on. She returned with a large black and purple chained flail. She wrapped her hands around his waist and grabbed his hard-throbbing phallus. "Hmmm, someone is enjoying their punishment, I'm just getting started sweetheart."

She held the chained flail backwards and unleashed it upon James' large back. This time he let out a large moan as he squirmed upon impact. The chain cuffs gnawed at his wrist while the flail left marks on his back. She unleashed a flurry of strikes upon his person, each one more severe than the last. With each strike, he moaned louder. His muscles tensed up, his toes curled, and his eyes bulged as he struggled to breathe. He let out a low-pitched scream as he reached climax. Eros walked in front of James and grabbed him by the chin while removing the elderwood from his mouth. She leaned in and gave him a passionate kiss on the lips. "Hmm...shame on you...you weren't supposed to enjoy your punishment THIS much." She winked and unleashed the chained beast.

James breathed rapidly while his eyes widened. He looked at Eros and grabbed her by the waist pulling her in closer. "I feel as if a huge weight has been removed from my shoulders. I don't know how else to explain it." Eros leaned in and rubbed herself against his chiseled chest. "You can repay me by coming to see me again." James nodded and gave her another passionate kiss, his mouth firmly pressed against her soft succulent lips. "I suppose it's about time I tell you what I know about the rapes and kidnapping of the guildless class." James scratched his head as he nodded slowly. "Yes, I would like to know about that." A single tear streamed down her left eye as James leaned in close to wipe it. "I don't know much, but I have seen my sister tend to some really young children brought in by men wearing white. She would do make up for these boys and girls and then the men would leave with the children through the back. I only saw half a crest but the one thing I could make out was a wing. I know there are many guilds that have wings as a crest. I'm sorry I wish I could be of more help!" James took a deep breath and pulled her in closer. "That is more than enough, I'll figure it out." Eros held him tightly for a few moments before walking over to the door and looking around. James placed his robe back on and gave Eros another kiss. "I will see you again," he said as he walked out to the exit with a wide smile on his face.

A voice could be heard from the right side. "James! Over here!" He looked in the direction of the loud voice only to be greeted with the image of Jarvan Hartengale VII and Azreal Glycerine. He leaned his head back and rolled his eyes. "Elephant dung," he mumbled to himself. Jarvan waved his hand motioning for James to come over. He ran his hand through his ponytail and slowly walked over to the table with several empty bottles of expensive wine. The Elephant Guild was one of the more modest guilds and frowned on frivolous spending, because of their modest views things such as expensive wines and foods were only purchased for traditional ceremonies such as weddings and the birth of a new family member. James also noticed a certain relaxing demeanor coming from both Azreal and Jarvan, something very akin to his own.

Jarvan gave James a big hug as the two embraced each other for what felt like an eternity. Although the two guilds were not very fond of each other the two successors remained very good friends. This was due to their strong relationship growing up while their fathers tended to official guild business. Jarvan released his old friend and beamed with satisfaction and exclaimed, "I can't believe your father let you out of the city!" James' arms tensed up. "Yes…I'm here on some official business." Jarvan nudged him in the ribs and quipped, "Official…I'm sure! Don't worry brother, you and your little friend's secret are safe with me." He glanced over at Azreal who promptly nodded his head. James took a seat beside the prince. He leaned back against the soft cushion and asked, "You seem to be in quite the festive mood, is there a special occasion?"

Jarvan laughed and placed a hand on his shoulder. "Well I'll have you know that I have been deployed to Tem, today is my last day in the city before I set forth on my journey. The scum who dare to call themselves a guild will taste my mighty blade and receive the weight of my glorious shield!" Jarvan stood up, raised his hand, and yelled, "Tem will quake before the teeth of the lion and quiver when they hear our mighty roar! For glory and honor, we shall feast!" The whole room chanted his name. James pulled his hood down while squirming. He turned to Jarvan and smiled with a meek expression, "I think it is time for me to take my leave…I have some other matters I must attend to."

Jarvan smirked, "I'm sure you do! Later this evening I shall expect you to see me off at the castle, my father and sister would be overjoyed to have your accompany! Plus, you can meet the queen, she is quite the delightful woman." Jarvan grabbed James by the neck and pulled him closer placing him in a headlock while ruffling his ivory hair. Perhaps I will have time to defeat you in a duel like old times." Azreal's eyes widened and asked, "You and James used to duel?" Jarvan smirked and replied, "Yes, and I always won. It was quite the sight even as children. My sister would always cheer whoever was winning at the time, while Octavius would sulk in the corner at his own ineffectiveness." James shrugged and said, "Sure, I'll see you this evening."

CHAPTER 11

ORIANNA

ORIANNA SAT IN the Skeksi drawn carriage shifting back and forth. She peered outside the window staring at the one in front that contained her mother and Malikai. She lowered her brow and sighed as she turned to Tamriel who was in mid-sentence. "I'm so glad they make you wear a veil. It covers that ugly face of yours," Tamriel taunted with a broad smile as he caressed his magical tome. Corvus who was sitting to his side shifted a bit in his sleep. Orianna sniffled slightly but kept silent. "Are you listening to me bar wench? I'm talking to you…If you like I could cast a spell or two to fix your face." Orianna mumbled, "No…thank you. I'm the way the deity made me." Tamriel cackled, "Well the deity must have created you with her eyes closed." Orianna lowered her head. "Why are you so mean to me? I have never done anything to offend you…at least I don't think I have." She clasped her gown firmly. Tamriel paused for a moment before responding. "Your very existence offends me. I see you as nothing more than a boulder that we must carry upon our shoulders. If you were any more useless I would have disposed of you myself. Your only redeeming quality is that you occasionally come out with a decent prophecy or two…but even that you can't accomplish consistently." Orianna lowered her head even more. "I see…but I'm trying to be better…doesn't that count for something?" Tamriel opened his tome, "It counts for a few verses in my tome. Allow me to put you out of your misery, they say death is rather peaceful."

Orianna remained silent for a moment. She stammered, "But I want to live...I want to help. I can be better...at least I think I can." Tamriel snarled, "Who cares what you think. What I think matters more. I am older and wiser, and I think we'd be better off with a new oracle." Orianna shifted in her seat and asked, "Someone like you?" Tamriel sat upright, his crooked nose wrinkled. "Yes, someone like me. I am well versed in the old tongue, even more so than mother. I have read all our magical tomes and have even created this one. It contains our most powerful spells." Orianna leaned in closer and taunted, "You mean the tome that you haven't even memorized. I mean...even I have memorized most of my required spells. Mother always rebukes you for needing to carry a tome around like an initiate."

Tamriel's face turned scarlet. He retorted, "Y...you...shut your mouth this instance!" Orianna crossed her arms and exclaimed, "You're not the boss of me!" She said stomping her feet. Corvus rustled again, mumbling in his sleep. Tamriel clenched his fist. "Quiet, don't wake that poor excuse for a healer. I refuse to hear more of his boring stories." Orianna continued, "His stories are boring, but I'd rather hear his stories than your vile words." Tamriel's face creased. "The truth is never vile. You're just a worthless piece of moss. Something that should have been dealt with a long time ago. One day when you realize this, come to me and I'll put you out of your misery." Tears streamed down Orianna's face. Corvus opened his eyes to see Orianna in tears. "Aww don't cry little miss. We will be back home before you know it. This reminds me of how I became a member of the high council. It's a long story, but we got plenty of time!"

CHAPTER 12

LORD VEGA

THE ELITE CLAN members stood in front of Volcanic Grove. The large geyser shot forth a blast of lava. The clan members gazed in awe at the dazzling display. Swell fish dashed in and out between the streams. Their sword like noses pierced through the water with great force while their red fins allowed them easy navigation. These fish are notoriously territorial and will send shocking attacks through anyone unfortunate to greet them. The eruptions caused huge puffs of blue smoke to manifest.

Sdogr placed a piece of meat in his mouth while one of his other arms scratched his head. "Mhmm, swell fish taste good, but dangerous to catch." His third arm scratched a large scab on his chest. Odessa shook her head and took a step-in front of the group. She pointed to the rift clamors stationed a few feet away from volcanic grove. They had sharp claws perfect for digging up the many creatures that slept in the ocean bed. Additionally, their large tails allowed for quick bursts in the water while running at the ocean floor. These medium sized beasts are exceptionally agile yet temperamental, even after being tamed.

"It is time for the challenger to choose his rift clamor!" Odessa exclaimed. The cretin danced side to side cheering for their glorious clan leader. Ayrsh raised his claws in the air and clicked his jaws together. He turned to his people and clicked both his claws against each other again. "Death to the Krynn!" he proclaimed. His Cretin people chanted his name. Ayrsh walked towards the first Rift Clamor whose eyes turned bright blue at the sight of the Cretin creature. He continued to walk to the second one which did the same thing. It wasn't until he got to the final Rift Clamor did he realize that none of them respected him enough to allow him to ride it.

Ayrsh grabbed the final beast and pulled on its reins, the beast pulled away and snapped at him. He struck the beast in the head and jumped on its back while the beast struggled to throw him off. Odessa covered her mouth as she let out a low giggle. "It is time for the champion to choose his Rift Clamor!" She exclaimed. Lord Vega threw down his trident onto the ocean floor causing a ripple of aura to disperse across the area. He walked over to the first rift clamor and grabbed it by the reins. He immediately climbed on top of the beast while it stood there patiently. Sdogr bit another piece of Swell Fish meat. "Ayrsh look strong but smell weak, I wonder what crab taste like." Both the Goba and the Undines laughed. Melas placed both his hands together as he stood there quietly observing the two Gauntlet contestants.

Odessa opened her large book and read, "The first one to navigate the entire grove without falling from their Rift Clamor is the winner." She pointed to her Undine follower. A large bodied Undine swam over to the middle of both Rift Clamors and raised her hands in the air. She shouted, "Ogha! Tokba! Threba!" She lowered her arms and both rift clamors jumped forward into the large ravine. Lord Vega stormed ahead swiftly, navigating through the first set of geysers. He took a hard left only to be blindsided by a Swell Fish which stormed right into his chest piercing his armor. The Swell Fish sent a large shock wave down his body as he grabbed it, snapping the fish in two. Sdogr could be heard from atop the cliff. He bellowed, "Bring me back food all mighty Lord Vega!"

Lord Vega pushed forward, determined to defeat the scum that would dare to challenge him. Ayrsh and his Rift Clamor were right on his heel pushing forward as he clicked his claws onto the back of the beast. Three Swell Fish came darting forward, grazing Ayrsh at the side of his head while the other two grazed his chest. Purple fluid streamed from his sides and cheek while the Rift Clamor pushed forward. He then extended his claws six feet ahead and clipped the back foot of Lord Vega's clamor caus-

ing it to veer left head first into a volcanic eruption. Ayrsh passed Lord
Vega and pursued ahead only to be blindsided by three more Swell fish
who picked up on his scent. This time all three pierced into his chest
causing several electric shocks to stream down his entire body. He let out
a loud scream. Miraculously keeping his Rift Clamor standing Lord Vega
pushed forward into the danger zone of the grove. He dodged left then
right, then left again only to have five Swell Fish dart forward aiming for
his head. He raised his left claw and created a whirlpool which captured
all five.

Another five flew towards Lord Vega but he moved his head to the
right at the last second. The fish kept spiraling forward straight into the
chest of Ayrsh who was knocked off his Rift Clamor. Lord Vega returned
to the group with only a piercing in his outer shell but received no physical damage. The Krynn all banged their spears on the sea bottom causing
the ground to shake. The Undines clapped with fervor while the Goba
laughed at Ayrsh whose Rift Clamor had abandoned him, forcing him
to climb up the ravine by himself. The Cretin leader took medium level
damage while steam spewed from his ears. The rules of the Gauntlet state
that a contestant who is injured is not allowed to be healed while the challenges are active. Odessa glared at the bleeding Cretin and covered her
mouth once again; she let out another giggle as her beloved beast returned
to snuggle beside her. Odessa opened her book and smiled as she turned
to whisper to her second in command. "It's time…"

The group now stood in front of the dreaded Hydrosta Lair. The Hydrosta
was one of the few known Elite Beasts in Pacifia. She is a massive sized
creature with the body of a female humanoid with twenty tentacles as
legs. For hair, she has thirty smaller tentacles and has no eyes. In replace-
ment of vision she has two large cylinders that shoot out poison gas. This
creature is deadly to all those who enter her domain. She lays one hundred eggs at a time and is said to be the mother of all Elite Beasts. Sdogr
raised all four of his arms and yelled, "The Hydrosta is no fun! She hides
all of her best eggs underneath her, and cowers in her vast cavern until it is
time to discard the worthless ones,"

Odessa tilted her head and commented in an even manner, "Yet you fight me for those discarded ones in hopes of consuming an Elite Beast." Sdogr revealed his yellow teeth and remarked, "No one has ever been brave or stupid enough to steal one of her crystalline eggs until now." Odessa licked her lips as she sneered at the great beast Hydrosta. She loomed over and rubbed her hands at the thought of retrieving one of the elusive crystalline eggs. "For this challenge, whoever enters Hydrosta's lair and retrieves a crystalline egg without dying is the winner. Challengers prepare yourselves and you may enter when you are ready." Lord Vega looked at the beast who could be seen throwing her eggs as hard as she could. The Goba members had all swam away to catch these rare delicacies. Lord Vega grabbed his trident and swam towards the monstrosity, while Ayrsh stood back slowly clicking his two claws together. Lord Vega arrived in front of the Elite Beast who screamed at him.

A massive shock wave was sent forth causing Lord Vega to brace himself with his trident. At this point the Hydrosta grabbed him with two of her tentacles and twisted him. He swung forth his weapon and cut the tentacles in half. At the same moment, he unleashed a massive whirlpool, destroying five more of her tentacles. She unleashed a large cloud of poison gas that filled his gills, causing him to go into a daze. Lord Vega placed his claw over his eyes as he felt the effects of the poison. Another tentacle came slashing forth grabbing him by his leg and pulling him higher up. The disgusting beast opened her mouth again to scream but this time Lord Vega twirled his trident again causing a massive wave of aura to push forward slicing the Hydrosta's head off.

It was at this point Ayrsh darted forward towards the cave for the crystalline egg. He grabbed the egg and swam back making a beeline towards the group whose mouths were all agape. Lord Vega turned to attack Ayrsh but the Hydrosta head had been reattached by her tentacles and she grabbed him once again. Lord Vega jammed his trident into the tentacles and freed himself. He activated the manta wings on his back and swam forth to the edge where everyone was waiting. By the time he arrived Ayrsh was standing there smiling as he held the crystalline egg in his hand. The Cretin did their celebratory dance once again. The tentacles on Lord Vega's head turned black and twirled furiously. His eyes turned black as he gripped his trident with all his might. The ground underneath him shook. Odessa declared Ayrsh the winner while staring at Lord Vega. His outer shell had been severely damaged, he was oozing purple liquid from his chest, stomach, and arm, as well as the poison appeared to have blurred his vision. It had dawned on her for the first time since meeting this creature they called Lord Vega that he was not some immortal deity. Odessa smiled to herself and waved the group over for the final challenge.

Odessa stood in the middle of the ring with her hands in the air. "As per our custom the third and final challenge of the Gauntlet is a duel until submission. Once again, if someone dies during the duel they are deemed unfit to lead and thus will forgo their clans position." Lord Vega walked to the circle with his trident in claw. He pointed to the Cretin elite members and yelled. "Fifteen!" Odessa turned to Lord Vega and asked, "Fifteen…what?" Lord Vega twirled his trident and slammed it into the floor causing another massive earthquake. He bellowed, "Fifteen of the Cretins strongest now!" Ayrsh took a step forward and laughed while clicking his claws. He taunted, "You fool, you will perish at the hands of my clanmates." He pointed to his personal squad and motioned them to join him in the ring. "All mighty Vega will die a miserable death," teased the Cretin leader. Melas' eyes opened wide as he stared at the massive rift that had been caused by Lord Vega's trident. Odessa stared at Lord Vega's eyes and shuddered. His eyes were now red like the red moon that often pierced their waters. The fifteen strongest Cretin surrounded Lord Vega and circled him with their mandibles held high ready to launch. They continued to circle though none dared to attempt the first blow.

Lord Vega dropped his trident and laughed, "Hahahaha, weaklings only know fear, but death will come regardless." He jumped forward and grabbed a Cretin soldier tearing his head off instantly. Another Cretin attempted to grab his trident, but his claw immediately snapped off upon touching it. Lord Vega stomped, and the trident instantly returned to his claw. He swung his trident forward in a cleaving motion taking off the heads of five Cretin members. He swam forward and twirled in the ocean water while swinging his trident backwards causing a whirlpool to emerge.

It sucked three Cretin members in, shredding them into tiny fragments. Five of the six remaining members jumped upon Lord Vega simultaneously only to perish at the tip of his trident. Each one of them lost their head one right after the other.

Lord Vega walked towards Ayrsh who had not moved once since the beginning of the duel. He pointed his trident at the cowardly Cretin and smiled. His eyes still burning red while the tentacles on his head still black. "Speak your last rights." Ayrsh went on both of his knees and placed his head at the feet of the Krynn. "O…oh…Lord…Vega…ple…" Lord Vega raised his left foot and stomped on the back of the cowardly Cretin leader, a loud crunch could be heard as liquid streamed out of the creature's pathetic body. Lord Vega walked over to the remaining Cretin members and grabbed the crystal egg from one of the members. He gripped it and placed his claw behind his head. He then launched the egg forward creating a loud popping sound as the water around his fist evaporated. Odessa and Sdogr both opened their mouth in amazement as they watched the egg fly away at a rapid pace. Odessa turned to her second in command and pulled her in by the neck and shouted, "Get that egg now!"

CHAPTER 13

JARVAN

JARVAN SAT ACROSS from his father doing his best to avoid eye contact. His father's disappointing glare always irked him. He stared at his champion piece as he contemplated his next move, he was always unsure of when to attack or defend with it. The emperor often told him a true general mastered the art of timing. A defensive strategy was mysterious to the great warrior because his tactics often involved blitzkriegs and reliance on his raw power. The time on the clepsydra reached critical condition as he contemplated this crucial decision.

Jarvan touched his piece and moved it forward to subdue his father's last royal piece. His father glared at him with a stone face and moved his peasant piece diagonally to subdue Jarvan's emperor piece. Jarvan stared at his captured emperor with his mouth agape and fist clenched. "I was... so...close...how can I lose to a meaningless peasant piece?"

The emperor clenched his fist as the rings on Jarvan's head danced. He stared at the light as it danced, his curiosity burned while his heart ached with desire at the sight of his son's halo. Not even the emperor knew the true meaning of Jarvan's secret weapon. "It seems you are quite mistaken my son. The peasant piece is the most important piece." Jarvan curled his lips upwards and furled his brow. "How can such a simple piece be the most important piece? It can only subdue the emperor and only under one circumstance." The emperor tapped his fingers on the Volute table and continued, "That is why it's the most important one, for the peasant to be useful it can only pursue one objective, which is to subdue the emperor and gain honor from doing so, because of this it is the most dangerous one. This is reflective of the guildless in our beloved territory. They are the hungriest for power and thus pose the biggest threat yet can be our most valuable asset in time of need."

Jarvan scratched his head as he reset the Volute board for another game. "Soon we need not worry about such things. We currently own sixty five percent of the world's territory. Once we conquer the Crocodile scum we will have seventy-five with the remaining being left to the Elephant Guild." An eerie expression crossed his father's face. The announcer blew the horn. "Enter the all honorable judge James from the Elephant Guild!" James entered the room and assumed the customary greeting stance of the Elephant Guild. He stuck his left hand out to the left and upwards while holding his right hand to his chest and nodded his head.

Lamia ran up to James and gave him a big hug. The queen returned James' greeting with a twirl and a bow while Octavius sulked in the corner continuing with his novel. James walked over to Jarvan who had started another game of Volute with his father. Jarvan glanced over at his father who nodded, thus he stood up and gave James a big hug. "Good of you to join us in the castle, it's been a long time since you've been here. I remember when our fathers would do business while we were up to no good," said the prince. James rubbed his chin. "Not like I had much of a choice, I could never say no to you." Jarvan laughed and pushed back his hair. Glancing at James' war hammer he asked, "Is that the famed war hammer of a thousand spirits I've heard so much about?"

Octavius' tiny ears perked up. He ran over to the two old time friends. He quipped, "You mean the war hammer that was created with the best part of a thousand different magical trees!" James' face turned red. "Y...yes...the only luxurious item an Elephant member can have is their weapon because a weapon is an extension of the oath that they have taken to protect their family. The only exception to this rule is my father who wears the sacred jewelry."

Octavius moved to touch it but Jarvan's glare prevented him from doing such a foul thing. Octavius sneered and then an unnerving smile crept across his face. "I would so…love to see such a beautiful weapon in action…perhaps you and my mighty brother could duel?" James shook his head. "I am not allowed to display my skills without good reason, for it is the duty of my guild to be the shining symbol of peace." The emperor walked in between the three men and smirked. "Yes, that is true, but I also would love to see a duel between the two of you. Is it not your duty to defend the honor of your guild at all costs? Your honor would be in question if you were to back down from such a challenge." James steeled himself and nodded his head. The emperor motioned for everyone to stand back. "First one to draw blood is the victor, and the use of magic is prohibited."

Jarvan smiled and grabbed his broadsword and shield. "Today I will show you some of the skills I've been practicing!" James responded with silence, his face stern as he took a defensive position. Jarvan charged in with his sword held high and shield lowered. James parried the blow by holding his war hammer diagonally and turning to the side. Jarvan stumbled but counter attacked by swinging his shield behind him pushing James forward. While using his war hammer for balance James caught himself before he could fall. Jarvan Immediately pounced leaping in the air with his sword pointed towards James' head. Once again, he stood in his defensive stance, as the pouncing Lion came closer he dodged and swung his war hammer upwards catching Jarvan in the mid-section. Jarvan landed face first into the marble floor, blood escaped his lips.

He stood up and wiped the blood from his face. His eyes twitched as the light underneath his feet and above his head grew brighter, his face burned red. James walked over to Jarvan with his hand outstretched. "If you could use magic I'm sure…" Jarvan pushed James' hand away and stormed off. Octavius snickered in the background as the room now filled with onlookers watched in amazement.

Jarvan pushed open his room door with such force that the door broke off its hinges. He picked up his dresser and flung it across the room shattering his crystal Lion. The prince let out a loud scream as the entire room filled with bright yellow light. He sat on his bed, sword in hand while his shield laid at his feet. He stared at his hands in amazement. *How can I*

have lost in a battle of skill? He gripped his sword and held it to eye level. He read the engraving aloud. "Draw me not without purpose, sheath me not without honor." He ran his hand through his hair. *I need to be the greatest...I* just *need to be.*

Octavius slinked in through the doorway while stepping atop the fallen door. He smirked at the sight of his younger brother sitting on the bed. "Hello brother," said Octavius. Jarvan squinted and glared at the frail man that was supposedly his older brother. "Why do you disturb me Octavius?" The frail man slinked closer while surveying the room. "It seems you've had quite the little mishap...I mean... who would have thought you'd lose a duel. Makes one think...you know?" Jarvan's left eye started to twitch. "Makes one think what?" Jarvan demanded. Octavius walked around the room caressing the remnants of the once great crystal Lion. "Aww...poor Akili. It seems he has suffered quite the little...accident." Jarvan stood up with his hands balled into a fist. "Makes one think what?!" he demanded again.

Octavius sat on the Lion's head and crossed his legs. "Well...I was just...thinking...oh never mind what do you care?" Jarvan walked towards Octavius and pointed his sword at his brother's throat. "Speak forward whilst you still have a tongue." Octavius yawned and pushed the blade slowly away from his throat. "Well brother dearest...It seems that one would think...after such a display of skill...that maybe James is the strongest warrior in all the land. I mean within the Elephant Guild...his forest magic is almost as revered as your holy magic. Who would have thought his physical power would be so refined?"

Octavius chuckled, "Then again...it makes me wonder what would happen if only you had a little more strategy to go with your physical prowess." He licked his lips as he reached for a piece of cheese that had been resting on a tray. Jarvan dropped his blade and grabbed his brother by the throat. His lungs ached as he gasped for air; Octavius held his grin and whispered. "That's all you know, you're nothing but a brute. One day the world will see you for what you truly are." Jarvan threw Octavius across the room. "Out!" Octavius made a whimpering sound as the air rushed forward into his lungs. Jarvan paced back and forth while stepping on crystal and marble shards. He took off his armor and placed it on its stand. The armor glistened in the sunlight as he stared at the dent that James has caused. He looked down at his boots and saw specks of his blood on it. He hadn't seen his own blood since he was a child. He used to climb trees and jump from them to see how much damage he could take. One time he broke his arm and still climbed back up a second time.

Jarvan chuckled to himself, remembering the long nights of training against the best teachers in the entire world. He was trained in thirty different types of weapons and had mastered the ancient art of holy magic, something that he was exceptionally proud of. Jarvan sat on his bed and placed both his hands on his knees while staring at the speck of blood on his boot. *What am I? If not the strongest…what am I…If not the best?* Jarvan stared at his two hands and marveled at how they trembled. Lamia approached the door slowly and knocked at the side of the arch. "C…can I come in?" Jarvan motioned for her to enter. Lamia walked in carefully as to avoid the broken shards and sat beside her brother. She grabbed his arm and held him tightly for a moment. "Do you remember when we were kids and you and James used to always duel?" Jarvan nodded. "Well I used to always cheer for who was winning at the time, but I always knew you would win." Jarvan shrugged. "Yes…I do recall that, what of it?" Lamia gripped him tighter. "No matter what obstacle comes before you; you will always return victorious. A simple duel doesn't matter when father has entrusted the fate of our world in your hands. This duel was merely the beginning of a longer journey for you, I know you will return victorious. You're my big brother!"

Jarvan smiled and ran his hand through her long golden hair. Lamia wrapped her arms around his head giving him a big hug, her large breasts pushed up against his cheek. "Besides, you have to return in time for my name day, everyone will be there!" Jarvan laughed and stood up. "Why yes of course. The great Jarvan Hartengale VII will return victorious and with a present for the all mighty Lamia Hartengale. I mean it is your twenty first name day after all!"

⁂

Jarvan had started to clean up his room when the air in the room suddenly became heavier. His back tingled as he turned around to see his father staring at him. "Yes…father?" His father walked in the room and sat on a chair while motioning for his son to do the same. "It is a weak man who lets his emotions overcome his rationality. I know with your condition, it is challenging." Jarvan lowered his head slightly. "My condition has nothing to do with it. It's just…," The emperor raised his hand. "I understand why you acted so, I am not here to berate you or antagonize you for it. I'm sure Octavius has already seen to that."

Jarvan balled his hands into a fist. "Do you know why I encouraged a duel between you two?" asked the emperor. Jarvan shook his head. "I encouraged a duel between you two because of the difference in fighting techniques. It all goes back to our game of Volute. You lack the ability to know when it is time to defend and when it is time to attack. This is something that may one day cost you many lives." Jarvan stood up and walked towards the bathroom where he washed his face. "I hear you father, but this was not some meaningless game of Volute. This was a live duel where I simply tested my new move too early." The emperor stood up and shook his head. "I have won countless battles without even stepping foot on the battlefield. This 'meaningless game' is a major factor in that. It would be wise for you to have taken the lessons you have learned to heart."

Jarvan slammed his hands on what was left of his desk. "That is the problem father. You have never lost a battle before. You have not tasted true defeat before, something that I have borne first witness to. What can you teach me of failure?" The emperor placed a hand on his son's shoulder. "With these eyes of mine I have seen to the destruction of countless hopes and dreams. I have seen what it looks like to give a man no reason to live repeatedly. One day you will learn what I have tried to teach you, but at what cost I do not know."

CHAPTER 14

JAMES

THE CROWD RUSHED in and out of the bazaar as the announcer shot off rainbow streams of light. James could see all sorts of guild crests. Some of the guilds he recognized and others he never knew existed. The guilds in Larimar were renowned for their choice of sanctioned guild armor. They varied greatly in color, but most contained rare and precious gems. These gems were not only for decoration as many of them were enchanted with various types of magic.

Virtually all types of magic could be found in Larimar. These ranged from extremely destructive to ones beneficial for all those who encounter it. The branches that can be found inside Larimar city are air, animal, artificial, celestial, healing, holy, insect, mineral, mythical, ocean, and curse. Certain guilds only accept members who have a natural affinity for a specific type of magic. The Raven, Lion, and Scarab Guilds are well known for this type of limitation.

"Come one come all! For the twenty first annual birthday tournament in honor of the great Lamia Hartengale, the Swan Guild is proud to present a special grand prize this year!" An onlooker from the Lion Guild yelled out. "Tell us what the prize is, you turtledove!" The announcer wearing the light blue robe with crystals hanging off the side blushed. "Well...this year's prize is something you'll find out if you have the pleasure of winning." The announcer continued, "This tournament is the chance for all to bring honor, glory, and respect to their guild. It will truly be a tournament of champions and I have it under great authority that last year's winner Jarvan VII will not be attending. This means that anyone could be this year's champion!"

James stared at the announcer and surveyed the large number of gatherers from all the different guilds. It was as if his proud Elephant Guild was nothing more but a grain of sand in the desert. The high strike operator walked over to James and handed him a sheet of paper. "Mr. Ivory, I assume you will be joining this year's tournament?" James raised an eyebrow. "How do you know who I am?" The operator smiled. "We in the Swan Guild know many things…I mean if only I had been there to witness the duel between you and the prince!" James placed a hand on the operator's shoulder and looked him in his eyes. "You'd be bright to keep that between you and your guildmates." The smile on the high strike operator's face broadened. He commented, "You really are new to this city your honor. However, I wish to give you a bit of advice. You will find what you seek if you were to join the tournament." James squinted while placing one hand behind his back. "What do you speak of?" The operator took one step back. "Oh…nothing at all your honor, I shall look forward to seeing you win!" The operator bowed and ran off.

James shrugged. *Me…win the tournament? That's not something I had considered. I wonder if father would approve of me entering this tournament for the honor of our guild?* Sadness filled his being. *But what if I were to lose…that would bring disgrace.*

James found himself standing in front of a small tavern with a rat on the door. *I suppose I can have a drink or two…I mean it won't bring me any harm.* He entered the tavern and nodded to the group that scowled at him. Without any further acknowledgment they continued with their conversation. James approached the empty table behind them and sat down. The bartender handed him a drink menu. "Warm beer and slightly warm beer…I see," James said. The bartender tapped his foot. "Hurry up and order or get out." James tapped his finger on the menu. "I'll have a slightly warm beer…I suppose." Without uttering another word, the bartender grabbed the menu and returned to the counter.

He surveyed his surroundings. The tavern had paintings of rats all over it. Some large, some small, some blue, and some green. He watched as the group in front of him arm wrestled. The hefty one slammed the slim one's hand into the wooden table. "Pay up!" the hefty one yelled. The slim one grudgingly placed a fistful of Lion dollars upon the table. Glaring at James the hefty one demanded, "What are you looking at?" James' face turned red. "I was just admiring your feats of strength, we're not allowed to arm wrestle where I come from." The hefty one flexed. "Try your hand…if you're not too scared of going broke." James winced but sat still. "I am not afraid…it's just…" The slim one picked his nose and teased, "It's just nothing…you sound like one of those docile Elephant Guild members." James clenched his fist and replied, "Please do not speak ill of my guild. Our vow of neutrality is not a sign of weakness, it is a sign of strength."

The hefty one laughed. "I knew it! You Elephant people all have an earthly rock chucking scent about you." James stood up with his fists clenched. "Oh…what are you going to do? Besides go and hug a tree," the hefty one continued with his banter. This question was met with silence. "That's what I thought…you guys hide in your fortresses because you are too scared to make waves in the real world. Living in a fantasy world is what I call it." The group of men stood up simultaneously. James' veins protruded as he clenched his fists tighter. He grinded his teeth and stormed out of the tavern.

James sat down at the guild sanctioned desk, like all things made by the Elephant Guild it was well made but nothing too extravagant. The wood was sturdy and would hold up over the years, but it left much to be desired for design. He sat staring at the paper with one hand on his chin as he attempted to update his father on the proceedings in Larimar. It had only been twenty days since he last spoke to his father, however a lifetime of events had passed him by.

Dearest Donta Ivory…, he crumpled up the paper and threw it into the Elephant sanctioned trash bin. *Hello, Father. I am writing you this letter to update you on the court proceedings and my activities since then. I deemed it necessary to execute a member of our family for they have violated one of our sacred tenets.* He paused and stared at the parchment for a moment.

James took out a blank sheet of parchment and started to write again. *Father, I have learned a lot following the proceedings for the execution of a member of our family. I believe that what was done was unjust. I strongly feel that it is time the guild makes changes for growth. It is foolish for us to think maintaining the status quo while the world evolves is to be honorable and just. In this city, our guild is nothing more than a group of saints who practice sin in secret. I have decided that I will join the annual tournament to demonstrate just how great and powerful our guild truly is. The world does not respect our forest magic and considers us a bunch of children playing tree planting. I strongly believe I am an honorable person and I will not stand for this. Once I become guild master I will make changes so that our guild can grow!*

James read over the letter. He stared at each word with fervor as he knitted his brows and clenched his fists. The words brought fire into his heart with each reading. He read it one more time before crumpling it up and throwing it in the trash. He pulled the previous letter and continued to write. *There is nothing left for me to do here. However, I have been instructed to remain in Larimar to conduct business with the Lion Guild. Your skills and expertise are needed for these proceedings and I would like for you to come in time for the meeting. The meeting is set to occur during Lamia's birthday party, much honor and respect, your son James Ivory of the Elephant Guild.* James stood up and punched a massive hole through the wall above his desk.

CHAPTER 15

ORIANNA

SOLAIRE AND A masked figure stood at the entrance of Larimar where they went over the details of their arrangement. Orianna stood nearby patiently waiting for the conversation to reach its end. She glanced over at the other group of masked figures. One had both of his hands positioned in an odd fashion while Tamriel was laughing at a tiny child who seemed to be constipated. Malikai was hunched against the carriage with a bottle of ale in his hands. *I wonder what they are talking about?* Orianna pondered. She walked towards the group when her mother took her staff and poked her in the back. "Where are you going one with large feet?" Orianna sniffled as she looked at her feet and mumbled, "My feet are not large...they are average." Solaire squinted her eyes and asked, "What did you say?" Orianna took one step towards her mother and lowered her head and answered, "Nothing mother." Solaire nodded her approval and continued with her conversation.

"We will meet tomorrow evening to go over the finer details. Ideally you can get Lamia to invite us into the party." Solaire raised an eyebrow. "That little fledgling is as dumb as this one. I'm sure I can convince her of such a thing." Orianna didn't notice the jab as she was too busy staring at the masked figures. Their robes had crystals hanging off them but had no insignia. A hand gripped Orianna's shoulder, the icy grip sent shivers down her spine. "Don't worry my child, you will see them again at tomorrow's banquet." Orianna managed a meek smile to appease her mother's gaze of fury.

❧

Lamia rushed over to the Duskbringers and gave Orianna a hug. Her long golden hair flowed in the wind. It glistened under the light of the sun matching the golden arch of the doorway to the courtyard. Her white and gold dress was unmatched in terms of quality. The sapphire necklace that she wore matched her eyes. Lamia was widely considered one of the most beautiful women in the world whose beauty was only matched by the Mora family. Lamia let out a loud gasp as she struggled to catch her breath. "When I heard you had arrived I ran all the way over here. It was so far…from all the way upstairs. Oh, my heavens light, I think we deserve some wine and fish for all the exercise I just did!" Lamia smiled, her pearly white teeth nearly blinded Orianna. "Sure…we definitely do," Orianna smiled brightly at her friend.

Solaire stepped in front of Lamia pushing Orianna to the side. "Before you go and have your fun, I would like to discuss something with you." Lamia shook her head and replied, "I'm so sorry grandma Duskbringer, but my father said you are to meet him in his chambers immediately. I don't know what it's about, but he did his weird eye thing when he said it. So…now my head hurts! We have to go and do some shopping, after all the pain I've been through!" Orianna giggled and answered, "Ok that sounds like a date!"

❧

The two friends walked through the bazaar with large shopping baskets. Lamia pointed at the jewel seller, her favorite shopkeeper in the marketplace. Lamia placed both her hands on the table and smiled. "What do you have for me today Remero?" The shopkeeper ran into his store, returning with a medium sized chest. His swan insignia was clearly visible. He opened the chest, revealing three massive gems. "I'm so pleased that you stopped by today. I have been saving this for you all week!" Lamia pulled out a white crystal loupe and inspected the gems.

She picked up a sparkling ruby. "Eh, this one has a tiny scratch on it, not good enough!" She threw it on the floor. She picked up a dazzling sapphire. "Eh, this one has a tiny little hole in it." She tossed the second gem on the floor behind Orianna. Finally, Lamia picked up a glorious alexandrite stone and licked her lips. "This one I'll take." She took out a medium sized sack filled with Lion dollars and placed the sack on the table. Orianna picked up the two stones off the floor and handed them to the shopkeeper. "No, no, no. Keep them I insist! This is more than enough to cover their cost. I can't see your face, but something tells me they match your eyes!" Orianna giggled and nodded her head.

"Thank you Remero and thank you Lamia." Lamia smiled and grabbed Orianna by the hand then pulled her towards the cheese cart. "See now this is the real treat, now that my brother has left all the good cheese will still be here!" Orianna's heart skipped a beat as a shock traveled down her spine. "Wh...which...brother...not...Jarvan..." Lamia tilted her head and laughed. "Octavius is supposed to be our older brother but he doesn't have an ounce of Lion blood in him. I swear it is as if a stork switched the babies at birth." She laughed hysterically. "Yes, him silly. Jarvan has gone to cleanse the world with his glorious holy magic. He is finally going to end the gruesome war against the Crocodile Guild!"

Orianna grabbed Lamia by both her shoulders as she struggled to find her breath. "Th...th...there is something I need to tell you." Lamia gently touched her hand. "You can tell me anything, you're like a sister to me." Orianna looked at Lamia while taking a deep breath. "The Raven Guild is planning...," Orianna's eyes widened while her throat started to close. Her tongue became tied in a knot. Tamriel closed his book and walked in between Lamia and Orianna. He placed his arm around both. "Hello, you two, I hope you're having fun!" Lamia let out a cough after getting a large whiff of his cologne. "Whatever could you two have been talking about, I'm ever so curious."

Lamia played with her hair. "Well...Orianna was just about to tell me something about what the Raven Guild is planning!" Tamriel smiled. "Oh, Orianna my dear. You sly one, you were supposed to wait for me to tell her. The Raven Guild is planning a special performance. We have hired a special troupe of entertainers to perform at your birthday celebration. We just need you to give the final approval, so the guards know to expect them." Lamia clapped her hands and jumped up and down. "Oh of course! I can't wait!"

CHAPTER 16

JAMES

JAMES JOLTED UPRIGHT. Beads of sweat ran down his face. He gazed at the thick walls that surrounded him on each side with eyes wide open. *It was just a dream but what does it mean?* He paced back and forth. *But it felt so real...as if someone had engulfed me in a tomb made of earth.* He glanced at his sweaty palms. *I killed a man with these hands. His blood will forever be intertwined with my spirit. How do I pursue on after committing such a sin?* Walking towards his mighty war hammer he paused half way. *Without life there cannot be death, without death there cannot be life. What the Elephant Deity gives in one hand he takes with another. Our sacred oath is as close to the Elephant Deity one can become, we are one with all of creation. From the carnivorous ferret, to the leaves blowing in the wind. The Elephant Deity will forever shine down upon us if we follow our sacred oath. For the world resides in our heart.* His father's voice whispered.

In the corner of his eye he saw a book that he was well familiar with. Removing the chains, he read the cover, *The Elephant's Creed A Guide on the Spirit Deities.* Flipping to the middle of the text his eyes scanned the page on the various ancient guilds. "With most of the world's territories under its control many view the Lion Guild as the dominant force in the world, however, very few understand the inner workings of the Elephant Guild and its customs. Additionally, little is known about the Aura Manipulation System that governs this world." James flipped to the next page. "A Spirit Deity grows more powerful based on the worshipping that it receives, which in turn grants said worshipper access to more powerful magic. Each Deity has different types of worship that they prefer. The Lion Guild is based on the number of their members while the Elephant Guild emphasizes the amount of dedication towards the five sacred tenets. These tenets are the foundation of the guild and can never be changed. The Raven Guild follows a unique doctrine where they channel much of their spirit power through their oracle, which changes every ten years. Members of the Crocodile Guild must undergo a series of trials to activate their inherent gifts."

He flipped to the next page. "Much credit is given to the sacred bloodline of the Elephant members which must be tightly regulated, for our forest magic is a rare and beautiful gift. Because of our few numbers one must practice safe awareness to ensure we continue to thrive." He threw the book onto the bed, causing it to open to another page. *I have followed this text closely for all my life, but I have so many questions. If the Elephant Deity never intended for me to pursue change why did he grant me an unsettled spirit?* The raspy voice returned. *Destruction. Destroy it all!* James clasped his head and started to hum a tune. The voice continued its onslaught. *Death begets rebirth, rebirth begets death. Without death, there is no growth.* He paced back and forth. The voices continued to haunt him. Looking up to the ceiling he issued a prayer to the Elephant Deity. *Elephant Deity grant me reprieve from these voices. My own thoughts continue to be drowned out by the whispers of my father and this mysterious voice. All I wish for is peace and justice.*

CHAPTER 17

LORD VEGA

THE GOBA'S LAUGHTER could be heard from where he laid his head. Odessa positioned herself at the entrance of the cavern, her arms became tense. She peered inside the cave where she saw Lord Vega laying with his eyes open. "L…L…Lord Vega…" Lord Vega turned to his side and placed a hand on the cavern floor, he raised his head. Staring at her with cold dead eyes he asked, "You disturb me for what purpose?"

She took a step backwards and gripped the cavern entrance. "I have come to inform you that the Mari have successfully defeated the Cretin during the Gauntlet. The Cretin will now be our first line of defense in case of an invasion by the Elite Beasts." Lord Vega laid back down and turned to face his cavern wall. "What point do you have to make? In order to be ruler of the land I must be viewed as ruler of the sea. The five clans still have doubts." The scales on Odessa's body turned yellow as she leaned in to see Lord Vega's battle spear had been broken in half, however, his Trident was in its usual spot.

"Perhaps you will join us for the feast as is our custom. In fact, that may aid in convincing the clans of your leadership capabilities." The tentacles on Lord Vega's head turned black; he stood up and walked towards Odessa. "The customs mean nothing to me. Convince? They will fall in line or perish like the Cretin elite. If I must wipe out the existence of another clan then so be it. How much longer do you think it will take until we can wage war on land?" Odessa looked up at the large figure and placed both her hands in front of her with her palms facing outwards. "I...don't..." Lord Vega raised his claw as a jolt of energy shot through Odessa's body holding her in place. She could feel the aura in her body leave her. Lord Vega grabbed her by the neck and brought her to eye level. "I don't know is not an acceptable answer." Odessa grasped at Lord Vega's claw as her aura levels reached critical conditions. "Soon...soon...I just need more blood sacrifices in the cursed area, I expect to have them soon." Lord Vega released her. Odessa dropped to the floor with her hands balled into fists. He placed his foot on top of her head and pushed it to the cavern floor. "I do not want to see you until it is time to leave for Lelanos." While kissing the cavern floor she answered with distain in her voice, "Yes...milord."

CHAPTER 18

JARVAN

AFTER THREE DAYS of travel Jarvan's massive army arrived on the outskirts of Passerine, the army consisted of 75,000 warriors. The warriors were divided between the two guilds. The Lion Guild provided 40,000 warriors while the Wasp Guild provided the remaining 35,000. Although the Wasp Guild was considered a strong militaristic guild their troops had little experience on the battlefield. Many of their duties consisted of maintaining their borders and patrolling these strict lines between their guild and the Elephant Guild territory. Jarvan spent as much time training the troops as he could.

Jarvan tensed up, his gaze fixated on the glorious gates of Passerine. He turned to the massive army that would follow him to victory. He placed a hand on Azreal's shoulder and smiled. "You seem to be in disarray, afraid you won't be seeing those lovely twins again?" Azreal turned red as a shiver ran down his spine. "It's…it's…just something you said is stuck in my mind." Jarvan smirked and tilted his head upwards. "I've said many a great thing in my short time with you! I wonder which sermon you have chosen to harp on." Azreal looked at the floor and started to kick the dirt beneath his feet. "Well…my guildmates…" Azreal lifted his head and stared at the Wasp Guild troops standing in perfect formation, their heads held high weapons on their back and wings prepared for the most evasive of maneuvers.

Jarvan turned Azreal around and raised an eyebrow. "Spit it out, we have heathens to eradicate!" Azreal took one more glance at his men before a single tear trickled down his face. "What...what...if the training you gave them isn't enough...what if we aren't ready?" Jarvan pulled him closer by the collar and whispered into his ear. "Suckle your fears and stem your worries, men don't cry! Besides...you are with the great Jarvan Hartengale VII, when in doubt stand behind me and watch as we emerge victorious!"

Azreal wiped the tear from his face and stood in ready position mimicking the stance of his men. Jarvan took a step back and raised his hand, all the Lion guild members raised their swords and shields and banged them together. Jarvan took one step to the left and raised his other hand. The Wasp Guild members loaded their weapons simultaneously and shot a round into the air causing a massive explosion. Jarvan smiled and looked at Azreal once more as his hair glistened in the sunset. The light reflected off his perfectly crafted armor. Javan declared, "There are those who walk with the eye of a tiger but often go blind, when you move with the heart of a Lion you will never miss a beat!"

The massive army had set up camp outside Passerine while the two generals attended to their business. They had one objective while in Passerine, inspect the boats they have purchased and make sure the changes they have specified have been made. The only member of the high council that remained in Passerine was the one known as Pinook. He was a frail old man whom many would call senile. If it was up to Solaire she would have kicked him out of the high council a long time ago. However, once a member has been granted access they are in the council until their death.

Pinook stood in front of Jarvan and bowed deeply, his body cracked several times as he attempted to complete the full bow. The stick he used as a cane seemed to be on its last leg just like the owner. Azreal whispered in Jarvan's ear, "I expected more of the high council." Jarvan nodded in agreement and asked, "Where is Solaire, Orianna, Malikai or the other high council members?" Pinook scratched his head and coughed hysterically. "My apologies milord, but it seems you must have missed them in Larimar.

They should have arrived already. Unfortunately, I am the only one who remains in the city." Jarvan nodded and waved the group forward.

Pinook led the group to a massive ship with a white Lion figurehead. Jarvan pointed at the ship's bow, "Pinook, explain to me why the wooden spirit on my ship is white and not gold!" Pinook coughed once again and shook his cane uncontrollably. "Well…milord, it is customary to use white for the figurehead, it is to appease the patron deity of the Dolphin. The great deity Olokun wishes for all those who travel her sea to use a white figurehead no matter their creed, guild, or spirit alignment." Jarvan flicked his hand to the side. The inspection was completed without any further inquiries. Jarvan nodded his head in satisfaction and smiled. "It seems you have built a wonderful flag ship. Take me to the Raven members who will sail our newly acquired ships." Pinook nodded his head and pointed to a group of forty Raven members in black robes with blue hats.

Jarvan placed a hand on the hilt of his sword while the veins on his head protruded. "You mean to tell me that I am to sail forty ships with these forty men!" Pinook smiled, revealing his only remaining tooth. "Yes, milord, it seems you severely underestimate the power of wind magic. Pinook pointed to one of the members and commanded, "You…young one, come here." The young boy ran over to Pinook and bowed, his black robe caressed the bottom of Jarvan's foot. Jarvan motioned for him to rise. Pinook placed a hand on the boy's shoulder and pointed at the flag ship, he then whispered in the boy's ears.

The boy stood in front of Jarvan, Pinook, and Azreal and clapped his hands. He chanted in what Jarvan recognized was the language of the deities. "Ilya mola voila journe! ilya mola voila journe! ilya mola voila journe." The flag ship rose above the water. Azreal and Jarvan clapped, they stared in amazement. Jarvan turned to Pinook and asked, "How long can they keep a ship moving at a time?" Pinook scratched his head and coughed, revealing his single tooth a second time. "They can keep the fleet moving for twenty-four hours at a time in a single direction or can make evasive maneuvers for twenty hours simultaneously. So essentially you have twenty to twenty-four hours of simultaneous movement of the entire fleet, after that they will need ten hours of rest, this includes food and water."

Jarvan nodded his head and continued, "How long will it take us to get to Tem from here?" The old man stood still for a moment and whispered in the boy's ears, the ship gently landed in the water while the boy went back to his previous spot. "Well…that depends…" Veins popped on the side of the prince's head again. Impatiently, he asked, "Well…that depends on what?" Pinook scratched the back of his head. "Well…it just depends on how far Tem is this time." Jarvan curled his hand into a fist and retorted, "I am not a fan of riddles old man, you are starting to sound like my coward of a brother." Pinook shook his head. "My apologies milord I do not mean to offend. It is…just…Tem is constantly moving. It is not difficult to find because the island is surrounding by a myriad of storms, however the island is constantly shifting its location. Sometimes it is five days away, sometimes it is three, there are even times where the island is visible from our coast, but there is no way to be certain how long it will take you to arrive." Jarvan clasped both of his hands behind his back and queried, "So then…how far is it now?" Pinook opened a small book and flipped a few pages. "Well milord…it seems the island of Tem is projected to be two days sail away!" Jarvan turned to Azreal and exclaimed, "Tell all of the troops to pack their things we leave before nightfall!"

CHAPTER 19
JAMES

JAMES STOOD IN the middle of the arena while his war hammer rested by his side. He looked up at the announcer as several Swan members ran back and forth in a frenzy in search of his next opponent. This next challenger would have made five to date. The first four challengers in the tournament were no match for James thus he dispatched of them with ease. The crowd was in awe of his dazzling display of forest magic and even more so amazed at how easily he defeated some of the more prominent figures in other guilds. So far, he had defeated the guild leaders of the infamous Dragonfly Guild, Shark Guild and Lynx Guild. He convinced the Snail Guild leader to surrender without lifting a finger. Because of this last victory the crowd has affectionately dubbed him, James the Merciful, a nickname that he wore with great honor for he knows it is one that his father would be proud of.

James stared at the royal family who had been watching all the matches. Lamia was clearly amused by James' participation and had been his loudest supporter. She looked elegant in her ivory colored dress and wore an Elephant broach that James gave her the day before. Her hair was tied back in a ponytail with single braids, the traditional elephant guild hairstyle for women of war. After an hour of waiting James sat down and meditated upon the things he had learned thus far. As soon as he sat down the announcer grabbed the marble of projection and casted a spell on his voice, "It seems The Puppeteer from an unnamed guild will not be joining us on this day. Victory by default will go to the great James the Merciful!" the crowd cheered. Lamia who had been seated next to her father dismissed herself and ran over to James, her massive breasts bouncing with every step.

James blushed. *Was she always this beautiful?* he thought to himself. His eyes revealed his deepest thoughts as he scrutinized the young princess from top to bottom. He composed himself as she drew close. "James! I knew you'd get this far. You're so amazing. Oh, my spirit, why is the arena so large?" He managed a weak smile and replied, "Thank you Miss Hartengale! I appreciate your kind words." Lamia wrinkled her nose and asked, "Why do you always have to be so formal when you speak to me? Ugh." James ran his hand through his ponytail. "I...don't...mean to be, I don't know," he said as he blushed.

Lamia poked him on his cheek and smiled, "You're cute when you're nervous. My father says you must join us to watch the next fight, supposedly the winner will be your next opponent!" James shook his head. "Right now, it is past the time for me to meditate on what I have learned during my time in Larimar. I would love to join you however, I must decline." Glancing downwards Lamia answered, "I had a feeling you'd say something like that. I will tell my father, good luck!" Lamia trudged towards her seat.

James walked towards the stage in the middle of the arena with his war hammer at his back, his grey armor gleamed in the sunlight. He crossed his arms and scowled. The meditation bared no fruit for the things that troubled him only managed to stifle his creativity. He didn't know what to do, but above all he didn't know what he must tell his father when he sees him. It took him a moment to look at the crowd but when he did he noticed that most were wearing masks. He checked the bottom of his boots and stealthily took a whiff of his under armor. The announcer also wearing a mask came to the stage.

He walked towards James and whispered in his ears. "Uh...I guess you weren't watching the last match. Good luck, you're going to need it!" James' eyes squinted as he took a step back and began to stretch. The announcer turned towards the emperor and raised his hand. The emperor nodded his head and waved for him to continue with the festivities. "First, I would like to say a few words for all of the fallen warriors up to this point!" The crowd yelled and screamed profanity. "The fallen soldiers have failed to impress you for the Lion does not accept failure!" The crowd chanted. "But fear not the next match is one that will shake the foundations of the tournament. We have good versus evil, honor versus dishonor, and glory versus cowardice. I give you James the merciful!" The announcer pointed to James and continued, "Next I would like to thank the great emperor who has graced us with his presence on such a monumental evening. "Emperor V! Emperor V! Emperor V!" The crowd stood in attendance as they continued to address the emperor.

The emperor kept his stern expression but stood up and raised his hand, silencing the crowd. The announcer following suit raised his hand as well. "We would all like to thank Lamia for allowing the Swan Guild to give her the gift of entertainment." The crowd chanted. "Lamia! Lamia! Lamia!" Lamia smiled and did the traditional lion bow. James stopped his stretching to gaze at her smile. It seemed to brighten the stage even more so than the Kazrite candles. *What if…she and I were to marry…could father truly object to such a thing? I know the emperor seeks a suitor…I mean…is it so vile of an idea that I seek a woman outside of the guild?* His father's voice countered. *An Elephant judge should never mate with an outsider much less marry one, to do so would bring dishonor upon the guild!* The raspy voice chimed in. *Trust your instincts. They are your connection to the divine.*

A repugnant scent crept into James' nostrils snapping him out of his daze. The members of the crowd who did not have the wherewithal to wear a mask coughed themselves into a frenzy. The announcer took a few steps to the opposite side of the stage behind James. "All welcome the infamous Molina Dae, the guild leader of the Skunk Guild!" A short skinny man with long black hair and a white stripe in the middle walked towards the stage. He carried a bag of peanuts in his hands. He wore black light armor with white stripes across the chest and the back. Molina smiled revealing a string of crooked yellow teeth. Walking over to James he did the customary skunk greeting by turning his back side to his opponent and letting loose a puff of air. Boos could be heard raining down upon the arena. James furled his brows but responded with the Elephant stance for honor. While holding his breath he placed his right arm across his chest and nodded his head. Molina laughed and then spat on the floor nearly striking James' boot.

His eyes twitched as his hands curled up into a ball, the ground beneath the arena shook. James felt warmth across his forehead and immediately locked eyes with the emperor. He composed himself and walked over to his corner; Molina laughed and did the same. "Well folks what a great display of…uh…well…let's just get this duel started shall we?" The announcer raised both his hands and a horn went off. James slammed his fist on the ground and created a ring of rose bushes around him. The poison dripped from the thorns as he sat in the middle. After setting up a defensive perimeter he slammed his other fist into the arena causing a large rift across the middle with ivory spikes at the bottom. Satisfied with his defense James went into his nature stance. He drew a tree symbol on his forehead and crossed his legs. James channeled his aura to his weapon and armor.

Forty minutes had passed before James opened one of his eyes. Molina sat on the edge eating nuts. He threw the remains down the chasm. James closed his eyes and began to channel his aura some more. He chanted the Elephant Guild mantra. "Solidarity, solidarity, solidarity…," another twenty minutes passed before James opened both his eyes. This time Molina pulled out his shaft and peed inside the gaping rift before them. Boos rained down like a thundering storm at the scraggly bush that surrounded his tiny member.

Molina laughed and picked his nose, flicking the snot as far as he could. When it landed atop a rose bush he smirked. James closed both of his eyes and went back to channeling. A member of the crowd shouted. "Do something! Someone! This sucks!" James twitched slightly. "Solidarity, solidarity, solidarity!" He chanted louder. Molina threw his peanut remains in the direction of James. The first one landed on the ground in front of the bush, the second on a rose, the third landed on James' knee. He chanted louder, "SOLIDARITY! SOLIDARITY! SOLIDARITY!" The fourth peanut remain hit James in the eye.

James stood up and stomped his foot. The ground beneath him shook violently as his eyes turned bright green. Tusks grew at the side of his jaw and his armor bulged as his physique grew larger. Green aura surrounded the once stoic judge and wrapped itself around his weapon as it gleamed under the sunset. War hammer held above his head he aimed it towards the dancing figure that was Molina Dae. Lamia yelled, "No!" but it was drowned out behind the crowd chanting, "Kill! Kill! Kill!" James in a deep thundering voice screamed. "You dine amongst the living no longer!" The catastrophic blow came within inches of hitting Molina but was met with an invisible force equal to that which came before it. The blow bounced back with incredible power sending James down the chasm landing on several spikes.

James awoke a few moments later with his head throbbing. He winced as he struggled to remove himself from the spike that lodged itself in his shoulder. Blood gushed from his shoulder and streamed down his back. Had James not reinforced his armor with so much of his aura he would have been killed upon impact. He landed directly on two other large spikes, one was located at the back of his head and the other located at his upper thigh. His father's words buzzed in his head. *One must never strike one's opponent in anger, for anger is the bane of victory.* Up until this point no man has ever been able to defeat James in a battle of patience for this was something he had spent his entire life mastering. *Not like this.* James snapped his fingers and the spikes turned into bushes, he snapped his fingers again and the ground rose. The crowd cheered upon seeing James stand up to face his smelly opponent once again. "So…I guess you are as hardy as you're made out to be," Molina snickered. "I suppose the women must love that about you, honorable sissy James."

This was not a tactic James would fall for twice. He walked over to Molina and attempted to touch him. A thin amount of reflective aura could be felt separating both duelists. James nodded his head. "Hmmm… I see…what kind of magic might this be Mr. Dae?" James asked. "I admit I'm not familiar with such tactics." Struggling not to cover his mouth he rubbed his nose instead. Molina shook his head and danced again. "I'm not telling, you're not going to figure out my secret!" James nodded and walked away to his corner; he sat down and thought. *What kind of magic could it be? Father had always said when deducing an unknown it is important to start with the known's. There are known knowns, known unknowns, and unknown unknowns. I know he uses a form of magic that reflects magic. I know knowledge of this form of magic is crucial to defeating it, but I do not know why. I do not know how long this magic can last nor do I know the limitations of it.* James stood up and snapped his fingers.

A large green rock appeared in his palm, he aimed and launched the rock at Molina, who smiled and pulled down his pants revealing his hairy buttocks. The rock bounced back at James who caught it. James looked up to Lamia who had a worrisome look on her face. *That pretty face somehow has a way of perking me up even in times of turmoil. I remember she used to always cheer me up when I would lose to Jarvan. He absolutely loves those aerial attacks. I wonder...* This time he aimed and threw the rock high above in an arch. Seeing the trajectory of the rock Molina took one step to the left and danced some more. *That might work...but my aerial skills are not fast enough...he is as nimble as he looks.* James stared at the floor beneath them for a moment. The ground beneath Molina had small cracks in it. *I wonder if that could be from the previous blow...it must be...but what if I am wrong?*

James remembered his father's most encouraging words. *Just do what feels right, for to do left is to dishonor yourself.* He picked up his war hammer and ran towards Molina, this time stopping short in front of the disgusting creature and slammed his war hammer on the ground. A large tree grew from underneath raising James up into the sky. He took off his helmet and threw it at Molina who dodged to the left once again. This time it would be his demise. He stepped into ivory vines camouflaged by the grey arena floors. The vines intertwined themselves around his body and raised him into the air. The Skunk Guild leader squirmed, kicked, and screamed but was unable to free himself. Once raised high enough James looked directly at Lamia and did the Elephant honor stance. She smiled as he jumped off the tree, war hammer raised above his head once again. The green aura streamed back as the crowd gaped at the dazzling display of forest magic.

In a flash of green light, the feint muffles of a scream emerged from beneath the mighty weapon of James. When the green light evaporated the tall figure of James the Merciful emerged with a massive grin across his face. The crippled body of Molina laid in a twisted figure as a few members of the Raven Guild rushed to take him to the healing quarters.

CHAPTER 20

ORIANNA

THE GROUP AT the table could be heard from down the hall, their merry singing filled the hallway. Orianna rushed to the dining room carrying the notes she had written about the twins. She has had several visions since leaving Passerine and she was determined to get her mother to listen to her. When she walked into the room she saw two masked figures doing back flips and cartwheels. Their bright pink suits threatened to blind her. A man holding a puppet was entertaining her mother with his scary puppets, who sat staring at the food ominously. The leader turned her head slowly and waved Orianna over to the empty seat at her left. Goosebumps emerged on Orianna's back. She sluggishly walked over to the empty seat. When Orianna sat down it dawned on her that there were several other empty seats. She swallowed deeply and turned to the masked figure. "Umm…are…are we expecting others?"

There was a long silence, the leader tilted her head to the side and finally whispered, "It seems they will not be joining us tonight." Orianna looked down and bit her lip. She looked up at the mysterious woman as her breathing became rapid. "I…see…" The female figure paused for a moment longer this time and then asked, "Perhaps I can keep you company?" She placed a hand on Orianna's shoulder. She jerked slightly and was hesitant to reply, "W…we…well…ok." She mustered a meek smile. Pointing at the small pink book the leader cracked her knuckles, "What do you have in your hands Miss Duskbringer?" Orianna blushed. "This…well…this…is my diary…it just has some notes on my…my…visions." The air between the two became heavier. It felt as if a weight had been placed atop Orianna's chest. Her breathing rate increased once again while the room seemed to have gotten a bit darker. "Yes…you are the guild's oracle are you not? I would love to hear what interesting things you have come to find." Orianna moved her chair slightly back and continued, "I don't…know…I'm not supposed…to show it to non-guild members."

The leader paused for a moment. "Well correct me if I'm wrong, but your mother doesn't seem to be quite fond of your visions lately and your brothers are constantly distracted. I have some experience with the old language, perhaps I can be of assistance." Orianna looked at Corvus who was passed out after a glass of wine. She glanced at her mother who was completely dazzled by the puppets. She observed her two brothers arguing over who was the more important high council member. Her hands shook as she cleared her throat and read what she had learned from her newest vision.

CHAPTER 21

JAMES

FANS BOMBARDED JAMES who was accompanied by several Raven members. The marks left from the healing remained visible. He shook the hands of as many people as he could, but was forced to continue his pursuit to the change rooms. Lamia approached him accompanied by a veiled woman. Lamia clapped her hands several times and commented, "That last duel made me a nervous wreck." James lowered his head and mumbled, "S…sorry…Miss Hartengale. I didn't mean to frighten you." Lamia sighed loudly and said, "Sometimes I wonder about you." James sighed softly and replied, "Sometimes I wonder about myself, who is your companion?" The veiled woman stepped forward and answered, "Allow me to introduce my good friend Orianna Duskbringer."

James outstretched his hand. Orianna crossed her arms and turned her head away. A few moments of silence passed before he returned his hand to his side. "What's wrong with you? This is the man I was telling you about." Orianna stomped both her feet, "I don't like him, I hope he loses." James raised an eyebrow and asked, "What have I done to displease you?" Orianna huffed and puffed. "I'm not telling, nor am I talking to you!" she said as she stormed off. Lamia twirled a strand of her hair, "I apologize for my friend.!.I don't know what has come over her. If it makes things any better, I am still talking to you…considering…" James saw the image of the lone tenet breaker wearing his dusty Elephant attire standing behind Lamia. He took one step back as beads of sweat dripped down his forehead. "This can't be...your dead...," he whispered. Lamia covered her mouth. "What are you talking about? I'm standing right here. Have you lost your wits?" Running his hands through his hair, he composed himself and mumbled, "I'm sorry, I have to go...I just...don't know what is happening to me." Lamia lowered her head while doing a curtsy.

James dashed forward wading through the crowd but found himself faced with a scarred face man. "I don't take kindly to losing. First, I had to discard my wife, next she loses the ring I purchased, and finally the Shark Guild forces me to step down as leader for suffering an embarrassing defeat to a mere Elephant Guild judge. How pathetic I have become. Arm yourself, I demand a rematch, this time to the death," the scarred faced man glared.

"I'm sorry for the series of unfortunate events, but I am not able to fulfill your request now. I need to get my mind in the right condition. Please allow me to pass you." The man withdrew his large mace, a Shark insignia glimmered on the front of his heavy armor. "Do you fancy yourself too good for me? I am no fool, I know all you Elephant members are sinners in the night. There is no way anyone can commit to such a strict set of tenets." He charged forward but James dodged the blow. James weaved several hand signs creating a wall of earth to separate the two of them. "I really do apologize for what has befallen you. May the Elephant Deity bless your future endeavors."

CHAPTER 22

LORD VEGA

LORD VEGA WOKE up suddenly, grabbing his trident of the divine he swam to the edge of his cavern. Peering outside he noticed that the dining area was empty. *The dining area is never empty...where are the other clan leaders?* Like a dart within the water he propelled himself to the base of the ocean floor where he could see his second in command approaching his position. "Caruktuk! What has occurred?" Caruktuk was severely injured, purple liquid oozed from his chest and shoulder. His spear was badly chipped and one of his arms was missing. "An Elite Beast has entered the gates and Odessa is nowhere to be found. The beasts that would normally assist in the defense of the stronghold are not in position. Additionally, the Undines have refused to assist us without the permission of their leader; they said that they are willing to withstand the wrath of Lord Vega when this is all done."

Lord Vega gripped his trident tighter and swam forth to the entrance of their stronghold. *Those insolent fish women! Could this be a plot to over-throw me once again? No...Odessa is loyal...she must have gone to the human world to speed up the process...but why now...how dare the Undines not assist the other clans.* Lord Vega's thoughts raced uncontrollably as he attempted to make sense of the situation. His armor pierced through the water at lightning speeds while the fins on the sides of his feet allowed for great maneuverability.

When Lord Vega arrived at the outskirts of the stronghold he was met with a gruesome scene. He demanded, "What kind of abomination is this?" Caruktuk stood beside Lord Vega with his damaged spear in hand. "Sdogr said this is the Testudine beast," replied Caruktuk. The Testudine beast was a massive turtle like creature with giant spikes spread out across its shell. Its long neck could extend and would reveal several plated scales at the top for added protection. The eyes burned bright orange while its humongous legs stomped the ground causing huge rifts in the ocean floor. The mouth was a gaping abyss that once opened revealed a stream of teeth capable of biting through armor as thick as the Krynn's. Lord Vega swam closer where he was met with the dead bodies from the different clans.

The Goba had successfully taken out both eyes of the creature. This caused it to flail about wildly, stomping several clan members each time. Lord Vega twirled his trident and sent a massive crescent of aura towards the beast. The attack hit its neck and dissipated into nothingness. "Most of our attacks are ineffective," Caruktuk commented. "I feel that I must make apologies my lord. I wanted to defeat the beast in the name of the Krynn, but it seems…I will…meet my end here." Caruktuk collapsed at Lord Vega's feet. Lord Vega looked down at Caruktuk and kicked the carcass away. He growled, "Pathetic!" He propelled himself towards the beast and stirred up a massive whirlpool. Sensing the large amount of aura accumulating, the beast paused for a moment before entering its shell. The clans took this time to remove their injured and clear the area. The whirlpool grew larger until it was almost the size of the beast itself. Lord Vega unleashed the massive whirlpool forward, sweeping up the creature and propelling it forward towards the exit. The Elite Beast in a flash of light was casted aside into the distance. A loud scream could be heard in the abyss.

CHAPTER 22

JARVAN

JARVAN WALKED TOWARDS the Raven Guild Captain, his hands at his side while his cape blew gloriously in the wind. "How much longer until we are at the outskirts of Tem?" he asked. The captain looked up while still maintaining his wind stance. "They are closer than anticipated, we will be there within a few hours." Jarvan nodded and turned towards Azreal who was vomiting over the side of the ship. He placed a hand on his back and laughed. "The winds of the sea do not agree with you I take it!" Azreal wiped his mouth with his forearm and nodded. "Unfortunately, few things agree with me. Just like the women back home they call me too weak for a Wasp member, yet too masculine to be a Bee, perhaps if I was taller like you or if I was more handsome I would be successful with women in my city."

Jarvan took a seat on the wooden floor of the ship. He beckoned to Azreal and said, "Sit with me for a minute my friend." Azreal lowered his head and sat down beside the great prince. "On my ninth birthday, my father placed a sword in my right hand and a flower in my left. He said to me, what do both things have in common?" Azreal listened silently but didn't respond. "Well? What do you think they both have in common?" He pinched Azreal. "Oh…umm…I suppose they both have the properties of the earth. The sword is a metal ore that can come from a variety of minerals while the flower…" Jarvan shook his head and ruffled Azreal's shiny hair. "No, see you're over thinking things, just like I was at first. My first answer was that they both are tools of the heart." Jarvan smiled. Azreal raised his eyebrows. "Tools of the heart?" Jarvan nodded. "Yes, tools of the heart. You see the sword is used for love of the battlefield while the flower is used for love of the bedroom." Azreal laughed hysterically and asked, "Even at the age of nine you were quite the ladies' man, weren't you?"

Jarvan nodded in agreement and added, "I suppose you could say that, but my father only stared at me and told me to try again. For days, maybe even weeks I sat in my room and contemplated the similarities between the two until I had lost all confidence in whatever answer I could possibly give to my father. Do you want to know what I came up with?" Azreal nodded his head in angst. "Well I wasn't about to give up, even at that age I could not accept a defeat. So, I went to my father and I told him straight. I said, no matter what answer I give you, you will tell me it's wrong, for I have lost all confidence in my ability to give you an adequate response. Do you want to know what my father did?"

Azreal kept silent waiting for the outcome. "Well…for the first time in my life I heard my father's laugh, but this was not a normal laugh, it was the laugh of a man who had been caught in his own game. It was the first and only time I had defeated my father in anything. To this day I hold onto that moment for he is my guiding principle for what it is to be a true Lion." Azreal scratched his head and asked, "So what about the flower and the sword?" Jarvan stood up and smiled. "The answer is quite simple my friend, both take confidence to wield. It takes confidence and grit to take the life of a man during battle, to taste the blood in the air and see the soul escape from the body. It takes confidence to step on the battlefield and risk your life, to look death in his cold dead eyes and tell him that today is not your day. The flower is the same concept off the battlefield. In matters of the heart it does not matter what type of woman you are dealing with. She will always love a man who exudes some type of self-assurance, whether she is an alpha, beta or new breed of woman. It does not matter. What matters is that you are confident in who you are and what you're capable of." Azreal smiled the brightest smile he could muster. "Really? I can do that…I can be more confident, at least…I think

I can!" Jarvan placed a hand on his shoulder and said, "It's going to take some work, but you'll get there."

Azreal ran over to Jarvan's cabin with his monocle in hand. The Captain's cabin was exactly what one would expect of a Lion Guild commander. It was filled with portraits depicting his previous accomplishments, a small crystal Lion statue, and a large commander's table made of elephant black wood. The chair was an elegantly designed ebony chair that had the Lion sigil on the back. Azreal flung the door open and entered the room. Jarvan was stooped over the table moving miniature pieces of the ship around. "Is knocking not something you do where you're from?" he snapped. Azreal's face turned red. He lowered his head and mumbled, "My apologies but we have encountered some sort of thick fog." Jarvan shook his head slowly and exclaimed, "You interrupted me because of some fog? Keep moving forward we don't have time to waste!" Azreal shook his head and entered the cabin. "There are ships deep within the fog and for some reason we can't turn, we can only move forward."

Jarvan pushed Azreal out of the way and went to the bow of the ship. He looked forward to see a large fleet of ships with a massive battleship dawning the Crocodile crest. Upon seeing the massive battleship Azreal ran to the side of the ship and relieved himself of his dinner. Jarvan signaled for the Raven captain to stop the movement of the ship. The Raven captain replied, "Sorry Milord but I stopped a long time ago. The ship is moving by itself." Jarvan turned around to see a thick fog at the back of the ship; it was as if it had a mind of its own. The flagship followed by the rest of the fleet stopped in front of the massive battleship. A large man with a pipe in his hand came to the edge of the battleship and waved at Jarvan.

The large man laughed hysterically and quipped, "The emperor must have gotten desperate; he has sent his son to die! Surrender your ships and tell your men to swim back to shore. This is the best I can do for my men are hungry for bloodshed on this cold evening. The sea is no place for a Lion cub." Jarvan unsheathed his sword and shield and yelled. "For honor, glory, and victory we shall conquer!" The Lion Guild members on the boat screamed, "Honor, glory, and victory!" A horn went off causing all the Wasp members on their respective ships to take aim.

Jarvan bellowed, "Submit yourself to me and your death shall be swift!" The Crocodile general pulled out some elder grass and placed it in his pipe, after a few puffs, the smoke merged into a grey orb. He blew the puff of smoke and it flew at tremendous speeds towards the adjacent ship's hull causing it to sink. "The day General Gatticus surrenders to a mere child is the day I dishonor the late great Dominus Bourbon, I think not." The crowned prince pointed his sword forward causing the Wasp army to fire their ammunition. The sound of Kazrite Ore meeting their target was a sound no one will ever forget. The destruction caused was tremendous, Crocodile members ran about in a daze to put out the fires but before Jarvan could signal for another attack General Gatticus was upon him. He launched his chained anchor towards the prince at blistering speeds. Jarvan raised his shield to block the blow but it was too late, the attack struck him in his chest causing him to slam backwards into the mast. Azreal rushed towards Jarvan to help him get up. Jarvan brushed him off abruptly and said, "Forget about me, I will handle him, my troops will protect the Wasp members as planned. Control your people and set their ships a blaze!" Azreal nodded in agreement and rushed over to his troops.

Jarvan stood up and charged forward sword held high. General Gatticus swung his anchor around him causing smoke to surround the two of them. "Welcome to my prison little cub, no one will come to help you now!" Jarvan banged his sword against his shield. "The battlefield is not a place for conversation, steel yourself," he replied. Jarvan charged forward once again with his shield held high. He lunged forward with his sword hand aiming for the heart. General Gatticus stood still as the blade pierced through him with ease. He laughed as he turned into a puff of smoke and floated in the air.

Jarvan furled his brows as he looked around for the second most feared opponent the Lion Guild has ever known. Jarvan stared above but could see nothing but smoke, the walls of the 'prison' seemed to be closing in. In a sudden flash of grey light General Gatticus came crashing down upon Jarvan, his anchor slammed into his helmet causing him to fall to his knees. He wiped the blood from his face. The general swung his anchor once again and hooked it on Jarvan's ankle. Pulling him towards the middle of the prison, he shouted, "Get over here little cub!" Yellow light emitted from Jarvan's eyes. He tilted his head towards the general and shot forth two beams. The beams pierced through the stomach of the smoky general causing him to drop to his knees. Jarvan stood up and gathered his shield, his eyes still glowing with yellow light. He crouched behind his shield and placed his sword on the floor behind it. Regaining his senses, the general took a few more puffs of his pipe. He taunted, "Oh…so now you're cowering behind your shield huh? What a joke. Your uncle would be proud!"

Jarvan clenched his teeth. He placed his hands over his sword and spoke the words that had ensured the death of many. "Prey on to my soul father spirit, for the Lion is within my heart. Grant me the strength to cut down those who will not submit to your will!" The words on his sword glowed bright yellow. Jarvan stood up and in a flash of yellow light he emerged in front of General Gatticus with his sword lodged deep inside the man's chest. He leaned in slowly and whispered, "For Jarvan Hartengale VI."

CHAPTER 23

JAMES

"THE WINNER OF this match will move on to the finals and be one step closer to the secret grand prize! Our first contestant James is a fan favorite and has been waiting patiently for quite some time. His next opponent has finally arrived. It is my pleasure to announce Scaa Cara, the guild leader of the Scarab Guild!" The announcer clapped both his hands together while the crowd remained silent. Scaa emerged from the dark hallways wearing a black mask, black shirt, and pants with a blue belt around his waist. The front of his clothing had a scarab crest on it. The Scarab Guild was a well-known guild within Larimar. It was famous for its focus on the advancement and the expert manipulation of insect magic. Anyone who had the ability to manipulate or communicate with any sort of hexapod was welcome.

From what I know the insects in the clan vary in terms of powers, but it is said that one bite from some of the more powerful insects could result in death. I will have to be careful. James walked over to the middle of the arena and shook Scaa's hand. A sticky residue attached itself to James while Scaa simply smiled behind his mask. Both contestants returned to their corners to await the emperor's words. Jarvan Hartengale V stood up and stared at the two contestants, he waited a few moments before speaking. "The two of you have entertained us greatly thus far; I look forward to a competitive match!" He nodded and sat down. Lamia sat in the corner clapping loudly.

Not one to wait for the horn Scaa displayed a series of hand gestures. Before James could set up a defense a swarm of black flies flew towards his hand. He tensed up, creating an aura shield around it. The flies chewed and gnawed repeatedly, each bite draining a small portion of his aura. "What kind of weak attack is this supposed to be?" He scoffed at his opponent. He shook his wrist free of the insects and marched towards Scaa, but his movements were notably slower. The massive war hammer that he had always found so light tugged at his back. Another swarm of insects approached, this time a group of mosquitoes. They buzzed around fluttering by his head as he attempted to swat them away. His aura imbued armor did little to stop the swarm from achieving their lofty goal. Slowly each one bypassed his armor and pierced into the soft flesh underneath. James winced, his movements slowed to a crawl as he was brought to his knees. He pulled out his war hammer and rested it on the floor using it for leverage.

The mosquitoes returned to Scaa releasing the stolen aura into his veins. He clapped his hands and created a large blue tree with rotten apples. James winced as he gripped his weapon tightly. He yelled, "You dare to make a mockery of my magic!" The masked opponent did a series of hand gestures. A swarm of scarabs swept him up, rising into the air he threw poisoned darts towards James. He draped his hand over his weapon and activated his spirit powers. *I call upon you to stampede upon my enemies, for with this war hammer I shall lay down the judgment of a thousand spirits.* Bright green light emitted from the glorious war hammer; the sound of stampeding elephants was heard throughout the arena. His eyes turned white and tusks appeared at the side of his jaw. He gripped his war hammer and smashed it against the arena floor. A massive green elephant with white eyes appeared.

Draped in vines the elephant charged forward grabbing Scaa with its long trunk. He smiled as he turned into a sea of scarabs and floated to the side. James charged forward shaking the ground with each step. He raised his war hammer and slammed it into Scaa's stomach causing blood to spew out. "Despicable!" shrieked a high-pitched voice. The scarabs caught his fall and carried him to the other side of the arena. The crowd erupted into a fit of laughter. "Shut up!" Scaa yelled. James charged forward once again this time ramming his two tusks into the chest of the Scarab leader and flipped him upwards; he pulled his war hammer back and charged it. Green aura flowed from his chest over to his arm and then into his weapon. Just as he was within striking distance the Scarabs caught Scaa once again and flew him to the side dodging the blow. The green Elephant grabbed Scaa again, with green aura surging through it, the Elephant slammed him into the floor repeatedly, blood spilling out each time. With each strike, he squealed louder until finally he gave up.

James stared at his final opponent, his mouth agape at the sight. *Surely... this must be a mistake.* He walked towards the announcer and tapped him on his shoulder. "Uh...is he...supposed to be my opponent for the finals?" The announcer widened his eyes and smiled. "Do not underestimate the elderly in our city, for they often have the most potent magic." James waited for the horn to sound before approaching the elderly man known as Sai Zakura. Upon further inspection, he was in exceptional shape. Although short he had very little body fat and carried an expertly crafted katana. He wore a straw Kasa with purple streaks across it. The Kasa had an inscription that read, 'There is joy in honor but life in duty.' His silk robe was elegant and glistened under the moonlight; pink, blue, and yellow flowers were plastered all over it.

Faced with the elderly Sai who dawned long grey hair and sporting a colorful silk robe James sheathed his weapon. "Perhaps you would like to surrender?" He teased. Sai laughed revealing several missing teeth. He placed a toothpick in his mouth and smirked. "Perhaps you would like to join me in the way of tea ceremony and we can discuss why you feel I should surrender." James raised an eyebrow but before he could answer the old man had already taken out a small table and poured two cups of ceremonial matcha. He sat down laying his war hammer beside him. With one hand on its hilt he picked up the cup and looked at Sai with his eyes slanted. Sai chuckled, revealing the gaping hole that was his mouth. "Oh...yes, you have faced many unseemly opponents up until now. Not to worry, I would never dishonor the great Armadillo spirit by poisoning the tea." James took a sip of the sweet hot beverage. "The Armadillo spirit?

I have heard of the Armadillo Guild, but I thought they were disbanded." Sai took a small sip of his beverage and answered, "Yes, that is true. I was left guildless for quite a time until a member of a prominent guild took me in. I am forever grateful to her I must say. What drives you to join this tournament if I may ask?"

James nodded slowly and took another sip of his tea. "I want to show the world of Lelanos the power of the Elephant Guild as well as bring further honor to my family. During my time here, it has dawned on me that the rest of the world view my guild as nothing more than a group of pacifists." Sai tensed up as he lowered his cup. "There is nothing wrong with peace my young man. Should not what matters most be what resides deep in your heart? I would have thought justice would be your true goal." James blushed as the hand holding the tea cup trembled. He stammered, "Yes…there…is something else that I do seek…" Sai finished his cup and placed it on the table. "Speaking of seeking something, you seem to have quite the troubled mind." James lowered his head and replied, "I have been hearing voices…my father's voice haunts me the most…and…" Sai refilled his cup, "and?" James continued, "and I have been…I don't know. I don't know how to explain it. I am starting to see things." Sai tilted his hat backwards and commented, "The scorching heat of our great sun has a way of playing tricks on the mind. I am sure it is nothing to worry yourself about."

James clenched his teeth and muttered, "I suppose…" Sai fanned himself and interrupted him. "I wish I had brought my white robe with me, for this weather is too humid for my liking." James placed his empty cup on the table. He swallowed deeply. "You…wear a white robe?" The elderly man raised his hand to reveal a Raven tattoo on his chest. "Yes of course, everyone in the high council of the Raven Guild wears a white robe." James' eyes widened as his hand gripped tightly on his weapon, the ground beneath them trembled as his eyes turned pure white. "You people will pay for your crimes, I swear it on my very essence!"

Sai laughed and exclaimed, "It seems our tea time has ended!" He backed off swiftly and withdrew his engraved katana. He placed a hand over his face and whispered a few incantations in the old tongue. The crowd clapped enthusiastically upon seeing the handsome face of a young man where an elderly one once stood. He bowed and quickly charged forward, each foot seemingly walking on thin air. He dodged the first blow sent forth by James' mighty weapon and ducked a second. The katana was used to block the third strike seemingly breaking in the act.

He pulled out a rose petal and plastered it on the side of James' stomach. With swift motions, he plastered two more rose petals one on the foot and another on his knee before receiving an elbow to the back of the head. Sai went crashing into the tiles creating a loud thud. James lifted his aura imbued foot to stomp on the head of his tea companion, but he was already gone. He scanned the arena, but he could only see faint pink streaks streaming around him. Rose petals emerged one by one then tens, then by the hundreds until there was a sea of rose petals surrounding the mighty James.

James clapped his hands together and created a stone barrier around himself. *This city is filled with such ill-conceived magic.* He looked down at the three petals stuck to his armor as they glowed bright pink. James tried to wipe them off, but they could not be removed. A few moments later the tip of a katana pierced through all three petals simultaneously. The blood poured out as he screamed in agony. "How?" he bellowed. The tip of the katanas twisted causing more blood to gush out until it disappeared along with the three markings. The sound of thousands of rose petals could be heard gathering around the shell of earth that James had created for himself. The blade of a katana pierced through the shell nearly striking his neck, a second shot forth at blistering speeds lodging itself in his stomach.

He closed his eyes and gathered his entire aura into a tiny green ball within the palm of his hands. A third blade propelled itself deep in his back. The blades cut through his armor as if it was made of parchment, blood continued to drip to the floor. "Flow without for I give you all that I have," he whispered. In a flash of green light, the tiny ball of dark green aura expanded destroying the shell and throwing Sai out of the arena. "Kuso!" yelled Sai. The announcer placed his hands on his head and exclaimed, "Wow...what a crazy turn of events! The new tournament champion winner is James the Merciful with a victory by ring out!" The announcer approached the bloody and broken James who leaned on his war hammer. He tried to help him up but James waved him off. Slowly he gathered his bearings and pulled himself to his feet. The announcer inquired, "Do you have any words for the audience, the whole city wants to hear what you have to say!" He placed the orb near James' throat. He looked at Sai who transformed back into his elderly form. It was clear he was completely unscathed. James gripped his weapon tightly and furrowed his brows, breathing heavily he yelled at the top of his lungs, "For justice!"

CHAPTER 24

ORIANNA

ORIANNA HAD ENJOYED the festivities leading up to Lamia's birthday extravaganza. So far, she bore witness to the great tournament that the city was known for, several massive feasts in the castle, and a city-wide scavenger hunt. She was concerned about the mysterious performers that were hired by her mother. However, these events only served to distract her from the visions of the twins with pointy ears. Her family members were too focused on the assassination plot to bother with her anymore; this was not unusual since an oracle is only considered useful during specific nights of the year.

Orianna stumbled into the dimly lit room with a glass of wine in her hand as she enjoyed her first experience with alcohol. Octavius was surrounded by several large tomes; his hands shook at the sight of the oracle. "H...hello...Orianna, it's so good to...I mean...glad to see...I mean what brings you to my quarters?" he blushed. Orianna took another sip of her wine and stammered, "Th...this...wine stuff...is gooood!" She plopped down on the chair across the forgotten son and exclaimed, "I was looking for you sillyyyy swannnn! I haven't seen you... since we were children!" She placed her wine goblet on top of a dusty tome. His cheeks still flush with red, he asked, "Y...you...remember me?" Orianna took off her veil revealing her full lips and elegant skin. "Ugh...I hate this stupid veil! Of course, I remember you...you and Lamia were good to me growing up,

Jarvan was a big meanie though!" She attempted to grab her wine goblet but touched Octavius' hand.

Upon contact he jumped, knocking the wine goblet into a large dusty tome. The two misfits both kneeled to clean up the mess, bumping heads at the simultaneous action. Orianna gripped her forehead and rubbed it profusely. "Ow!" she chirped. "I'm so sorry, p...p...please...allow me to read you a story like I used to when we were kids," said Octavius. Still rubbing her forehead, she smiled sweetly at him. Octavius scrambled through the tomes until he picked up a large purple tome that read, 'Land of the Fae'. He flipped to the middle page. "Ok...so...um...this story is about a world far away called Crestonia. It is a place like ours in that magic is bountiful, however, the magic they do is well...different. They do something called spirit bonds and spirit magic. I'm not sure what that is but it sounds scary." Goosebumps emerged across Orianna's forearms and back. "Oh, that sounds good, tell me more."

Octavius licked his lips as he stared at her round jaw and alluring eyes. "W...well...umm...they call themselves the Fae people and they have wings on their backs that they use to fly as high as a castle." He raised both his arms to illustrate how high. Orianna clapped her hands together excitedly. "Oh...wow. More!" she exclaimed. "Well they are all extremely beautiful and are said to live for hundreds of years, also they are known for having twins and those twins can communicate without even speaking a word to each other. What's odd about them is that they all have pointy ears. Supposedly at night their wings turn brown and they turn into hideous creatures."

Orianna choked on her spit, a serious look crossed her face as she grabbed the tome from his hands. "Let me see!" She stared at the picture of a Fae person with her jaw opened. Orianna flipped through several pages, each containing more pictures of the same people she kept seeing in her visions. "This is it! These are the people!" Octavius furled his eyebrows. "What...what do you mean?" he asked. "Can...may...I borrow this please?" she said. Octavius clenched his teeth and bit his bottom lip. "Umm...I don't know...this is from the queen's personal library and I wasn't even supposed to go in there...," Octavius stammered. Orianna went on her knees and placed both of her hands together. "Pretty pweas-eeeeee!" her round eyes sparkled under the dim light.

Octavius coughed hysterically. "Oh please…don't do that…please get up!" Orianna stood up and gave him a kiss on the cheek. "Thank you! You're the best!" She took the tome up and ran off nearly tripping on her gown on the way out. Octavius placed a hand on his bright red cheek. "Oh…oh…well…shucks." He sat there for a moment smiling to himself before going back to his reading.

CHAPTER 25

JARVAN

THE FLAGSHIP WAS severely damaged during the battle against the Crocodile fleet. When General Gatticus was killed his remaining troops flew into a frenzied rage and pushed the fleet back causing the ships to go into a disorganized formation; for these reasons, the flag ship was now in the middle of the fleet in opposed to the front. Even when faced with unsurmountable odds the Crocodile fleet fought right down to the very last man.

Jarvan stood leaning against the bow of the ship. His eyes glazed over as he peered out onto the passageway that laid before them. The passageway was thin and thus caused the remaining twenty-two ships to move in a file of two ships. "I can't believe they didn't surrender...did you see the look in their eyes when Gatticus died? I wonder if my men will fight or surrender should I fall..." Azreal's eyes widened and his breath increased rapidly. "P...please...don't talk like that. If you die then...I have to lead... and oh please Wasp spirit shine upon the Lion!" Jarvan clasped his friend by the neck and laughed heartily, "Don't worry. I won't fall anytime soon. There are many battles to be won and too many women to bed before I meet the grave." Jarvan squinted as he tilted his head to the side. "Why does it seem like we're missing ships?"

Azreal tilted his head as well. "Perhaps they have made it to the island and have fanned out to create more space. That is something my members would have instructed them to do. We are very good at formations as you know, I mean…" Jarvan raised a hand completely silencing the Wasp Guild general. He tensed up and placed a hand on his sword. The ship beside them trembled fiercely, before anyone could react massive teeth emerged from the water creating a massive sized whirlpool.

The creature engulfed the large ship. Upon seeing the creatures gaping mouth Azreal attempted to take out his weapon, but Jarvan stopped him. "It's too close to the ship." Without another word, he unsheathed his mighty broadsword and jumped overboard into the mouth of the creature. Several moments passed before a flash of yellow light escaped from the watery depths. Jarvan emerged from the water in a display of light. Azreal squinted and covered his eyes with his forearm. Everyone within visible range of the daring attack cheered. "W…wow…that…was amazing!" he said.

The crowned prince climbed aboard the ship with ease. Azreal ran over to Jarvan. "Wow…I can't…believe you just jumped into the mouth of that monster without hesitation. I mean…what if you died?" The veins on Jarvan's neck throbbed, his jaw clenched, and he lowered his eyebrows. "When will you learn this is not a game? A man who is not willing to die on the battlefield is nothing more than a tree waiting to be cut down! It would be a disgrace to the way these people have fought if I wasn't willing to sacrifice my life to defeat them. Quit acting like a fan and start acting like a general!" he yelled. The Lion and Wasp guild elite squad members on the ship stared in awe at Jarvan.

Azreal looked down and away while blinking back tears. His shoulders slumped as he walked away slowly, periodically looking back. Jarvan massaged his temples while running his hand through his hair aggressively. He walked over to the bow where both of his hands gripped the head of the lion figurehead. *The great Lion Deity must be testing me…I know not how to reach this man.* He grimaced and caressed the elegant figure. *Is my back strong enough to carry us both? It must be. I have no choice. I am the mighty…*

Jarvan quickly raised his shield. A sea of arrows rained down upon the flag ship. The screams of the Wasp members who had no means of defending themselves echoed between the narrow passageways. Jarvan made his way to the Raven captain who had been struck in his ankle, covering them both with his mighty shield he dragged the man inside the ship. The rest of the Lion members took cover underneath their shields and followed their general's lead by protecting the Wasp Guild members.

Jarvan tried to pull out the arrow but it would not come out. Seeing the Raven captain laid out on the table Azreal rushed over. He widened his eyes and twisted his mouth in a grotesque manner and asked, "What's going on?" Azreal poked his head outside, an arrow grazed his nose. Jarvan tapped his fingers against the table. "Help me with this arrow, we have to move out of this death trap!" Azreal moved closer and ran his hand over the arrow, the wound oozed a dark purple liquid. "This arrow is enchanted with curse magic." Jarvan fixed his gaze at the wound. "A pox upon those heathens for using such foul magic, and here I was beginning to respect them."

Azreal shrugged and replied, "I believe that all magic is the same, it's the usage that determines whether it is foul or not. Some people equate our mineral magic to be foul magic, additionally we use curse magic on the tips of our daggers." Jarvan pounded his hands on the table and declared, "I don't care about your beliefs on magic and its practical uses, some of my men are still out there on the defensive. Can you disenable or disenchant or whatever it's called?" Azreal rubbed his nose, hiding a smile he replied, "Yes, I can. I certainly can disenchant this magic. I'm not an expert or anything but in this instance…" Jarvan grabbed him by the collar gripping tightly and shouted, "Do it now!"

CHAPTER 26

JAMES

IN THE DAYS following the tournament James has had no shortage of fans who sought out his magical imprint on their artifacts. The Elephant Guild allows the use of force to defend the honor of the guild, but it looks down on excessive pride or tributes of the ego. Because of this James would bring dishonor to his guild if he were to oblige to such a personal request. A magical imprint is to inscribe a special artifact with one's aura signature. By doing this they essentially are giving a portion of their aura to that person to use however they wish. This can result in allowing them the ability to use that person's magic if they managed to get the artifact sealed.

To stay hidden James had attempted to lock himself within the confines of his guild's fortress. Unfortunately, the emperor requested for his presence in the Lion headquarters for a victory feast. Anyone who knows the emperor knows that he does not accept the word 'no' from any person more than once in their lifetime. James bit his lip and swallowed deeply. With each step he took towards the main hall his breathing increased in pace. His mind became a daze as the raspy voice questioned. *The play is set as your journey begins to unfold, will you choose death or life? Are they not the same thing?* James paused a moment as his sweaty hands clasped the handles of the large metal door. Opening the door to the main hall his jaw dropped. The mind that was previously racing became frozen in time.

Before the illustrious James laid a large crystal statue of him holding his war hammer. The crystal statue was placed on top of the banquet table containing every single delicacy from his home city of Grande. There was root milk, boar tusk soup, and even the extremely complicated hog tongue pie to name a few. The aroma of the delicacies titillated the nostrils of the stocky warrior. He licked his lips and rubbed his hands together. He smiled broadly. Lamia who saw the burly figure in the corner of her eyes swung her arms and did a little spin before skipping towards James. "Hello mister champion! Do you smell anything different about me?" she cooed as she caressed his arm.

James furrowed his brow and leaned forward. His eyes fixated on the tight grey dress with gold trimmings that she wore. This was the typical Elephant Guild dinner dress; additionally, he could smell the glorious scent of Elephantine perfume number one. He licked his lips and nodded slowly. "You're wearing Elephantine perfume, how did you acquire such a rare scent? I mean I haven't smelled it since I was a child." Lamia giggled and replied, "A true lady never reveals her best kept secrets. Now come before the food gets cold. She grabbed his hand and brought him to the massive marble table. The dinner guests clapped their hands enthusiastically, showing their appreciation for the tournament champion. Some of the most prominent figures in the world sat at the table waiting to be introduced to the warrior who dazzled everyone with his forest magic.

James graciously said, "Thank you...please...no need...seriously... you are all too kind," Lamia introduced him to each dinner guest one by one; there were so many that James couldn't even remember who was from which guild and what role they played in their guild. Finally, he looked to the end of the table where he saw a familiar face, one that he didn't expect to see. Lamia pointed to a woman dressed in an elegant red dress topped off with a gold chained necklace and red leather gloves.

Lamia continued with her introductions. "Well...you already know Sai from the Raven Guild, we also have Tamriel from the Raven Guild, the little boy with them is a protégé or something, but anyways they are both high council members, oh and finally we have Eros Mora the final Mora to join us this evening, Eros why are you all the way down there when your sisters are over here? Please come closer and sit beside James.

He fidgeted in his chair. His hands became clammy while a single bead of sweat dripped down his forehead onto his dinner suit. Lamia continued with her monologue. "But wait, where are Orianna, Malikai and Solaire? Oh, for heaven's light, the food is getting cold." She turned to her father. "Father should we just eat without them?" The emperor who was already half way through his pie raised a thumb.

The entire group dug into the amazing feast that was spread out in front of them. James stared at Eros as she approached the empty chair that was next to him. She gave him a wink and sat down placing a hand on his thigh. Nearly jumping out of his seat he sat upright and attempted to eat his soup while the dominatrix caressed his inner thigh. Lamia called out to him, "James! James! Hello, can you hear me?" James scratched his nose and shuffled around uncomfortably in his seat. He stammered, "S…s… sorry…what was the question?" Lamia sighed and placed both her hands on her hips. "I said…are you enjoying your soup? I handpicked every dish here myself. I wasn't sure what you wanted so I made sure they made everything! I don't like soup, but it smells good, so I don't know…what do you think? Gosh…you're such a big head sometimes!" Trying to ignore the gradual bulge in his pants, James replied faintly, "Yes, I enjoy it very much. Thank you, milady." Lamia rolled her eyes and shook her head. Turning to the queen she let out a loud sigh, "Mother Aeterna! Do you see what I mean, he is hopeless!"

CHAPTER 27

ORIANNA

ORIANNA COULD HEAR her mother banging on her door, the surprisingly heavy fist of the elderly woman repeatedly slammed against the iron hinges. "Get out of that room now, we are late for the banquet dinner!" Orianna pressed her lips together and rolled her eyes. *I wonder whose fault that is?* She stood up and placed the book about Crestonia down on her cabinet. Walking over to the mirror she placed her hands on the cabinet and stared at the mirror where the Raven Deity once paid her a visit. Her lips quivered as she wrapped her arms around herself. *What...what am I to do? How can I find the twins when I can't even get a minute to myself? I hate the people in this guild...I hate them all...except...well...Malikai. I mean he is the only one who listens to me and doesn't want something from me. Corvus thinks I'm a fool and just wants to go against my mother...That mysterious woman wants me to leave the guild and join her band of miscreants! I wear this veil to hide my face while everyone is the one hiding their true intentions. Above all...*

Tears poured down Orianna's willowy face. *Above all...no one cares about the prophecy! I know it is my purpose to fulfill the prophecy, why is everyone against me?* She slammed her fists on the cabinet, her aura shot out wildly causing the mirror to break. Looking at the mirror she grabbed her hair and tugged it slowly. *Ahh! My mother is going to kill me!* Placing her palms against her head she gathered the pieces of glass. *You know what...she...she can...she can go screw herself! I hate her most of all, the only thing she ever does is hit me and yell at me for being clumsy. I mean...I know I am clumsy but...but still...I...deserve better...at least I think I do.*

Her hands flowed through her hair in aggression. *No! I know I deserve better, I'm...I'm going to leave!* Orianna grabbed the gemstones that Lamia bought her along with all her savings; she placed them in a bag with the rest of her precious belongings. She walked up to the door then stopped and stared at the door knob. Her shoulders hunched down while her knees shook. *B...but...where do I go?* Orianna closed her eyes and furrowed her brows. She held this position for a few moments before snapping both her fingers together. *Malikai...he has been all over the world, he must know some place that I can at least find more information on these Fae people!*

Malikai has never been the same since his early days in the guild. In his youth, he was a child prodigy, something the Raven Guild had never seen before. He showed great promise with wind magic as well as had the ability to wield two blades effectively. This made him one of the most feared duelists from a young age. The Raven Guild speaker at the time personally took him under his wing and taught him several advanced wind techniques. Having this advance knowledge at such a young age enabled Malikai to receive plenty of attention from the Fox women, however, one day he changed for the worse. He started to drink heavily and would lock himself in his room for days, often without showering or eating. He would walk around with his eyes glazed over seemingly lost in another world.

Orianna was the first to notice her older brother had strange bruises on his person that had not been healed. When she approached her mother about these bruises she said that he was chosen, and that was the end of it. To this day Orianna has no idea what happened to her once joyful and talented brother. When the Raven Guild broke away from the Fox Guild, he started to spend even more time with the guild speaker. Around this time his drinking habits worsened, eventually he consumed the most toxic of all alcoholic beverages in the land. His love for toxic beverages was so well known that vendors would line up at the Raven headquarters to sell their goods to the renowned drinker, 'Malikai strong liver.'

Orianna walked into the open room and covered her mouth, the stench of vomit and alcohol threatened to steal her lunch. Malikai sprawled out across the floor with several bottles of Kinderstar Ale, one of the most putrid ales on the market. His swords were sprawled out on the floor while his armor was tucked away in the corner. His undergarment was defiled with blood and chunks of fish. She took out her silk napkin and wiped the vomit from his mouth. Pinching his nose, she whispered, "Please wake up brother." Malikai groaned and turned over to his side. Pinching his nose once again she yelled, "Wake up brother!" Malikai stirred and sat upright in a flash with both his fists clenched in front of him. "Who goes there? You want a piece of this?" Orianna shrugged and took a seat on the bed. "Brother…it's me…may we talk for a minute?"

Malikai rubbed his eyes and yawned, he reached over for a bottle of ale and chugged it down. "Of course, little sister…what ails you?" he said. Orianna lifted her head and puffed her chest out. "I'm leaving, I'm going my own way!" Malikai threw his head back and laughed. "You have only ever been to two cities and never without a chaperone. Where do you think you're going alone?"

Orianna looked down at the floor and fiddled her thumbs together. "I…I…don't know…but I need to find the Fae twins…the ones with pointy ears." Malikai scratched his chin. "Well…hmm…I don't know anything about Fae twins with pointy ears but if information is what you're looking for then your best bet is to go to Ladle." Orianna tilted her head and shrugged. "Ladle…what is that?" Malikai laughed holding his stomach, "Not a what, but a where…or even more so a who. Ladle is the Owl city far north from here; it is a place where a large portion of the world's natural resources are collected. The Squirrel Guild collects berries, nuts, and other fruits and vegetables. They also collect books, tomes, and rare artifacts for The Great Owl. If you're looking for some weird class of people, then your best bet is to visit the largest library in the world."

Orianna grabbed her brother's hands and looked him in his eyes. "Please brother…help me escape…the guards won't let me leave the quarters without you, Tamriel, or mother. I just want to be free of all of this!" Malikai grabbed her hands and lowered his head. "I can't do that sister I'm sorry. I have a duty to the guild to uphold its customs. You are too important to the guild for us to let you wander off on your own. After the situation with the Lion Guild is settled, I promise I will take you to Ladle but above all don't blame yourself for the prophecies. The Raven Deity controls the magic, you are not responsible for what the Deity tells us to do. Please remember that." Orianna wiped a tear from her eyes and nodded. "Okay…I'll…I'll wait."

CHAPTER 28

JARVAN

THE CROCODILE GUILD is a guild unlike any on the mainland. They are a self-sufficient society that does not rely on trade or commerce to satisfy the needs of the group. They are a warlike people that train their members from a young age. Failure to pass this training regime resulted in being exiled out of the guild sanctuary or being offered to their sea beast. Being exiled was essentially a death sentence because the island was filled with wild animals with varying degrees of aggression. The trees on the island of Tem were so numerous that even its inhabitants found themselves lost.

Jarvan and his medium sized army had set up a beachhead to defend against any attacks from the center. A large bodied Lion soldier whispered to Jarvan, "Sir…I have the status report you requested." Jarvan turned to him with a stern face and said, "Well…get on with it." The man nodded and began reading the parchment. "Well…of the 75,000 soldiers that we left Passerine with we have approximately 34,690, of that 34,690 only 8,000 of them are Wasp Guild members. It is exactly as you suspected, the Wasp Guild's formation was unable to withstand the attacks during the passageway; our guild members did their best to protect them but being under fire themselves it was difficult. Finally, we lost a large portion of our supplies as our reserve ships were capsized during the attack."

The hefty man rubbed his growling stomach. Azreal lowered his head and kicked a rock across the sand. Jarvan nodded and waved the man away.

He turned to Azreal. "This may make things difficult, I was relying on the projectiles to reduce our casualties. It is even more important now that we know they have expert marksmanship." Azreal raised his head and bit his lip before speaking, "How can you tell they have expert marksmanship?"

Jarvan furrowed his brows and widened his stance. "I suppose you couldn't have known since you were inside the cabin pouting. They could target the Wasp Guild members from behind the safety of the ledge, the entire time they were invisible to us. What made matters worse was that they would strike your members solely. The first few volleys were to put my men into a defensive stance while the next few were aimed directly at the hearts of the Wasp, whichever man is at the helm of this army, he is a force to be reckoned with in terms of tactics. Azreal widened his eyes and shook violently. "Perhaps…perhaps…we should turn back and get more reinforcements."

Jarvan clenched his fists together. "When will you understand, It is better to die in the hands of the enemy than it is to live in the bosom of your mother? We will pursue on." Jarvan turned towards the army with a smile on his face. "Today we have touched the sands of the mighty island known as Tem. It is a great island, one said to possess jewels and crystals of unparalleled beauty. It is a land where the women are said to have an earthly green taste, something like that of a kiwi or a strawberry. Well men…soon we will feast on the fruit of our hard labor!"

The men cheered and raised their hands in salute. "First thing is first, I want everyone to break into their squadrons. I will be taking several squadrons into the forest by evening's sun to forage for food." One of the Lieutenant Generals raised his hand. Jarvan pointed at the stocky man with a long beard. "Yes, LG what is it?" The man stroked his beard and said, "Perhaps I should lead the men into the forest, it is rumored that the Crocodile Guild forest is filled with dangerous animals such as giant bears and crocodiles not to mention the cursed traps that could cut a man in half!" Jarvan laughed and grabbed his growling belly. "Should a bear find me in the woods you should fear for the bear!"

Jarvan and his squadron navigated through most of the forest without much cause for concern; in fact, it was eerily quiet. The trees sparkled in a variety of colors, some of them dawning rainbow colored branches. In truly a skilled fashion the Wasp members easily killed the birds in the trees using their throwing daggers. Azreal even caught himself a rainbow-colored raven. "Jarvan, perhaps we should head back we have enough food for everyone besides, it's getting dark," Azreal said as he stepped in front of the crowned prince.

Jarvan shook his head, tension running down his spine. "You're not thinking like a general, we have enough food for everyone here but what about the men back at the beach? We need more rations. Those supplies that we have need to be saved for an emergency." Azreal nodded in agreement and turned around, a rustling sound could be heard in the distance. "It could be another rainbow raven! I'll go check it out!" he said with a smile as he ran off into the distance. Jarvan reached his hand out to grab Azreal but it was too late. "Fool, let me lead the way it could be...ahh never mind," he continued walking. A few moments later a loud scream could be heard a few feet away.

The squadron ran in the direction of the scream. To their dismay there was a giant bear laying over Azreal with blood on its claws. Azreal was sprawled out on his back, blood oozing from his forearm. "I tried to warn you...lions, tigers, and bears oh my!" he said with a grin. Azreal screamed, "Please...get it off me!" Jarvan shook his head. "It's just a bear, you should be able to handle that with your bare hands." Sweat pouring down Azreal's face he yelled out once again, "This isn't the time for your puns, help me please!" Jarvan sighed and banged his sword on his shield. The bear looked at Jarvan and charged towards him. When the bear came within striking range the general of the army dropped his sword and shield to the ground. The large beast pounced upon the general and the two became intertwined.

The two rolled around for several moments until the crowned prince grasped the giant bear into a choke lock, removing the oxygen from its lungs. It groaned and moaned before going limp. He stood up and said a Lion Guild prayer for the animal. Azreal slowly made his way over to the group clutching his bleeding arm. He stuttered, "Why...why...didn't you use your weapon?" Jarvan raised an eyebrow and pursed his lips. "It wouldn't be fair." Jarvan looked behind Azreal staring into the colorful bushes. He placed a hand on Azreal's shoulder, "It's time to go...don't forget to bring the bear!"

⤐

Upon returning to the beachhead they noticed a large crowd surrounding an arrow stuck in the sand. Jarvan approached the crowd with his chest held high. "What is going on?" The Lieutenant General ripped the parchment off the arrow and brought it to the crowned prince. "This arrow landed over here a few moments ago," said the LG. Jarvan glanced at the paper then crumpled it. He clenched his teeth and threw the parchment into the water.

Azreal tapped the prince on his shoulder. "What did it say?" he asked. Sneering he scratched his mustache and replied, "Someone named Niloticus Bourbon claims we are trespassing infidels and that WE should get off their island! How dare he call me an infidel when HE is the one who is a heathen and must surrender to the might of the Lion Guild. Additionally, it makes the claim that their numbers range in the hundred thousand and that they will descend upon us like locusts." Azreal gasped and exclaimed, "What...a hundred thousand!" He bit his lip, placing both of his hands on his head. The prince narrowed his eyes while creasing his brow. "I highly doubt it, their actions to date do not support that claim. In fact, this tactic does not seem to match up with the tactics they have used prior. Traditionally the Crocodile Guild likes to fight head on with their skilled warriors. Now that I think about it, the battle in the ravine was rather unusual."

Azreal shrugged and muttered, "I don't see how...I mean...he simply wants to avoid needless bloodshed." Jarvan laughed and answered, "We are long past that juncture. No general in his right mind would surrender once he has successfully established a beachhead. That is the curious part, I mean if he had such troops he would have been waiting for us at the exit of the passageway; that would create a bottleneck situation essentially winning the war. Instead he allows us to reach the beach then tells us to leave? There is much to be desired from this Niloticus character. I would surmise from this letter that they have fewer troops than we do." Azreal lowered his head placing both his hands behind his back. "I see...no general in his right mind, well in any case what next?" he asked looking down at the sand once again. Jarvan caressed the hilt of his sword. "Tomorrow we will enter deep into the forest and find their stronghold." Azreal nodded in agreement.

Jarvan woke up early in the morning and started to map out the pathway that they took the previous evening. A few hours later Azreal joined him in the General's tent to assist. Azreal widened his eyes in amazement and asked, "You did all of that in a few hours?" Jarvan's smile filled the room, "They don't call me the chosen one for just my battle acumen. I'm actually a pretty good artist. See this is where we are now, and this is the area we covered last night. This only leaves here and over here as places that they can have a stronghold large enough to fit a sizeable army," he said with a smile on his face. "Ok…so I guess we will be going here first then if that doesn't pan out we can go over here. This way we have an easy time coming back to the beach head after we've secured a victory." Jarvan nodded in agreement placing a hand on Azreal's shoulder. "There you go, now you sound more like a general." Azreal smiled and responded, "I did a lot of spirit searching last night. For the first time in years I spoke with the Wasp Spirit, she came to me in a dream and it was amazing, I mean…" Jarvan put a hand up, interrupting him. "I'm sure it was…anyways it's time to go."

Walking with fervor in every step that he took Azreal moved through the forest struggling to maintain the pace set by the chosen one. He chugged along, sweat dripping down his face to the collar of his armor. "So…who is that Niloticus Bourbon guy anyways?" Jarvan raised both his hands in the air. "I have no idea, I have never heard of him. I'd assume he is the son of the great Dominus Bourbon." Azreal raised an eyebrow and asked, "What do you mean great? Wasn't he an enemy of the Lion Guild?" Jarvan nodded in agreement and replied, "Yes, he was the greatest enemy we ever had. In fact, he was the one who killed my grandfather, supposedly he was the greatest warrior to ever live." Azreal stopped dead in his tracks. "I thought your late uncle held the title of the greatest warrior to ever step foot on the battlefield...I mean that's what all the books stated." Jarvan laughed and stated, "You can't believe everything you read in books. According to my father the only man greater than Jarvan Hartengale the VI was Dominus Bourbon. He was a man so feared that at the mere sight of his battle axe legions of men would turn and run. He could summon a thousand giant crocodiles to do his bidding and above all he had a war cry that would freeze men in their tracks. I actually modelled my own war cry after his."

Azreal scratched his head and asked, "You mean that crappy animal magic was once capable of something so fearful? How inspiring." The two-continued walking. "Yes, but it is quite sad that he has passed. I mean by now he would have been in his sixties, but I was still hoping to meet him on the battlefield. It would have been a true honor to cleave him down with my glorious sword of cleansing but perhaps it is for the best. I'm sure many of our men would have met their end even in his old age." Azreal furrowed his brow and asked, "Do you really think a man could be that powerful at such an advanced age?"

Jarvan shook his head. "You my friend haven't met Sai Zakura, after being trained by him in the art of combat I would say any man is capable of anything." Azreal's mouth dropped. "I have heard of him, I sure hope to be trained by him one day, I know I'd make an excellent student." Jarvan smirked and teased, "You still have some of my training to go through but sure, when we get back I'll introduce you." Jarvan placed a hand to bar Azreal from moving. "Don't take another step." He bent down to look at a string that was tied across two trees, behind one of the trees was a massive sharpened log imbued with curse magic and secured with lock magic. Infront of the string was a barrier that was used to drain the aura of anyone who passed by.

He motioned for the head scout to disarm the trap. The man ran over to the tree and drew the sigil of a golden key with a skeleton as the bow. "Open thy lock for I am your master." The man walked over to the string and kicked it. The wooden piece held in place while the barrier that was in front disappeared. Continuing to walk forward the man stepped on a rock and kicked it away. Immediately several arrows shot forth from both sides of the forest lodging themselves into his chest and stomach. He dropped to the floor as blood dripped onto Jarvan's boots. Jarvan frowned while crossing his arms. "That's not good…not good at all," he said with a straight face. Azreal moved his head frantically. "What do you mean…please tell me he wasn't the only one capable of doing advanced key magic?" Jarvan placed both of his hands on his head and knelt to the floor. He looked at the man and said a prayer. "Ok…I won't tell you."

CHAPTER 29

JAMES

LAMIA WAS KNOWN for her expensive taste in clothing, jewelry, and food, but above all she was known for her love of parties and the ability to throw a party that was so expensive that it would far surpass some of the other guilds yearly budgets. In the case of James' tournament after party she took the reins from the Swan Guild and decided to throw the party herself; something Octavius pointed out as being peculiar, considering the tournament was in her honor.

The room was decorated in white silk thread made from the web of the rare ivory spider. A large blue Kazrite flame was lit in the middle of the room giving the entire room a blue tint. The music was so loud that it could be heard from outside the castle. James sat in the corner watching Tamriel conversing with a masked figure. The little boy identified as Piet was standing right by his side; he was wearing a white robe with a pearl necklace and black shoes. His face was an unusual pale blue with small freckles dotted throughout his face.

James frowned and crossed his arms when he locked eyes with Sai Zakura. Tamriel ran his hand through the young boy's hair. James immediately stood up and approached the three Raven members. Upon seeing the massive figure approaching them Sai placed his hand on the hilt of his katana. Tamriel licked his lips and sneered before speaking, "Well… well…well…if it isn't the magnificent judge James, or perhaps I should call you James the Merciful. How smart of you to be graced by our presence. I would have expected you to introduce yourself to us sooner."

James clenched his teeth and remarked, "I was not aware the Raven Guild allowed children in the high council. From what I understand only the high council members wear white robes." Tamriel smirked and replied, "Muahaha, what keen eyes you have. I suppose all those vegetables must be good for something. If you must know, he is a special exception. Aren't you good little Piet?" The boy stood there frozen with a pale expression. James continued, "He seems rather in disorder." Tamriel tilted his head to the side and asked, "What are you getting at?" James took one step forward causing Sai to do the same. "What I am saying is…" Lamia poked James in the back, "There you are! I've been searching for you everywhere." James raised his eyebrows while biting his lip.

"Well…," Lamia grabbed his hand and tugged him forward. "I don't want to hear it Mr. You're coming to dance with me." She walked him over to the middle of the dance floor and started to do the traditional Lion Guild dance. She twirled around James while he stood there awkwardly. "Move your feet, gosh you're hopeless!" she exclaimed with pursed lips. She took his hand and placed it on her hips then started to rock side to side in his massive arms. James turned red as he brought her in closer; her scent filled his nostrils with bliss. He leaned in closer and placed his hands on the back of her waist. Lamia rested her hands on his broad shoulders and hummed along with the song.

The two embraced each other for several songs, even the ones that were solo dance songs. James looked Lamia in her beautiful blue eyes. "Lamia… what would you think if I were to tell you that I…" Lamia tilted her head forward and smiled, revealing pearly white teeth. "Yes…James? Go on… you know you can tell me anything." James blushed while his palms perspired. "That I…" In the corner of his eye he saw Tamriel, Sai, and Piet leaving the after party. He clenched his teeth and said, "I have to go."

᪥

Tamriel ran his hand across Piet's pelvis. Sai closed his eyes completely shut; turning away slightly. Tamriel caressed the boy's neck. "You're a good boy Piet, keep being a good boy and I will continue to treat you well." Piet kept silent. Tamriel tapped the pearl necklace on his neck and whispered something in his ear. "Will you keep being a good boy Piet?" The boy turned to Tamriel and smiled. "Yes master, Piet will continue to be a good boy, forever and always." Tamriel stroked him on the head. He placed both his hands together forming an arch. "Excellent," he said. Sai covered his mouth before spitting on the floor. "Perhaps we should make our leave, it seems James Ivory is not fond of us these days." Tamriel narrowed his eyes and twisted his mouth. "You dare to bring up that Elephant scum's name? He is from a guild of self-righteous fools, besides their tenets prevent them from interfering in the operations of other more reputable guilds like our own!"

James slammed the top of his war hammer into the marble floor. He then crossed both of his arms and glared at both Tamriel and Sai. The three Raven members turned around to see James walking towards them. Sai stepped forward and placed a hand on his katana but Tamriel held him back with a smile. "What did you say about my guild!" yelled the heroic James. While maintaining eye contact Tamriel chuckled, "Which part…the self-righteous fool or the scum part? In fact, I was about to say how cowardly your guild must be since you sat out of the Great War. Since then you have done nothing besides hide in your territory accumulating dust and eating tree bark. Frankly, I was shocked to see the all mighty judge James leave the confines of his hut. I would have thought this city to be too civilized for you." Tamriel licked his lips and smiled.

James stood tall and clasped both of his hands behind his back. "You're right…" Sai furrowed his brow and tilted his head. "What?… Don't say that…" James shook his head, "No…he is right…all of that is true. Things will change soon and the likes of you…," Pity filled his eyes as he continued, "You people will truly feel the weight of justice crash down upon your shoulders like a thundering storm." Pink aura surrounded Sai as he unsheathed his katana. Green aura surrounded James as he gripped his mighty war hammer. Lamia ran up behind James and gave him a hug, her large breasts squeezing against his muscular back. She exclaimed, "Oh James! They are playing my favorite song…come and dance with me!" Sai sheathed his sword while the three made their exit.

꙳

James collapsed on his bed with a loud thud. The soft feather bed absorbed his body. The muscles that he had worked so hard to maintain ached. *Who would have thought dancing would take so much out of me? Lamia has the stamina of a Gazelle.* Rolling around in the bed he finally sat up. *The beds in this city are too soft. I miss the confines of my fortress already. The soil beneath my bare feet, the trumpeting of the Elephants, but above all I miss the quiet solitude. In Grande I flourish in the deep recess that is my mind, while in Larimar I am drowned by them. Nothing could have prepared me for this.* He took a sip of coconut water. A beverage that was abundant in his home territory. *But I have a mission to complete. I will not let the Raven Guild continue with their depravity.* His father's voice penetrated his thoughts. *If you ever interfere with another guild's activities your death will not be swift. You are my son and thus an example will be made of you.* James clasped the leather jack. *If I must forfeit my life, then so be it.*

He peered outside into the yard where he could see a large crowd gathering. The music filled his ears causing him to enter a slight trance. *I wonder who is playing that magnificent tune...* The music grew louder as if it was coming towards him. He glanced outside the window to see the crowd was standing outside of it. A familiar voice began to speak, "James honey, I certainly hope you weren't sleeping because I have a surprise for you."

James bit his bottom lip. "Eros you look absolutely stunning...I mean...you always do...but you're wearing the special Elephant party gown. I haven't seen such a thing since I was a child." Eros struck a pose and said, "Yes, I changed hoping that we could go for a walk. You were so preoccupied with Lamia that I didn't have a chance to spend time with you." James blushed, his palms filled with sweat. A soft expression appeared on her face. "I'm not going to let you go so easily, please come and join me for a walk." James gathered his things and made his way towards Eros. Noticing the group of masked figures surrounding her, James queried, "Who are they?" Eros replied, "These are a group of entertainers, would you believe it? They appeared out of nowhere; I saw them performing in the city square and I hired them to do a special act for you."

A masked figure approached him wearing all black. "I am Madam Dupont and these are my entertainers." She pointed towards a man holding two puppets, and two men wearing pink suits with stripes on them. Madam Dupont's aura inched towards James. A gruesome expression came across his face. "Eros, let's go!" Eros furrowed her brows slightly, "What about the entertainment? Do you not like my surprise?" James shook his head. "I can't place words on it, but I just know we have to go, please come with me."

CHAPTER 30

JARVAN

JARVAN'S ARMY CAME to an open clearing in the middle of the vast forest, most of his troops laid across the ground clutching various parts of their body. The poison from the cursed objects ran their course immobilizing a large portion of his army. Azreal and the Wasp members were left largely untouched, this was due to the Lion members being the first ones to clear a patch of forest ensuring that it was safe. To make matters worse Azreal's aura was dwindling making it very time consuming for him to disenchant the cursed objects so that the Lion's members could be healed.

Jarvan turned to his men, looking at all the injured soldiers and remarked, "There is fresh water coming from this river, we will make camp here." He planted his shield down into the ground. Azreal wrapped his arms around himself and rocked from side to side. "Here? I mean... what if this is another trap?" Jarvan narrowed his eyes and pointed to the Wasp general. In a low-pitched tone he asked, "What's your point? My men are dying, both armies are tired and hungry, and it is coming onto nightfall. Do you suggest we travel through this...this...death trap of a forest blind?"

The Wasp general lowered his head while rubbing his neck. He stammered, "I suppose...not..." Cutting him off Jarvan took a step closer to the Wasp general and interjected, "Your cowardice is truly testing my patience, do not open your mouth unless it is to provide valuable information. In fact, assist the Raven Guild members in healing my men so that we can leave at first light." Azreal nodded in agreement, feeling slightly flustered. Nightfall descended in what felt like mere moments, the cold air swept through the camp at an alarming rate. Jarvan and the most skilled of his men took the first watch in anticipation for an ambush. After finishing his duty of disenchanting the cursed arrows Azreal volunteered to join the first watch. This act of bravery was met with shock but Jarvan ultimately turned him down.

Jarvan's eyes darted back and forth as he listened for any sign of an attack. He knew better than anyone that the first attack is often the most devastating, something he learned from his late uncle. A soldier walked up to Jarvan and handed him a bowl of bear soup. "Here you go sir, it is time for the second watch." Jarvan shook his head and placed the bowl of steaming soup at his side. "I'll take a second watch, something…something is not right." The man nodded in agreement and nudged the second watch awake.

Swoosh! A glass arrow careened in Jarvan's direction. In a split second the crowned prince caught it before it could pierce his neck. "Ambush! Formation Zero!" he yelled. All the able-bodied lion members stood in a circular formation with their shields up, followed by the Wasp members in the inner circle, followed by the injured troops in the middle. Jarvan joined his men in the outer layer with his shield raised high and yelled, "Come out and face us you cowards!"

There was a long drawn out silence, then a high-pitched voice yelled out, "Leave the island now!" Jarvan lifted his head while pushing his chest out. "The mighty Crocodile Guild will perish soon enough, surrender now and your deaths will be swift." More arrows launched out of the pitch-black forest catching several Lion soldiers whose shield was not raised high enough. The outer circle closed the gap within an instant, just in time to block another volley of arrows aimed at the Wasp Guild. "We will fight to the death for we embody the spirit of the great Dominus!" the voice yelled back.

A whistling sound filled the clearing. The army stood in formation for several long moments before a Wasp member shuffled around uncomfortably. The tiny figure with Wasp wings on his back placed both his hands behind his back and stood on his tip-toes, "I think they are gone, if I just fly up a little bit I can probably see…" A glass arrow surrounded by dark pink aura in the shape of a Crocodile flew forth at blinding speed taking the Wasp members head off. "Stay in formation!" Jarvan yelled. High pitched laughter and giggling could be heard throughout the forest. A different high pitch voice spoke this time. "You will all die miserable and pathetic deaths worthy of you men for you are not trained properly. I pity your master." Several whistling sounds could be heard throughout the forest this time followed by rustling of the leaves.

At first light, the group that was still able bodied progressed forward into the final area on the map. Considering they have traveled throughout the entire island without finding a stronghold it was safe to assume that this area would be where they would find the bulk of the Crocodile Army. Jarvan's massive army had dwindled significantly, however the ones that remained were the strongest and the most experienced. Jarvan was silent after last night's ambush; he said not one word to Azreal or to his troops. Azreal knew better than to interrupt Jarvan's silence. The light below his every step flickered violently while the halo above his head shone bright yellow.

Azreal took this to mean that for the first time since they have embarked on this campaign Jarvan was enraged. The two generals came to a massive clearing at the end of the island with a large wooden fence at the back. A few structures towered over the wall, in front of the massive wall was a medium sized army of women and young men. The men all carried heavy battle axes that seemed too large for them, while the women carried expertly crafted glass bows and similarly fitting glass arrows. They all had green war paint on their faces; the men wore green and black medium armor while the women wore green and black glass armor.

Azreal stared in amazement and stuttered, "Wh…you…mean… all this time…the archers…the archers…that have been plaguing us all this time have been women!?" With the dryness of his tone evident Jarvan commented, "That makes your army's inability to fire back during the passageway even more pathetic. Fear not for I am to blame." Jarvan sheathed his sword and placed his shield on his back. He walked forward and barked, "Azreal come!" Azreal took his weapon out and loaded it with ammunition. "I'm not going to let them catch me off guard this time," he whispered as he followed behind Jarvan.

A tall sickly man with a large nose and small eyes carrying a wooden staff stood in front of their army. He was accompanied by a short and slender woman who had a pink Crocodile sigil branded on her glass armor. Her gorgeous face was perfectly symmetrical, yet she continued to hold a fierce expression, diminishing that beauty. "I am the great Niloticus Bourbon! Who dares come upon my island?" Jarvan attempted to hold back his laughter but failed. He laughed uncontrollably grabbing his stomach. "I have never heard of you above all I presume you're the fool who wrote that ridiculous letter. This is the mighty leader of the Crocodile Guild?"

Jarvan turned to Azreal and winked then placed a hand on the hilt of his blade. "Dominus Bourbon must be turning in his grave!" The moment the words left his mouth the slender woman had her bow nocked with a cursed arrow aimed directly at Jarvan's throat. A split moment afterwards Azreal had his weapon aimed at Niloticus' head. "Should that name leave your mouth once again you will find your body laid to rest where you stand!" said the woman. Jarvan glared at the woman with a hand on his hilt, then redirected his attention to the 'great' Niloticus.

"I propose we settle this without any unnecessary bloodshed. My army is greater than yours and you have a frontline made of little boys. I will not disrespect the battle acumen of your archers for as I'm sure you already know they surpass my own army of Wasp members. He looked at Azreal with sullen eyes. "If you defeat me in battle then my army will leave the island. Should victory come upon me then you will all surrender to the Lion Guild and be placed under my wardship." The woman lowered her weapon slightly, "How do we know your men will honor this agreement?"

Jarvan raised both his hands and clapped twice. The entire army including the Wasp members chanted, "Jarvan! Jarvan! Jarvan!" He stood erect and arms crossed, "I swear it upon my honor as the crowned prince of the Lion Guild, for I am the great Jarvan Hartengale VII. Do you accept? Perhaps this fierce companion of yours is a better choice for this duel?" Niloticus took a step back blushing slightly. "N…no…I accept. I am the guild master," he said. Jarvan clapped both his hands together and waved Azreal back. The woman lowered her bow and placed her arrow back in its quiver.

Jarvan unsheathed his sword and readied his shield with a stern expression on his face. Niloticus muttered a few words as his staff melted into a green goo like substance. It oozed slowly and formed a circle in front of him. All that was left of his staff was a short sword with the Crocodile sigil on the hilt. "You shall perish under the might of the great Niloticus," said the guild master. This threat was met with silence as Jarvan charged forward sword in hand. He jumped over the puddle, but it rose, grabbing him by the foot. Swinging him straight into the ground he came crashing down. The goo moved forward and engulfed the heavenly warrior swarming over his legs then his torso, and finally his head covering him completely; the crowned prince was all but gone.

Niloticus raised his dagger in the air and laughed, "All bow before the dominant Niloticus Bourbon!" The Lion army stood still while the Wasp members spoke amongst themselves. Beads of sweat trickled down Azreal's face as he stared at the green goo. A stream of pure yellow light erupted from beneath it; the goo shattered instantly. Jarvan stood with his hands glowing pure yellow light while the light beneath him danced chaotically. He opened his mouth to speak and yellow light escaped, "You dare to disgrace me by thinking such a pitiful attack could defeat me? You will die in a crumpled heap of your filth." Jarvan walked slowly towards the pitiful sorcerer each step creating a pillar of light.

Niloticus dropped his dagger and ran towards his army pushing them aside. "You guys stop him!" he said. Jarvan unleashed a massive beam of light into the sky. "Blast! What a waste, if only Dominus Bourbon were here to face me in battle!" A massive Crocodile shaped arrow careened into Jarvan pushing him across the field, as he stood up he began to dust himself off. He looked at his shield and noticed that it now had a massive dent in it. He smiled as he approached the woman who shot the arrow. His men unsheathed their swords while the Wasp members readied their weapons. The chosen one waved for his army to ad ease. "Men on this day we are victorious! Subdue the women and these young warriors. Do not take the women for yourselves! They are prisoners of war and are to be treated as such!" The woman with the Crocodile badge slanted her eyes while approaching him. "You won't be raping the women and killing the young, that is the policy of the Lion Guild when they conquer a guild, is it not?"

Jarvan shook his head. "What you say is true, those are my orders because my father believes the children today are men to be faced in battle tomorrow, but after facing such a gallant and courageous people with such unique tactics I would dishonor myself if I bore witness to such a thing." The woman blushed slightly before covering her face with a scowl. "I don't believe you…we will see." Jarvan motioned for his men to apprehend the Crocodile Guild soldiers as he walked into the walls. Turning to the woman he said, "Would you accompany me…umm…your name?" The woman furrowed her brow. "I…suppose…and it's Din Tei Bourbon, what's it to you Lion scum." Jarvan twitched his eye slightly, "You would be wise to watch your tongue when speaking to me. I shall not spare that coward, for a Lion must always stalk its prey." Jarvan pursued onwards into the village. Once inside he was met with a short woman in sorcerer's robes holding the head of Niloticus.

There were several small children holding daggers standing behind her. He tilted his head backwards and approached the woman slowly. "What is the meaning of this?" The woman dropped the head on the floor and kicked it towards him. "My son thought it was a better idea to come running into his mother's bosom than it was to stand and fight against the heavenly Jarvan Hartengale VII…he thought wrong!" She sat down on a bench, indicating to her daughter to sit beside her. She looked at Jarvan and continued, "Shall we discuss the terms of our surrender?" Din Tei sat beside her mother with a scowl on her face. "Yes…perhaps we should," Jarvan answered, approaching her with his entire body tense. The woman placed a dagger on the table. "Should you find my terms disagreeable you will have to take the life of everyone here because this is non-negotiable," she said in a calm and even manner.

Jarvan's eye twitched once again while the light beneath his feet flickered on and off. An immense amount of aura oozed from this woman, she was no normal sorceress. Jarvan tilted his head back, shifting uncomfortably and asked, "Perhaps…are you Viva the Sorceress?" Seemingly taken aback, the woman answered, "Yes…I am… do you know of me?" He placed a hand on the hilt of his sword and answered, "Yes…my father had spoken of you once…he said…" He looked at Din Tei. "He who will not be named was the greatest warrior to step foot on the battlefield while his wife Viva was the greatest sorceress." She smiled revealing perfect teeth. "I don't know about the greatest, but I have been known to cast a spell or two." Din Tei retorted, "Why are you being so courteous to this heathen!" Viva twirled a strand of her hair and replied, "In battle, one should not hate the ones who fight it, but the ones who start it. What you feel is my fault, for you do not even know what it is we were fighting for." She snapped her fingers and a small tome appeared before them. "After we have finished our negotiations I should like to tell both of you a story. Sir Hartengale…has your father explained to you the ramifications of your victory today?" Jarvan shook his head in acknowledgement.

"Very well, this will be an informative conversation, but first here are our terms. The Lion Guild will allow our precious island to combine against the mainland once again and the Crocodile Guild will swear undaunted loyalty. We will never rebel nor will we speak ill of the Lion Guild and the deaths that we have incurred. Additionally, we will share our secret knowledge of primordial magic with the Lion guild and the Lion Guild alone. In return, you will allow us to continue to practice our own spirituality and grant us access to your trade routes on the mainland." Jarvan raised an eyebrow and licked his lips. "What if a member of your guild does speak ill of the Lion Guild or harbors resentment? This can lead to things such as a revolt."

Viva snapped her fingers. Everyone within the village had their hands tied together with green aura, including Jarvan. "Then they will face my ire." She snapped her fingers once again releasing everyone. Jarvan opened his mouth in awe. Din Tei pointed a finger at Jarvan VII and declared, "He isn't even the leader of his guild, the emperor is a ruthless man who does not accept bargains. We should continue to fight!" Jarvan stood up and placed his hand on his chest. "I Jarvan Hartengale VII swear upon these terms with my life, should my father not see it fit to honor these terms I will take my own life with my own blade!" The mighty sorceress stood up and placed a hand on her daughter's shoulder. "To seal this agreement my daughter will become your wife," she said while taking off her emerald ring and handing it to Din Tei. Jarvan looked at Din Tei's exotic features, her perfectly aligned face, her slim yet curvaceous body, her green eyes and thought of her wild demeanor, something that intrigued him greatly. "I accept, should she have me as her husband," said the warrior. Din Tei screwed her face into a grotesque manner but kept silent.

Jarvan's glare shot back and forth as if some phantom had appeared; he stood up and placed his hand on his hilt. This caused Din Tei to grab her bow and point a nocked arrow at the crowned prince. Viva tilted her head and asked, "What's wrong?" Jarvan shook his head. "I don't know but something…something is coming." At first it seemed as if the trees themselves shook but they soon realized it was the entire island. Viva clapped her hands and her eyes rolled to the back of her head. Jarvan looked at Din Tei with a raised eyebrow and asked, "What is she doing?" Din Tei scoffed. "Don't you people have clairvoyance magic where you come from?" she asked while squinting. "She is checking to see what is going on with our beloved Turtle Island. Jarvan scratched his head and creased his face. "I thought this island was called Tem." Din Tei spat on the floor the moment those words left his mouth. "Tem is a derogatory term; it stands for The Emerald Mainland, a play on our green armor. You people are so unrefined."

Jarvan looked up to the sky and took a deep breath. "The lord truly tests my spirit," he said removing his hand from his hilt and sitting down. Viva returned from her journey with a grim face. "You all need to leave this island immediately." She turned to Din Tei with tears streaming down her face, "Gather the young warriors, take your father's battle axe and our most valuable tomes, the Sea People are coming!" Viva snapped her fingers and a large path opened leading from the village all the way to the beach head where the lion ships were docked. She turned to Jarvan with hopeful eyes and declared, "Beware the Sea People they can't be trusted!" Din Tei turned to her mother, with the special magical tomes in hand. Tears streaming down her face she asked the question that she already knew the answer to, "Mother, aren't you coming with us?"

CHAPTER 31
JAMES

SOME WOULD ARGUE that the Raven Guild's communication service was the backbone of the Lion Guild and not their massive army. The Communication Hub in Larimar is the second largest Hub in the world preceded only by the Great Hub located in the Raven Guild headquarters of Passerine. The members who worked there oversaw the letters sent from every single citizen in the city. In Larimar the primary use for a Raven was to pass on secret messages between the elite members of guilds as well as for guilds to conduct business either internally or externally. Because of the sensitive information that passed by via Raven it was very important for the employees of the communication hub to be reliable and trustworthy. Very few people have ever set foot in the Communication Hub as it was off limits to anyone who was not a trusted guard or a member of the high council; this was a place that even the Emperor himself could not step in without special permission from the high council.

James poked his head out from the wall separating him and the entrance to the hub. There were ten guards standing outside of the entrance. *Hmmm...Security is tighter than I anticipated...* He drew a square on the ground then placed both of his hands in the middle of the square, immediately a large nightshade plant sprouted from the ground in front of the guards. The plump berries sprouted out at the side and sparkled. One of the guards taking notice of the small tree walked over to the berries. "Hey guys...come and check this out...they smell...so... good," his eyes glazed over as he walked closer.

Resisting the devious aroma of these magical berries one of the guards pulled out his sword. The other nine guards surrounded the tree and ate the berries. James narrowed his eyes while pressing his lips together. *Here I thought I had mastered this tree formation. Although nine out of ten will have to suffice.* He withdrew his mighty war hammer. The strong-willed guard searched around the entrance before coming to the corner where James was hiding. As soon as he turned the corner James grabbed him and slammed his head into the wall, knocking him unconscious. He turned his attention towards the other nine guards who were walking around in a daze. Many of them jumped up and down flapping their arms in a futile attempt to fly, the rest were rolling on the floor clutching their stomachs. James walked up to the large dome shaped building and opened the Oak-wood door. Upon entering he immediately turned around and covered his mouth, letting out a gagging sound. *This...this...is atrocious!*

Sai jumped down from the second level landing in front of James. "You have finally arrived. I have been expecting you. I take it you're as repulsed by what you see as I am." He motioned for James to follow him. "What is this place?" The elderly man took a deep breath and sighed deeply and replied, "This unfortunately is the heart of Larimar." James covered his mouth once more. "The heart? This is wretched...this is unjust...this is..." Sai interrupted, "This is life." Covering himself with his robe he continued to walk forward. "These children...they are all guildless...unlike myself they have no magical acumen...thus they were left to die on the street. We in the Raven Guild rescue these children and give them food at the cost of their labor."

Veins protruded at the side of James' head. "You mean you steal children from their parents then rape them. Once you've defiled them you force them to work for you by placing cursed objects on them. I have seen those pearl necklaces before. My guild uses them on unruly Elephants... this is horrible." Sai slammed his fist on a table and yelled, "NO! We... we...rescue them...can't you see...this is the best I can...the best we can do for them. As for the other activities that occur...I admit it is wrong. I have pleaded many times to Tamriel, but he and his associates of various guilds have their own exotic tastes."

James took his war hammer and slammed it on a nearby desk, destroying one of the tables a child was working at. "Exotic tastes! Your blood will be spilled before this day is over!" he screamed. The children all continued to work, the one whose table was destroyed simply sat there silently. "I had hoped you would see things my way but perhaps I was being too optimistic. It's tea time perhaps you will join me in one last ceremony before one of us meets their end." James sneered while his eyes turned pure white. "I will not! You will answer for your crimes here and now!" Sai took a another deep breath and continued, "I suppose…that was wishful thinking as well…perhaps it is for the best."

He clapped his hands. Simultaneously all the children made their way to the second floor. James' jaw dropped at the sight of so many children trapped in such a small building. "How many children are here?" Sai scratched his head and reluctantly answered, "Well…to answer your real question…this building was built to fit five hundred people…yet we house about nine hundred children." James twirled his weapon above his head and clenched his fist and declared, "I Judge James of the Elephant Guild have taken into consideration your actions. I have weighed your heart, mind, body, and spirit. I have considered your deeds presented to me on this day. I sentence you to death!"

Sai took another deep breath and unsheathed his elegant katana. "I Sai Zakura choose to fulfill my duty as a Raven Guild high council member. Under the protection of the great Raven Deity I will defend this facility with my life." He placed his hand over his face, turning young once again. Their auras clashed causing the tables surrounding them to smash into the walls. James slammed his war hammer forward causing a huge rift. Expecting this attack Sai darted to the side and lunged forward. James deflected this attack with the hilt of his weapon and countered by slamming his fist into Sai's back. The young man winced in pain but managed to tag a flower petal on James' fist. "Curses…not again!" he yelled.

Sai lunged forward once again but this time James was ready for him. He placed his hands in a square trapping Sai in a tomb of earth. Using this opportunity, he retreated to the other side of the room. *How do I defeat him? There has to be a weakness.* Before James could gather himself, Sai cut through the walls with his katana and darted at lighting speeds towards him with his katana held to the side. Using the tables that remained as leverage he jumped and dodged the streaks of green aura that came his way. Once within striking distance the Raven member struck at James' heart. Reading the attack, James used his war hammer to deflect the blade but it was too late, he had already been tagged at the side of his arm.

Curses...I can't afford to be tagged once again...this isn't a tournament. Sweat poured down his face as he took a deep breath and closed his eyes. *I need to use a different strategy.* James clapped both his hands together springing forth an orchard of small nightshade trees. Sai stopped to observe them. "Do you think I am so weak willed that I would eat one of those berries? Surely you underestimate my willpower!" Pink aura flowed from his arms into his blade. The young man darted forward once again with a stream of pink aura trailing him. As he approached the orchard he bent his knees in preparation for the jump. James placed his hands in a spade formation causing the trees to transform into a large spike.

Sai attempted to stop in time, but it was too late; the tip of the spike lodged itself into his chest. James charged his war hammer with green aura and made his way to the renowned Raven Guild trainer. "James..." Said Sai blood spewing out onto the floor. Crossing his arms, he answered. "What?" Sai pulled himself off the spike and landed on his knees. "This isn't the end...the abyss that is the underbelly of Larimar runs deeper than you could ever imagine." James squinted. "It seems pretty clear what I must do. First, I must dismantle the Raven Guild piece by piece and bring to light these atrocities. Then I will convince my father to accept these children into the Elephant Guild." Sai shook his head and stammered, "It isn't that simple...they...they won't let you." James raised an eyebrow and asked, "Who is they?" Sai began to speak when his throat started to close. His face aged back to its original elderly condition. James lowered his weapon. "Speak...who are they?" Sai grasped at his throat as his lungs ached for oxygen. A masked figure appeared in a puff of black smoke. His black robe decorated with crystals gleamed under the dim light. "How fortunate for you that you still have a role to play in the grand stage that is our world." James attempted to grab his war hammer but his hand only twitched slightly. Pain shot through his neck as his eyes closed.

James awoke in his bed with his weapon laid to his side. Soft knocking could be heard outside the large door to his bed chambers. "Mr. Merciful...Mr. Merciful...I humbly request that you wake up. It is time for you to leave for Lamia's birthday extravaganza." James shot up to his feet. Looking around in a daze he attempted to regain his senses. The image of the children ascending the stairs of the hub appeared before him, as if reenacting some sick play. He backed into a wall as he clenched his fists. Swirls of black aura surrounded him as he looked around wildly. The raspy voice returned. *Focus.* While his father's voice countered. *Weakling.* Regaining his senses James composed himself and began to get dressed. "I am nearly ready. Thank you for waking me up." He took out his ceremonial armor and glanced at it. Caressing his hand against the giant Elephant crest in the middle it dawned on him what it truly meant to be a member of the Elephant Guild. *It isn't about the tenets...*

James stood there in his ceremonial armor awkwardly fidgeting with the straps; he bit his lip while constantly swallowing. His father had arrived, he could sense the cool, calm, and collected aura of the well-respected Elephant Guild leader. The man known as the Elephant's Sorrow was a man known to be unwavering. The emperor was feared for his devious tactics on the battlefield, but the Elephant's Sorrow was known for his persuasive demeanor off it. Once Donta placed down his mighty claymore a large portion of the world ceased to fear the Elephant Guild, but his business acumen was something of legendary status and has allowed his guild to acquire a large portion of the most powerful magical artifacts in the world. Together the two guild leaders owned the entire mainland, this was not a fact that was lost upon the massive crowd that attended this special occasion. Donta Ivory entered the room to a standing ovation. This is the man who has not left Grande for over a decade, the last time he and Jarvan Hartengale V had important business to discuss.

The tall elderly man walked in with a glorious ivory cane. His beard stretched seemingly forever to the ground while both his hands dawned five rings of varying stones. Apart from the extravagant rings and the cane he possessed nothing of note. His clothing appeared to be something one could find in the guildless quarters. The brown shirt was too baggy even for his hefty figure and the grey pants were aged almost to destruction. While pacing himself he inched his way to his son who was standing upright with his hands behind his back. He had dumped the alcoholic beverage he was drinking and filled his cup with water instead.

The Elephant's Sorrow inched closer as the applause died down. He poked his son in the stomach. "You've gained two pounds…we shall have to remedy that when we leave this filthy place." James glanced over at Eros and then over at Lamia. "Yes sir, I understand," were the only words James could muster. His father took the seat that James had been saving for him and crossed his legs. He glanced at the plate that his son had left out for him but touched none of it. "Rat poison…all of it!" James immediately took the plate up and dumped the food in clear sight of his father.

He came back with a cup of water and several sticks of celery. "Here you go father." James placed the plate in his father's hands. Donta sneered at the plate but took a bite of celery and commented dryly, "I suppose… it will do." Lamia ran over to the two Ivories with a special treat in hand. She bowed deeply and did both the traditional Elephant Guild salute and the traditional Lion Guild salute. "It's so good to see you Mr. Ivory. I am so glad that you have graced us with your presence. I certainly hope your trip wasn't too troublesome!"

Donta smiled revealing his well-maintained teeth, "Of course not little lady, your twenty first name day is an occasion that deems such an arduous journey. My old bones would gladly make the trip twice over!" He took off one of his rings and placed it on the plate with the dessert. "This my little lady is for you, it is a cherished family heirloom that belongs to you now. It will grant you a long life and prosperity for it is imbued with the spirit of the great Elephant Deity." Lamia's eyes widened to the size of saucers. "Oh…my…great spirit. Thank you ever so much. You are too kind!"

Donta beamed a ray of white aura in her direction. "Don't mention it my dear, I've known you since you were this high," he said pointing his cane low to the ground. Lamia giggled, "Oh dear, it is time for me to go cut the cake! Please excuse me, I will be back soon. I would absolutely love to hear stories about James." Donta clapped his hands and smiled greatly, beaming an abundance of white aura. "Yes of course, this man was quite the little rogue elephant growing up. He was on his best behavior when you saw him!" Lamia placed a hand over her mouth. "Oh my, oh my!" she said as she skipped over to the banquet table.

Donta slanted his eyes as she skipped away. "Ugh…I hate that puffy pompous little brat." James bit his tongue before speaking, "What…do you mean sir?" Donta leaned back into his chair. "A true Elephant woman would have refused to take the ring, for it was a family heirloom," he said sneering. "This is another reason we shall find you a good wholesome Elephant woman, one with strong and sturdy thighs to bare me many grandchildren." The veins at the side of James' head protruded, his hands shaking he whispered, "But…but…you gave it to her…" Donta clapped his hands and laughed, "Ahh yes son, not to worry. I gave her some meaningless jewel, like I would ever leave our great city with our precious heirlooms to come to this…this…cesspool of debauchery and mayhem." Donta stared at Lamia then darted his eyes towards the emperor. "Disgusting…all of them!"

James' eyes quivered as he clenched his fist. "But father…they have always been good to me…and is it not you that said you should judge one by their actions and not the things other people say?" Donta looked at his son for a moment before clenching his jaw. He stomped his cane on the floor causing a single thorn to rise up from beneath James' shoe piercing his heel. "You forget yourself boy, it seems all the time you've spent here has made you quite uppity. This is something we will rectify when we return to Grande." James clenched his teeth as blood dripped onto the floor beneath his shoe. "Yes…sir."

CHAPTER 32

ORIANNA

ORIANNA TWISTED HER ring as she sat staring at the great emperor. She bit her lip, her gaze darting back and forth between her guildmates and the masked entertainers. She counted ten Lion guards standing vigilantly over the emperor. *Is…that enough?*. A Deer servant walked in her direction with a large platter of Fishbits, a fish delicacy that was quite popular in Passerine. She beckoned the Deer servant over to her. The man was well aged with a beard. He wore the typical yellow hat that the male Deer servants wore when serving the Lion Guild elite, upon closer inspection, he had what appeared to be two claws tattooed at the side of his head.

Orianna fiddled with her thumbs as she grabbed several Fishbits off the plate. "That…is umm…an interesting tattoo…is it real?" she commented. The Deer member slanted his eyes while pulling his hat further down. He sneered and said, "That's an interesting veil…is it there to cover your ugly face?"

The man walked off with the platter before Orianna could grab more. She placed both her hands at the side of her hips. "Well then…that was rude…here I thought everyone in the Deer Guild was sweet and savory… mhmm like those Fishbits!" Tamriel saddled up beside his little sister and placed a hand on her shoulder. He leaned towards her and whispered in her ear, "Don't you be your normal clumsy self and mess this up for the guild. If you do…I'll have a gang of…" Tamriel's train of thought was lost when he saw a Deer Servant speaking to a young boy dressed in white.

He picked up his spell book from the table where it rested and left without another word. Orianna took a deep breath. *I wonder what that was about…well at least that vile brother of mine is gone.* Malikai walked up to the great oracle with two bottles of ancient wine in his hand. "Sister… sister… look what I got! Ancient wine…I didn't know there were still any bottles of this left…I mean… you can't drink any but…I'll drink a bottle or two in your honor!" A Deer servant with face paint on his face walked by and said, "Umm…this party is in honor of Lamia…not Orianna… I mean…milady over there, no disrespect intended." The Deer servant bowed deeply spilling some of the Fishbits that were on his platter.

Orianna stood up and walked towards the man with the goodies. Malikai clenched both his fists and grabbed the servant by his collar, spilling the rest of the food on the floor. "I know… leave us…fool you!" The face painted man stuck out his tongue as he took his leave. Orianna sat back down with her arms crossed. Solaire walked up to her with her staff clenched tightly. "Didn't I tell you to sit still and look elegant? The Raven Oracle must appear graceful and elegant at all times!" she yelled as she pinched her daughter on the arm. Muttering underneath her breath Orianna murmured, "You're going to kill him anyways…what does it matter." Solaire's eyes gleamed as she asked, "What did you say? Foolish little girl…as if we would soil our hands. The masked figures will take care of the dirty work, and we will fail in our attempt to heal the emperor."

Orianna's eyes widened. "Who are these masked figures?" Solaire paused for a moment. "You're quite a mouthful on this day. I suppose you would not have noticed since you can barely walk two steps without stumbling. The masked figures claim to be from an unnamed guild, however, these mysterious figures are from the Swan Guild. Thus, they are the ones who truly have an iron grip on this world." Orianna shifted uncomfortably in her chair. "That isn't possible, the Lion Guild has the mightiest army in the world." Solaire sighed and replied, "Your lack of wit forever displeases. The Swan Guild creates the gold that we use as a medium of exchange while the Lion Guild enforces the law of the land. I ask you then, who really owns the world?"

Orianna bit her lip and asked, "So where do we fit in this equation?" Solaire squinted and answered, "If you must know our guild is in the best possible position. We appear to serve the Lion Guild and reap those benefits while we work with the Swan Guild to gain our freedom. With the emergence of the Sea People, things will tip further in our favor. We will pit them against each other while we pick up the pieces of their fallen souls." Orianna gasped and asked, "How can you be so despicable?" Solaire cackled, "Since when did you grow such a long tongue? How dare you speak to me in such a manner. I am your mother and as much as I regret it, I birthed you!" Orianna clasped her mouth and exclaimed, "You're...you're...horrible!" She stood up to walk away but Solaire whispered a few incantations, "Ilmarrrr vunam nok toe." Orianna felt her blood start to boil. Blood seeped from her eyes. "Sit back down or so help me Raven Spirit that is holy we shall have a new oracle soon enough." Orianna wiped the blood that was dripping down her face and sat back down. Her mother looked her in her eyes and placed a hand on her hand. "Everything I do...I do for my children...one day when you're older and have children of your own you'll understand. Now stay here and don't move, things will get very dangerous very soon."

CHAPTER 33

JAMES

JAMES STOOD PATIENTLY waiting for his father to finish his meal. His heel continued to ache as he shifted it slightly. Crossing his arms, and biting his lip, he asked his father, "Father...would you like more celery sticks and water?" His father nodded in acknowledgement. He limped over to the banquet table where his eyes locked onto Lamia, she quickly filled her plate then walked over to the behemoth of a man. Lamia twirled several strands of her hair. "Hey you, did you enjoy the cake? Mother dearest picked it out, it's supposed to be a Swan Guild secret recipe, isn't it somehow otherworldly?"

James glanced at his father while stroking his ponytail. He turned to Lamia and shrugged, "Yes, I suppose." Lamia shook her head. "Why... why do you always act like that towards me?" James looked down at the ground, struggling to maintain eye contact. "Whatever do you mean Miss Hartengale?" Lamia plopped her plate on the table and crossed her arms. "Like that! You act so professional as if we haven't known each other since we were children...I mean...I know we haven't seen each other in a long time but ever since you came back to this city you've acted like the stuck up pious man that everyone says you are!"

He clenched his jaw before speaking. "Because...I'm not supposed to feel this way about you..." She leaned in still maintaining a stern expression. "What way?" she asked. "He took a step forward and whispered in her ear. "I...want...you...I have always wanted you...ever since the day I first laid eyes on you...but it has grown ten times over since I have returned to the city." Lamia grabbed his hand. "I want you too James...I just wish...you hadn't taken so long to say it...my father has promised me to Tamriel Duskbringer from the Raven Guild. We are going to be wed a month from now."

The stoic man's heart dropped to his stomach. "But...but...that... can't be..." Tears streamed down her face. "Yes...I'm sorry James...I... can't...be with you." She turned and ran off into her father's arms. He was accompanied by Malikai, Tamriel, Solaire, and several other Raven high council members. James stood there for several moments with the plate in his hand, his eyes fixated on the Duskbringers. His body filled with killer intent as his green aura flowed throughout his body. He walked towards the table where the Duskbringers were enjoying their meal.

Donta Ivory poked him in the back with his cane, snapping him out of his frenzy. "Boy...what do you think you're doing?" James clenched his teeth and looked his father in his eyes. "Not right now father." Donta tilted his head to the side. "Boy...if you don't get back to your seat right now we will leave this filth of a ceremony immediately." Clenching his fist, James repeated, "I said not right now." He walked off towards the table where the emperor sat. "Sir...may I interrupt for a moment of your time?" The emperor winced but he motioned for James to pull up an empty chair. "Normally I'd be infuriated at being interrupted but this young Duskbringer has quite the steamy scent." James managed a smile before running his hands through his ivory hair. "There is something you must know..."

The emperor forced a smile as he stood up to greet Donta. "Donta! so great to see you, we have important business to discuss! That agreement we made a while back...I believe the time for you to honor those terms has come...has it not?" Donta swallowed deeply but maintained his grin. He looked at his son with cold eyes. "You're in my seat...boy." James fidgeted for a moment before giving up his seat to his father. "Of...course... father...here you go," he said, clenching his teeth. "That will have to wait for now, it seems it is time for the main event," said the emperor. He raised his hand in the air. The entire room erupted into applause as several masked figures walked to the middle of the room. Madam Dupont raised both her hands and snapped her fingers. "Greetings ladies and gentlemen of the varying guilds, it is my pleasure to present to you our first act, The Sand Dancer!"

᠗

James shifted uncomfortably in the jewel encrusted chair. The guests in the room engaged each other in conversation. Piet could be seen standing beside Tamriel while Malikai conversed with his beloved Lamia. James' eyes darted back and forth as he shifted his gaze from Tamriel to Malikai, and finally Orianna who approached him. Clenching his fist, he struggled to contain his ire. Orianna beckoned to James. "E…excuse me…Mr. Ivory…" she stammered. "If you please…I am not in the mood for conversation. I would appreciate it if you let me be," replied James. Orianna lowered her head. "I don't have much time, my mother is busy with the members from the Swan Guild." James sighed and answered, "Excuse my being curt but I fail to see what this has to do with me." Orianna clutched her gown as she leaned in to whisper into his ear. "I am too scared to do it myself, but something must be done…"

James' demeanor shifted slightly. "What is troubling you so? You're shivering." *Just kill her. She is a nuisance. Put her out of her misery.* His father's voice whispered. James slapped his forehead repeatedly. "Quiet, I don't want to hear you anymore!" he bellowed. The entire room glared at him. Tears streamed down Orianna's face, past her veil. She dropped to the floor as the salty droplets followed suit. Lamia rushed over clutching her friend by the arm. Turning to face James with scarlet cheeks she furrowed her brows, "What's wrong with you? How can you be so cruel? Orianna is the sweetest person I know. Please leave, you're ruining my party!" *Hahahahaha,* whispered his father's voice. James stood up slowly. "I'm…s…" Lamia slapped him. "I don't want to hear your sorry. Sorry is a sorry word. Just go." *Kill her too, she is rather rude.* Once again, his father's voice whispered.

Feeling the gaze of everyone in the room he approached the door. His father's aura surrounded him in a tornado of fury. His hands clasped the large golden doors. A low chuckle could be heard in the background as his gaze fixated on Tamriel who smiled with glistening eyes. As he pushed open the doors his legs became numb. Each step becoming more difficult than the last one; he finally arrived at the guard's station. "Leaving already Mr. Ivory?" He struggled to speak, "Y…yes…I will have my war hammer back." *Kill…kill…kill.* He attempted to rub his eyes, but his hands were frozen. "Not a problem. Here you go…is something the matter? You're sweating a mighty storm," said the guard. Losing control of his breath all James could muster was one word. "Help!"

The guard looked at him with one eyebrow raised. "Oh…you must be quite intoxicated. Here let me get one of my guildmates to escort you to the Elephant Guild fortress. The guard placed the heavy weapon on the ground. The large hands of James weaved several signs as vines surrounded the guard. "Wh…what are you doing? Release me…I can't… brea…" Blood spurted onto the floor as the vines tightened their grip. Black aura surrounded the mighty James and entered his mouth filling his lungs. *Hahahaha, it took a group effort, but we have finally deconstructed your will. Now you shall do our bidding. Puppeteer…carry out your mission to its fullest.* Moving on their own his hands clasped the War Hammer of Justice. He turned around and faced the door to the event room.

Green and black aura emerged from James. The ceremonial armor glowed dark green as it became imbued with spirit power. The eyes on the Elephant Sigil turned black. *Don't let them…We will do what we choose. Begone uncouth Elephant.* His father's voice vanished into the nothingness as the raspy voice drowned it out. Unable to control his body James continued to walk towards the entrance. He entered the room, weapon in hand to see ten Lion Guards blocking his way. "We meet again James. Lay down your weapon and enter captivity!" yelled Captain Warda. A smirk crossed James' face. He opened his palms causing poisonous vines to shoot out at rapid speed.

Bypassing their armor, the guards turned purple as the poison worked its way into their bloodstream. The man identified as Captain Warda cut through the vines with his rapier. He lunged forward with his rapier aiming at James' heart. Deflecting the blow with his war hammer James stomped his feet causing ivory spikes to rise from the ground impaling the captain. In the corner of his eyes he saw the look of horror on his father's face as he launched towards the emperor with his war hammer held high. With green and black aura trailing, the war hammer came crashing down upon the emperor's shoulder. A loud crunch could be heard as half of his body collapsed into a crumpled heap. The last thing he saw was Lamia's eyes rolling to the back of her head as she fainted. His eyes closed as thundering footsteps could be heard from behind the door.

CHAPTER 34

JARVAN

THE GUARDS IMMEDIATELY bowed at the sight of the crowned prince. Their eyes widened when their gaze landed upon a company of Crocodile women, followed by several children. Jarvan turned to one of the castle guards, placing a hand on his shoulder. "I need you to take these women and children to the guest chambers, make sure they are fed, and treated as our worthy guests." Biting his lip, the guard squirmed uncomfortably and muttered, "But…but milord…" Jarvan tightened his grip on the Lion Guild guard. "I don't recall saying you could speak freely. Now do what I am commanding you to do without fail. Should I find that they have been treated unfairly you will find yourself living in the guildless quarters."

The guard nodded then proceeded to lead the Crocodile members inside the castle. Jarvan turned to Din Tei who was standing beside him with a scowl on her face. "I assure you he will follow my instructions. Your people will be taken care of." Crossing her arms Din Tei sneered, "Don't expect me to thank you." Jarvan smirked and replied in a sarcastic tone, "I wouldn't even dream of it. Now please accompany me to the royal chambers. Today is my sister's birthday and I'm sure she would love to meet my bride to be." Din Tei winced, screwing up her face in a grotesque manner. "I suppose I don't have much of a choice."

Jarvan and Din Tei walked into the grand castle of the Lion Guild.

Din Tei's mouth opened wide as she stared at the numerous banners that were laid out across the castle walls, the gorgeous paintings, and the elegant statues. Jarvan smiled to himself and asked, "Do you like what you see? This will be your home from now on." Din Tei spat on the floor and retorted, "This will never be my home." Her eyes welled up with tears. Blinking in order to stem the tears, she sighed and spoke barely above a whisper, "My home is gone." Jarvan lowered his head. "I know this situation is difficult for you…" Din Tei spat on the floor once again and yelled, "You know nothing oh glorious Jarvan Hartengale VII!"

Jarvan's eyes quivered and the veins on his forehead protruded. "Would you kindly stop spitting on my floor?" Din Tei locked eyes with the heavenly Jarvan VII. Without any sign of hesitation, she spat in his face. Jarvan grabbed her by the collar and pushed her up against the wall, raising a hand to strike her down. She looked him in his eyes and yelled, "Do it…I know all you Lion Guild warriors are nothing but brutes!" Jarvan sighed and released the woman that he had agreed to marry. "Whether you like it or not we are now betrothed. This arrangement between the Lion and the Crocodile Guild was your mother's last act for the survival of your guild. I certainly intend to honor her wishes. If you'd rather be cast aside by my father into the Lion Guild catacombs let me know and we can forget this little arrangement right now. If you choose to act this way in front of my father no one will be able to save you from his ire, not even me. He is far less sympathetic to your plight than I am, in fact, he would certainly revel at the thought of feeding you to The Warden."

Din Tei softened her posture and asked, "The Warden?" Jarvan clenched his teeth and remarked, "Yes…that despicable man. He is a vile creature who treats the prisoners like wild animals that are to be hunted." Din Tei looked at Jarvan with sullen eyes and asked, "Do you know why this war was started?" Jarvan shook his head. "I will ask my father about that when things die down. Why…was there something in your mother's grimoires?" Din Tei nodded. "Yes…the true origins of this war…this supposed Great War." Jarvan raised his hand and whispered, "Shh…I sense a battle going on upstairs." Din Tei screwed up her face and retorted, "Ok…but don't shh me!" Ignoring her comment, he unsheathed his mighty broadsword and ran towards the throne room.

Din Tei following suit had her bow and arrow ready. Each step made the sound of thunder under the weight of Jarvan's enchanted weapon. He pushed the door open with his shoulder. When Jarvan entered the room, he grasped the situation immediately. His father laid on the floor in a crumpled heap while James Ivory with his weapon in his hand loomed over him. His sister laid on the floor unconscious while his brother was cowering in the corner. The rest of the guests stared at him in a daze. His eyes turned bright yellow as the veins popped at the side of his head. The lights beneath his feet formed a large circle. Jarvan unleashed a flash of light, blinding everyone in the room. He charged his sword with yellow aura while running towards James who turned towards him with a menacing grin. His blow struck James' war hammer causing him to fly backwards. James went crashing into the wall; several bones could be heard breaking.

Jarvan twirled his sword around as he charged once more for the killing blow. Just when he reached within striking distance James Ivory rolled to the side dodging the deadly blow. A massive amount of aura emitted from James causing Jarvan to steel himself. The two weapons clashed together causing an explosion of aura pushing everyone in the room back against the walls. The green and yellow auras danced viciously while the ring above Jarvan's head spun furiously. The only word Jarvan could muster was, "Why?" James' pitch-black eyes flickered between white and black. "Help me!" James whimpered. Jarvan looked at his father's bloody corpse. "I will help you die a slow and painful death!" Ramming his shield into the face of James a loud crunch could be heard; James stumbled backwards, his eyes turned back to its normal hazel hue. James widened his eyes as he dropped his war hammer to the floor. Jarvan approached his best friend, his sword placed firmly against his throat.

CHAPTER 35

JAMES

THE STINGING OF the elderridge cuffs made its way across James' arms. He sighed heavily as he inched closer towards the light of the cell. He squinted in his attempt to read the parchment placed against the brick wall. *List of executions*, he read. *James Ivory from the Elephant Guild, and Zane Grey from the guildless class.* James slumped in the corner. *What happened?* High pitch laughter erupted from the cell next to him. "Oh… James the Destroyer has finally awakened. I was beginning to think I would meet my end all by my lonesome." James winced. "James the destroyer? Is that what they call me. How long have I been here?"

Zane chuckled and said, "I mean it is quite the fitting name for someone who killed the emperor and ruined the prissy princess's birthday party. I'd say you have been out of it for fifteen moons or so. It's hard to tell with this tiny excuse for a window they give us. I shall have to file a complaint to the warden." Standing up James gripped the bars through his cuffs and exclaimed, "I didn't mean to kill the emperor! Something…someone entered my body and took control of me." Zane danced around under the dim lighting. "Quite the compelling story, I think I just may have to use it as well. I didn't mean to dig up the bones of the Lion Guild's pride and joy, someone else made me do it." James kicked the bars and replied, "I'm serious. First it started with me hearing my father's voice then I began seeing things, sometimes there are two voices in my head.

Zane raised an eyebrow. "Hmmm…I see. I'm no longer amused with your story. Maybe you should try adding clowns or something. They always make things more interesting." Pacing back and forth James breathed heavily and continued, "I need to convince Jarvan and everyone that I am innocent. It must be the Raven Guild and those masked figures. They did something to me at the hub." An eerie expression came across Zane's face. "What do you mean at the hub? What do you know about the kids?" James stopped pacing momentarily and replied, "I know that I'm the one who defeated Sai Zakura and was about to set the children free, but something happened. I don't recall. I just know there was this masked figure." In a flash of purple light, the figure of Zane appeared in the cell with James. Upon closer scrutiny, this man was oddly dressed, short, and slightly overweight.

What was exposed of his body was painted white with a moon on one side while dawning a teardrop on the other. His clothes were a combination of bright pink, blue, and purple. One eye was purple while the other blue. "Hmm…let me take a closer look at you," he said as he examined James' face. He snapped his fingers and his elderridge cuffs dropped to the floor. James' jaw dropped in amazement. "How can you perform magic through elderridge? They are specially designed to drain one's aura to minimal levels. Zane snickered and replied, "I don't know, maybe I'm special or something. My teacher often gave me special education." Raising an eyebrow James screwed his face in a grotesque manner and asked, "What?"

Zane pulled a large flute out of his pocket. The musical instrument had an odd design on it. A mysterious tune filled the cell as one red snake and one white snake swirled around James. A bulge pushed against his stomach causing him to keel over. The bulge rose to his chest and finally his throat where he struggled to gasp for air. His eyes turned black as black aura erupted from his mouth entering the flute. James collapsed to his knees coughing up black ooze. "Interesting, what a marvelous specimen. It nearly resisted my song of cleansing," Zane commented. "This will make a valuable addition to my collection." James inquired, "What just happened?" Zane snickered, "Hehehe, I suppose you don't know of such occult magic. That my stocky friend is an egregore. Basically, it is a thoughtform created by a group of people who maintain a single purpose. It manifests as a dark cloud of aura and allows a member or several members of that group to tap into that frequency. In simple terms it allows someone or a group to control you from a set distance. The more powerful the egregore the more powerful the wielder. It seems you made some very powerful enemies."

Using the bars as leverage James climbed to his feet and asked, "Am I free from these voices and hallucinations?" Zane placed a finger upon his nose. "No, I rather think not. They won't be able to control you anymore, but the barrage of voices will continue. The magic must be dispelled at each source to accomplish such a feat. You see, the voices come from one place, the hallucinations another, while the creator and the one who possessed you are most likely different entities as well." James stepped forward. "It seems I must endure these voices for now. Can you use that magical flute and this egregore thing to prove my innocence?"

Zane nodded and asked, "Perhaps, but why would I want to do that?" Zane circled the massive James. "I mean...I was kind of looking forward to seeing your head get chopped off by the sword of your best friend. What a great addition your skull would make to my collection." James winced. "Collection...you continue to talk about a collection. What do you collect?" With his hands at his hip Zane did an awkward bow. "Allow me to introduce myself. I am the great Zane Grey also known as the Great Collector. I am sure you have heard of me." Forcing back a chuckle James shook his head and commented, "I have never heard of such a person before." Zane sighed heavily and continued, "I suppose that is to be expected. I mean I just opened my business today. This egregore is only the second piece of my collection. One day it will be a massive collection filled with the universes most powerful magical artifacts." Placing his hands forward a grim expression crept across James' face, "I know a place where you can get plenty of powerful magical artifacts, but you will have to free me and help me clear my name first."

CHAPTER 36

ORIANNA

ORIANNA STOOD IN her room grasping the book containing the tale of the Fae people, her arms shuddered. She glanced at the broken mirror that her mother failed to have replaced. *These people are monsters.* The young woman threw her book against the stone walls, it landed with a loud crack. "I hate you all!" she yelled aloud. Orianna tightened both her hands into a fist and closed her eyes. *Raven Deity…if you're there… strike them down now! Strike them all down with the power of the wind!* She waited a few moments before kicking the dresser, injuring her foot in the process. *Argh! I hate my mother the most…that evil witch…that poor excuse for a cleric, may she find herself sleeping in a dusty grave!* Suddenly a surge of aura rushed throughout her body sending a tingling sensation through her fingers. *I'm going to give her a piece of my mind!*

Orianna picked the tome up and headed towards her mother's quarters. The stomping of her feet echoed throughout the huge halls as she travelled to the master bedroom. She saw Tamriel in the distance, she furrowed her brows as she locked eyes with her vile older brother. The two Raven high council members walked in a straight line neither giving way to the other. Waving his hand Tamriel remarked, "Move you clumsy bar wench." Orianna exclaimed, "No!" Tamriel widened his eyes but continued his path. "Move or I will move you myself." Without uttering another word Orianna tightened her fist, swung back and punched Tamriel in his large crooked nose, his nose cracked upon impact. He dropped to the floor releasing his tome of spells. Orianna kicked him in the stomach repeatedly before picking up his tome and marching towards the room where her mother was asleep. She pushed the door open and peered inside. At first glance, the room was vacant. Orianna picked up her mother's precious artifacts and smashed them against the floor, one by one they crashed towards the ground. She screamed as she kicked the cabinet.

A buzzing sound could be heard as blue aura spewed out of her body. The aura drifted towards her mother's staff laying on top of her bed. The staff gleamed in a spiral of bright light causing Orianna to shift her attention. She placed a hand on the elegant staff made from the rare Glimerwood. Picking the staff up she filled it with a large amount of her aura, blue light emitted from her eyes causing ancient markings to appear on the handle. *Alma jean, take noromo!* she said in a thundering voice. She made her way to the entrance of the Great Hub. Upon seeing her aura, the three guards stationed there called for assistance. Orianna waved the staff and the three guards became unconscious. *I...I...will be a prisoner no longer...by the grace of the Raven Deity!*

CHAPTER 37

LORD VEGA

LORD VEGA SAT on the back of the gigantic creature with his trident by his side. The tentacles on his head laid still while his free claw tapped the shell of the Testudine. He turned to Odessa with squinted eyes and asked, "How did you tame this beast?" Odessa caressed her arm slowly before her scales turned orange. "Well you see milord, the Hydrosta egg that you threw was in good condition. We found that a fresh Hydrosta egg could be enchanted. We then fed this enchanted egg to the Testudine and as such it became tamed," She said holding back a mischievous smile.

Lord Vega knocked on the shell of the beast with his free claw. The tentacles on his head moved wildly as he stood up and took a step towards Odessa. Standing her ground, she stood up straight with her arms folded. Lord Vega grabbed her by the chin as the other members of the army watched in awe. "The next time you keep a secret from me will be the last!" Odessa glared at him with cold dead eyes but managed to nod her head in agreement. Sdogr could be heard snickering in the background. He exclaimed, "I guess there will be no surprise party for Lord Vega! Hehehehe." The rest of the Goba members erupted into laughter. Melas looked onward in silence as his Mari tended to do. The Undines scowled at the blatant disrespect their leader had been shown but made no move to avenge her. The Cretin were notably left off the giant sea beast and were ordered to swim instead.

Sdogr did a summersault and pointed towards passerine with all four of his arms. "Oh Land! Oh Land! I hope humans taste oh so grand!" he said while licking his green lips. Odessa whispered to Lord Vega. "My lord, it would be unwise to allow the Goba to eat our allies." Lord Vega turned his head slowly towards Odessa and smiled. It was the first time she had seen him smile in a long time. "Allies? These humans are merely fodder. What does it matter whether we eat them, or they perish at the hands of the fledgling prince. They served their purpose and have killed the emperor. I have no other use for them but to keep our bellies full, entertain my clanmates and to serve as shields of meat! Surely you seem to forget yourself…number two!" Odessa nodded her head once again and made her way back to the comfort of her Undines. This Lord Vega was not the same Lord Vega that she had spent time with in Pacifica; this was the Lord Vega of bloodlust, a creature with insatiable appetite and one who knew no limit to his wrath.

The Testudine arrived at the cliff of Passerine, where the beast towered over most of the buildings. The Undines who were singing switched with a second group of singers. Upon seeing the large beast being ridden by these hideous creatures the Raven members bowed deeply with their heads touching the floor. Lord Vega smiled, revealing large jagged teeth. He had been practicing the common tongue for decades just for this very moment. "Humans of Pastarise! I am Lord Vega Zkhaosncin your new lord and master. Tremble in your domination!" A small voice from the back could be heard giggling. Lord Vega's gills twitched at the sound and made his way to the source of the giggles. His large shadow overlooked a young girl in her teens with red streaks wearing a black raven cloak. "Girl…why you laugh at Lord Vega?" The girl turned apple red and bit her lip, blood dripped onto her clothing. "M…Milord?"

Lord Vega's claw twitched as it opened and closed slowly. "Girl… why do you laugh at Lord Vega?" he repeated slowly. The girl stammered, "You…said Pastarise…we live in Passerine. It's a simple mistake I'm sorry Milord." Lord Vega curled his lips into a grotesque smile, revealing his jagged teeth once more. "Heheheh that was a funny? Lord Vega made a funny?" He turned to the onlookers of Raven members who still had their heads bowed. "Laugh…everyone laugh at Lord Vega's funny!" The entire city of Passerine erupted into a nervous fit of laughter. Odessa and her Undines shook their head slowly while the Goba danced wildly and licked their lips, the Mari as always were silent. The young girl giggled hysterically until Lord Vega gripped her by the locks of her hair and held her up six feet into the air. He ripped off her clothes and placed her back on the ground. "Now dance!"

Tears rolling down her face, the young girl whimpered and asked, "Milord? I don't understand." Lord Vega dropped to both of his knees causing a loud thud to echo. "I made a funny...now you make a dance. I can feed you to Sdogr instead." He pointed to the green Goba who brandished a sharp weapon in each of his hands. The young girl started to dance, eventually she tripped over one of her guildmates. The Goba elite and the Krynn booed the young girl. Lord Vega sneered, picked her up by her stomach and threw her to Sdogr who immediately dug his teeth into her flesh. The Sea Lord turned to the still bowing Raven Guild and clapped both his claw like hands together. "Does anyone else find me funny?"

CHAPTER 38

JARVAN

THE THRONE ROOM had but a few candles lighting the way. Jarvan walked towards his father's seat. His hand caressed the throne. The gold Lion figures gleamed in the dimly lit room. The base of the chair was decorated with white velvet. Light emitted from the base of his feet as he climbed upon the massive seat. He looked at the portrait of his father that hung to his right. *A pox on the man who had a hand in your demise. To think…that the man I called best friend would be capable of such a thing.* Jarvan slammed his fist against the Lion figurine. *I shall not weep tears for your body…your spirit lays with the great Lion Deity and it will be avenged.*

Leaning backwards he shifted slightly. *I must divert my attention to the matter at hand. James will be executed by my blade…as our custom. But can I bring my blade to such a level? To sully my glorious sword of cleansing with the blood of a despicable assassin. I do not know why he did such a thing. The only thing I can think of is the Elephant Guild desires war.* Jarvan stood up, light flickered around him. *It makes sense from their perspective. The Lion Guild's battle power had diminished greatly, while the Elephant Guild still stands strong. Could their vow of neutrality have been a long-term ploy to gain the upper hand?* Jarvan ran his hand through his golden locks.

We have had a rocky relationship through the decades but to devise such an atrocious tactic. To sacrifice your only child to kill the emperor…could Donta Ivory truly be such a despicable man? Jarvan lowered his head. *There are so many questions yet so few answers. I must have answers before I push forward. My desire for bloodlust lures me to the battlefield, but I am emperor now…I must think about my people.* He descended the golden steps. *What perplexes me most is why he would cry for help and then surrender? Yet to act out the most devious of actions moments prior. I must have answers before I end his life, my spirit will not rest. Then there are these Sea People that are coming. What am I to make of all of this?*

Soft knocking could be heard from outside the throne room. "Enter and speak quickly because I wish to be alone in my thoughts." Tamriel and Malikai entered the dark room. "Why have you disturbed me?" asked Jarvan. Malikai did an awkward bow as he struggled to maintain his balance. Tamriel did a half bow. "We have come to see how we can be of assistance in the coming days." Jarvan waved them off. "You could have been of assistance during the party. You failed to heal my father and you failed to intervene. What use do I have for you?" Malikai mumbled softly, "I was asleep." Tamriel stepped forward and answered, "It all happened so quickly. Mother did her best to heal your father, but the damage was too great." Tamriel took another step forward. "Where is the all glorious cleric now? I wish to speak to her of these shortcomings!" Jarvan exclaimed.

Tamriel crossed his arms and scowled. "She has returned to Passerine. She was so embarrassed by this failure that she couldn't bear to be seen." Jarvan stomped his feet causing light to spray out in all directions. "How fitting that she would abandon me in my time of need. Is the Raven Guild speaker not the appropriate person to turn to in times of turmoil or am I stuck with you two?" Tamriel bit his tongue as he did another half bow. "Milord…perhaps if you were to direct your ire towards the Elephant Guild. They have cleared out their fortress in Larimar and have made their way to the Elephant capital of Grande. Did you not order Donta to stay in Larimar while you decided the fate of their guild?"

Jarvan clenched both his fists. "That coward Donta Ivory! He dares to disobey me? I will have his head on a pike next to his son's. The red soil of Grande will pale in comparison to the blood that will be spilt." An eerie expression came across Tamriel's face. "If you were to send what remains of your glorious army towards Grande you could catch them by surprise." Jarvan clenched his teeth and replied, "When I need someone of the likes of you to give me advice I will ask, but in this instance, you may be right. I can't delay any longer. I will issue a decree and we shall slaughter the Elephant Guild and hang Donta Ivory for treason." Lamia barged into the throne room with her hands at her hips. She walked past Tamriel and Malikai without saying a word. "Brother, I have been listening from behind the door. I know I shouldn't have but I am glad I did. I think you are rushing things, as you tend to do." Jarvan squinted and asked, "What do you mean?" Lamia grabbed his hand. "I don't want to see you make a grave mistake. We are not in a position of power. I would watch your games of Volute with father and he always said the Lion must only fight when we have the upper hand. Please do not forget his wise words."

Jarvan paced back and forth. "This is true, he did say these things." Lamia grabbed his arm and pleaded, "If we are to be truthful you never listened to him in life…at least listen to him in death." Jarvan's eyes watered. He turned away from his sister and blinked rapidly to prevent the tears from flowing down his face. Lamia clasped him from behind. Removing her hands from his waist he spoke gruffly, "Everyone begone from my sight…I must be alone with my thoughts." Lamia nodded and stood in front of him. "Before I go…there is one more thing." Jarvan softened his posture and asked, "What might that be?" Lamia bit her lip, "Well…Orianna gave me this letter to give you before she left to Passerine. She said it was very important and that you must read it as soon as possible." Jarvan scowled and replied, "I don't care what that imp has to say, It's probably a love letter or something of the like." Lamia pushed forward the sealed piece of parchment. "Please…just read it. She was shivering when she handed it to me, it must be important."

CHAPTER 39

JAMES

ZANE STARED AT James with a piercing gaze. Several moments passed by in silence. "Ugh...if I must...I supposeeeee," said Zane. "If it isn't worth my time I will put this egregore right where the sun refuses to glimmer." James winced but nodded. "Perhaps we should start with you getting these cuffs off me?" Zane sighed once again and continued, "You're really making me work for these artifacts, aren't you? Speaking of which ...I want my payment first. So, we will have to go to this hidden trove of yours before I lead you to Tamriel and these masked figures." James grimaced and answered, "That would be a massive waste of time. Tamriel is most likely somewhere in the city along with the masked figures. I will not agree to this, I could never return to my home of Grande a runaway and a murderer. How could I face my father without my name being cleared?"

Zane furrowed his brows and replied, "Well then...I suppose I'll just leave you here to rot. I am starting to think you'd like to have your skull used as a goblet." James tightened his fists through the cuffs. He let out a loud grunt as he attempted to break free. Zane leaned back against the wall with his hands caressing his flute. "All it would take is a snap of my fingers...we could have already been well on our way to Grande by now." James shot him an errant glance, but he knew he was right. "Fine...fine... free me from my captivity," he said through clenched teeth. Zane snapped his fingers and the cuffs dropped to the floor. James turned to the bars and grabbed them. A surge of energy shot through his hands causing him to fly back into the wall. "Tehehehe…it seems you aren't the brightest horse in the stables. Naturally they would curse the bars to the exit."

Loud footsteps could be heard from down the hall. "What's with all that noise? Criminals are to be quiet at all times." The guard approached the cell to see the two men facing him with their cuffs on the floor. Grabbing his golden horn, he blew it loudly, "Prisoners attempting to escape!" he bellowed. James weaved several hand signs causing vines to spew out from his hands. The guard struggled to dodge the attack, one of the vines grabbed him by the neck pulling him into the bars then sending him backwards into the wall. "I apologize but I must clear my name." Zane played an odd tune causing the golden keys to rise from the pocket of the guard. The key entered the socket and unlocked with a low click. The two men ran outside the jail room. Faced with three different passageways they stopped; upon seeing the guards rushing towards them Zane grabbed James by the forearm and pulled him towards the one on the left. The two escapees ran down the hall however they encountered a brick wall. "I thought you knew where you were going!" argued James. Zane shrugged and retorted, "Whenever I'm in doubt I just go left. I shall have to file another complaint to the warden, I mean there really shouldn't be any dead ends in dead man's land."

James' eyes turned green as green aura circled his feet. "This isn't the time for your jokes. Now we must fight our way out. I seek as few casualties as possible." Zane snickered and replied in an even tone, "I won't be fighting…that sounds too troublesome." James clenched his fists and replied, "This journey is trying my patience, may the Elephant Deity grant me solace. If only I had my war hammer…" Zane's eyes perked up. "Ohhhh yesssss…the war hammer that is made from a thousand different magical trees. It is imbued with their spirits is it not? Quite the rare artifact it must be. I surely would like to see it with my own two eyes." James exclaimed, "Assist me in finding it!" Zane pulled out a long piece of rope and laid it upon the floor. He played another odd tune from his flute causing the rope to dance towards the brick wall. It stopped just short of the wall and continued to dance about side to side. "It seems the quickest route to the weapon is through this wall." James slammed both his hands onto the stone tiles. "Part the way towards my path for none can stand before the honorable judge James!" The stone tiles split apart revealing a passageway.

A company of guards approached from behind with their weapons unsheathed. "Stay where you stand and allow yourselves to return to captivity!" one of the guards bellowed. James slammed both his fists together causing the ground in front of them to erupt, blocking the path between the guards and them. "Let's go!" yelled James but Zane had already started walking. They emerged from the passageway into a large cavern layered with steel chains. The ceiling had several large axes attached to black chains. A tilted portrait of a slender man wrapped in chains hung on the wall. His helmet was decorated with one black feather, one yellow, and three red. He clung onto a strange looking weapon with a six-part segmented blade. The portrait was signed, 'The Warden.'

Zane fixed the tilted portrait pushing it to the side. James stared at him with a raised eyebrow. "What? I dislike when things are out of place. In any case the weapon should be through that door," said Zane, pointing at a large metal door with chains wrapped around it. "All you have to do is part the metal seas like you did with the stone and we will be fine." James winced and retorted, "It isn't that simple. My forest magic is limited in that regard. This entire room is made of metal. I am unable to bend, break, or separate metal." Zane sat on the floor with his legs crossed and replied, "I see...ok." James furrowed his brows and asked, "That's it? Can't you do something?" Zane tilted his head to the side, causing James to do the same. "I am doing something...I'm waiting for The Warden to come out."

James sighed and sat beside Zane. He folded his arms and began to channel his aura, "Solidarity...solidarity...solidarity..." Zane pursed his lips and asked, "What are you doing?" James shrugged and replied, "If I'm to face The Warden I ought to be prepared. He is an accomplished tournament champion, has killed over a hundred men off the battlefield and has been awarded the Emperor's Medal of Honor three times." Zane raised an eyebrow and sneered. "You surmised all of that from simply looking at his portrait?" James nodded in agreement. "Yes, I read something about these feathers when they gave me my own." He untied his ivory hair revealing a yellow feather. Zane's eyes widened, "Ohhhh…how interesting… what does it do?" James shrugged and answered, "Do? I don't know if it does anything. It was supposedly my prize for winning the tournament." Zane examined the feather with his purple eye. "Hmm…ahhhh yesssss… I see…interesting…very interesting…" James grabbed the feather from him and examined it. "What? What do you see?" Zane cackled. "I don't know what it does but it does have an unusual kind of aura in it…pure." With a wide grin Zane said, "Give it to me." James shook his head and replied unable to hide his distain, "I think I'd rather hold on to it. It's the only positive thing that has come from my entire stay in this treacherous city."

The metal door swung open with a loud thud. "My oh my…oh so grand. I have been blessed with two criminals who come to feast on my steel. My oh my…oh so glee. You know nothing of paradise and what it means." James and Zane raised their eyebrows. Zane was the first to speak, "What an odd character…" A slight smirk crossed James' face. "That is certainly a riot coming from you." He turned to The Warden and said, "Excuse me warden sir but there has been a huge misunderstanding. I have been framed and do not wish to fight you. I just came for my weapon so that I can defeat the ones responsible. Justice must be carried out by my hand for I will finish what I started."

The Warden's eyes turned grey. "My oh my…oh so rude. You must state the whole thing child before we are through. The Warden is my name and rhyming is my game, to toy with the criminals as I spew out my syllables. My oh my…oh so slow. Paradise can be found when one has a yellow flow. Channel your aura and imbue it with spirit. A desperate plea for gain is the only path to true fame." James stood up with his arms crossed, "I don't know what you're talking about." Zane danced around in a circle, "He is right, you are kind of slow. He said when you have the yellow feather you can find your Paradise and gain immense power." Zane picked his nose, flicking the snot on the floor. Grey aura surrounded The Warden as the cavern condensed. He withdrew his jagged blade and charged forward at rapid speed. Chains trailed his back as they dragged across the floor.

James dodged the blow at the last second but was blindsided by a chain. The large string of metal wrapped itself around his neck throwing him into the wall. He crashed with a loud ring as his armor met with steel. Blood escaped his lips as he let out a low cough. Weaving several signs, he shot forward ivory spikes from his palms. The Warden surrounded himself with his tail of chains causing the spikes to bounce off harmlessly. James was already upon him. Green aura leaking from his fist he slammed it into The Warden's chest, pushing him back. Clapping his hands together the mighty James grew larger causing his armor to bulge. Ivory tusks emerged from the side of his jaw as green aura surrounded him. The ground trembled with each step as he charged forward, vines spiraled wildly around him.

The Warden dropped to his knee and whispered several incantations. "My oh my...oh big tree, cut you down before you flee. I call upon the Lion Deity to shackle my foe and bring retribution upon thee!" The cavern condensed once again. The metal chains attached to the warden shot forth towards James grabbing him by the arms, legs, and torso. He broke the links with his aura. Upon seeing the chains on the ground, The Warden lunged forward, bladed weapon in hand. James caught the weapon with his bare hand, grimacing in pain. A smile crept across the warden's face as grey aura seeped into James' hand.

James glanced at his hand made of solid steel, he attempted to close his fist but to no avail. "My oh my...how does it feel to be one with steel?" The Warden taunted. James struggled to keep his arm up high however the weight of the hand unbalanced him. The Warden dashed forward once again this time launching his blade towards the feet of James. The blade extended itself forcing James to jump at the last second. The sharpened weapon met with the floor slicing a massive chunk of metal, revealing soil underneath. The cavern condensed a final time. "My oh my...oh so fine, looks like you've finally ran out of time," The Warden continued his taunt.

A surge of grey aura surrounded James as liquid metal surrounded his feet. It oozed onto his boots turning them into solid steel. The liquid continued to ascend towards his torso turning it into steel. Sweat poured down his forehead as the liquid threatened to engulf him. Zane appeared in a puff of purple light. "Sorry it took me so long...well not really sorry.

I was able to obtain plenty of items for my collection. Did you know the warden has a stockpile of contraband hidden away? Quite the naughty person he turned out to be. He is supposed to return all contraband to the Lion Guild vaults where they are locked away under tight guard. When this is over I'll have to file a complaint to the emperor himself," Zane chuckled.

James bellowed, "Give me my war hammer!" Zane shrugged and replied nonchalantly, "Sigh…how rude. I thought all you Elephant members were supposed to be patient." Zane reached in his pocket and pulled out the mighty war hammer. Handing it to James he licked his lips and exclaimed, "Quite the beautiful weapon!" The liquid metal had just about covered James' entire body except for one of his arms and his neck. He threw the weapon against the ground causing ivory spikes to pierce through the floor lodging themselves into The Warden's stomach. "Release me from your foul magic or I will imbue them with poison," James ordered. Blood gushed onto the spikes. The Warden mocked, "My…oh my…If you do that we will both meet our end." James clenched his teeth and retorted, "I am fine with that. My name will go down in disgrace, but I will be free from my turmoil. Death is but one path to the all mighty Elephant Deity, one that I will gladly take if that is his wish." The Warden dropped his weapon to the ground, it clinked against the steel floor. "My…oh…my…it seems today is not my day," The Warden sighed.

CHAPTER 40

JARVAN

JARVAN REACHED FOR the last piece of cheese but was beaten by Din Tei. She shot him a satisfied glance as she consumed the last piece of cheese, their eyes locked. "As the emperor I have summoned you all here because you will all play a vital role in the war to come," His eyes surveyed the entire room; he locked eyes with each member of the war council. "It is natural that I will be the Supreme Commander, as such I have come up with a brilliant plan that will grant us a swift victory over all of our foes. I believe we should take an aggressive stance by taking our fastest units and crushing the Elephant Guild at their fortress; something my father wanted to do for a long time. Then we continue from Grande and make our way over to Passerine where we will defend the port against this Sea Lord, Sea King, or Sea Walrus, whatever he wants to call himself and be back within a week. I call this a Lionkrieg." He beamed unwilling to hide his smug demeanor.

Din Tei shook her head drawing the attention of the entire room. "That won't work, what a foolish idea," she said. Jarvan's eyes twitched rapidly. Tamriel scowled at Din Tei. Oblivious to the serious business at hand, Malikai downed a pint of ale. In his attempt to break the awkward silence in the room Octavius questioned, "Why won't it work?" Taking a handful of meat from the plate, Din Tei replied, "Well, a tactic like that would require expert coordination between the units needing to act as one cohesive unit. Correct me if I'm wrong but this fortress of Grande has been built specifically to withstand a large siege. I have seen the one they built here in Larimar and it is impressive. If they took this much care with a fortress built in your territory I could only imagine how much effort went into their capital city. On top of all of that this Lionkrieg tactic sounds to me like it needs light armored men who can move swiftly amongst an urban environment. How do you expect the heavy armored Lion soldiers carrying massive spears, swords, and shields to accomplish that? If the rest of the Elephant Guild is anything like the man who murdered your father all your men are dead." She took a bite out of the meat in her hand.

Jarvan's cheeks became flushed. "Well what do you suggest?" he retorted, grinding his teeth. Din Tei shrugged and continued to eat. Beads of sweat dripped down Azreal's nose. "W…well…she does have a point… I have been to Grande before and it is incredibly secure. The fortress is made of reinforced ivory, said to be stronger than any material on the mainland. It is a layered city with each division separated by massive walls. On top of that there are ravenous plants surrounding the outskirts that attack any non-Elephant member on sight. That is unless you have been granted a fortress pass."

Light flickered wildly beneath the table from Jarvan's feet. "So, what do you suggest!?" he exclaimed. Azreal paused for a moment. "What if instead of going to war with the Elephant Guild we try a different tactic?" Jarvan clenched his teeth as his eyes turned bright yellow. "Are you suggesting I forgive the scum Elephant Guild for their blatant declaration of war?" A smirk crossed Tamriel's face and a gleam crossed Malikai's eyes. Azreal bit his lip causing blood to trickle on his chin. "N…n…no milord. What I'm saying is we try something different…that is all." Jarvan clenched his fists and remarked, "Does your cowardice know no end? Am I to suffer your incompetence for as long as I breathe?" Tamriel took a sip of his tea and questioned, "Why is he even here? The Wasp Guild's army is all but eliminated, what possible use could they serve, maybe they should return to Sentia and amass another army with another general."

Azreal lowered his head as tears flowed slowly down his face. "I'm s… sss…sorry…don't send me back in disgrace. I like it here. I was just trying to be useful." Jarvan turned to Tamriel with slanted eyes. "I have still not forgiven you for your ineptitude during the party, you will be bright to keep quiet." Octavius opened a large dusty tome, and commented, "Well...father did write down his favorite Volute tactics. I am sure we could find something of use here." Jarvan grunted, "Once again with that silly game of Volute. What use of it on the real battlefield? The real world is where a man's true spirit is tested. It can't be dictated like pieces on the board." Din Tei leaned forward and replied, "My mother once told me of your father. She said he never stepped foot on the battlefield but won countless battles by playing a board game. Is this the Volute you speak of?"

Octavius nodded in agreement and stated, "Here is an interesting tactic, what if we issue a truce between the Lion and the Elephant Guild. Requesting that Donta Ivory return to Larimar to complete an investigation where he will be allowed to speak his side. Father called this the Lion's Den Tactic. When the opponent enters the Lion's den he will be kept under close guard for his 'protection' and brought to justice before the emperor. Naturally the emperor will pretend to listen to the opponent's side but his mind will already have been made up. Execution by the gallows is the most common result."

Din Tei, Octavius, Jarvan and Azreal stared at Tamriel who erupted into a fit of laughter. Malikai bit his tongue. Jarvan's ire crept towards the Raven Guild high council member. "What's so amusing?" Tamriel stopped laughing to take another sip of tea. "Tis a sad day when I see the Lion Guild consider such a childish tactic. Especially against an opponent such as the Elephant Guild. They are nothing but a bunch of tree planters with a giant house made of clay. The great Lion Guild that I know of could easily topple such a structure and do so in an honorable manner. Excuse my crudeness but I find it hard to believe that your father would 'request' the presence of an assassin if something were to befall one of his children. No, I think not. I rather believe he would crush that assassin and everything he stands for with the entire might of the Lion Guild and its allies...as cowardly as they may be," he said glancing at Azreal and Din Tei.

Jarvan paced back and forth. Octavius was the first to speak. "Ever since your return from Passerine you have expressed quite a large amount of bloodlust for a cleric. Does it have something to do with the scar on your nose?" Tamriel's face turned scarlet. "Leave me and my nose alone. I tripped and it broke…there is nothing more to say on that matter." Jarvan slammed his fists on the table splitting it in half. "His motives matter not…he is right. I will not 'request' anything of these traitors. I shall command that Donta Ivory leave his fortress and return to Larimar where he will face his punishment like a man. Malikai, how many soldiers can you raise underneath the banner of the Raven?" Malikai stopped drinking. "Hmmm…" He shifted around in his seat placing two fingers in the air. Jarvan winced. "Two?" Malikai nodded in agreement. "I believe 20,000 soldiers can be arranged. They will mostly be from the lower-class guilds but they will fight for the Raven Guild with much fervor. We have healed many of their members at discounted prices and they do owe us that much."

Tamriel leaned forward with a sly grin and asked, "Why do you ask?" Jarvan stopped his pacing to face the man with a crooked nose. "You will arrive to the doorsteps of Grande with a large army of 20,000 under the Raven Guild banner. They will be accompanied by the range-men of the Wasp Guild, totaling an army of 28,000. Should Donta Ivory refuse the Wasp Guild will set their fortress ablaze in a storm of orange aura." Tamriel and Malikai nodded barely able to contain their glee.

Azreal shifted in his seat uncomfortably. Din Tei opened her mouth to speak but didn't bother. Jarvan bragged, "I will take on these Sea People and their ruler with the Crocodile Guild at my back for range support. They will quake in fear at my battle cry while they crawl back to the salty depths where they belong." Octavius whispered in Jarvan's ear, "Is it a good idea to trust these people so soon?" Din Tei stood up and spat on the floor. She exclaimed, "I can hear you! These Sea People destroyed my beloved Turtle Island and killed my mother. I hate them more than I hate you and your filthy Lion Guild ways!" Jarvan smirked and continued, "I suppose that settles it." Octavius turned to Din Tei and asked, "What can you tell us about these Sea People?" Din Tei lowered her head and whispered, "There was some information about them in my mother's grimoires. It seems she took detailed notes on them, based on her conversation with the one they call Odessa. The Sea People come from a world called Pacifia. They can travel to our world via a crystal portal."

Azreal scoffed and remarked, "A crystal portal? How outlandish. How illogical...how..." Jarvan raised his hand, interrupting him. "Quiet you!" he snapped. Din Tei continued with her findings, "The one she interacted with was what they call an Undine. Along with the Krynn they are the only ones capable of manipulating aura. There are five clans in Pacifia that are all united under one leader known as Lord Vega, a vicious Krynn lord who can drain the life force from your body with one touch. That is all she was able to gather." Octavius sighed and continued, "That isn't much to go on..." Drenched in sweat Azreal stammered nervously, "W...with... one touch?...That sounds painful." Jarvan shook his head and declared, "It matters not...this Krynn Lord will taste my blade while his carcass is left to rot in the sun!"

CHAPTER 41

JAMES

THE ESCAPED CONVICTS emerged from the Lion Guild prison covered in dust. Brushing his armor off James turned to Zane. "We are fortunate that it's dark, we must get out of this cesspool while we can. Do you have any friends that we can turn to?" Zane laughed while clipping his toe nail, "I don't have friends, at best I have like-minded individuals. Considering they are like me, they won't lift a finger in my direction. In fact, they would be the first one to betray me for an artifact or two." James raised an eyebrow and answered in a dry tone, "I see." *Keep an eye out on him, he will turn on you. Everyone will turn on you. You're going to die alone in a pit drenched in your own blood,* said his father's voice. "Not again!" exclaimed James. Zane placed both his hands on his hip. "It seems those voices have returned. What did it say this time?" James shook his head. "It doesn't matter...I think I know a place where we can find refuge." The two escapees made their way through the guildless quarters.

Zane took a deep breath. "Ahhh...I love the smell of the guildless quarters. Something about the blood, guts, and mold beckons my being." James replied, "I suppose now is when I should harp on your odd taste ways but all I can think about are the children." A perplexing expression crossed Zane's face, "Oh...Mr. merciful. How honorable of you. To think about the guildless children who have been mercilessly taken advantage of when you are in a deadly situation. Your kind heart makes me ill," Zane replied. James winced as his father's voice returned. *Kill him, he is despicable. You're going to kill everyone anyways. Death follows you wherever you go. You're a cursed being who will never know peace.* "What do you know about the children?" Zane replied, "Well I don't know much. I just know I heard a bunch of abducted children were returned to their families. They all had pale skin and wore odd necklaces."

An elderly woman with several teeth missing ran up to James grabbing his hand. "Please give me a loaf of bread Mister! I must take care of my sick grandchild, he is ever so pale." James reached in his pocket only to reveal the yellow feather. "I'm sorry they took all of my money. I have nothing to give you." James turned to Zane with his arms crossed. "I'm sure you must have something of worth in those deep pockets of yours." Zane tilted his head and asked, "Who me? I couldn't dream of parting ways with one of my items. I only just collected them. I haven't even examined them yet!" The ground beneath the three shuddered violently. "Give her something now!" James exclaimed. Zane sighed as he reached into his pocket and pulled out an emerald necklace. The gemstone glowed bright green. "Ugh...here...take it." The woman kissed Zane's painted hand. Turning to James she did a bow. "Bless your kind heart sir. May your deity bring you many blessings!"

The two escapees arrived at the entrance of the Pilgrim's Inn. The purple door had an 'open' sign on it. Zane giggled and commented, "I like the way you think, we ought to wet our whistles before we depart for Grande." James sneered, "We aren't here for THAT. This is where...my... umm...friend works." Zane smirked and replied with a wink. "Good, your friend shouldn't have any qualms taking care of my friend." James grabbed the collector by the collar. "You will treat her with respect. She is a lady of the highest caliber." Zane mumbled, "Could have fooled me." James released his traveling companion abruptly and retorted, "What was that?" Zane shrugged and replied while rolling his eyes, "Nothing...of note." Upon opening the door to the Pilgrim's Inn James and Zane were met with the scent of lilac. The facility had recently been redecorated. It was filled with ivory colored couches, grey and purple curtains, and the floor was made of marble tiles. Several patrons crowded around the stage where the renowned Ludus Mora twirled her body around a blue pole.

"You stay here...I'll be back," James said. Zane nodded with fervor. "Gladly!" James approached the bar. The bartender smiled revealing pearly white teeth. "What can I get you?" James shook his head. "Just a little information if you don't mind. Where may I find Eros?" The bartender leaned in closer and whispered, "Ahh I see...one of her special clients. She is in her dungeon." She added with a wink, "I'm sure you know where that is." James turned to leave when the bartender grabbed him by his forearm. She glared at him for a few moments and said, "You know...you look strangely familiar..." James' face turned red. "Y...yes... I've been here a few times before." The bartender nodded in acknowledgement and answered, "Hmm...I suppose that explains it, enjoy your stay." He approached the door and laid his hand against the handle. *What if she won't help me? No one will help you...no one can help you. It's all for naught...just kill everyone and put them out of their misery.* He ran his hand through his hair, tugging at several strands. The door swung open causing him to step back. Eros emerged from the door. She looked in all directions as her gaze shifted back and forth. "James, you look like a mess. Come inside."

She embraced him tightly before brushing off some dust off his ceremonial armor. "Last I heard, you were taken to the prison and awaited execution." James lowered his head. Sweat poured down his face as he dropped to his knees. "I didn't mean to do it...something was controlling me. Please believe me..." Eros grabbed him by his head, engulfing him with her body. The scent of lilac filled his lungs as he inhaled deeply. Fighting back tears he blinked repeatedly. Eros ran her hands through his hair and whispered in his ear, "I believe you." James looked up and stared in her eyes and asked, "You do?" Eros grabbed him by the cheeks. "I could never believe that you would do such a dishonorable thing. The entire situation was just...just so odd. It was unlike you." James rose slowly. Eros clasped his hands holding them with all her might. "Tell me what you need of me and it will be done."

❦

James gazed in horror as the gates of Grande laid sprawled across the ground. Orange flames flooded the land as far as he could see. Blood stained the hooves of his enchanted horse. He urged the beast to move forward but it would not take another step. The flames danced across the land as he watched tree after tree collapse to the ground. *This cannot be…* a loud explosion echoed in the distance causing the horse to fly up throwing its two riders off. Tumbling to the floor James landed on his side. Zane nimbly landed on one foot. He did a half jump as he gazed at the dazzling display of destruction. A twinkle crossed his eyes. James stood up removing his war hammer from its strap. "The battle is still going on in the distance. I can sense my father's aura."

Running towards the entrance of Grande James was met with several members of the Raven Guild army. Slamming his weapon into the ground several tombs of earth encased his adversaries. "I don't have time for you! I must help my father." *Just give it up, he's going to die!* His father's voice rumbled in his head causing James to drop to one knee. Using his weapon as leverage he rose to his feet. Each step seemingly carried him farther from his destination. A large gust of wind careened in his direction as he grasped a nearby tree. Sweat flowed down his brow as he clenched his teeth. He gazed into the distance to reveal his worst fear. *Your father is going to die and there is nothing you can do to try to change that!* His father's voice echoed in his brain.

Blood trickled down Donta's face as he gripped Tamriel's neck with his bare hands. Tamriel's eyes bulged while gasping for air. He took out a small dagger and jammed it into Donta's eye causing him to release the pedophile. Malikai limped forward with two blades. Drenched in his own blood he jumped in the air and unleashed a flurry of wind waves in Donta's direction. Donta slammed his cane onto the floor causing the ground to rise. Tamriel opened his book and spoke words that James couldn't make out. Donta struggled as blue aura surrounded him. As the aura tightened its grip Donta became paralyzed in time. Malikai rushed forward with surprising speed.

Focus! Cried the raspy voice. A surge of green aura flowed through

James' body as he regained his composure. He charged forward with his war hammer held high and unleashed a massive wave of green aura, but it was too late. Malikai had already descended upon Donta as the blades sliced through his neck, causing his head to drop to the floor with a loud thud. James' eyes widened in disbelief. Tamriel turned to him with a sinister grin on his face. Malikai stumbled towards his brother gripping his shoulder for leverage. The two erupted into a pair of ravens as they ascended into the air, followed by what was left of their army.

CHAPTER 42

ORIANNA

ORIANNA LAID ON the straw bed covered in an old wool blanket, her head rested on a straw stuffed pillow. The smell of manure filled her lungs causing her to stir. Rubbing her neck, she stood up and walked towards the room. She entered the hallway only to find a large burly man staring her down; she immediately went back to the room and draped herself with a soiled blanket. Upon exiting the room, the burly man was gone. *What a disgusting place but at least it is far away from home.* Staff, magical tome, and coin purse in her possession she made her way to the dining room. "Well o'l good day young lady!" exclaimed the old inn keeper. He was a frail man with a large wart on his nose but had a smile that was mesmerizing.

Orianna managed a faint smile. She was about to do the customary Raven bow but stopped herself. The inn keeper clapped both his hands with glee. "The bread is almost ready. I trust you slept well milady," he said with a broad smile. Orianna rubbed her neck once again. "I suppose...you could say that," she replied shifting her eyes. The inn keeper, while maintaining eye contact leaned in closely. "Don't worry milady, your secret is safe with me," he said with a wink.

Orianna's face flushed. "W...w...whatever do you mean?" Orianna took a step back as the words left her lips. "A few men from the Raven Guild came in here looking for a young woman carrying a staff, they were very uppity and pushed me around but I didn't say peep. It's surprising to find that a guild of healers would be filled with such ruffians. I can see why you left," the inn keeper commented. Orianna shook her head furiously and replied, "I know nothing of this Raven Guild and their search…I am merely a traveling guildless." The inn keeper winked and smiled before whispering, "I hear you loud and clear missy. Please have a seat, breakfast will be served shortly." Orianna sat in the corner with her back against the wall. She scrutinized the room, her gaze shifting from person to person. There was a young couple sitting ahead of her whom the waitress knew by name. The two patrons sat whispering and giggling while they fed each other cornmeal porridge. The burly man sat across from Orianna with a hand on the hilt of his mace. He had a large scar across his face along with a blue cape. *Could he be Raven?* She withdrew the staff and placed it in front of her on the table.

The burly man stood up and walked towards her with his brow furrowed and eyes slanted. "I want to sit here," he said in a thundering voice. Upon closer inspection, he was much larger than she thought. His biceps were the size of her head while the shield he carried at his back was the size of her torso. "I'd rather you didn't…" Ignoring her response he sat down and placed his mace on the table. It wasn't as expensive as one of the noble guilds, but it was enchanted with ocean magic. "How much?" he asked. Orianna raised an eyebrow as she shifted back a bit, one hand resting on her mother's staff. "Whatever do you mean sir?" she responded. The man cleared his throat and leaned forward pushing the table towards her. "How much for me to keep quiet Miss Duskbringer?"

Orianna's eyes widened but she remained still, "It seems you have mistaken me for someone else kind sir, now please I wish to eat my meal in peace." She pointed towards the empty table beside her. The man scoffed before spitting on the floor. "Listen here missy, I ain't no sir and I ain't kind. Pay me to keep quiet or I'll have quite the song to sing to the Raven Guild members who are staying over at Plimith inn down yonder." He stared at her with blue eyes like the ocean that caressed the edge of Passerine. Orianna reached into her coin purse and pulled out five lion dollars. "This is all I can afford. I have a long journey ahead of me."

The man laughed loudly and answered, "I care not for your journey;

you keep the five coins and give me the rest of the bag. We will call it my hush hush fee. Things are bound to get unfortunate for you if you press your luck. I had to discard my wife, I lost my guild position, I failed in the tournament, and I come home to find my home has been pillaged. Something tells me bumping into you will make it all worth it," he said reaching for her coin purse. "Please sir...this is all I have," Orianna said as she grabbed her coin purse from the man. "Listen here you senseless wench, give me the coins or I will take it from you...after I've had my way with you right here on this table!"

A surge of blue aura filled Orianna's body causing the young cleric to get up abruptly, grabbing the staff in the process. "Perhaps you would do well to lose that ill-mannered tongue of yours!" she said as she took a step back and raised her hand. The inn door flew open as a large gust of wind entered the building. The man turned to face his demise, the wind sliced at his arms, legs, face, and stomach simultaneously. He tried to bellow out in agony but a large ball of blue aura entered his mouth stifling his voice. Struggling to speak he whispered, "Don't kill me...please."

The burly man dropped to the floor causing a loud thud to echo throughout the room. Orianna lowered her staff causing the door to slam shut. "I am not a murderer...I am not like them!" Towering over her fallen foe she gripped the staff tightly. Breathing heavily she walked over to the inn keeper whose gaze was fixated on the stocky, scar faced man on the ground. "How much for one of your enchanted horses?" she said as she rummaged through her coin purse. She gripped the counter for leverage. The inn keeper turned bright red as he struggled to speak. "T...t...take it...it's round back Miss Orianna Duskbringer," he said bowing his head deeply. "Once again you are mistaken...I am simply a traveling guildless."

CHAPTER 43

JARVAN

THE TWO ADVISORS walked up to Jarvan. Octavius tapped him on the shoulder; with his back erect he handed Jarvan a piece of parchment. "Here is the speech we have prepared, it discusses in length the topic of the war we are about to embark on and why we will need to activate martial law. It also tackles other issues such as the gathering of resources from every guild in the city. It discusses the concerns that they are expected to have, and should make for a very functional speech," he said.

Jarvan winced as he read the speech but kept quiet. He turned to the former Queen consort. "Pragma…what do you make of this?" Pragma ran her hand through her hair. "If I may ask…why do you care to hear my opinion on this? Your political and court advisors have given you their recommendation." Jarvan took a step towards Pragma holding her hand gently. "You knew my father better than anyone, what would he think of such a speech?" Pragma nodded in agreement and took the parchment from his hand. She murmured to herself as she read the speech nodding her head when she finished.

"Your father would approve of this speech however…" Jarvan caught her gaze directly. "Speak freely…mother." Pragma smiled deeply. "You are not your father nor will you ever be." The political advisor's face became red as he took a step forward crossing his arms. "The seventh will be as great a commander as the fifth ever was." Jarvan raised a hand and asked,

"Whatever do you mean by that?" Pragma tightened her grip on his hand. "Your father would approve of this letter because he was strongest when he spoke from the mind...you are strongest when you speak from the heart, your passion is what moves these people...it is why they have always loved you and looked to you for inspiration."

Jarvan caressed his face slowly. "I will not need this...thank you," Jarvan said as he returned the parchment to his political advisor. The advisor shot a quick glance at Pragma but took a step back. The emperor walked over to the balcony where the citizens awaited his second royal decree. "On this day my men and I will embark on a campaign unlike any other. We will make our way to the great city of Passerine to defend our world from these unknown creatures. These Sea People will feel the full brunt of our ire and kneel before the Lion banner. Their crimes are heinous for they believe..."

Lamia rushed forward grabbing Jarvan by the arm. She pulled him from the balcony looking him in his eyes. Sweat drenched her dress. While heaving heavily she attempted to speak. "What is the meaning of this sister?" Lamia grabbed him by his collar. "Did...did...did you read the letter?!" Jarvan freed himself from her grip. "I didn't have time to read such a worthless letter, I opened it but decided it was not the time to spend on such foolishness." Lamia thrusted the parchment into his hand. "Read it now!" Jarvan sighed heavily. "I find it disheartening that you would interrupt my second royal decree to read this..." Jarvan turned to Pragma who raised an eyebrow. "What is ever the matter my dearest son?" Jarvan unsheathed his weapon and pointed it at her throat, "Speak the truth whilst you still hold your tongue!" Pragma clutched her stomach as she raised an eyebrow. "What troubles you so...have you gone mad?" Jarvan's grip upon his weapon tightened. "Orianna makes the claim that the Raven Guild is in league with the Sea People and that they manipulated James Ivory with the assistance of the Swan Guild...your guild!" Pragma Aeterna gripped her chest. "Oh, my dearest Jarvan, how blind your family has been all of these years. I assure you...this latest sin is not our greatest but it was the most pleasurable. I got to play the lovely doting mother to such a precious Lion cub," she giggled.

Jarvan launched forward to pierce Pragma's neck but her body collapsed to the floor. Black aura escaped her mouth as the cloud of black smoke hovered above her dry carcass. It began to speak, "One day we shall meet again, that is if he doesn't kill your first." Jarvan shot forth a beam of light causing the black aura to disperse into nothingness. A low chuckle filled the room. "If only it was that easy!" said the entity. The emperor approached the balcony once again. To his horror several hundred blobs of black aura rose to the sky causing several hundred bodies to collapse to the floor. His jaw dropped as they merged into one and disappeared into nothingness. Lamia bit her lip, "Wh...what...what now?" Jarvan's eyes burned as the halo above his head rotated. "Passerine will crumble beneath my feet and I will swim in the blood of their fallen."

The two armies stood a short distance apart from each other, the wind blowing in Jarvan's direction. The dry air seeped into his lungs causing him to let out a low cough. Malikai was the first to make his move. The long-haired man dressed in white made his way to Jarvan, his face fixed into a grimace. With his hands tightened into a fist he approached Jarvan holding a blue flag, signifying his wish to parley. "May we discuss a few matters?" Jarvan's eyes quivered rapidly as he placed one hand on the hilt of his sword. "What could you and I possibly have to discuss?" Malikai took one step forward and replied, "I ask that we settle this dispute between the two of us. Should I fall my men will surrender to your ranks defecting from Lord Vega's army. There is no need to see a multitude of bloodshed on the sacred ground of Passerine." Jarvan sneered and said, "Oh...I see...you wish to preserve the sanctity of this great city you have built. How very noble coming from the vilest of creature to walk this earth. Perhaps you wish to save your men from slaughter as your army has clearly dwindled." Malikai placed his hands on both of his swords. "Perhaps...should you fall..." Jarvan stomped his foot on the ground, causing the dust around them to scatter. His aura spewed forth engulfing Malikai as his killer intent began to manifest itself.

"Hear this you putrid mongrel. There will be bloodshed...I will not be satisfied until every single citizen of Passerine kisses steel. I will not rest until you have paid for your heinous crimes ten times over and your mother's body dangles as she hangs by the noose of my gallows. I will not sleep until this precious city of yours is burned to the ground and the tree you love so dearly is turned into kindle to bless my feet with warmth!" bellowed Jarvan. Malikai took a deep breath and asked, "So that is your answer then?" Jarvan took one step forward and withdrew his sword raising it in the air. "There will be blood…there will be death…and you will perish upon this soil…this is my vow as Jarvan Hartengale VII!" Malikai turned around and made his way back to his army of turncoats. Jarvan turned around and made his way back to his army of paragons.

The wind dissipated for a moment as the heat became unbearable, both armies stared each other down. Jarvan turned to his men and raised his sword, "Tonight they will embrace their loved ones in the afterlife!" Every man banged their weapon across their shield. The emperor turned to Malikai's army and aimed his sword. "Charge in the name of the Lion!" The men rushed forward as a stampede of gold careened across the Passerine soil. His Excellency locked eyes with Malikai before slamming his shield onto the ground. A large beam of yellow aura shot forward in Malikai's direction. Malikai dodged the massive attack at the last moment however the men standing behind him were not so fortunate.

Malikai rushed forward at blazing speed with both blades drawn. Blue aura spiraled around him, his eyes turning bright blue. "For the Raven Guild!" he yelled as his blades came crashing down onto Jarvan's shield. Before Jarvan could counterattack Malikai was already at his back both blades aimed at his neck. Jarvan dodged but was nicked. A few drops of blood fell to the floor as he backed off. Malikai jumped into the air causing the ground beneath him to emanate blue aura in the form of a raven. The giant raven emerged from a sigil surrounding the traitor. The aura hardened creating armor with giant wings. Jarvan opened his mouth as he took a defensive position against the large figure that peered over him. *He isn't supposed to be this powerful!* Malikai opened his mouth as a screeching sound emitted. The emperor's ears started to bleed as his vision started to blur; in his daze he dropped his shield to the ground.

Malikai crossed both of his swords. A giant tornado formed as the air around Jarvan swirled violently. The emperor dug his sword into the ground while he held on to its hilt. Malikai dropped down with his swords raised and slashed at Jarvan's chest easily bypassing his enchanted armor. Jarvan winced as blood oozed out. *Finally, I have met a worthy opponent... who would have thought it would be that drunken fool, but death will not take me on this eve.* Clutching his chest Jarvan knelt to the floor placing his head against the hilt of his sword. *Lion Spirit grant me the power of the divine; cast forward your strength so that I can vanquish my enemies!* A large surge of aura rushed through his body, the aura exploded in all directions emitting vibrant rays. His eyes became yellow while the sword glowed brightly. In one motion Jarvan cut the tornado in half.

Malikai swooped down once more this time a giant tornado followed behind him. *Curses!* Jarvan swung his sword back and cleaved in the direction of the Malikai. A crackling sound shot forward as a large ray of light sped across. Malikai tried to dodge but it was too late. Receiving the brunt of the damage the wings disappeared causing Malikai to fall at a rapid pace. The emperor dashed forward at lighting speed with his sword pointed forward. While still in the air the renegade parried the attack causing a massive shockwave killing soldiers on both sides. Jarvan stood up blood trickling down his face and chest. Malikai stood up blood trickling down his hands and shoulders. "You are tougher than I expected but your life will end with the next blow," taunted Jarvan. Malikai retorted, "Well for the first time in decades I'm sober but it's humorous that you say that. I was thinking the same thing. It will be a shame that you will not achieve a glorious triumph!" The two warriors dashed forward, causing a sea of aura to trail both combatants. The two fighters clashed causing another massive shockwave, killing thousands.

Jarvan took a few steps before dropping to his knees, blood oozing out of his chest. His eyes glazed over as he looked in the direction of the blue sun. Malikai took a few steps forward and smiled emphatically. "It seems death is in my destiny. All praise be to the Raven Deity for releasing me from my oath," he whispered as he dropped to the floor, drenched in a pool of his blood. Upon seeing the demise of their leader, the remaining members of Malikai's dwindling army ran to the gates of Passerine. Using his sword to prop himself up Jarvan screamed at the top of his lungs, "Charge forward, we shall win this war on this day!" His men rushed forward swords and shields raised ready to deal a decisive blow.

The Passerine gates opened. Several squadrons of green monsters emerged from the gates. They slashed and clawed their way through the Raven members. Upon seeing the massacre of the remaining Raven members some of the Lion Guild troops retreated. Unfortunately, much of the army remained steadfast in their pursuit of victory. The green creatures shot out streams of green liquid. The liquid oozed all over the soldiers causing them to clutch their faces as their skin washed off their bones. The screams of his loyal soldiers could be heard from where Jarvan was standing. An errant soldier ran up to him with tears in his eyes. He yelled, "Please sir...we must retreat!" He shook his head and stumbled towards his dying men. "No...we must save them!" The errant soldier grabbed another cowardly soldier and yelled, "Help me bring him back!" The soldier nodded in agreement and the two men grabbed their emperor by the arms. "Let go of me. We...must...," Jarvan whimpered.

CHAPTER 44

JAMES

JAMES PACED BACK and forth. The large hut was decorated with various plants. Vines encompassed the walls. The red soil caressed his bare feet. His thoughts raced as his hands clasped his war hammer. *Hahaha I told you he would die! You will bring death to everyone you love. We will make sure of it.* His father's voice boomed. James clutched several strands of his hair and pulled them out. The ivory strands tumbled to the floor. *What a sorry life I live...he can't be dead...by my own doing...* The raspy voice responded, *Not...your fault. I allowed these foul demons to take advantage of me, had I have been of iron will we would not be here. Perhaps if I had not swayed from the tenets...this must be punishment for seeking to make changes. Change...is good...change begets growth,* the raspy voice returned. James stomped his foot into the soil, causing a small crater to form. *Enough! I don't want to hear anymore!*

He went down on one knee and lowered his head, tears streamed down his face. *Father...forgive me...I have failed you time and time again...I am a failure.* Soft knocking could be heard from outside the hut. "Please... whoever it is...please go. I am in no condition to receive anyone." The knocking persisted. "Please...just go!" he yelled. The knocking continued. James approached the door of the hut and swung it open with all his might, causing the door to detach. "Captain Forge, why do you disturb me?" he demanded. "I'm sorry sir but there are several matters that I must bring to your attention." Captain Forge lacked the imposing figure of the typical Elephant member. His scrawny figure was only highlighted by the massive battle boots that he wore; with every step he took the ground beneath him would threaten to give way.

"Why me? There are many generals that still draw breath," James queried. Captain Forge raised an eyebrow and asked, "You don't know?" James crossed his arms. "What are you alluding to?" Captain Forge dropped to his knees placing his head into the soil. "As is our custom when the current guild leader passes without naming his successor, the population has voted. It was a slight victory decided by only a couple votes, but it has been decided that you lead us in these troubling times." James shook his head in denial and commented in a dry tone, "I'm in no condition to lead anyone anywhere. Who was the other leading candidate?"

Captain Forge bit his lip struggling to speak. "Well...spit it out... who was the other candidate?" James asked. The captain raised his head slightly and replied, "General Arminous." James' jaw dropped. "You mean my father's most hated general. The one that wishes to unite all Guilds under the Elephant banner? The one who believes every Elephant Guild member should spill their blood for the sake of the guild?" Captain Forge rose slightly. "Y...yes...sir. It seems he proposed that after driving back the Raven Guild and their army we should strike at the hearts of the Lion Guild. He makes the claim that his spies from Larimar returned with great news. The emperor has taken what's left of his army and began the long journey to Passerine. It would be easy for us to march upon Larimar and capture the city."

James tightened his fist and exclaimed, "How dishonorable!" Captain Forge bit his lip once again. "There is more..." James raised an eyebrow and uttered, "Continue." Captain Forge placed both his hands behind his back. "The emperor was the one who sent the Raven Guild's provisional army to Grande with two demands. One Donta Ivory must return to Larimar immediately to face judgement for your crimes. And two...he must bring your head on a pike if he wishes to receive any chance of absolution." The earth beneath them rumbled and James' eyes became a blood curdling green. "That Jarvan...not once has he heard my side of the story, to think we were once best friends is almost laughable."

Beads of sweat dripped down the captain's face. "If I may ask sir… is it true what they say…that you…you killed the emperor under the orders of your father. To liberate us from our pact?" James' eyes widened. "Is that the story that has reached Grande? What pact do you speak of?" Captain Forge mumbled, "We…well…as your father's head of security I have often heard him grumble about the pact he made with the Lion Guild. Something about assisting them in a universal war once the world is united under his banner. If the Lion Guild managed to own seventy five percent of the world's territory the Elephant Guild will turn over all of their magical artifacts, including each and every members' weapon.

James ran his hand through his unruly hair. *Lie to him, it's your only way out of this mess. Liberation can be yours if you lie,* his father's voice whispered. *Truth, justice, and honor must be upheld,* countered the raspy voice. "I see…" Sweat poured down James' face. "Well…" Captain Forge nodded. "I understand sir." James raised an eyebrow and asked, "You understand what?" Captain Forge nodded again. "I understand. You shouldn't have to tell me what I and a little over half the population already knows. General Arminous tried to make it seem as if you disobeyed your father under his orders and that you work for him. He said that he would make the Elephant Guild great again and purify the entire land of the cesspool that is the Lion Guild. One thing is clear to the entire guild, both of you want the same thing but only one of you is fit to lead." James' grip tightened around his war hammer.

Coward, whispered his father's voice. *Coward,* whispered the raspy voice. James lowered his head slightly. Captain Forge tilted his head back. "There is one more thing…I hope you will be proud of me sir. I have managed to capture someone that I suspect is an assassin for the Lion Guild. He wears a mask and a robe dawned with crystals. I tried to remove the mask but it would not budge. It is enchanted with lock magic. James' ears perked up and he asked, "Where is this assassin now?"

James opened the door to the prison and walked over to the guard while glancing at the prisoner. He recognized him as The Puppeteer from Lamias' birthday party. Handing the guard an apple he spoke, "Take a break, I will be interrogating the prisoner alone." The guard hesitated a moment but nodded in agreement. James turned his attention to the assassin and said, "Now that I have you alone I am going to make one thing very clear. You are going to tell me how this curse was created, who created it, and where I can find them and you're going to tell me now. Either it will be after I have broken all of your bones or before, but you will tell me." The prisoner tilted his head to the left but remained silent.

James took off his ceremonial armor revealing his muscular physique. While flexing he charged aura into his left fist. James opened the gate as the prisoner backed away into the corner. "You people think this is a joke? You think I am a play thing that can be used for your schemes? We will see if I can't change your mind." James entered the cell. With one smooth motion he slammed his fist into The Puppeteer's stomach causing him to spew out blood. "What have you to say about my ailment!" he yelled. The man looked at him this time tilting his head to the right. James winced as his eyes filled with green aura. This time swinging back his right hand he catapulted his fist into the man's chest, causing a crunching sound to echo throughout the room.

The prisoner dropped to his knees but continued to be silent. A high-pitched voice spoke from outside the jail cell. "He won't talk until he has been recognized as the greatest puppeteer of all time, that is his Paradise," it said. James turned around swiftly in search of the voice. His gaze locked onto a wooden puppet sitting on the chair where the guard was sitting moments prior. He grabbed The Puppeteer by the throat and shouted, "Quit the games fool…I don't know how you made that puppet move and I don't care…tell me about the curse or I will destroy your prized possession." The man's eyes blinked repeatedly. "That is right…it is clear that you love these puppets in some sick fashion." The prisoner furrowed his brows and licked his lips. "You disgust me, but I will have my answers." James walked over to the puppet and picked his weapon up. "Don't do that…I'm oh so scared. What a big and scary war hammer you wield," cried the puppet. James filled his weapon with his aura, raising it high above his head he glanced in the prisoner's direction. "Are you ready to answer for your crimes!" he yelled.

The Puppeteer remained silent only serving to infuriate James further. With thundering force James brought his mighty war hammer down upon the wooden puppet. Sparks flew out as steel met with wood. James flew back into the cell causing a massive dent into the bars. Instantly The Puppeteer launched forward wrapping a string around the guild leader's neck. James grasped at his neck as he tried to free himself, but his other hand was tied securely to the bar. "Hehehehe…hahahaha…hohohoho… what an unseemly sight…the great tournament victor James Ivory all tied up…would you like a…hand?" the puppet cackled. James could feel his lungs begging for oxygen as his vision became blurred. The last words he heard were ones that sent shivers down his spine. "Lucky for you I was instructed not to kill you, however, everyone you love will die a slow and painful death one fitting for humanities crimes, fare thee well Mr. Ivory," said a high-pitched voice.

CHAPTER 45

AZREAL

THE AIR AROUND Passerine was unusually humid. The once green grass was soaked with blood as carcasses laid out across the once sacred ground. Bodies stacked upon each other from both guilds. Green figures dragged the dead bodies into the gates of Passerine. Azreal was the first to make out what the green figures were. He gasped as he covered his mouth. "Those...those aren't human," he whispered. His captain squinted and asked. "I can barely make out anything...are you sure?" He nodded in agreement. "Yes...they have four arms and long pointy ears." Azreal tugged on the collar of his cloak. "Th...th...this isn't g...good." The captain tapped the Wasp General on the shoulder. "What now sir? You said that it was best that we make our way to Passerine to meet with Jarvan, but he is nowhere to be found." Azreal tugged on his collar again. "Uhhh... umm...perhaps they are inside and the Sea People have already surrendered?" The captain sighed and said, "Sir...that is unlikely, take a gander at the bodies that lay there would you say there are more Lion Guild bodies or Raven Guild bodies?" Orange aura filled Azreal's eyes activating his true vision. His breathing increased as he inhaled deeply. "Oh no...oh no...this is..." He purged himself by a nearby bush.

Struggling to speak Azreal touched his captain's face with his hand. "What is it?" Orange aura entered the eyes of the captain. He exclaimed, "Oh...that is...that is disgusting! They are eating the bodies." Azreal continued to relieve himself spitting out chunks of his lunch. "Sh…should… m…maybe we should head back to Larimar?" The captain shrugged. "I don't know, that is up to you to decide…you're the general. I keep telling you that sir. It isn't fair for you to continuously defer to me." Azreal scowled but nodded in agreement. "Ok…ok…I got it. You will capture one of these creatures so we can examine it and make notes on how to defeat them. That way we don't return empty handed." The captain crossed his arms and said, "I think you mean…WE will capture one of these creatures. I don't care if you're the Queen's nephew, I'm not going out there alone nor am I taking my squadron with me into that death trap." Azreal turned red. "Me being the Queen's nephew has nothing to do with anything. I earned this position with hard work and productivity." The captain rolled his eyes and commented in an uneven tone, "Yes…whatever you say." Azreal sniffled and muttered, "Does no one respect me?" The captain shrugged and stated, "I think one of them is coming."

A large green creature approached the group with its nose in the air. It licked its lips and withdrew three daggers and a sickle. The captain widened his eyes and commented, "How amazing, they really do have four arms." Azreal pulled out his weapon and loaded it with a charged Kazrite Ball. "I'll…I'll handle this. Just you watch. You will learn to respect my abilities!" Azreal took aim and breathed deeply. Perspiration dripped from his brow. The captain pushed the weapon down with fervor, "Are you mad! The noise will draw more of those creatures to us. We can't possible fight another battle. Look at our men…they are still traumatized from the battle against the Elephant Guild."

Azreal turned to his men. His eyes widened as he analyzed the few thousand that remained. His men shivered repeatedly, some remained in a catatonic state. The battle prior left them both in a daze and amazed at the raw destructive power of the Elephant Guild's forest magic. Although at first their barrage of Kazrite Ore allowed them to breach the great walls of Grande, the battle quickly turned against them. The Elephant Guild although small in numbers plowed through the Raven Guild's army with ease. Just thinking about their glowing white eyes sent shivers down Azreal's spine.

"O…ok, what do you suggest?" Azreal asked. The captain sighed heavily and replied, "There you go asking my opinion again. I don't know, you lead the way I'll follow, as is our Wasp custom. Just don't blow it. We don't have Jarvan to bail us out this time." Azreal took out his poisoned dagger. The serrated edge dripped purple ooze. "Ok…I got it. You go from the right. I'll go from the left. When it gets within range we charge in with our daggers and pincer attack it. All we need to do is strike it once and the poison should paralyze it. The captain nodded in agreement. The green creature approached the bushes where Azreal and the captain hid. Sniffing the air, it spoke, "Gargle gargle, humans. Nom nom nom."

Azreal raised an eyebrow. "What primitive speech, it hurts my ears." The captain placed a finger on his lips. "Shhh…I think it can hear us." The creature walked right up to the bush and looked down upon the two Wasp members. The putrid smell entered Azreal's lungs as he turned to run, the captain followed suit, but it was too late. The sickle lodged itself into the back of the captain as he dropped to the floor with a thud. With his eyes closed Azreal lodged the dagger into the creature's abdomen. The green monstrosity stopped and looked down at the dagger that stuck out. It pulled the dagger out and licked the blade. "Gargle gargle…tasty gargle gargle poison?" The Wasp general nodded slowly as the monstrosity grabbed him by the throat, dropping one of its daggers in the process. "More?" Azreal rummaged through his pockets to reveal a vial filled with Wasp Grade Poison. "H…here…take it. Take it all. Just don't kill me please." The creature tilted its head. "Eat you I must!" It opened its mouth to reveal several jagged yellow teeth.

In a blur of pink aura three arrows pierced the neck of the creature causing it to tumble forward landing on top of Azreal. The weight of the creature threatened to crush his very existence. Din Tei and a small squadron of Crocodile women made their way through the river of Wasp members, their green tinted glass armor gleamed under the sunlight. Din Tei approached the creature and spat on its face. "Disgusting Goba!" she exclaimed. Struggling to move Azreal begged for assistance. Din Tei and several women hoisted the creature on their shoulders. She looked at Azreal's disfigured face and stated, "How does it feel to be saved by a woman?" Azreal shrugged and answered, "Actually, in my society we are ruled under a matriarchy. The women are typically the most gifted of our people and the Queen controls all our productivity. In fact, it feels kind of good. Feels almost like home...I mean..." Din Tei rolled her eyes, "I didn't request your life story. We should leave before more of them smell your urine soaked scent. Mother said the Goba are especially attracted to fear."

CHAPTER 46

JAMES

ZANE APPROACHED JAMES who dawned a scowl. He asked, "What about those magical artifacts for my great collection." James shook his head and answered, "Not now. I have to find that high pitched puppet wielder!" Zane tilted his head and asked, "Oh the guy with a puppet? The egregore left his body and rose to the sky. I thought you and him worked out some kind of deal." James clenched his fists and inquired, "What do you mean rose to the sky? You mean to tell me he is dead?" Zane shrugged and said, "Well the host is dead but the consciousness lives on." The guild leader ran his hand through his messy hair. "Now what am I to do, that was my best lead to these mysterious figures." Zane shrugged, "Now you can give me my artifacts." Sighing heavily, he took one step towards the collector and exclaimed, "Is that all you care about!" A twinkle crossed Zane's eyes. "Yes, that is correct." James winced but marched towards the Elephant Guild vault. He approached an apple tree in the middle of the city. Zane pouted, "I'm not hungry." James placed his hands on the base of the tree.

The tree glowed bright green. A sigil appeared across the base. "Grace the mighty hands of the Elephant chosen. May the vaults open up in wake of the worthy!" The tree opened revealing a spiral staircase descending into the depths of the earth. Approaching the end of the staircase they entered a room filled with various artifacts. A twinkle crossed Zane's eyes once again. "I have never seen such a beautiful sight. I want it all!" James tapped him on the shoulder. "You can only take one thing. These are some of the most powerful enchanted items in the world. While the Great Owl in Ladle has the largest collection, my father has the most powerful."

Zane looked at James with a puzzled look. "Had…" James winced. "Yes…had…" Zane walked forward caressing several objects causing them to glow varying colors. He walked towards a vase with the Elephant Guild sigil on it. "There is no aura coming from this item, what does this do?" James inched closer and picked up the object, "That is the Vase of Containment. You can load your aura into it to store it for later. Father called it a useless piece of junk." Zane exclaimed, "I'll take it!" James shrugged and replied, "Sure." The two emerged from the vaults to the vision of Captain Forge and what remained of the Elephant Guild army. General Arminous was not present with them. "Sir, we wish to know what your plans are for the immediate future. Word has reached us from Passerine that Jarvan has engaged the Raven Guild in battle but what makes matters more confusing is that there is an army made of odd creatures occupying the city. Do we march upon Larimar and lay the final screw to the Lion Guild or aid them in this mysterious war?" *March to kill them all…just kill everyone,* his father's voice said. *March to defend your world,* the raspy voice echoed. Struggling to maintain his sanity, James could only muster a few words. "I'll let you know."

CHAPTER 47

DIN TEI

THE GROUP ENTERED the sparkling gates of Larimar city; there were no guards there to greet them. The first thing they noticed was a sea of grey and brown. The Elephant army seemed relatively unscathed from their earlier battle but there was no sight of the golden lion banner. Each soldier had their faces twisted into a grotesque manner; many stood firm with their arms crossed as the Elephant members glared at their group. Azreal gasped, "I fear we are no longer welcome in this city." Din Tei took a shallow breath, "Let's not jump to conclusions." She raised an eyebrow as they passed the sea of angry men. Din Tei tapped one of the higher-ranking soldiers. "Where might I find the emperor?" she asked. The soldier pointed towards the Elephant fortress where the highest-ranking members of each group remained visible. In a small pile there was a company of forty Lion Guild soldiers, none of them ranked higher than sergeant. Azreal lowered his head. "What a sorry band of soldiers, they look like they have been stung by the Wasp queen herself," he whispered.

Din Tei was the first to step into the fortress however she wished she hadn't. Once inside the fortress she immediately made note of the situation. A clown was pacing around with his hands on his head, Octavius sat on a chair with his head slumped into his arms, a large man with ivory hair was pale while his eyes were burning green, but the most discouraging sight was Jarvan who was slumped in the corner with enchanted bandages wrapped around his arm, chest, and head. He had a bottle of ale in one hand and stir mushrooms in the other.

Din Tei walked up to the ivory colored man who shook his head. "When I heard the news, I marched towards the city with my army," he said as he shook her hand. "I am James. I trust that you are Jarvan's ferocious bride to be?" Din Tei nodded in agreement. "Yes…I suppose one would call me that but a more pressing manner is what happened in Passerine?" James shrugged and replied, "I don't know much. A message came from one of my guilds spies in Passerine. It informed us of the battle between the Lion Guild, the Raven Guild, and the Sea People."

Din Tei walked up to the Supreme Commander. "What have you to say for yourself?" she said, nudging him with her foot. Jarvan slumped backwards into the corner. Azreal saddled up beside Jarvan and peered over his shoulder. "So I'm guessing it was a failure then," Din Tei sneered. "A victory with forty-one men could not be a victory." Azreal lowered his head. The face painted man approached the group of warriors and said, "I'm guessing this great Supreme Commander of yours decided he would secure glory and honor and all that hogwash by defeating their whole army in one fell swoop. A tactic that would make sense coming from a novice general." Jarvan winced as he took a swig of ale. Azreal took out his weapon and pointed it at the painted man, "Show some respect stranger!" The stranger laughed in hysteric fashion, "The name is Zane and you must have me mistaken for your little ragamuffin friends. Fire that weapon and you'll be blind before you can pronounce your last name."

Din Tei turned to James and said, "Do something about those two… please." She placed a hand on his arm. James sighed and poked Zane. "Let it go…when he is ready to talk he will until then we need to think of a plan." Zane crossed his arms, "Is he not the reason your father is dead? Perhaps you forgot he didn't even come to see you to hear your side of the story? Sounds to me like a poor excuse of an emperor but an even worse excuse of a friend." James clenched his teeth and said, "That is true, we still have open wounds that need cleansing but now is not the time for that conversation."

Azreal kicked a chair to the floor and asked, "And? What does that matter now…what does anything matter? We are doomed. The entire

Lion Guild has been massacred!" James placed a hand on his chest, "We still have the Elephant Guild, we are just as formidable. You have seen firsthand the true might of my guild. We still have a chance!" he said furrowing his brows. Din Tei picked up a chair laying on the ground and sat down, "We all have old wounds that need to be healed. But none of that can take place before our current reality. These Sea Creatures are here, and they wish to unleash themselves upon our land. Whether we are Lion, Crocodile, Elephant, or Wasp. We must unite under one banner and survive for the sake of our world. These Sea People feast upon our dead. There is no way they have come here for anything but bloodshed."

James sat beside her. Stroking his hair, he spoke, "A war of attrition might work. We could turn this city into a fortress. First, we would build a contravallation..." Azreal scratched his head and asked, "A contra what?" Din Tei chimed in, "A contravallation...it's a ring of forts surrounding the outside walls behind traps." Azreal slapped his forehead. "Oh! Ok... sorry...continue," Azreal murmured. James continued, "We will then enchant the city walls with earth magic giving them an added layer...say eight inches thick. Our long-ranged soldiers will be well protected." Din Tei nodded in agreement, "That could work, all we have to do is gather all resources from the surrounding villages." She glanced at Jarvan with sullen eyes and continued, "Naturally we would have to house the citizens of these villages." Azreal chimed in, "What about the Squirrel Guild? Those paranoid people have been gathering resources for such an occasion for years. Who would have thought they were right?" James turned to Din Tei, "I have heard of your guild's swift movements in the forest. Can you send a couple of your squadrons over to the north and convince them to share their resources? We will house all of their people and keep them safe from this disaster that has befallen our land." Din Tei nodded in agreement.

Jarvan stumbled towards the table and mumbled, "It won't work... it all won't work...you didn't see what I saw...those...those...things it was as if they had sprung up from the seed of death himself. They slaughtered my army within minutes!" Zane raised both his hands in the air, "See what I mean...he's pathetic...you guys need a new Supreme Commander." Jarvan took another swig and shouted, "Take it! I don't care, this is all meaningless, a war of attrition always favors the larger army. They will just throw bodies at our defenses until they collapse."

In one swift motion James punched Jarvan causing him to fly into the wall and exclaimed, "Go back to being quiet!" The blow knocked Jarvan unconscious. Din Tei placed a hand on James' shoulder and said, "I nominate James. He controls the largest army, came up with the plan, and is aggressive enough to lead us to victory." James turned scarlet and asked, "Me?…lead the united army…I could never dream of such a thing. My mind is not where it needs to be." Din Tei clasped his hands firmly. "You must…it is your duty to lead. I have seen the fire in the eyes of the men outside. They won't follow anyone else into battle." James winced. *Arminous could lead them…I'm sure that would make your father soooo proud. We would rather see him lead. You're just going to end up dead,* his father's voice whispered. James winced again and sighed, "If there is no one else, I suppose it is my duty to take the position." Zane crossed his arms and exclaimed, "It's settled then. The Elephant's Association shall be the name!"

CHAPTER 48

JAMES

A SHOOTING STAR shot across the nights sky, the large rock left a trail of red as it careened across the sky. The warm breeze of the territory indicated a storm was coming. "I wonder if this is a good omen or a bad one," James commented as he noticed a cloaked figure, with weapon drawn, approaching them. An odd sensation filled James' being. He asked, "Who are you and why do you have your weapon drawn?" The figure outstretched his arms causing James to feel disrupted. "If you are to become what you need to be, you need to know where your strength lays."

James picked up a handful of dirt, crumbled it into pieces and allowed it to scatter in the wind. "If you are referring to my leadership abilities, it is not power that defines a leader, it is the direction they choose to spread that power." I make no claim to be a powerful person nor am I so humble as to call myself weak. I simply forge ahead and do what I feel is just." The figure sighed heavily, "The hands of justice burden your soul without purpose. I shall liberate you in time." James raised an eyebrow and quizzed, "What do you mean by that?" The cloaked figure wrote James' name into the dirt with his odd weapon. "You are lost because you don't know what it means to be James Ivory." James gasped, "You do not know me. Who are you to say what I know and what I don't know?"

An odd red substance encircled the two men. "You need not know who I am, but you must know who you are. If you are to secure a victory you can't be trapped in the mind of a wanderer. There is no room for a nomad on this journey. Either you will find answers, or you will meet your death, this is the conclusion I have reached." The cloaked figure darted forward towards James. He danced around in an odd formation creating a red circle underneath him. "I don't want to fight you. I have other things on my mind," James replied.

The warmth below James' feet increased, causing the Supreme Commander to take a few steps back. The circle followed his trail. The figure was upon him launching a devastating blow with his fist. James caught the blow with his hand but felt a surge of pain catapult its way through his arm. Wincing he threw the figure to the edge of the arena and withdrew his weapon. "It seems words will not end this façade. I will knock a flurry of senses into you," James teased. The cloaked figure dashed forward, this time he dragged his foot on the ground. With a flick of his ankle he sent soil in his opponent's face causing him to drop his weapon. Without reprieve, he was behind James with a blade to his throat. James clasped the blade with his bare hands. Blood dripped down his palms onto the soil. In one swift motion, he leaned forward catapulting the figure forward into the fire. *You killed me…you killed me. I thought you were the hand of justice.* His father appeared in place of the cloaked figure. *Begone foul illusion!* James cried out.

James clenched his fists as his body filled with bright green aura. Stomping his feet, he caused the ground to rip apart. The cloaked figure rolled to the side at the last second, but James was already upon him. His war hammer came crashing down onto the opponent's stomach, causing him to gasp for air. Heavy breathing escaped as James dropped his Hammer of Justice to the ground. "I'm sorry…I don't know what came over me. I didn't mean for things to go that far." The cloaked figure stood up, his face contorted, "If you continue to hold back things won't bode well for you. The universe doesn't need the stoic James, it needs something that only you can provide." Din Tei rushed forward with her bow and arrow nocked, she demanded, "What are you doing wrestling with the ground!" James turned to where the cloaked figure once stood but he was gone.

CHAPTER 49
LORD VEGA

LORD VEGA SAT on the giant sea beast with his legs crossed. His trident laid beside him glimmering under the sunlight. The smell of sizzling flesh filled his lungs. Revealing his teeth, he peered down onto the floor where Sdogr was ripping to pieces the corpse of a Lion member. He looked up with a wide grin. "Want some?" he asked. Lord Vega shook his head and retorted, "Humans are filthy beings, I refuse to put such trash into my stomach!" Sdogr continued to munch on the leg of the Lion member. "Taste good though nom nom nom," he cackled. Odessa twisted her face as she walked past the green monstrosity. "Milord…the witch woman refuses to teach me her wind magic. The humans may be primitive beings, but their magical abilities far surpass our own. I believe with her magic I can complete the spell needed for transition to the final phase of our plan," Odessa said. Lord Vega jumped down causing the Goba beneath him to scatter. His tentacles twisted violently, he demanded, "What do you mean refuse? Bring it to me now!" Odessa bowed deeply.

A few moments later she returned dragging Solaire by her hair. "Remove your filthy hands from my person. How dare you, do you know who I am?" Her wrinkled face was exceptionally red. Odessa threw Solaire at Lord Vega's feet, his towering figure casted a massive shadow over the once great council woman. "You disobey…you seek death?" he inquired. Solaire stood up straight stamping her feet against the floor. "How can you expect me to teach magic when Orianna my sweet is missing, Malikai the ever loyal son is dead, and Tamriel the wealth of knowledge that is has fled the city? I miss them so much that I cannot function without them." Lord Vega tilted his head to the side. He turned to Odessa and raised both his claws. "What does it mean?" Lord Vega asked.

Odessa grinned and said, "You see milord…this is a human emotion called grief…she is filled with negative emotions, so she can't concentrate on teaching magic." Lord Vega took a step forward with his claws in front of him. "I care not for your guh-reef! You will teach Odessa your mystic ways or have your skin peeled off your tiny bones." Solaire took a step back only to bump into Odessa. "Without all my children…I have nothing…can't you understand that…is there no heart in that shell of yours?" Solaire pleaded. Lord Vega cackled, his sharp teeth glistened. He exclaimed, "I have three hearts! It makes a funny…perhaps death will not be your fate." He turned to Odessa and said, "Take it to the Cretins… they can make use of its feminine qualities." Solaire protested but she was dragged away.

Lord Vega clapped both his hands causing a shockwave. "I want entertainment. Now!" Melas emerged out of nowhere. "Yessss Lord Vega… I have arranged something quite delightful for your viewing pleasure." Lord Vega motioned for him to begin. Two humans walked up to the lord dressed completely in feathers. "Dance for the great Lord Vega, lord of Pacifia and king of this pathetic excuse of a world!" The shivering couple embraced each other tightly as they did the traditional Raven dance; the creatures from Pacifia erupted into a fit of laughter. Melas clapped both his claws together and shouted, "Next!" This time a young woman approached the lord. She wore a collar around her neck and had scratches all over her body. Lord Vega tilted his head slightly and sneered, "I see she spent time with the Cretins." Melas whipped her with one of his tentacles. "Sing…thing!" With tears streaming down her face she started to let out a few high-pitched notes. However, her voice cracked several times. Lord Vega's eyes widened. "Horrible…death!" Melas pointed to one of his squad members, who removed her from the lord's sight. "Next!" he yelled.

Corvus Jackdaw made his way slowly to the feet of the lord, his old bones creaking with every step. "What do you want with me? Is this how you treat your allies?" he said pointing his cane at Lord Vega. The lord grinned. "Allies? I believe the word you misheard when Odessa first approached you was dominion. You are mere cattle...some of you will be farmed while the rest will be sent forth onto the battlefield, this is the best your pathetic race can ever hope for, be grateful that you humans have such great magical acumen." Corvus shuddered, clutching his chest he took a step backwards and stammered, "This can't be...I thought..."

Lord Vega leaned forward, the stench of his breath created a cloud of blue vapor. "Show me how you humans make coitus." Turning to Melas he said, "Bring me a female human." Melas rushed forward into the crowd of Passerine citizens. The men and women were separated. Some wore collars while others were given daggers and swords. Melas picked up a young girl and dragged her over to where Corvus stood. "Make coitus! Now!" He said pushing the girl towards Corvus. He gazed at the young girl who had been badly beaten. "You can't be serious...she is but a young child... how can you expect me to...to...have relations with her?" Corvus stuttered. Lord Vega turned to Odessa once again and inquired, "What does it mean?" Odessa ran her hand down the young girl's body, "It seems the humans count world turns and identify their age that way. Whereas we count age based on whether we are alive, or we are dead, because of that I suppose they make it taboo on when two humans should be allowed to mate." Lord Vega's tentacles turned purple. "I still do not understand... she is over child bearing age is she not?" Odessa nodded in agreement, "Yes but they have odd customs that I admit I do not fully grasp myself milord." Lord Vega picked up his trident and pointed it at Corvus. "Make coitus now!"

Corvus threw down his cane and raised his fist and shouted, "A pox on you!" Lord Vega turned to Odessa and inquired, "What is this pox and why does it come to me?" Odessa leaned forward and whispered, "I believe that is an insult milord." Lord Vega widened his eyes. He grabbed Corvus by his collar and bit into his neck, ripping out his Adams apple in the process. With blood dripping down his face he turned to Sdogr and exclaimed, "Excellent!" The Goba chanted, "One of us!" Lord Vega turned to Odessa and said, "Go to the humans of Larimar and tell them of our terms!" Bowing deeply, she motioned for her Undines to follow her. Melas slinkered beside Lord Vega with a cooked Raven arm. "They taste better once we add the thing they call fire to it my lord." Lord Vega nodded in agreement, dropping Corvus to take a bite out of the Raven arm. Melas bowed and said, "Perhaps I should go with Odessa. These humans are proving to be rather insolent." Lord Vega waved him away. "Go on...I care not who goes. The result will be the same." He said with a mouth full of flesh.

CHAPTER 50

JAMES

JAMES SAT AROUND the large ivory table polishing his cherished weapon while massaging his temples; he took a deep breath and sighed, "I am tired of all of this waiting, even I have my limits." Azreal took a seat beside the mighty guild leader and asked, "I can't remember the last time I polished my weapon, it is ever so soothing." He pulled out his long-ranged weapon and placed it on the table. "Mind if I join you?" he said. While taking out the Kazrite Ore he shook his head and said, "I just don't know man…" James glanced up to see Azreal's eyes brimmed with tears. "What don't you know?" Azreal placed his hands on his head and sighed, "I just don't know if I can do this. I mean it was one thing when we had the numbers but fighting a battle where we are bound to lose? What if we surrendered, would it be that bad?"

James curled his lips, "Don't even say such a thing. If the others heard what you were thinking they would gut you." Azreal leaned forward and whispered, "That's why I'm telling you…it's something worth talking about isn't it? I mean surrender is a viable strategy. My guild surrendered to the Lion banner immediately when they arrived at our doorsteps. It's been decades and things worked out very well for us." James sighed and replied, "That may be true, but this is different. This is a foreign invader we are talking about…some…some…entity that is supposed to be from another world, if that is to be believed." Azreal widened his eyes and asked,

"You don't think the stories are true? That they come from another world, some sea planet made entirely of water?" James shrugged and answered, "I don't know what to believe. I believe anything that I can see with my own two eyes. I don't trust in these stories…fables…and mythical creatures. All I know is that if it can be struck with my war hammer then it can be defeated, besides we don't know what this Lord Vega will do when he arrives. We have no clue as to what his intentions are or why he is doing any of this."

Din Tei walked up behind James. While taking the seat beside him, she replied, "I believe I can answer that." Zane glanced at Din Tei and quipped, "When did you get here?" Azreal shot up immediately and demanded, "When did you get here? I saw her walk in but you…you weren't there a moment ago!" Zane smirked and retorted, "Perhaps you should change your guild name to the Chicken Guild?" He sat down and played his flute. Din Tei glanced in Zane's direction and commented, "You find humor in this don't you?" Zane chuckled, "Of course, in fact I find all of this amusing." Din Tei raised an eyebrow, "How can you find all this death, destruction, and mayhem fun? What kind of monster are you?" Zane shrugged and replied in a nonchalant manner, "The kind that is bored with this conversation, call me when things get interesting." He played a note and snapped his fingers, within a few seconds he disappeared in a puff of purple smoke.

Din Tei slammed her fist onto the table and shouted, "Ugh…he is just so…ugh!" James placed a hand on her shoulder and asked, "What do you know about their intentions?" Din Tei shook her head and answered, "I don't know anything about their intentions, but I do know a bit about their motives." My mother wrote about it on the last page of her tome, which is odd, because it talks about the beginning of all existence." Azreal tilted his head and asked, "Why is that odd?" Din Tei continued, "Well, why would you put the explanation of the beginning of existence at the end of your book?" Zane appeared behind Din Tei with his head resting on her shoulder. "It's a surprise!" he yelled. Pushing him off she continued with her story, "In the beginning, there was the entity known as The Absolute. The Absolute had consciousness yet was completely alone in its existence. The Absolute was an entity that took neither shape nor form.

The Absolute had neither the ability to move or talk, however it had the ability to think. At first The Absolute thought of something and nothing, something manifested in the form of energy and nothing manifested into the form of the void."

Azreal leaned forward while scratching his head and asked, "What's the void?" Zane shook his head and answered, "Don't they teach you anything in your cluck cluck classes? The void is everything that is not, it is what surrounds our planet, but we can't see or interact with it. Some say that is where we go when we die!" Din Tei nodded in agreement. "Well something like that. After a series of thoughts, the entity known as The Absolute suffered from a sensation that has no name. The closest thing to describe it is boredom. In the new creation known as time, The Absolute tried to create the one thing that the Absolute could not create, another Absolute. What made matters worse was that in the attempt to create a second Absolute it created something that it could never feel, this was the creation known as Esprit De Corps."

James leaned back into his chair and stated, "I don't know what that is." Zane yawned, and mumbled, "I don't know this one either." Octavius walked into the room carrying a large tome and interjected, "Esprit De Corps is a common spirit existing between members of the same group inspiring feelings of enthusiasm, devotion, and strong regard for honor of the group." Zane raised an eyebrow and asked, "Ew...why would anyone want that? That sounds horrible!" Octavius sighed deeply before taking the empty seat beside Din Tei, "Don't mind me...continue." Din Tei rolled her eyes and then continued, "You people interrupt a lot...anyways...with each attempt at creating a duplicate of itself The Absolute would create another concept that it could never experience. One eternity The Absolute ran out of concepts to create. The Absolute decided to destroy itself for being a single consciousness held absolutely no meaning. During this process of destruction, the entity known as The Absolute created five versions of itself; sensing the vast and limitless power that appeared before it The Absolute created the worst thing that could ever exist...fear.

To alleviate its fear The Absolute banished these five entities to five separate dimensions in the void. Within each dimension contained one planet where that entity would reside and be able to create without interference. These beings began calling themselves gods, to create a conscious being a piece of their own energy would be transferred. For many centuries, these gods would create everything on their respective planets until they no longer held consciousness themselves. Once again The Absolute was alone in its limitless power."

Azreal widened his eyes and asked, "So, you mean to tell me there is a piece of god in all of us?" Din Tei nodded in agreement. "According to my mother yes…I mean…that would explain what aura is." Octavius interjected, "Yes…but that doesn't explain why Lord Vega is here." James slammed his fist on the table, his eyes glowing bright green, "This Vega creature thinks he can become a god by killing us all!" Octavius shook his head, "There has to be more to it than that…why not just unleash his massive army on us from the beginning. Why make up some complicated plan involving the Raven Guild?" James grinded his teeth and grunted, "Then what could it be?" Octavius shrugged, "I don't know…but something tells me we are about to find out." James withdrew his war hammer, "I sense it too…it's powerful…an aura like I've never felt before."

Azreal loaded his weapon before speaking, "I'll…st…stay here and man the fort." Zane was about to speak when James nudged him and said, "We don't have time for that." The group made their way outside where the men had their weapons drawn. General Forge stood at the gate with a monocle in his hand. "What do you see?" asked the Supreme Commander. "I see a blue woman…I suppose…with a small octopus." James raised an eyebrow, "Show me!" Grabbing the monocle out of General Forge's hand he gazed. "That does appear to be a blue woman with a small octopus." Din Tei remarked, "That would be what my mother calls an Undine. They are very formidable and wield very powerful ocean magic. They also have the ability to heal and can cast primordial spells, many of which we don't even know exist."

James nodded slowly, "I see…what about that black and blue octopus?" Din Tei opened her mother's tome and flipped through the pages, "Well that would be a Mari." James raised an eyebrow and asked, "And…?" Din Tei shrugged and continued, "That's all it says…that the thing is called a Mari." James took a deep breath. "Well…I suppose we should pay these creatures a visit. Zane, I want you to get Azreal, when the time comes have all of his men fire a volley at the sun, make sure the ores are imbued with forest magic." Zane shot James a puzzled glance but before he could inquire James and Din Tei had already left.

CHAPTER 51
DIN TEI

DIN TEI GLANCED over at her comrade and remarked, "You seem quite calm in the face of the unknown." James shrugged and commented, "I suppose that is a good thing." Upon closer inspection Odessa was clearly not human; she had blue scales that gleamed a certain gold tint. Her pupils were tiny but were a vibrant blue and her ears were pointed; her facial structure was shaped like a beautiful woman in her thirties, but her aura said otherwise. "Do you speak our tongue?" James asked. Odessa nodded to him and answered, "I am versed in all the languages of the five worlds; yours being the most primitive." James raised an eyebrow, and continued, "Very well...then this will go smoothly. How may we be of service to you...miss..." Odessa perked up, "You are quite pleasant...you humans have proven to be an obnoxious group of people so far. You can call me Odessa, my last name would be too difficult for your primitive tongues to pronounce." Din Tei bit her tongue while glaring at Odessa.

James opened his palms and asked, "Well what can I say maybe we aren't as advanced as we think we are?" Odessa grinned revealing yellow teeth, "We are here to accept your unconditional surrender." Din Tei covered her mouth hiding a scowl. James nodded slowly, "Hmmm...that will be quite troublesome...you see...we have no intentions of surrendering. Perhaps we can ask you to leave our world and return to yours." Odessa's scales turned orange. "I do not understand...why would you not surrender. Your emperor is dead, your military is in shambles. The only military force you have left are the Elephant Guild's which are untested in true battle and those miners with wings. What sense does it make to fight a futile war?" Din Tei clenched her fists and asked, "What about the Crocodile women?" Odessa chuckled, "What about you? An army of human women is not an army. It is at best a breeding ground." Din Tei made movements to grab her bow but James restrained her.

"I am curious though if we were to surrender what would happen to us?" James asked. Odessa stared at Din Tei for a moment before answering, "Some will be farmed and others will fight the next war." It was James' time to chuckle, "I was never a fan of small spaces and fighting under those conditions doesn't sound very appealing. I think we'll have to pass on your generous offer." Odessa nodded and turned to leave but the blue octopus pushed past her and pointed his tentacle at James, "Sir...reign... dur or die! Lord Vega cuh...mands it!" Din Tei erupted into a fit of laughter. James maintained a solid expression and asked, "And what might this be?" Upon closer scrutiny, the octopus resembled a cross between an octopus and a fish. Most of the body was made of water including the tentacles while his head resembled a fish. Odessa stood upright and said, "This is Melas, the leader of the Mari clan." James raised his fist and stated, "Perhaps I should show you a little demonstration." Within moments thousands of Kazrite Ore flew towards the sun exploding in glorious fashion. The remnants scattered across the sky in a blaze of green and orange fire. Odessa's eyes widened at the sight as she took a step back. Melas took several steps back as well. Odessa clasped her hands over her mouth. "You can damage the sun?" she whispered. James clenched his teeth. "Yes, and the sun will come crashing down to start the world anew before we give up our freedom!" Odessa stared with her mouth agape.

"Before we end our negotiations I do have one more question for you," James remarked. Odessa nodded in acknowledgement, "Yes...what may that be Mr..." James remained expressionless, "My question is why have you declared war on us in the first place? You can simply call me Supreme Commander; my name is too primitive to pronounce." Odessa squinted and replied, "Hmmm...you ask a question that you should already know the answer to. Are you making a funny?" James shook his head. Din Tei sighed.

Odessa's scales turned red and she continued, "Well...it is how you humans say...quite simple. We declare war on you because your world is where our next crystal is. The game dictates that the ruler of a world must conquer the worlds in order of their crystals." James raised an eyebrow and asked, "Game...what game?" Odessa shook her head and commented, "If you do not know about the game then your world is truly doomed. You have no great leader and thus you have none that can oppose the great Lord Vega. Conversation is done!" The two groups went their separate ways. "What do you make of this game?" Din Tei asked. James stared up at the sky, remnants of Kazrite Ore still trickled down. "I don't know, but what I do know is that our chances of victory are greater than we thought."

CHAPTER 52

ORIANNA

ORIANNA STUMBLED INTO the wilderness. Using her staff as a walking stick she took a few steps forward. The sound of clicking surrounded her on all sides. *What is that noise?* Struggling to take another step she sat down to rest her weary bones. "I wish I knew where I was! I think I am close...the city should be around here somewhere," she murmured. The clicking sound grew louder forcing the young sorceress to cover her ears. "You're in Ladle," said a high-pitched voice. Orianna looked around wildly. "Who said that...and that can't be...this is just a clearing surrounded by a few apple trees." Rustling could be heard in the trees. "Hoot? Hoot? Hoot? Who could it be if not the one who knows where he is?" Orianna sighed and stated, "I'll have you know I am not in the mood for your riddles sir." Orianna wiped the sweat off her brow. "Hoot...hoot...hoot, are you?" Orianna rolled her eyes. "Me... I'm a traveling guildless who is looking..." The clicking sound returned. Covering her ears, she yelled, "Stop that! Please!" The trees started to shake violently. "Lies! You lie...why lie? It is not I who wish to bring you harm miss wanderer! I ask you again...who...are you?"

Orianna pulled out the last remaining bit of food out of her bag. "I'm not answering to someone that won't show themselves." She took a bite out of the sweet cake that she had been saving. More rustling could be heard from the trees. "What is that? It smells good!" Orianna revealed a reserved smile, "Oh it's absolutely delicious! It's a sweet cake." She broke off a piece and held it up to the sky. "If you show yourself I'd be willing to share some with you." The clicking sound returned though much lower. "I don't know, this could be some sort of trick to capture me." Orianna placed the piece she broke off into her mouth. "Mhmm its sooooo good," she said with a mouth full of cake. "Throw some at the tree across from you please," the voice replied. Orianna shook her head, "Nope, you have to come and get it, this is the last piece."

A young boy jumped down from the tree across from her. He had pink hair and wore a pink vest with a squirrel sigil on it. "Please madam, may I have the last piece," he said doing an awkward bow. Orianna handed him the piece of cake and watched as the boy gobbled it up. "Thank you! That was quite delicious!" Orianna pulled out the bottle of spirit elixir she had been saving for when she arrived in Ladle. "I guess this counts, considering it's a fake city." The boy stated, "Ladle isn't fake. This is Ladle, I wasn't lying. The Great Owl doesn't like liars. He says anyone who lies must be banished from the city." Orianna nodded. "I see, well then I won't lie to you, my name is Orianna." The boy raised a finger to his lips, and whispered, "I know who you think you are Miss Orianna Duskbringer. The Great Owl said you were coming but for what he does not know. I just wanted to see if you knew who you really are." Orianna creased her brows and asked, "What is with you and these riddles young lad?"

The boy giggled and replied, "I'm practicing my Great Owl impression. If you think I'm bad wait until you meet him. By the way what is that you are drinking? It looks tasty," he said licking his lips. Orianna remarked, "This is spirit elixir, I'm not supposed to be drinking it for it is a psychoactive beverage that is supposed to bring one's aura more in line with their Spirit Deities, but because I am the oracle I am forbidden from drinking it." The boy widehed his eyes and asked, "You're breaking the rules? Why would you break the rules? The Great Owl says rules should never be broken. Anyone who breaks a rule need to be banished from the city!" Orianna placed the bottle down and stated, "The deity has chosen me for a special purpose and I feel that this elixir will play a special role in fulfilling that purpose." The boy took a step closer and picked up the bottle and inspected it. "May I have a sip? I have never had spirit elixir before." Orianna nodded. The pink haired boy took a sip of the elixir, the sweet liquid washed down his throat. "Oh my, this is rather delicious even better than the cake!" the boy exclaimed, dawning a broad smile. "My name is Raine and it is a pleas…" Raine shook his head wildly, clutched his temples and clawed at his forehead. "Ouch!" he bellowed. Dropping to his knees, he screamed causing the trees to shake violently. Raine's eyes turned pitch black as his body dropped to the ground.

CHAPTER 53
JAMES

JAMES LOOKED AT the fortifications with a stern expression; the massive structures could house hundreds of range-men granting the safety of the black ivory walls. James called his first general over; every step that he took quivered the ground beneath him, his black ivory boots caused cracks in the earth. James glanced down at the cracks. "I see you are still wearing your Battleboots, do you ever take them off?" he asked. General Forge did his own version of the Elephant salute. "No sir! Never. These boots are worth more to me than my own life, besides as a general I must be prepared to do battle at any given moment. I can't expect to lead my men and hold them accountable if I do not hold myself accountable. Sir!" he said bowing deeply. The boots were expertly designed with small tusks at the tip, they glistened under the moonlight revealing a slight bluish tint.

At first glance, the weapon may have seemed unusual. However, they have proven to be very effective under the most dangerous of situations. The generals kicking acumen was something of a legend within the Elephant community and that reputation has garnered him a General's position at the young age of nineteen. The last person to accomplish such a feat was James. He placed a hand on the general's shoulder. "Excellent, that's exactly what I like to hear. Now...I'd like you to go over the plan we have issued out to every legion." General Forge nodded and answered,

"Yes sir! The plan is as follows, the Elephant army will defend the forti-fications at all costs, giving up their life to save the life of a Crocodile or Wasp member if necessary. They will provide the long-range fire power."

James nodded in agreement. "Excellent…now why have we chosen this strategy?" General Forge raised an eyebrow and asked, "Sir…I do not understand why the question is necessary to ask?" James smirked and replied, "I figured as much…you see when it comes to battle it is impor-tant for a general to know why a strategy is employed so that they can make on the spot decisions if necessary." General Forge stared at James with wide eyes. "I see…so that I will be prepared in case communication is interrupted between us." James nodded. "That's better…so back to my question. Why?" The General tapped his foot lightly for a few moments. "I see… From our limited knowledge, we have discovered that the enemy does not use long range tactics, at the very least you could determine that they do not have advanced technology such as ours. In the form of the new explosives we have created a tech that they do not have and do not know how to counter." James smiled and continued, "There you go… because of that it is imperative that we protect the long-range firepower at all costs for they are the key to our strategy. It is also why there will be a melee specialist stationed in each fort."

Eros called out to James. Her seductive voice sent chills down his spine. He glanced over to see her walking over with a large pie. "Oh, James sweetheart, may I have a few words with you?" James looked at General Forge, his mouth agape. "I suppose but please make it quick we have final preparations to carry out." Eros smiled revealing her perfectly straightened teeth. Her face had an unusual glimmer. "A few moments is but all I need my dear, it is about the emperor," Eros said. James turned to General Forge whose bulge had been sticking out. "Uh…finish the last two forts, make sure you get with the…ahem…Wasp Guild and place an appropriate curse on them both." General Forge whose face had turned bright red nodded and ran off, his feet crashing upon the ground with every step." Eros smiled and said, "Hmmm…he's cute although a bit thin." James remarked with a sharp tongue, "Don't get any ideas, my men are off limits and they have priorities." Eros winked, "Oh, James sweetie there is no need to be jealous now. I'll never forget the time we spent after your victory party." James blushed as he pursed his lip, "W...wha...what happened with the emperor?" he said looking at the ground.

Eros giggled and answered, "Well...I suppose there is no easy way to say this but he has become a menace." James widened his eyes and asked, "A menace...what do you mean?" Eros handed him the pie placing her hands in front of her. "All he does it sleep, drink, and complain. He doesn't shower, and he doesn't allow himself to be entertained. He just sits there on one of our couches complaining all day and night; what makes matters worse is the rest of the Lion Guild. They have become aggressive to say the least, a few of my guildmates have been bruised. I don't know how much longer we can house them, but that is not the worst part about all of this." James furrowed his brows and asked, "There's more?" Eros nodded in acknowledgement. "Yes...the other patrons who come to our establishment see the emperor in such a state and they are scared. They think we are all going to die, I mean who can blame them? To see him rambling on, he talks about cursing the spirits and how the Lion Deity has forsaken his people. Please, I urge you to do something!" James nodded in acknowledgment and stated, "I will...I just need to finish a few things here and I will be over there to help. Is there anything else you wish to discuss with me? You seem unusually stiff." Placing her hand on his arm gently she lowered her head and whispered, "There is something else yes, but I am too ashamed to discuss it here in the open, perhaps later when you come to visit?" James bit his lip. "Sure...I suppose."

CHAPTER 54

JARVAN

THE WOMEN SITTING beside the emperor covered their noses as he picked up another bottle of ale. One of the fly girls bit her lip before speaking. "Ex…excuse me your excellency but perhaps you have had enough to drink?" Jarvan glared at her and retorted, "How do you…uhh…what?" With spit flying everywhere he attempted to finish his sentence. "I'm… the emperor…more drinks!" Reaching for another bottle he spilled ale on the woman closest to him. "Sorry…madam…blame the spirits! They… betray…everyone!" Jarvan tried to stand up but only managed to make it halfway. He felt a punch to the stomach causing him to kneel to the ground. Looking up from the ground, he drawled, "Oh…it's you. What do you want James? I don't appreciate being punched!" He fanned off his former best friend and struggled to get up.

James outstretched his hand, "I was hoping I'd be able to knock some sense into you! You are making an ass of yourself." Jarvan knocked away his hand and exclaimed, "Remove yourself from my sight at once! You only draw breath because I have stayed your execution…temporarily. I will never forgive you for killing my father. If you weren't going to die in this war I'd cleanse your body myself." James shook his head and continued, "I suppose now is the time to have that conversation. I was being controlled by this thought form thing. It's hard to explain but…" Jarvan raised his hand cutting James off. "I know all about the thoughtform.

Your friend Zane came to visit me. That means nothing to me. Your mind is volatile and can explode at any moment. Keep your distance and allow me to perish in peace."

He's right and you know it. Perhaps now is a good time to stop. His father's voice echoed. *You've already been through the pain…hold out for the pleasure.* The raspy voice boomed. James furrowed his brows and stated, "I'm taking you back to the castle so Lamia can watch over you." He pulled Jarvan from the floor and wrapped his massive arms around him. Hoisting the emperor over his shoulder, he headed towards the exit. The crowd of onlookers watched as their emperor was carried off like a mere child. Some had tears in their eyes while others merely covered their mouths at the repulsive stench. Eros approached James while wearing a black mask. "Please don't forget when you have time we have that other matter to discuss." He nodded in agreement. They stepped foot onto the streets of Larimar. "Don't you have a futile war to fight?" Jarvan slurred. "We have a war that will determine the fate of this world, to give up is to accept death. Where is the Lion's pride you so hold dear? Where is the golden fist of the great Jarvan Hartengale VII? How weak you must be to have lost your will after one defeat," James rebuked.

Jarvan struggled and stated with furrowed brows, "I see what you are trying to do, and it won't work. You know nothing of my plight. Unhand me this instance…I'll walk!" Placing the emperor on the ground James slapped him. "Then enlighten me!" Jarvan vomited on the ground. He struggled to talk but more vomit spewed on the ground. "Your heavy hand holds no weight in this conversation. The death of your father pales in comparison to my torment. It is more than just the murder of my father, it is more than just the loss of my entire army. Can you not see? The Lion Deity has abandoned me, and I am not the true descendant of the Lion Deity. I have turned our great legacy into the story of a lamb laid to slaughter."

James lowered his head as he thought about both their parents. He moved to place a hand on Jarvan's shoulder but stopped. He asked, "What do you mean true descendant?" Jarvan clenched his fists and continued, "It is prophesied that there will be a child born of holy light that will carry forth the Lion Guild to heights previously unknown. I was taught to believe that person was me, yet here I stand waiting to be slaughtered by creatures from the abyss. Who am I really?" James shrugged and stated, "I wish I had the answers to that question, but I don't…in times like this I would contemplate these things but for you I would suggest you do something more…Lion like…have you paid your respects to your father or prayed to the Lion Deity?" Jarvan hung his head low and replied, "I couldn't face my father after such a defeat. There is so much that he was trying to teach me, but it fell upon deaf ears. I don't know…I just don't know about anything anymore." Lowering his head, he blinked as tears welled in his eyes. He continued, "As for the Lion Deity…I curse the Lion Deity with all my heart because he has abandoned me. There is no room in my heart for the Lion Deity. I cast him out as if to cast out those wretched sea creatures. I rebuke him as if to rebuke those shadow villains!"

James placed a hand on Jarvan's chest and said, "Then help me cast them out with your blade that shines under the darkest of nights." Jarvan raised an eyebrow and asked, "There is no hope, why can't you see that? Destruction of my people and destruction of my honor is all that remains in my future. I ask you one question all honorable judge James. Why should I pray to the Lion Deity when he has forsaken me…left me to clamor along with the guildless with my tail between my legs?" James pondered for a moment before placing a hand on his friend's shoulder. "The spirits test us to see if we are worthy of their blessing, it is not up to us to decide when these tests arise, but it is up to us whether we overcome them." Jarvan nearly toppled over in laughter. "What's so funny?" James inquired. "You are quite the eloquent one when you choose to be…I will take what you have said under consideration," Jarvan replied.

CHAPTER 55

ORIANNA

ORIANNA SHOOK THE boy repeatedly and shouted, "Raine! Raine! Wake up...great Raven Deity...please save this child!" She sighed heavily. "I wish my mother was here to heal him. I know she was mean to me, Malikai, and Tamriel but I do miss her. I miss Malikai and his drunken self...even Tamriel had his good moments. He taught me my first healing spell." She tightened her hands into a fist. "No! They didn't listen to me and will all get what they deserve. In whatever form their punishment takes on it will be the will of the Raven Deity. I don't need my mother and I don't need anyone but the Raven Deity...this is another part of my mission. I can feel it." Orianna placed both her hands on the boy's temples and closed her eyes. "Great Raven Deity I call upon your light to bless this child with your gift of health. I ask you to bring forth his illness and cast it away into the shadows."

A massive gust of wind passed over the boy's body causing him to stir slowly. "Huh...what happened? Who are you? And where is Vayne?!" The boy sat up, looking around wildly his face contorted, he shouted, "Vayne! Vayne! Where is my sister...you! Woman...give my sister back now!" Orianna widened her eyes. "My name is Orianna Duskbringer and according to you we're in Ladle home to the Great Owl." Raine grinded his teeth. "The Great Owl! I remember now...that...that...Owl has my sister. Human woman, I command that you assist me in my mission to recover my sister." Orianna furrowed her brows. "You're quite the uppity little brat now that you have been healed. I miss the old Raine already and why do you call me 'human woman' as if you are not human?" Raine raised an eyebrow turning bright red. "Foolish human! Do you not see my gorgeous pink wings? I am the great Fae prince Raine, first of his name and last of his name. Twenty-fifth in line to be the king of all Fae. You shall show me some respect human woman."

Orianna bursted out into laughter. "Well first...you don't command me to do anything...secondly there are no wings at your back...all I see before me is a scrawny little boy with pink hair. Besides, even if you are who you say you are, you aren't much of a prince considering there are twenty-four other people ahead of you to be king. Frankly, I am not impressed." Raine clenched both his fists while his face turned scarlet. "I will show you the great power of the Fae...pick any sentient being and I can transform into it." Orianna pondered for a moment. "What if it is something that is said to be a myth like you Fae people supposedly are?" Raine placed both of his hands on his hips. "Human woman ask no more questions, I will show you my mighty powers." Orianna bit her lip while furrowing her brows. "Hmph, how rude you have become. Fine then all-powerful Fae prince turn into a pink dragon with feathered wings." Raine smirked and replied, "We used to have dragons like that in my home world. That is an easy task for one as great as I." Crossing his legs Raine made a series of hand signs for several minutes.

Passing her hand through her long black hair Orianna commented in a dry manner, "This is taking quite a long time. Do all your magical abilities take this long?" Raine grinded his teeth, "It is taking long because my connection with my soul bond is weak, my soul partner is all the way back in Crestonia, do not rush me child." Orianna raised an eyebrow and replied, "Child? You are at least ten world turns younger than I. How can you refer to me as a child?" Raine sighed, and answered, "You know nothing about my people do you?" Orianna shook her head. "I know a bit, assuming what the stories say are true. I know that the current king is Avalon and he is an entity that loves shiny objects. I also know that the Fae use some unique kind of magic that we have no understanding of. That is about it."

Raine laughed and answered, "Figures your primitive species would make everything sound so barbaric. The great Avalon is an entity who knows no equal, well except for the queen." Orianna raised an eyebrow and asked, "You have a queen? The stories make no mention of a queen." Raine laughed and retorted, "Of course not, who do you think wrote the stories for you humans to read? As if we would allow you people to ever set foot into our precious world." Orianna sighed and replied, "I certainly hope all Fae aren't as condescending as you are. I am still waiting to see this all-powerful dragon."

Raine's body started to stretch as if being pulled from an unseen force. His eyes glossed over becoming lizard like. Pink fireflies started to surround his body covering him in a bright pink light. His body grew four times over as feathered wings emerged from his back. What was once a humanoid face now became a dragon's head. What was once a humanoid body became the body of a giant dragon. The tail had spikes running up to its spine with two small horns at the top of its head. The rainbow-colored wings flapped furiously causing a massive gust of wind to blow past Orianna. She stood there with her staff in hand mouth agape. *Oh, for spirit's sake what a sight!*

"Hahahaha do you believe me now? Human woman!?" Raine taunted as he stomped his massive legs. Slowly he shrunk back to his normal size, returning to his humanoid form. Orianna stood there staring at the Fae boy for a moment. "I think you're the one I've been sent to find!" Raine shrugged nonchalantly and stated, "I wouldn't know anything about that, my sister was the one who communicated with the king back home. It was the Great Owl who took my memories and imprisoned my sister."

Orianna shook her head in a slow manner. "How horrible, why would he do such a thing?" Raine leaned forward and said, "I'm not sure, but my best guess is that we will find out when we go to see him. He wants to meet you because of what you are." Orianna raised an eyebrow. "What do you mean because of what I am? Do you mean because I am an oracle?" Raine clutched his chest. "He cares not for such pathetic things. Nor would the mighty Fae, you humans are so obsessed with time. Time is irrelevant when it can be manipulated at a whim. The only thing that matters is the now, being present in every individual moment is what brings joy to any entity. Whether they are Fae, Zulu, Human, Sea Creature or Shade it matters not. The past is the past and the future is the future. You can hold value in the now when the now is directed towards a specific and beneficial goal." Orianna widened her eyes and exclaimed, "Such...such...profound words from a child...I am in awe!"

Raine replied with his arms crossed, "Listen here little girl, I am a hundred and thirty-four in your human world turns. But in my world, all who live are called age one, because either we are dead or we are alive. Either we breathe the glorious air that is Crestonia or we don't." Orianna scrutinized Raine's face closely. "Why are you looking at me like that!" Raine demanded. "I am trying to see if you have any wrinkles," Orianna answered." Raine slid a few inches backward and replied, "This matter is of the utmost importance. Will you assist me in my endeavor or shall I commission another sorceress?" Orianna nodded in agreement and said, "If you'll have me I'd be glad to help, something tells me this is exactly what I have been sent here to do."

CHAPTER 56

JAMES

JAMES WALKED INTO the main fort where Din Tei was stationed. She had sent one of her guild members to retrieve him. The Supreme Commander entered the fort with his weapon at his back and inquired, "I'm here, what was so urgent that you summoned me?" Din Tei replied, "You know, you don't seem very thrilled to be the Supreme Commander." Din Tei started to apply poison to the tip of an arrow. James shook his head and continued, "Of course not, the fact that we need a Supreme Commander means we are at war. This is not something that I enjoy. I have been attempting to meditate once again, yet I continue to experience a sort of blockage, among other things." Din Tei raised an eyebrow and commented, "It sounds to me as if you do not know what your Paradise is, but I find that hard to believe. On my island that is...was...the first thing they teach you, how to find your Paradise and awaken your kundalini."

James withdrew his weapon and placed it on the stone floor. "Death, destruction, and mayhem continue to plague me wherever I go. I can't focus on anything with these voices that enter my being. It is as if they have attached themselves to my spirit and won't let go. The Swan Guild used a powerful form of magic that I have failed to dispel. I just have this feeling that things will get worse before they get better," he sighed. Din Tei lowered her head and said, "That is a lot to struggle with. I don't think I can be of much help. The only thing I can think of is, forge through.

When in doubt you must attempt to align your thoughts, body, and spirit. That is the quickest path to achieving your Paradise. One of the many things my training has taught me is that one must rely on their own spirit when they have reached the lowest point. It is better to fall on your own sword than to fall on the sword of another."

James winced and asked, "What does that mean?" Din Tei reached forward and placed her hand on his chest. "You have to focus your will and block out this foul magic. You are in a disarray, I can sense it just by looking at you. Your aura levels are so powerful but your heart wavers back and forth." James replied in a bitter tone, "As far as I'm concerned I will feel better when everyone responsible receives my hand of justice, until then I suppose I will continue to bathe in the shadows that are my thoughts. What was it you wanted to see me about anyways?" Din Tei flailed her hands in the air and inquired, "Before we get into that, what do these voices say?" James clenched his jaw then replied, "They tell me things…" Din Tei asked, "What kind of things?"

James dazed out into the sunset before continuing, "Sometimes the voice of my father enters my head and tells me how dangerous I am, as if he is driving me to kill once again. Then there is another voice…a raspy voice that seems to help me. I don't know anymore. What I do know is that I am losing my sanity as each day passes." He turned to face Din Tei. The feeling of hopelessness clearly visible in his eyes. "These visions and voices come to me when I least expect it. It's like they know when my guard is down. Just when I feel comfortable as if I am making progress… they return."

Din Tei touched his forehead lightly. "I don't feel anything unusual. I have never heard of a magic that allows one to implant thoughts." James creased his face and replied, "Neither have I. The only clue I have is this egregore thing that Zane has trapped in his flute." Din Tei crossed her arms. "So that's why that guy is around. I was wondering about him. He is quite the unusual fellow." James shrugged and continued, "Now it's your turn, what did you need of me?" Din Tei moved towards the front of the fort. She pointed to the fort beside them and asked, "Why are these two forts smaller than the other's and why are they cursed?" James gripped the walls firmly and answered, "Well…Zane convinced me to place curses on these forts. He said he would combine it with an item from his collection causing it to do something we have never seen before. I honestly do not know what they do, but he assured me it would be useful to our endeavors."

Din Tei squinted then asked, "I suppose that answer will have to do. What of our chances for victory? I know you know, otherwise you wouldn't be meditating all the time." James shrugged and replied, "If you count laying in bed with your eyes closed hoping to fall asleep as meditation then sure. You are right I have a general idea of what our chances are. Before I met with Odessa and the half pint, it was at about ten percent. However, after meeting with them and actually getting a grasp of what they know I'd say it is about fifty percent." Din Tei widened her eyes and exclaimed, "So, a mere coin toss is what separates us from death!" James bit his lip. "One thing I have learned recently is that we are always a mere coin flip from death. Most of us just can't feel it. I suppose that's the benefit of basking in the light that is a normal life." Din Tei looked at him with wide eyes, "You know sometimes you say the most peculiar things. It's quite…" James turned away from her. "Something is coming…" Din Tei followed his gaze. The sound of the battle horn erupted. The soldiers moved to their respective stations.

James stared at the strange objects approaching them. "What…what are those red things? We haven't seen those yet." Din Tei sifted through the pages of her mother's tome, "That's a Cretin. They are crab creatures with ironlike shells. My mother theorizes that their claws have so much force that they can crush any type of substance with them. We can't let them approach the forts or they will destroy them within seconds!" James commented, "I had a feeling they had something like this, that's why there is a melee specialist in every single fort as a last defense."

The ground shook as the Cretins moved side to side while clicking their claws. General Forge could be heard from below ordering his men to hold position. James frowned his brow and asked, "What in the world are they doing?" Din Tei shrugged and stated, "I don't know, maybe that is how they prepare for war. It's rather distracting though." James clenched his jaw. "What's wrong?" asked Din Tei. "I was just thinking about my father." She lowered her head and sighed. "I take it you think about him often. If I could do…" James interrupted, "They are coming! Have your women ready their arrows." The archers nocked their arrows and aimed ahead. Din Tei took the lead position with her own arrow nocked. The Cretin clan rushed forward with their claws open. The two groups clashed into each other as steel met hardened claw. "Fire!" Din Tei yelled.

The sky turned pink as a sea of arrows rained down upon the Cretin army, each arrow hitting its mark on the neck. The arrows pierced through the tough outer shells causing the screams of the Cretins to echo. "Excellent!" Din Tei yelled. "Again! Ready…aim…fire!" Another volley rained down upon the Cretin army. This time their members hunched over with their claws sticking out. "What an awkward pose, what could they be doing?" asked Din Tei. The red shells of the army turned a bright red. "I don't know…fire again. Their first wave is a lot smaller than I anticipated," said James. The archers rained down another volley. This time the arrows bounced off their targets falling harmlessly to the ground. The Elephant Guild members held their ground to a devastating result, their weapons bypassed the hardened shells of the Cretin causing the ground to drown in blood. "For Crocodiles thunder…the arrows no longer have an effect!" Din Tei exclaimed. "It should be fine…my guild members should be able to handle the rest," James replied.

James started to walk away when Din Tei tapped him on the shoulder. She pointed to the middle section directly in front of them. "Look at that group over there, the one with black stripes across its chest. That group has broken through and is making its way to us." James widened his eyes in astonishment and said, "Their claws are glowing. I don't like the looks of this, I'm going down there. No matter what happens do not let an enemy touch this fort." Din Tei nodded in acknowledgement. James made his way to the bottom of the fort. Jumping down from the top he landed with a thud.

"Cluh cluh claw…Is this a worthy adversary that stands before me? You humans prove to be weaker than I had thought!" the Cretin clan leader exclaimed. James withdrew his weapon. "You should look around, in a few moments your group will be the only one standing…though not for long." The Cretins danced side to side while clicking their claws. "For Lord Vega, I gladly lay down my life, but I shall take countless humans with me," the Cretin clan leader continued. Widening his stance, James took a deep breath and asked, "If you say so…though I am curious. Why do you guys do that clicking thing with your claws?" The Cretin leader opened its mouth revealing countless tiny teeth. "It is a dance ritual we use to intimidate our foes…are you not terrified?" Smiling at the Cretin's claws James smirked and replied, "It would take more than a few dance moves to scare the leader of the Elephant Guild. Lay down your mandibles and agree to be prisoners of war."

The creature clicked its claws together in response. James aimed his war hammer forward as the Cretin army drew in closer. They danced around him clicking their claws together chanting, "Death…death… death." The Cretins continued to chant and click. James sighed and quipped, "I suppose it is up to me to make the first move, I have no interest in prolonging this battle." He ran his hand over his war hammer causing the following inscriptions to appear: 'Woe is thee that who fear the unknown, for judgement falls on those who fear the throne.' Green aura surrounded the mighty weapon as he pulled it back behind his head. He slammed the weapon into the ground causing giant boulders to crash upon the heads of all who surrounded him. With a loud thud, the Cretins' bodies landed across the floor in a circle, the same circle where they had been dancing a moment before.

CHAPTER 57

JARVAN

JARVAN HAD ON his father's favorite robe; the one he wore the night before his death. The gold and white robe was his father's prized possession. His father had always said it was his thinking robe. *Perhaps this thing will help me.* Jarvan made his way down the stairs to the inner sanctum where his father rested. On his way down, he heard the voices of both his brother and sister who often frequented the gravesite. Octavius looked up with raised eyebrows. "I didn't expect to see you…with the war going on and all," he said lowering his head. Lamia gave her brother a feeble smile and asked, "Hey…how…are you doing?" Jarvan shrugged. "Surviving… so I suppose that is something," he said as he took a seat in front of his father's casket. The glorious solid gold casket had white coins, goblets, and other artifacts placed in a large bowl in front of it. It was said that if you didn't pay your respects to the Lion Deity when a loved one passes he will haunt you from beyond the grave. To satisfy the deity, one must place anything made of white gold in a glass bowl.

Octavius turned to his brother blinking in quick succession. "Do you have anything to offer the deity?" he asked. Jarvan shook his head. Octavius rummaged through his pocket, revealing a ring made of white gold." Jarvan widened his eyes and exclaimed, "That's mother Hartengale's ring!" Octavius nodded in agreement. "Yes, the day she was taken from us she had given this to me. It was as if she knew she was going to be kidnapped."

Jarvan moved closer to inspect the ring and then asked, "You've kept it all this time?" Octavius nodded his head in agreement and then continued, "It is all I have of her. If I'm not mistaken, it's the only thing we have of her. Here...take it. You should be the one to put it in the bowl. You were always his favorite." Jarvan smiled and commented, "That may be so but you were always mother's favorite." Lamia placed both her hands on her hips and asked, "What about me?" Jarvan quipped, "You don't count, you're the only girl. Of course, they had a special place for you. It was always Octavius versus me." Octavius sighed and said, "Yes...and now it's just us." The room became quiet for a few moments. Lamia was the first to break the silence. "Well...If I have to share a kingdom with anyone I'm glad it's you two, even though you both will never be as beautiful as I!" Jarvan and Octavius both smiled. Jarvan raised an eyebrow and asked, "If I place the ring in the bowl, what will you offer the Lion Deity?" Octavius opened his palms. "I have been here many times, each time I have dropped something of value. I'm sure this one time won't hurt."

Jarvan nodded and said, "If you guys don't mind I'd like to do this in private. I have some things I wish to say to father and the Lion Deity." Octavius nodded and grabbed his sister's hand. The two Hartengale siblings took their leave. Jarvan knelt before the casket with his palms forward. He bowed his head and prayed: "Dear Lion Deity heed my prayer. I ask that you grant my father safe passage into your sanctuary and that you watch upon his soul for he has served you honorably in life. I also ask that you hear my personal prayer and guide me in the path that I have laid out before me. I am having doubts about my Paradise and I can feel my powers weakening. The strong connection that I once had with you is withering by the day. Please show me a sign so I know that you are still watching over me!"

Jarvan placed his mother's ring in the bowl. He waited a few more moments before bowing his head down again. "Father I ask that you also give me a sign. Please, anything...to show me that this wasn't all just a waste of time. I don't even know why we have been at war for several decades now. I don't know what to do now that the Swan Guild has disappeared from our world and these Sea People have emerged. What am I to make of all this? There is so much I should have asked you father." He rested there for a few more moments. Jarvan stood up and turned to the stairs with his head bowed low. A voice whispered from the direction of the casket. *Pride!*

Jarvan turned around to see his father's spirit before him in full form. Jarvan exclaimed, "Father, you're here!" The spirit smiled and said, "Yes son but I haven't much time. There is only one thing I have come to teach you." Jarvan bowed down on his knees. "Anything father...I am willing to listen." The elder Jarvan floated closer to his kneeling son and asked, "What have you learned about your pride?" Jarvan's palms became sweaty. He stammered as he spoke, "Well...well...my pride...my pride has been my downfall. If I had been thinking with a clear head, then I wouldn't be in this mess to begin with. I could have accepted your decision, I could have approached James when he was in captivity, and I could have retreated when I had the battle won." The elder Jarvan nodded and inquired, "Excellent...what about your Paradise?" Jarvan's forehead dripped with sweat. He continued, "Well...my Paradise...what is there to say about it...my Paradise is to raise the Lion Guild to heights previously unknown...at least that was what I thought it was."

Jarvan V nodded in agreement and asked, "So, what has changed?" Jarvan VII slammed his fist against the floor. "I was defeated...It was more than a defeat...it was a massacre! How can I surpass you when I was defeated?" The former emperor phased away slowly. "One battle does not make the man...it is the war that completes him. There is no shame in defeat for only in defeat can we learn of the demons that haunt us. We all have our demons. In my living moments I had many, some of which I failed to overcome, that is your task now. You will accomplish things far greater than I. You will experience things that I could never have imagined. The Lion's pride is but a double-edged sword, it is with true defeat that you learn to master such a tool," said the spirit.

"What things...? I don't understand," whispered Jarvan. "It is time for me to take my leave son. Remember what we have discussed." The spirit did the customary Lion farewell. Jarvan rushed forward to embrace his father and exclaimed, "Please...I still have questions! How will I know the right path to take?" The spirit glimmered as it added, "You must see these things for yourself," were the last words he heard from his father. Jarvan tried to move but some unseen force kept him from doing so, it was as if a huge amount of pressure pushed down upon him. He rubbed his burning eyes furiously, but they only burned more. After a few moments, the pressure relieved, and he stood up. He walked over to the casket and looked at his reflection, he now had the golden eyes of a True Lion.

CHAPTER 58

JAMES

JAMES PICKED UP a handful of dirt and threw it into the wind. He kneeled onto the floor and drew the Elephant sigil. The sigil started to glow dark green. Zane tapped James on his broad shoulders and asked, "Why are you drawing in the dirt? James raised his eyebrows and replied, "Do they not honor their fallen warriors wherever you're from?" Zane shrugged and replied in an nonchalant manner, "I'm from a place called nowhere, it is our belief that when you die you return to the soil that birthed you." James lowered his head and uttered, "How cryptic…" Zane scratched his head and quizzed, "What do you mean cryptic? It's very simple. It is all a cycle of give and take. It is quite liberating when you think about it. We pillage the land during our lives and then return our essence to it when we die feeding the next generation in the process. We already know where we are going. There is no mystery and no fear of the unknown."

James sighed and continued, "That may be true but there is also no wonder and no hope. Those are two of the most powerful traits one could ever possess. Spiritually speaking how do you explain the existence of aura and all of the wondrous things we can accomplish if not for the deities and them existing in another plane of our own?" Zane scoffed. "That is an easy one. This is fundamental knowledge that we are born with." he said crossing his arms. James retorted, "Well, care to share what you've learned at this nonexistent land of yours?" Zane shot him an odd look and replied, "I'm surprised the ever-skeptical Elephant Guild Leader would want to hear about such things. Traditionally your people have been closed off to the rest of society." James nodded in agreement. "I cannot argue that however I plan on taking the guild on a new path. Thus, it is important that we understand the customs of our allies and even incorporate some of their concepts into our teachings. I have learned a closed mind is not a mind that leads to proper growth."

Zane hopped around on one foot and continued, "You seem to be learning swiftly, I am impressed. But to answer your question it is very simple really, it is all about consciousness and energy. Are you familiar with these terms?" James nodded in agreement and answered, "Yes, we are taught these things at an early age as well. Consciousness is our thought. It is awareness of the mind of itself and the world around it. Energy is power, something that cannot be destroyed only transferred." Zane agreed and said, "Here is the thing, where I'm from we believe that consciousness and energy are on the same spectrum. Although they are not the exact same thing they like to play together for lack of better words. The combination of both consciousness which is power of thought and energy which is power in its rawest form is what creates the thing we call aura. All this happens right here." Zane ran both his hands all over his body. "The only external force to concern yourself with is the power of...actually... never mind."

The Elephant Leader glanced down at the oddly dressed man. "So, you've chosen to be coy on this topic? Very well. What are your beliefs on the mind and the inner workings?" Zane pondered for a moment then replied, "Well that is a complicated topic. But in simple terms we believe the brain is simply a vessel for consciousness. This often manifests into the form of an ego, which is like a character in a play. It can be transferred, manipulated, and even killed repeatedly. This death happens in the form of paradigm shifts also called the death of the ego." James inched closer towards Zane and asked, "Paradigm shift?" Zane replied, "Yes, that is a fundamental shift in perspective or underlying assumptions. But there are times when the mind becomes fragmented, why do you ask?" James' hands perspired as he opened and closed his hands. "I believe I have gone through one of these paradigm shifts and my mind has…" A blue speck caught James' attention. He withdrew his war hammer from its holster. "Head to your position, they have arrived."

Zane crossed his arms. "Yes, I'll go back to the seat I have chosen. I look forward to another entertaining battle," he said as he rushed to the top of the gate. James glanced at the main fort where General Forge could be heard stomping back and forth as he prepared for the incoming attack. James chuckled and stated, "He is quite the energetic one. I'm glad I promoted him." The guild leader slammed his fist into the ground causing the earth to tremble. Large ivory spikes emerged. The blue creatures approached slowly with long whips in their claws. They had tentacles for legs with bodies made primarily of water. Their massive claws were armored, and they had tiny fish heads. In the middle was an extremely small one with no weapon in hand, its yellow eyes seemed strangely vacant. Recognizing the small one as Melas he thought out loud, "It seems Melas was not an appropriate representation of their clan."

Melas raised a claw, signaling to his army to charge forward. Rushing body first the creatures impaled themselves into the spikes. Their bodies turned into pools of water leaving behind their claws and head. The Elephant members chuckled to themselves. General Forge walked up to James and asked, "Is this a joke?" James furrowed his brows, gripping his war hammer tightly and replied, "Something is wrong. Go back to your station and await my orders." General Forge stomped back to his position. The entire army of water creatures had been decimated at the hand of James' spikes, all except Melas. The little creature walked up to the spikes and tilted its head back and shouted, "No surrender!" James glanced down at Melas and asked, "You will not surrender? I take it you shall die by the spike as well." Several red bubbles swirled within the creature's body. "We the Mari will not accept your surrender. No surrender for you!" Everyone in the Elephant Guild erupted into a fit of laughter. James snickered and commented dryly, "Umm…ahem…in case you haven't noticed…you're alone." Melas climbed on top of one of the spikes. "We the Mari are never alone!" Its tentacles wrapped around the spike causing it to turn blue. "Mari return!" the creature yelled.

A flash of blue rays shot out in all directions, blinding the soldiers.

When the light disappeared there stood a massive creature made completely of water. Its legs were massive tentacles while it's arms giant geysers of liquid. The water creature lashed forward with its tentacles killing hundreds in an instant. It tilted forward aiming its arms at the ground. With a blast of hot water another large chunk of the army was decimated. A volley of Kazrite Ore came flying out towards the entity. The Mari laughed and blasted another shot of water, this time at the fort. "The Mari will never die!" bellowed the creature. James unleashed a vicious attack on the entity. With tremendous force, he severed one of its tentacles. Suddenly James froze. His father appeared before him with his eyes bulging out of its socket. *You shall meet your end the same way that I met mine, James Ivory.* His body tensed up causing him to perspire. "Fa…father?" The Mari turned towards James' direction and dropped to the ground. The creature swallowed the mighty James. General Forge leaped forward, managing to sever another tentacle, this time causing the creature to tilt into a fort destroying it in the process.

"Stop that…pathetic human!" the creature cried out. The Mari shot forth a large stream of liquid catching General Forge in the chest. Flying backwards he slammed into the ground with a loud thud. The Mari stood up and walked towards the main gate, ignoring the projectiles being shot at it from all directions. It shot forth two massive waves of water forward putting a large dent in the reinforced gate. Green light emitted from the center of the creature. It staggered backwards with its tentacles attempting to grab at the source, but it was too late. Bulges pushed out repeatedly until the creature exploded. Water gushed in all directions drenching the surviving soldiers. James went spiraling into the ground barely missing a spike on his way down. With a loud thud, he crashed to the floor causing a massive crater.

CHAPTER 59

ORIANNA

RAINE LED ORIANNA to a small gooseberry bush. He picked off two berries and handed one to the sorceress. "Here…you have to eat one, otherwise you'll lose all your memories when I unveil the illusion." Orianna raised both eyebrows, "What illusion?" Raine smirked and continued, "It is the strongest of all the illusions in their city. The Squirrel Guild does not believe in pride but if they did this would be their pride and joy." He led her to another bush this time a blackberry bush. "What do you mean they don't believe in pride?" Orianna continued. Raine explained, "Yes… they are a pious people. They do not believe in committing any of the seven deadly sins. Are you familiar with this or perhaps this is a Squirrel Guild custom?" Orianna responded, "No, we do not have such a concept in the other territories, not that I am aware of." Raine smiled and said, "Well it is quite something really. They are lust, pride, greed, sloth, envy, gluttony, and wrath. I'd go more into detail about them, but I honestly don't know more than that. I'm not sure anyone in the guild truly knows." Orianna questioned, "How can they believe in something that they don't really understand?" Raine replied, "Do you not believe in the deities but not truly understand how they work? How is this any different?"

Orianna lowered her head and muttered, "I admit the Raven Deity is somewhat of a mystery to me." Raine shrugged and commented dryly, "You humans are at the same time the most simple and primitive species yet the most complicated." Orianna looked at him and asked, "Whatever do you mean?" Raine clapped his hands and an entire city appeared before them. The inhabitants all had large fluffy tails and large teeth. They wore silver straw robes with tiny squirrel sigils across the chest. The inhabitants stared with wide eyes and furrowed brows. "Why are they staring at us like that?" Orianna inquired as she looked at the inhabitants in amazement. Raine scratched his head and explained, "Well human, I failed to mention one thing, I have broken their cardinal rule. Never bring a member of another guild into Ladle; this is punishable by expulsion from the guild and banishment." Orianna gasped and asked, "Are you not afraid of being punished?" Raine waved her off and scoffed, "I care not for human rules and customs anymore. Now that I am whole I remember my true mission, which is to find the rest of my people, the ones that came decades ago." Orianna's eyes bulged, "You mean to tell me there are more of your people here in Lelanos? How did you get here? Why did you come here? I have so many questions."

Raine puffed out his chest and retorted, "I'm sure you do. For the Fae are a great people and we have many answers to the problems you people encounter daily. However, now is not the time. We have arrived at The Great Owl's chamber." Orianna asked in an nervous tone, "Why have they been following us anyways?" She looked back to see a crowd of Squirrel members standing behind them with their arms crossed." Raine sighed and answered, "You are full of questions Miss Duskbringer. You see none are allowed in the Great Owl's chambers unless it is to bring him a tome at his request. This is another one of their sacred laws, one of which I intend to disregard."

As they entered the room Orianna gasped as she saw the room filled with books as high up as the ceiling. In front of them stood a giant silver Owl with piercing green eyes. Upon approaching the Owl Orianna took out her staff. The Owl uttered, "Click…click…click….you will not need that. I know what it is you have come for." Raine picked up a book and threw it at the Owl, the book bounced off the large creature. "Give me back my sister or you will evoke the wrath of the Fae." The Owl turned its head in a circle. "Hoot hoot…you believe threatening me is the best way to retrieve your sister? Oh, poor Raine La Fleur…have you not learned anything during your time with us? The sins are deadly for they mislead the emotions in the opposite direction of where you want to go. That is of course unless they are left unhindered."

Raine clenched his fist and shouted, "I don't care for your riddles! Where is my sister?" The Great Owl turned his head around once more. "Orianna, I shall release the Fae woman if you are willing to make a trade with me." Orianna raised an eyebrow and replied, "I don't have much, but I will do my best." She walked closer to inspect the Owl. "Excellent, I ask you to give me your brother's magical tome. I wish to wet my appetite with your guild's secret spells and customs." Orianna widened her stance. She glanced over at Raine who still had his fists clenched. "But…but…I still need this tome so that I can learn how to become a great sorceress. Is there nothing else I can offer you? Perhaps the remaining bit of spirit elixir?" The Great Owl's eyes glowed in vicious fashion. He asked in angst, "You have spirit elixir with you? But how can that be? The plant necessary to create this liquid has been extinct for hundreds of years." Raine scoffed and retorted, "So, there are things that even the so called Great Owl doesn't know!" Orianna nudged him and whispered, "Shh…It's best not to antagonize him." Ignoring the Fae boy, the Owl walked over towards Orianna, kneeling he demanded, "Pour the liquid in my mouth little girl." She leaned forward and poured the remaining spirit elixir into the mouth of the massive bird. "Excellent, now leave! I have no more use for you!" Orianna exclaimed, "What about the Fae girl!"

The Owl tilted its head and replied, "Hoot? I do not recall mentioning any Fae girl. I think it is time you take your leave. I have limited time to spend with my new-found powers and I do not wish to spend it on you." Raine pointed his finger at the Owl and shouted, "I will give you one last warning Owl! Return Vayne to me this once or I shall have your pelt!" Flapping its wings furiously the Owl started to screech. Orianna covered her ears in time but Raine was not so fortunate. His ears began to bleed as he fell to the floor with a thud. Orianna's vision became blurred as she struggled to maintain consciousness. She bit her lip and whispered the only words that came to her mind. "I invoke the Raven Deity to merge with I, Orianna Duskbringer the true vessel of the spirit. Cast upon me your light and wash away all my sins for I am pure of heart!" Orianna could feel her bones beginning to crack.

The loud screeching became a low humming sound. The pain she initially felt became a numbing sensation. Her eyes widened as her vision become clear. A tattoo of three ravens began to etch itself onto her arm. The Owl rushed forward with its talons directed at her throat, but she stood there waiting. Time slowed down as she raised her hand pushing the Owl back into the wall. She walked over to Raine who had begun to stir and touched his forehead, blue light emitted from her palm.

She glided towards the Owl while her feet hovered above the floor. While pointing her staff at the creature's head she whispered. "Return Vayne to us this instance!" The Owl opened its mouth and a young girl crawled out. Her blue robe was soaked with saliva. Her long blue hair had strands of straw in them. Raine rushed forward and embraced her. "Vayne, I'm so sorry I left you trapped for so long!" Vayne shook her head and replied, "It is I who is sorry. While in the Owl's body I could watch you as he watched you. I was not strong enough to return your memories to you but things are better now. I just wish we were united with our family." Raine lowered his head and said, "I have no idea where to find the glorious scouts." Vayne smiled and replied, "Fear not brother, we have been watching others as well and I know where they are."

Using a table for balance Orianna interjected, "Perhaps now that he cannot watch us we should not grant him anymore information?" The Great Owl squawked, "Please do not hide such information from me. I apologize for my actions…for imprisoning you. There was just so much that I had to know." Orianna silenced the Owl by glaring at him. The group made their way outside where they were greeted by a large group of Squirrel members bowing before a group of women dressed in green glass armor. Orianna curiously asked, "Who are you?" One of the women crossed her arms and retorted, "I do not answer to you."

Vayne stood between them with her hands in the air. "Fight not, we must discuss the real matter that is at hand, the wave of Sea creatures that are on their way here. We all must leave, or we will be killed." She turned to the bowing Squirrel members and continued, "This includes all of you. Please gather the food you have collected and come with us."

A Squirrel member with a sash stepped forward. "We heard everything that went on inside the chambers. Although the Great Owl is not the god we had thought he was, we will not abandon our home. You may take all the food you need for we have ample, but we will stay here and trust in our illusion." Vayne shook her head and replied, "Please, I urge you, these creatures have already sensed our presence. They will find the hidden entrance." Raine tugged on his sister's garments and asked, "Who cares? These are nothing but mere humans. Let us go where our family is."

Orianna walked over towards the Squirrel leader whom immediately started to bow in front of her. "Why do you bow before me?" she asked. The leader whispered, "Because you defeated The Great Owl. You must be a god as well, for only a god can subdue a god." Looking at the grim expression on Vayne's face she started to pace back and forth. "Well as your god I order you to gather all the food and head to Larimar." Raine turned to his sister and asked, "Is this Larimar convenient for us?" Vayne nodded in acknowledgement. "It is the center of everything that we wish to accomplish. We must unite with our sisters and complete our mission in time." Orianna lowered her head and said, "I'm glad you guys are reunited but I don't think it's a good idea for me to return to that city, too many bad things happened to me in Larimar." One of the women in green licked her lips and asked, "You are a member of the Raven Guild are you not? Can you perform healing magic?" Orianna nodded and answered, "Yes, it is one of my gifts." The woman circled Orianna for a few moments then stated, "It is your spirit bound duty to assist in the war. Try not to annoy us along the way, you smell of weakness."

CHAPTER 60

ZANE

THE GREAT COLLECTOR laid in his bed with his eyes open. The moonlight pierced the ivory structure that was the Elephant Guild fortress. A loud voice could be heard from inside the main hall. "Where is he?" the voice said. Zane stirred, rolling over to his side. With a loud sigh, he rolled his eyes as he began to put on his garments. James Ivory entered the room with sweat trickling down his forehead. "Oh…you're changing. Perhaps it's best if I wait outside," he said while glancing at the purple markings across Zane's chest. "Never mind that, what brings you to my quarters. More items for me to collect?" he said as he grabbed his flute. James swallowed deeply then said, "There has been a situation, the curses we placed on the two main forts at the north gate have been destroyed but there is no sign of an enemy. What exactly were those curse traps supposed to do?"

Zane caressed his chin. "Interesting…did all personnel withdraw back inside the city. We will need to make use of the higher ground to take out the Goba." James raised an eyebrow and asked, "How do you know it's the Goba that are attacking next? It could easily be another wave of Cretin or the Mari. Maybe even one of the other races." Zane tensed up as he made his way towards James. "Elementary my dear Ivory, the curse trap was designed to instantly poison any enemy combatant who is in range of it once activated. It is a master level trap that could only be resisted by something like the Goba. According to Azreal they are immune to poison, as such I surmised they would be immune to curse magic as well. I was hoping we could save the traps until it was the Goba who attacked," he said with a mischievous grin.

James furrowed his eyebrows and asked, "I don't understand. Why would you hope for the trap to fail?" The two continued to make their way to the entrance of Larimar. "Well you see, in the case that the curse fails to poison the target group it does something even more useful to us. It becomes a living curse which eats away at their insides." James stopped abruptly, placing his hands on his head. "What kind of horrible curse is that?! It would fail on the Goba but work on our men. Have you gone mad?" Zane shook his head and replied, "Just the opposite, Din Tei found one very interesting thing about the Goba. They are an extremely cautious race and do not particularly enjoy battle, because of this it was safe to assume that they would send out scouts to survey the area and get as close a look as possible. Keep in mind every single enemy they have sent to our door step has been eliminated. Those scouts being unaffected by the trap would return to their base carrying the curse. It may not affect the Goba but it will affect the other clans."

James covered his mouth and exclaimed, "That is horrible! Your cowardly tactics know no end...no honor...no justice!" Zane tilted his head and retorted, "There you go with your talk of honor and justice. Don't you have the citizens to think about? I have myself to think about. Together we are facing an enemy that wishes to enslave us or eat us. I think the time for your honorable war is over." James tightened his hands into a fist and stated, "That may be so, but this war will be won by the mighty hand of justice not by devious tactics. I swear by it." Zane shrugged, "You can swear by whatever you want as long as victory is assured. Feel free to thank me when all of this is over."

James glared at Zane but kept silent. General Forge approached with a slight limp, "Uh sorry to interrupt sir but we see feint green shadows out in the distance. They are darting in and out of our range. The men are getting anxious because they wish to forgo the support of the long-range specialists and launch an offensive strike." James placed a hand on the general's shoulder and asked, "Approximately how many do you see?"

The general paused for a moment and answered, "About a hundred…we could wipe them out easily with me leading the charge." Zane raised his hand and interrupted, "No, keep the men in place, it's a trap. If I were you I'd focus my attention on how the Goba got in close enough to set off the trap without being detected." General Forge started to turn red. "That was my fault. There was a lapse in shift change which left the forts vulnerable for about two minutes." James' mouth dropped open. He asked, "Can they really be that fast? This uncanny ability to close in such a distance and retreat in the span of a couple minutes?" Zane shrugged and responded, "Time to investigate, I suppose."

The group arrived at the gate where whispering could be heard amongst the men. Zane began playing a somber tune. "Something has happened," said James. "Go and find out what the men are whispering about," he said to General Forge. When the general returned he began to rub his clammy hands together. The general dropped to the floor and placed his head on the ground. "My apologies sir but three squadrons of my men ignored their orders and rushed forward to meet the Goba in battle. There has been no sign of them ever since they passed the archery range." James stomped his feet causing the ground to shudder. He stated in a dry tone, "Perhaps it was too soon to promote you. Your men are disobedient, and you may be lacking in other areas."

Zane grabbed James by the arm, "If I were supreme commander I'd have my men fall back right about now, somewhere like the confines of the city." James shook his head and responded, "I'm not leaving my men out there. There is a chance they are still fighting." Zane quipped, "You wish to go out there and risk more men just to save a few squadrons?" The Elephant Guild leader grabbed Zane by the collar and bellowed, "These are my men and I will not abandon them!" Zane released himself from James' mighty grip with a smile. "You dishonor yourself then because you have the rest of your men to think about. We don't know how many Goba are out there. You are more than likely rushing your men to their death. What sense does that make? The needs of the many outweigh the needs of the few, or are you unfamiliar with basic tactics?" James' eyes started to glow bright green.

General Forge whose head was still on the ground raised it slightly. "Sir, if I may add in my own opinion, allow me to go in and investigate. I am the fastest member of the army with these enchanted boots of mine. I can run in and get a good look at what's going on. Would that satisfy your concerns?" James nodded in agreement and commented, "Fine... make it so." Before General Forge could take his leave, James grabbed him by the shoulders and said, "Take care of yourself." General Forge nodded in acknowledgement. A few moments passed by as the two companions stood there, neither of them saying a word to each other. General Forge emerged from the shadows with a small hole piercing through one of his boots. The men rushed to his aid, but he pushed them aside as he made a beeline to James and Zane. Dropping to his knees he took deep breaths. "What happened? Are you ok?" James asked with his eyes still glowing. The young general panted and said, "I'm just...tired...I've never had to run so fast in my life. They possess incredible speeds but above all that poison they spew out. It will eat right through our armor over time; we may be able to survive a direct hit from it but not for long. However, Larimar does not stand a chance, even with the enchantments we have placed on it. Not even the great walls of Grande could stand up to such an attack for a prolonged period."

Zane widened his eyes. He turned to James while rubbing his neck and asked, "What do we do now?" James looked up to the stars before surveying the area. "Kill them as fast as possible. It's going to be tricky but with the aid of our ranged personnel it is possible to defeat them. The changes we made to the squadrons will be successful." Zane asked, "What if the line falls like it did with the Cretin?" James took a step towards him and replied, "Then we'll be living with the spirits soon enough." James slammed his foot into the ground and continued, "Think not of what can go wrong, think of only what will go right. We shall be victorious. I just wish Jarvan was here, I'd feel much better if he was fighting at my side." Zane simply played another somber tune.

CHAPTER 61

JAMES

JAMES LOOKED BACK as he walked into The Pilgrim's Inn; the scent of the lilac caressed his upper lip. With bags underneath his eyes he surveyed the room before taking his first step inside. Eros stood behind the bar with a cup in her hand. The half empty bottle laid to rest atop the table. She smiled meekly and waved the behemoth of a man over. Sluggishly he made his way over to the Fly Girl and asked, "It's so empty here, what happened?" Eros lowered her head and replied, "In these hard times, it seems even our business has suffered. Do you know when this siege will end? It's almost been a year." James caressed his beard and said, "I wish I could give you a solid answer, but the situation is bad. I just don't know what to do." Eros grabbed his hand and leaned towards him and asked, "How bad is it?" James wrapped her in his arms, her scent filled his lungs. "This has to stay between us. If word of this situation gets out there will be panic." Eros nodded in agreement. James lifted Eros onto the bar stool where he leaned in closer. The two locked eyes while he took a deep breath. "The rations are running out...soon we will have to stop feeding the guildless, after that, I don't know."

She lowered her head and muttered, "I had a feeling the rations have been getting smaller." James slammed his fist against the table, "If only these creatures weren't so cowardly. They only attack at night and they are so fast that they are able to dart in kill some of my men and dart out."

He began to pace back and forth. Eros grabbed his hand and pulled him in closer. "Come here, allow me to take your mind off these green goblins." She unstrapped his helmet nearly nicking herself on the edges. His long ivory hair flowed wildly underneath. Next, she undid his breastplate revealing his rippled chest. James kissed her lips, the soft texture pressing against his. Working his way down he began to bite her neck, her moans filled the room. Grasping her by the waist he removed her gown with ease. He bit her lip as she grabbed at his belt, causing it to loosen. His tasse fell to the ground with a thud. He pushed her back into the bar table. His mouth became filled with her breasts as he sucked and nibbled on every single inch of them. She placed a hand on his head urging him to bite her harder.

James picked her up with one arm and placed her on top of a table. Holding her hands, he kissed her stomach making his way lower. Hovering around her torso his warm breath sent shivers down her spine. "Wait, I thought that was taboo in your culture?" James licked her. Her moans became screams of ecstasy each time his moist tongue touched her lips. "I don't care...I just want to make you feel good, every single inch of you." Tears began to stream down her face. James stood up wiping his mouth. "What's wrong...did I hurt you?" Eros stood up wiping her eyes. "No...I'm sorry...let's continue." James held her hands. "Tell me...what is the matter?"

Eros took one of the chairs and sat down. "I just wish you knew the truth." James raised an eyebrow and asked, "What do you mean? You can tell me anything." Eros shook her head causing tears to fly out. "No, I don't think now is the right time. It will only make things worse. There is something I have been hiding from you." James pulled her closer kissing her on the forehead. "Whatever it is you can tell me. I love you. The thought of you keeps me going in these hard times." Eros' eyes widened as she stated, "You're just saying that...love is but the most powerful human emotion, no one has ever said they loved me before. They love what I do to them sure... but not me...for they do not know me." James held her in his grips. "So, show me...the real you. Whoever that may be I can handle it."

Eros took a step back and snapped her fingers. Her ears began to stretch turning into pointed ones, while large purple wings with rainbow colored spots started to emerge from her back. Rainbow colored aura circled her in a fury as the room filled with sparkling dust. James widened his eyes as a warming sensation filled his body from head to toe. "I have never seen something so beautiful. To say you are breathtaking would not do you justice." Eros smiled. "This is my true form. You don't think I'm a freakish creature like the green ones?" James shook his head as he held her hands with all his might. "How can you ever think such a thing...if I may ask...what are you?"

Eros floated in the air causing more sparkling dust to trickle down. "I am a Fae...the third princess to the throne to be exact." James sat down causing the chair to crack. "But...but...how did you get here? Why are you here? What about the rest of the Butterfly guild?" Eros twirled around in the air. "It has been over fifty years since I've been in my true form. I will answer all of your questions for you are my true love and...the father to my child." James dropped to his knees. "Me...a father?"

Eros landed in front of the large man gently caressing his hand with her wing. While circling she began to speak. "We astral traveled here and thus I am only partly here. Because of this my powers are limited. We initially came here to scout out this land for one of our seers had a vision. Yes...every single member of the Butterfly Guild is a Fae. But above all...I am pregnant. I have known ever since that fateful night but I have kept this hidden from you. You have been so busy with this war that I didn't want to distract you." James covered his mouth. "I knew you looked slightly larger than usual...I thought you had simply gained weight."

Eros covered her face as she asked, "Are you mad?" James kissed the Fae woman. "How can I be mad? You are the mother of my child and future wife. If you'll have me. I do not have the words to convey the joy that I feel. The joy that resides in my spirit." Eros ran her hands down his arms. "Of course. Anything to be with you." James got down to one knee. "We will provide this child with everything this world has to offer. He or she will be born into a world of peace. I swear it." Eros smiled. "I'm glad you are overjoyed. I have wanted to tell you for so long. There is one negative...," she looked down as a tear trickled to the ground.

"What is the negative? Remember you can tell me anything." Eros took a deep breath. "When a Fae has a child with a human the birth can be exceedingly difficult." James took a step back. "We will not worry about such things. I still believe the Elephant Deity watches over us. These circumstances are a test that we will overcome." James wiped her eyes with his finger. "The average life span of an Elephant Guild member is ninety. We are the hardiest of all the bloodlines." She took a deep breath. "I feel so much better now that I have told you." He pulled her closer towards him. "Things will work out, I swear it. When shall we expect the child?" Eros grabbed his hands and replied, "Soon…very soon. I feel it."

James emerged from the Pilgrim's Inn beaming. He walked out onto the tile floors of Larimar causing green aura to escape at his every footstep. His thoughts raced as he thought about spending time with his future child. *You a father? How amusing. That child is going to grow up a grave disappointment like his father.* His father's voice whispered. A loud scream erupted breaking his chain of thought. He withdrew his war hammer from its holster and rushed towards the center of the outburst. Another scream emerged from the south gate as citizens began to rush forward from all directions.

The north gate had been withered down to a stub. The walls eroded and the bodies of Larimar citizens laid sprawled across the once beautiful marble floors. General Forge limped towards James blood spewing out from his stomach. James held the young general as he collapsed to the floor. "Wake up…I need an update…wake up damn you!" he yelled as he slapped the young man across his face. Regaining consciousness General Forge opened his eyes slightly. "I'm sorry…I'm so sorry…we tried to hold the line but…they came in swarms. One of them…he called himself Sdogr…he cleaved through us like we were made of butter. I engaged him, but I was no match."

The general closed his eyes once again, this time was his last. "He was so young…may the Elephant Deity grant you safe passage," James whispered. Green streaks surrounded the guild leader. He made his way to the group of Goba that had passed the gate and entered the city. One of them turned its attention towards the swirling green colored monstrosity that was James Ivory. Each step he took caused the ground behind him to rupture. Green aura oozed out of the cracks. The Goba rushed forward with its four axes in hand. James shot forth a large blast of aura in the form of an Elephant. It rushed forward running down the entire group of Goba save one. The sole survivor tilted its head to the side. "I am Sdogr! I eat you!" yelled the beast.

James sneered. He swung his war hammer towards the beast causing another wave of aura to shoot forth. The creature easily dodged the massive blast, but James was already upon him. With his free hand, he grabbed the Goba by his neck slamming him into the ground. The Goba made gargling sounds as it tried to spew out its poisonous innards but to no avail. Using one of his free hands he stabbed James in the chest with a dagger. The blade had no effect, bending against the imbued armor of the mighty James. Sdogr's eyes turned black as he started to hum. James furrowed his brows as he dropped his war hammer and began to squeeze tighter with both hands. "You will pay for your actions...I sentence you to de..."

James' ears started to ring as his vision became blurred. He turned around to see a large Goba standing above him with all four hands wrapped around his war hammer. The Goba prepared for another onslaught. At the last second both James and Sdogr dodged the hefty blow. The massive power behind the weapon caused the ground to split into two. James started to weave signs but Sdogr was already upon him with the war hammer in his hand. "Your weapon, rahahah." James dodged strike after strike as he witnessed firsthand the feeling of being pursued by such a destructive weapon.

A third Goba approached from behind ramming its head into the legs of James causing him to fall backwards. He clapped his hands together causing a massive spike to emerge from the ground impaling the third Goba. Sdogr halted his attack momentarily. "I see...you not so weak." Sdogr started to hum again. James while breathing heavily started to weave several signs. Surrounding himself with ivory spikes he began to draw a sigil onto the ground. This time blackish sap bubbled from the ground behind the spikes. A few moments passed while Sdogr stood there with the war hammer in hand humming. This time a group of twenty Goba came to the aid of their leader.

James widened his stance and begun to charge his aura. Green colored aura emerged but it started to fizzle away. "Curses...I am running dangerously low." James slammed his fist to the ground causing a massive chasm to surround the spikes. Placing both his fists together he dropped to one knee. "Elephant dung...what bad timing." Struggling to stand he raised his fist. "Come forward you ugly creatures...there is no reason for pause!" At the urging of the tenacious James two Goba ran forward making the leap only to be impaled onto the spikes. Their screams echoed the thoughts of their leader.

Sdogr pointed at James with his eyes pure black. "He is cattle...cattle will be slaughtered. Attack!" Blood curdling shrieks rushed forth from the Goba elite. Ten Goba rushed forward some making the jump only to be impaled by the spikes others falling to their demise. One made it past the spikes only to land on the black ooze. "No...we...are...stuck!" the creature cried out. James pulled his fist backwards and launched forward with a devastating blow, shattering the rib cage of the creature. Instantly it flew backwards falling to the bottom of the chasm. Sdogr twirled the weapon around his head then slammed it on the ground. A massive ripple shot forth towards a group of running citizens killing them in the process. "No! Stop!" yelled James. Sdogr cackled manically. "Come out...human!" Raising the war hammer once again Sdogr smiled revealing sharp yellow teeth. James nodded in contempt. He snapped his fingers causing one of the spikes to form a bridge between himself and the Goba. "You come here...and face me...like...a Goba...or are you so cowardly that you must send your men in to defeat me?"

Sdogr cackled. "Goba not cowardly. Goba smart. We no fight unless we must, unlike other clans. I kill you and keep war hammer for myself." The other Goba all lowered their heads simultaneously. Charging forward at lightning speeds Sdogr slammed the weapon into James' chest. Blood gushed forward as several ribs broke upon impact. Collapsing to the floor James looked up as Sdogr stood over him with his war hammer in hand. The creature smiled as he held the weapon above his head. "Goodbye... human!" In a sudden flash of yellow light, the large Goba's head dropped to the floor rolling to the edge of the spikes into the sticky ooze. Jarvan appeared above James with a bright smile on his face. "It seems you've landed yourself into a sticky situation!"

CHAPTER 62

JARVAN

JARVAN LEANED OVER James who had his hand over his chest. "Why are you smiling?" he asked. The injured warrior rolled over to his side. "I'm glad to see you have rejoined us on the battlefield, that's all. It felt quite empty without your shining light and obnoxious personality." Jarvan winced, his pure golden eyes seemed to constantly survey the room. "Well…I must say I don't think I would have broken out of my slump if not for you and your choice words. Though I hope you know this doesn't change much between us. I did see him…" James raised an eyebrow. "Saw who?" Jarvan leaned in closer. "I saw my father. He came to me at his gravesite." The large man sat up and said, "I see…that is something…"

Din Tei walked in and crossed her arms. "Why are you sitting up? I thought I told you to stay put." James directed his attention to the Crocodile leader. "I feel much better. My head is a little sore but I feel good. My chest feels incredible. What did you do?" Din Tei smiled. "Orianna healed you. I then added a paste made from the plants left over from my homeland. The healing was not expert level, so you should take it easy for a while. I'm worried about your head. When I was applying the paste, an odd sigil appeared on your forehead, reducing the effects. That weapon of yours sure deals quite a blow."

James blushed. "That was the first time in my life I've ever been struck by my own weapon, I will make sure that it is the last." Jarvan turned away in disgust and asked, "How did you allow such a disgraceful thing to occur anyways?" James sighed. "When General Forge died it was if I had lost another piece of my spirit. With each passing death I feel a certain loss of self. I continue to see those that I care about leave before their time. I had been grooming him for years to take up that position, perhaps it was too soon. The Goba all had this smug expression on their face at the sight of his dead body. I didn't manage my aura levels properly and ended up running dangerously low as the battle wore on. It was a novice mistake one that I will not make again." Jarvan nodded in agreement and stated, "I've learned that none of us are infallible no matter how hard we try." James stood up at the protest of Din Tei who attempted to push him back. "I must check on the rest of my men," he argued. "What of the Goba…what happened after you carried me to the sick bay?" asked the commander.

Jarvan took a deep breath and answered, "That quirky companion of yours dispatched of them in the most gruesome of ways. It seems he wasn't too happy to hear of your potential demise. It was as if the whole city was under his spell. It seems he does possess some unique power. I will be keeping a close eye on him." James quipped, "They say when you speak the devil's name he appears before your very eyes." Jarvan turned around to see Zane standing behind him with a mild expression on his face. Zane entered the room with his flute in his hands. "James there is something I must tell you in private." James retorted, "We are among friends, anything you can say to me you can say in front of them." Zane took a step forward. "Do you remember that Eros woman who assisted us?" James turned scarlet. "Of course, how can I forget her? I know her very well. Why do you ask?" Silence swept the room. "Is she waiting outside for me? She does have a habit of showing up when I least expect it."

Zane shifted around slightly before speaking. "There is no easy way to say this, apparently she was killed along with a group of civilians fleeing from the Goba. It happened during your battle with their leader." An expression unlike any other covered James' face. His lips quivering, he only managed a few words. "But I was just with her…" Zane placed the flute to his lips. "Perhaps if I were to play you a tune, that would cheer you up." Din Tei glared at him and asked, "Foolish clown do you know nothing of how emotions work?" Azreal rushed into the room with his weapon drawn and exclaimed, "G…guys…it…it's humongous!"

Jarvan clasped the hilt of his sword. "What do you speak of? Another wave of those green ghouls in search of another taste of my blade?" he said standing upright. Din Tei grabbed Jarvan's arm as she trembled violently. "I feel it too…this is bad…it feels like it did on my island but worse." Jarvan looked the princess in her eyes and nodded in agreement. "It's best if we investigate this mystery creature. I understand if you want to stay here," he said turning to James. *Hahahaha, I told you death would follow you wherever you go. Did I not say that everyone would die? How does it feel?* His father's voice echoed. Silence was all he could muster.

CHAPTER 63

JAMES + JARVAN

THE GROUP PEERED outside the broken gate that once marked the entrance to Larimar, they were joined by Azreal and Octavius. The group of warriors watched with their mouths agape as the blue figure approached, followed by a giant wave of water. Din Tei swallowed deeply and stammered, "If that…were to land on Larimar it would drown all of us." The figure stopped in the middle of the battlefield brandishing what appeared to be a trident. James retorted, "I think it wants us to greet it in battle." Jarvan scoffed. "All of us? Who does he think he is?" Din Tei took a step back. "T…th…this must be Lord Vega." Azreal stared in amazement. He threw his weapon to the ground with all his might. "You can't make me! You can't make me fight that…thing. I can see it clearly. It's monstrous, three times my size!" Jarvan grabbed Azreal by the collar and rebuked him. "You coward, have you not learned to steel yourself after all this time!" James placed a hand on Jarvan's wrist. "I think he is right. I can sense this entities aura and it is far beyond our own. Anyone else will just get in the way," he said looking at Jarvan.

Jarvan released Azreal and spat on the floor. "Very well, I shall show you my redemption song for the Lion never loses twice. My men shall be avenged, this Lord Vega king of the seas will wish he had remained in the bottomless pit that is his world. My broadsword will be the last thing he bears witness to!" James placed a hand on Jarvan's shoulder. "It's good to see we have the old Jarvan back. I know things are not like they used to be, but we must unite as one and defeat this foe." Jarvan pulled out his weapon and raised it into the air with a nod. James turned to the remaining group raising his war hammer into the air. "Balance in all things and justice for all those who have fallen. The death that has occurred upon this land will not go unanswered," he proclaimed, as he headed towards the Sea King when Din Tei clasped his arm. "What troubles you?" Din Tei took a deep breath. "Your state of mind worries me…just remember…you must stay focused if you are to emerge victorious." She handed him the yellow feather. "I found this in your pocket. It is an awakening feather. Very rare and very powerful. If you are ready, it will activate."

James sighed. He glanced up at the clear green sky. *She is right, I must stifle my emotions and focus my mind. That is what Eros would expect of me.* The two heroes approached Lord Vega who had been waiting patiently in the distance. Once they arrived at his feet he slammed the end of his trident into the ground, a small pool of water bubbled. "You two wish to die for the sake of your world?" James stood steadfast, "When you put it like that it makes us sound like fools." Lord Vega shook his head, "Fools you are not. I commend you for making it this far. You have eliminated the Cretin, the Mari, many of the Undines have fallen ill, and you have drastically weakened the Goba. You humans have done well, you will make good cattle and great slaves. Surrender now and I shall let you two live because you are the strongest your world has to offer."

The two heroes looked at each other. Jarvan withdrew his sword. James tapped his war hammer onto the floor. Simultaneously they both spoke. "Never shall we give up our freedom!" An eerie smile crept across Lord Vega's face. He picked up his trident and assumed his battle stance. Jarvan was the first to make his move. He darted in with his shield held high waiting for the counter blow from Lord Vega. When met with stillness he launched forth his sword into the creature's stomach with all his force. Having no effect Lord Vega stood there with the same eerie smile. James rushed forward at a slower pace than normal with his weapon held high. He struck a devastating blow towards Lord Vega's head, but no damage was detected. Lord Vega laughed and taunted, "Is this all you have to offer? I hope not, I went to the trouble of learning your language, so I could understand your screams of agony. Perhaps my efforts will go to waste."

Jarvan made movements once again. He passed his hand along his blade reciting the sacred incantations of the Lion Guild. With lightning speed, he lunged forward aiming upwards towards the massive creature's throat. This time Lord Vega blocked with his trident. "Oh…how marvelous, it seems your magic would be effective against my armor. But I find myself still wanting more." James passed his hand over his hammer reciting the sacred incantations of the Elephant Guild. His eyes turning green he launched another attack imbued with aura. While defending against the flurry of blows from Jarvan's broadsword Lord Vega deflected the attack from James with his claw.

James snapped his fingers causing a massive spike to launch forward. At the risk of being impaled Lord Vega dodged the attack only to receive a shocking blow from Jarvan's blade. Lord Vega laughed as a tiny drop of his blood leaked onto the ground. "You have drawn first blood…I am impressed. Perhaps it is time I stop toying with your essence." Lord Vega twirled his trident into the air causing a massive whirlpool to emerge. The whirlpool dragged James into the ground as he clawed the earth for grip. Jarvan rushed to his assistance but was knocked back with a massive blast of water. Lord Vega twirled his trident above his head causing a massive amount of blue aura to accumulate.

Turning towards James Lord Vega approached slowly. Jarvan shot forth a beam of yellow light towards the back of Lord Vega causing him to fall to one knee. The tentacles on his head twirled in every direction. "You dare make me fall to my knee? I will eat you and spit out your spirit!" Lord Vega shouted as he rushed forward launching an attack aimed at Jarvan's chest. At the last second Jarvan pulled up his shield to defend against the brutal attack. The shield snapped in two causing the tip of the trident to pierce through the emperor's armor connecting with a vital organ. Blood sprayed in every direction.

James freeing himself from the whirlpool sent forth a massive Elephant which thundered across the earth ramming itself into Lord Vega. Lord Vega was hurled into the air flying off into distance. James pulled himself to his feet. Jarvan limped towards his companion with his hand covering his stomach. "He's coming…stand back." Lord Vega lunged forward with his trident aimed towards Jarvan. He stabbed his sword into the ground and kneeled to the floor. "I call upon the Lion Deity to crush my enemies, for it is I Jarvan Hartengale VII and I shall cast out all evil, divine retribution!" he yelled. The halo above his head enlarged into massive swords made of light. The swords launched forward in a dazzling display of light piercing through Lord Vega's armor with ease, stopping him dead in his tracks. He let out a loud growl. With the holy swords sticking out of his body he collapsed to the floor. Jarvan widened his stance. "We are victorious!" he said coughing up blood. Rain clouds started to form as the sky darkened in color. James pointed at Lord Vega's body. "He is still breathing!" Rain started to fall as the heroes became drenched in the unusually cold water. "Attack him while he is still down!" said the Supreme Commander.

James ran forward with his war hammer held high. The green aura swirled in a blur of chaos around him. Jarvan took aim as he charged his sword for another destructive attack. The water caressed Lord Vega's body as he rose to his feet surrounded in dark blue aura. "Fools! You have yet to bear witness to my final form!" he yelled. Lord Vega's armor casing dismantled to reveal a scaled monstrosity underneath. The manta wings on his back turned into a large shield. The tips of his trident turned bright red as water surrounded his feet allowing him to glide. Lord Vega swung his trident forward sending forth a massive shockwave causing both heroes to stop dead in their tracks. Beads of sweat dripped down each of their faces. In a low voice Jarvan whispered. "Th…this isn't finished yet…we can still…defeat him."

Before another word could be uttered, Lord Vega was upon them. He set his sights on Jarvan once again who had been charging a massive amount of aura. He sent forth the massive ball of light at blistering speeds only to have it deflected by Lord Vega's shield. "We need to do something about that shield!" said James. Lord Vega cackled, "Foolish human…resistance is futile." James furrowed his brows. "You are nothing more than a fish, go back to the sea where you belong!" Lord Vega grimaced. "Insolent!" he yelled as he dashed forward, appearing in front of James with his hands clasped around his neck. Feeling the moisture leave his body James struggled to grab Lord Vega's wrist. While unleashing a flurry of vines he yelled out, "Now!" The vines wrapped themselves around the lord of Pacifia rendering all his movements null. Jarvan unleashed an enormous beam of light engulfing the two warriors.

Lord Vega dropped to both his knees before collapsing face first on the ground. "How can this be?" he whispered. Jarvan kneeled on the ground in too much pain to move. He glanced over at James whose breath was shallow. The voices of angels entered his ears as they filled him with a tingling sensation. "It seems now is when I meet my end. I hear the call of the sirens. At least honor has been restored..." Jarvan's jaw dropped as the massive figure that was Lord Vega climbed to his feet. His purple blood seeped back into the wounds. The wounds closed leaving Lord Vega virtually unscathed. The monster approached Jarvan as he dragged his trident on the ground. Each step he took sent shivers down Jarvan's spine. The honorable emperor struggled to gain his composure. Using his sword as leverage Jarvan pulled himself to his feet. Feeling the warmth of his blood descend his body he spoke, "I shall die standing upon my own two feet, for that is the way a man should go." James' eyes widened as Lord Vega continued his pursuit of Jarvan, "Lord Vega...stop this. You have won. We will fight for you," James said as he dragged his body towards his best friend. "Insolent cattle, my bloodlust must be satisfied. Death is the only outcome." Still dragging his body forward, James replied. "If you must satisfy your bloodlust take me instead." Lord Vega turned to James brandishing his weapon. "You will meet your architect soon enough."

The monstrosity approached Jarvan. Thrusting forward he knocked the sword out of his hand. He drove the tip of the weapon into Jarvan's chest, causing him to hunch over. He raised the trident in the air and slammed it into the ground, causing another crater to form. The emperor laid there in a crumpled heap. James arose to his knees. "I won't..." blood spewed out preventing him from speaking. Lord Vega's tentacles tensed up, "Muahaha, you can barely speak, and you believe you can defeat me? Lay down at my feet and your death will be swift." While sneering he approached James. "I won't let you get away with this. You have caused so much death. If not for you my father, fiancé, and child would all have beating hearts! All this destruction over some game?" James uttered.

Lord Vega paused for a moment. "Some game? Your ignorance knows no end. You displease me. Torment will be your fate. I will kill you last," he said pointing behind the commander. James glanced at the group standing at the edge of Larimar. *Focus your spirit, for it is your spirit that guides you upon this day,* the raspy voice thundered. Clenching his fists, he rose to his feet with much difficulty. The beating of his heart intensified, his eyes turned dark green. A ray of green light emerged from his person surrounding the Supreme Commander. The rocks surrounding him began to rise. The dead leaves that caressed their feet started to hover. His War Hammer of Justice glowed bright green. Vines enclosed the glorious weapon as strange markings appeared all over his body. "I will not permit you to harm another soul. There will be justice!" he bellowed, causing dark green aura to surround them both. Lord Vega took one step back. The tentacles on his head froze. "It…it…seems the snake within has awakened…It matters not. Your death will come regardless."

James stepped forward collapsing the earth beneath him with each step. He bellowed, "I banish you back to the abyss where you came from, you will impose on us no longer!" James swung his war hammer to the side causing Lord Vega to brace himself with his shield. In a flash of green light, he appeared behind his opponent. Swinging his weapon into his back a loud crunch could be heard, Lord Vega dropped to his knees. Vines engulfed the monstrosity limiting his movements. With his war hammer held high it came crashing down upon the head of the deadly Sea Lord. Before he could strike again, Lord Vega ripped through the vines enabling him to retreat. Clasping his trident, he launched forth several whirlpools putting James on the defensive. Holding his mighty war hammer to the side James exclaimed, "You will die a hundred times over before I am satisfied!" He shot forward with his war hammer aimed steady at the monster. Lord Vega shot through the water with his trident aimed towards his opponent. The two warriors clashed causing a massive crater to form. Looking up at the world above them James smirked. He slammed his weapon into the soil causing the earth to close, engulfing them both. Upon seeing the crater close Lord Vega attempted to climb his way out but it was too late, their tomb was set. Several moments passed by before a hand emerged from the soil.

"The greatest injustice is the one that prevents growth"
– Negus Lamont

If you enjoyed the experience, a constructive review would be most appreciated. Please head over to Goodreads, Amazon, or Kobo and leave a review.

About the Author

My mind is a chaotic place to dwell. The dark thoughts that clamor for freedom spill out onto the pages of art. You have entered the mind of a Bipolar author. Many have inquired as to why I bother to write in the first place. Some say it is a dying art form, while others claim it is simply a waste of time if I want to be successful. Truth be told, I write because that is what I have been called to do. Mental illness is a topic that still has stigma attached to it and I wish to aid in the removal of said stigma. My novel Rise of the Abyss from The Search for Paradise series is my first step towards that. Diving into the depths of one's abyss is the best way to heal for all those involved. It is my greatest wish that you continue with me on this journey. There is more wisdom to be revealed and more healing to be done.

If you wish to maintain a connection feel free to interact with me on social media or catapult an e-mail my way.

Facebook: Negus Lamont
Instagram: Negus Lamont
E-mail: neguslamont@gmail.com
Website: www.neguslamont.com

www.ingramcontent.com/pod-product-compliance
Lightning Source LLC
Chambersburg PA
CBHW030635110726

47901CB00002B/448